SCHOLASTIC

GRADE 3

CW01667872

Morning Jumpstarts: Reading

100 Independent Practice Pages to Build Essential Skills

Marcia Miller & Martin Lee

New York · Toronto · London · Auckland · Sydney
Mexico City · New Delhi · Hong Kong · Buenos Aires

Teaching Resources

Cover design by Scott Davis

Interior design by Sydney Wright

Interior Illustrations by Maxie Chambliss, Rusty Fletcher, Mike Gordon, James Graham Hale, Anne Kennedy, and Sydney Wright; © 2013 by Scholastic Inc.

Photo credit: page 64: © Ken Catania/Visuals Unlimited/Corbis

ISBN: 978-93-86313-40-9

Published by Scholastic Inc.
Reprinted by Scholastic India Pvt. Ltd. January 2017
Printed at JJ Offset Printers, Noida.

Introduction

In your busy classroom, you know how vital it is to energize students for the tasks of the day. That's why *Morning Jumpstarts: Reading, Grade 6* is the perfect tool for you.

The activities in this book provide brief and focused individual practice in grade-level skills students are expected to master. Each Jumpstart is a two-page collection of six activities designed to review and reinforce a range of reading and writing skills students will build throughout the year. The consistent format helps students work independently and with confidence. Each Jumpstart includes these features:

- Word of the Day
- Sentence Mender
- Cursive Quote
- Analogy of the Day
- Ready, Set, Read!
- Brainteaser

You can use a Jumpstart in its entirety or, because each feature is self-contained, assign sections at different times of the day or to different groups of learners. The Jumpstart activities will familiarize students with the kinds of challenges they will encounter on standardized tests, and provide a review of skills they need to master.

The Common Core State Standards (CCSS) for English Language Arts serve as the backbone of the activities in this book.

Generally, we have kept in mind the CCSS "anchor standards" that should inform solid instruction in reading literary and informational texts. In addition, the activity pages provide students with practice in developing and mastering language skills, summarized below.

ANCHOR STANDARDS
FOR READING
- Key Ideas and Details
- Craft and Structure
- Integration of Knowledge and Ideas
- Range of Reading and Level of Text Complexity

LANGUAGE
- Conventions of Standard English
- Knowledge of Language
- Vocabulary Acquisition and Use

A Look Inside

Each two-page Jumpstart includes the following skill-building features.

Word of the Day The first feature on Side A builds vocabulary. Students read a grade-appropriate word and its definition. A brief writing task asks them to use the new word to demonstrate understanding of its proper usage.

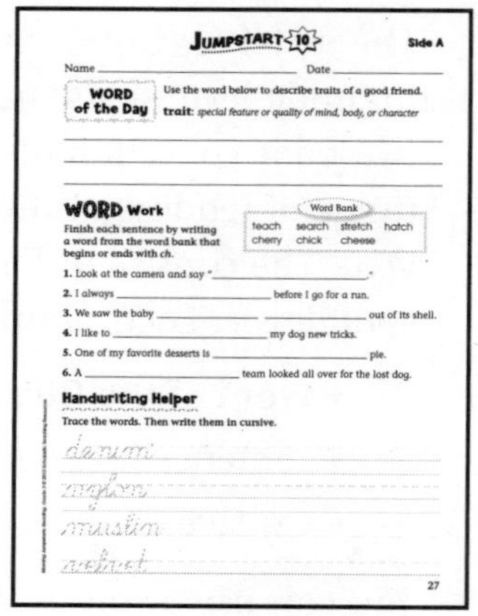
JUMPSTART 10 Side A

Name ______ Date ______

WORD of the Day — Use the word below to describe traits of a good friend.

trait: *special feature or quality of mind, body, or character*

WORD Work

Finish each sentence by writing a word from the word bank that begins or ends with *ch*.

Word Bank: teach search stretch hatch cherry chick cheese

1. Look at the camera and say "______."
2. I always ______ before I go for a run.
3. We saw the baby ______ ______ out of its shell.
4. I like to ______ my dog new tricks.
5. One of my favorite desserts is ______ pie.
6. A ______ team looked all over for the lost dog.

Handwriting Helper

Trace the words. Then write them in cursive.

27

Fun Phonics Every Side A presents a grade-appropriate word-study feature that focuses on a key phonics or word-study topic. For more capable learners, this activity may provide review. Students who need more support may need guidance or hints to help them succeed.

Handwriting Helper This feature rounds out Side A by offering students a chance to practice cursive handwriting. The words and phrases encompass practice of both lower- and uppercase letters.

Ready, Set, Read! Every Side B begins with a brief reading passage, followed by two or more text-based questions. Passages include fiction and nonfiction, prose and poetry, serious and humorous writing, realistic and fantastical settings. Dig deeper into any passage to inspire discussion, questions, and extension.

Tell students to first read the passage and then answer the questions. Show them how to fill in the circles for multiple-choice questions. For questions that require students to write, encourage them to use another sheet of paper, if needed.

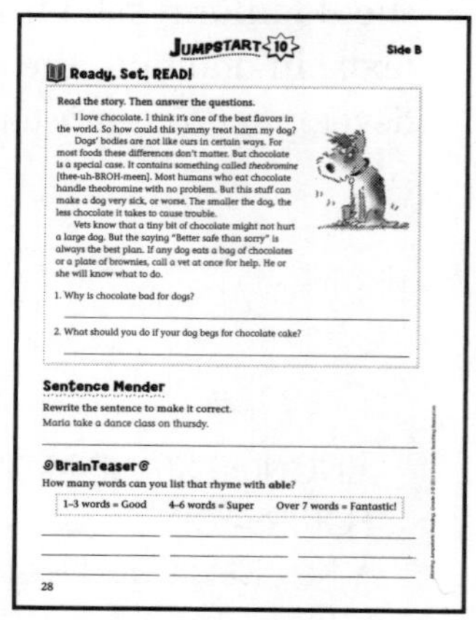
JUMPSTART 10 Side B

Ready, Set, READ!

Read the story. Then answer the questions.

I love chocolate. I think it's one of the best flavors in the world. So how could this yummy treat harm my dog?

Dogs' bodies are not like ours in certain ways. For most foods these differences don't matter. But chocolate is a special case. It contains something called *theobromine* [thee-uh-BROH-meen]. Most humans who eat chocolate handle theobromine with no problem. But this stuff can make a dog very sick, or worse. The smaller the dog, the less chocolate it takes to cause trouble.

Vets know that a tiny bit of chocolate might not hurt a large dog. But the saying "Better safe than sorry" is always the best plan. If any dog eats a bag of chocolates or a plate of brownies, call a vet at once for help. He or she will know what to do.

1. Why is chocolate bad for dogs?
2. What should you do if your dog begs for chocolate cake?

Sentence Mender

Rewrite the sentence to make it correct.

Maria take a dance class on thursdy.

BrainTeaser

How many words can you list that rhyme with **able**?

1–3 words = Good   4–6 words = Super   Over 7 words = Fantastic!

28

Sentence Mender The second Side B feature addresses grade-appropriate conventions of standard English, especially spelling, capitalization, punctuation, and grammar. Children will see a sentence with errors. Their task is to rewrite the sentence correctly. A sample answer is given in the Answer Key, but it is quite possible that children may devise alternate corrections. Link this task to the revising and proofreading steps of the writing process.

Brainteaser Side B always ends with some form of an entertaining word or language challenge: a puzzle, code, riddle, or other engaging task designed to stretch the mind. While some children may find this section particularly challenging, others will relish teasing out tricky solutions. This feature provides another chance for group work or discussion. It may prove useful to have pairs of children tackle these together. And, when appropriate, invite children to create their own challenges, using ideas sparked by these exercises. Feel free to create your own variations of any brainteasers your class enjoys.

Name ______________________ Date ______________

WORD of the Day

Use the word below to describe a story you like.

plot: *the main events that tell the story in a book, play, poem, or other work*

____

____

____

WORD Work

Read each pair of words. Circle pairs that rhyme.

1. honey funny	**2.** jeep jeans	**3.** chief reef
4. dear bear	**5.** chair dare	**6.** pink brink
7. arch porch	**8.** beach leech	**9.** finer dinner
10. rode toad	**11.** foot boot	**12.** room plume

Handwriting Helper

Trace the words. Then write them in cursive.

jet

rub

list

bulk

JUMPSTART 1

Side B

Ready, Set, READ!

Read the story. Then answer the questions.

Toby was excited and also a little scared. Today he was exploring his first cave with Dad. Both wore hiking books and gloves to protect their feet and hands. Each put on a hard hat with a light on it. Their headlamps would shine ahead of them in the dark.

Dad and Toby drove toward Cave Creek. They parked near the creek and followed it into the woods. Soon Dad pointed out a little rock pile. "This cairn marks the opening," said Dad. Toby looked, but he didn't see any cave. What he saw looked more like a rocky hole in the ground.

"We're going down . . . there?" Toby asked.

"Yup," said Dad. "This cave opens up once we're inside. But no running, son. The rocks are slippery, and some wiggle. We'll have to duck so we don't bump our heads. Stay close by me and step where I step." Then they turned on their headlamps.

1. What is a *cairn*?
   - ○ A. a cave
   - ○ B. a creek
   - ✓ C. a rock pile

2. Why was Toby excited and scared at the same time?
   - ○ A. He did not like the dark.
   - ○ B. He had a new pair of hiking boots.
   - ✓ C. He was going into a cave for the first time.

Sentence Mender

Rewrite the sentence to make it correct.

i walkd the dog when I woke up

I walked the dog when I woke up.

BrainTeaser

An *anagram* is a new word made using all the letters of another word. **Act** is an anagram for **cat**.

Make an anagram for each word.

1. pace ⇔ ~~space~~ cape

2. sour ⇔ ours

3. lump ⇔ ~~plump~~ plum

4. wolf ⇔ fowl flow

5. dusty ⇔ study

6. charm ⇔ ~~marth~~ march

Name ______________________ Date ______________

WORD of the Day

Use the word below to describe a way you are active.

active: *with much action; lively; busy*

____

____

____

WORD Work

Read each word in the flag.
Listen for where its /f/ is.
Write the word where it belongs.

fantasy	infant	sheriff
defend	drifter	knife
enough	fireproof	graph
fountain	belief	coughing

beginning /f/	middle /f/	ending /f/

Handwriting Helper

Trace the words. Then write them in cursive.

hip

rust

push

wheel

JUMPSTART 2

Side B

Ready, Set, READ!

Read the story. Then answer the questions.

Jacy was on the rug, petting her cat, Scout, when the rug began to jiggle. Was it an earthquake? Scout hissed and arched her back. Jacy tried to calm her. Then the rug rose up above the floor. Jacy and Scout were floating, too!

The frightened cat clung to Jacy, who didn't know whether to be scared or excited. Scout wanted none of this floating. So off she jumped, and hid under a chair. Jacy was now alone on the rug as it gently sailed around the room, dipping down, spinning, rising up. Jacy didn't even hold on. Too bad it's a small room, she thought.

Just then, one wall of the room spread open like curtains on a stage. The rug and Jacy swooped outside and headed into town.

1. What kind of story is this?
   - ○ A. science
   - ○ B. mystery
   - ○ C. fantasy
2. How did the room change?
   - ○ A. There were new curtains.
   - ○ B. A wall opened up.
   - ○ C. It got smaller.
3. What does the word *arched* mean in the story?
   - ○ A. curved
   - ○ B. straightened
   - ○ C. stretched

Sentence Mender

Rewrite the sentence to make it correct.

granddad moved back to canada

Grandad moved back to Canada.

BrainTeaser

Use the words in the word bank to make a tongue twister. It has two sentences. Both sentences begin with *Sheep*. Write your ideas below. Then try to say it three times in a row!

Word Bank

shack	should
shed	shouldn't
Sheep	sleep

Sheep Should sleep in a shed.
Sheep Shouldn't sleep
in a shack instead.

Name Vivaan Date 8/11/22

WORD of the Day

Use the word below to describe how to vary your breakfast.

vary: *change or make different*

I had a very choices of breakfasts

I will vary my breakfast everyday

WORD Work

Notice the sound of the underlined part of each word.
Write a rhyme with the same sound, spelled the same way.

Not round, but squ<u>**are**</u>	Not a cub, a big b<u>**ear**</u>	Not a table, a ch<u>**air**</u>
1. Not common, but rare	**2.** Not an apple, but a pear	**3.** Not just one, but a bear ~~tiar~~ stair
4. Not dressed, but bare	**5.** Don't cut, just ~~tear~~ tair	**6.** Not on land, but in air

Handwriting Helper

Trace the words. Then write them in cursive.

kilt kill kill kill Rill Rill Rill kill

skip skip skip skip skip skip skip

where where where wher wher

tissue tissue tissue tissue tissue

JUMPSTART 3

Side B

8/11/22

Ready, Set, READ!

Read the invitation. Then answer the questions.

Join Us for a SURPRISE Party!!!

Ethan Clary will be 10 years old soon. Of course he knows when his birthday is. But he doesn't know about this party! Come help us celebrate.

DATE: Saturday, May 12

TIME: 1:15 PM to 4:00 PM.

PLACE: 53 Oakmont St.

PHONE: 555-4321

Dad is taking Ethan to run errands while we set up the house. Please arrive on time! We want to shout a loud "Surprise!" when he walks in.

DON'T SPILL THE BEANS!!

1. What is the reason for the party?

To surprise Ethan

2. What does DON'T SPILL THE BEANS mean?

dont tell him

Sentence Mender

Rewrite the sentence to make it correct.

wear do you keep the kitty Litter.

Where doy you keep the killy litter?

BrainTeaser

Knock-knock jokes use the same pattern:
Read the example here aloud.
Now make up a funny answer to this knock-knock joke:

Knock-knock!

Who's there?

Hatch.

Hatch who?

hatcheroo

Knock-knock!

Who's there?

Abie.

Abie who?

Abie C D E F G…!

JUMPSTART 4

Side A

Name Vivaan Date 9/11/22

WORD of the Day

Use the word below to describe standing at a brink.

brink: *the very edge of a high place; the spot just short of*

The dinosaurs are at the brink of extinsion

WORD Work

The box has nine phonograms (sound groups). Write nine words in the chart—three for each *l* blend. Use every phonogram *once*.

Phonograms

-ade	-are	-ash
-each	-ed	-iff
-one	-own	-y

bl	*cl*	*fl*
blend	clever	flower
black	clover	flow
blue	cloud	flounder

Handwriting Helper

Trace the words. Then write them in cursive.

self self self self self

fewer fewer fewer fewer fewer

fifth fifth fifth fifth fifth

ukelele ukelele ukelele ukelele

JUMPSTART 4

Side B

Ready, Set, READ!

Read the story. Then answer the questions.

Vincent Van Gogh (GO) grew up in Holland. Days in Holland could be rainy and dreary. When he began to paint, he used dark colors.

Van Gogh often painted people at work. Some paintings show stooped farmers digging in brown fields. Some show peasants at home. In one, people are eating potatoes in a gloomy room. Van Gogh also painted everyday things like old pots and shoes.

In 1888, Van Gogh moved to the south of France. There, most days were sunny and bright. What do you think happened? His paintings changed! Now he painted bright yellow sunflowers and blue skies. He painted colorful boats and gardens. He painted portraits of smiling children. The everyday things he still liked to paint were now bright and cheerful. Even his night scenes shone.

Van Gogh sold only one painting in his lifetime. Today many of his paintings hang in famous art museums. He was truly a great artist.

1. What does *stooped* mean?
   - ○ A. smiling
   - ● B. bent over
   - ○ C. running
2. Van Gogh's paintings
   - ○ A. got darker when he moved to France.
   - ○ B. got more colorful when he moved to Holland.
   - ● C. got more colorful when he moved to France.
3. The last sentence of the passage is
   - ○ A. a fact.
   - ● B. an opinion.
   - ○ C. not true.

Sentence Mender

Rewrite the sentence to make it correct.

Do you know Dr reeds first name?

Doyou know Dr Reed's first name?

BrainTeaser

Some verbs make the sound they stand for. Finish each simple sentence with a sound verb.

The hen **clucks**.
Fried eggs **sizzle**.

1. Bells chime.

2. Brakes screech.

3. Soda fizzes.

4. Pigeons Cooing.

5. The Tin Man bangs.

6. The kettle hisses.

JUMPSTART 5

Side A

Name ______________________ Date ______________

WORD of the Day

Use the word below to describe a dreary morning.

dreary: *gloomy; dull; without cheer*

____

____

____

WORD Work

G can have two different sounds.
Soft *g* sounds like /j/, as in **gym**.
Hard *g* sounds like /g/, as in **gate**.
Sort the words into each can below.

Word Bank

ginger	garden	genius
dragon	danger	wagon
gem	regular	village
gourd	strange	giggle

Hard G	Soft G

Handwriting Helper

Trace the words. Then write them in cursive.

iris

just

pill

issue

JUMPSTART 5

Side B

Ready, Set, READ!

Read the story. Then answer the questions.

When Rupert planted a boot in his garden, his neighbors sneered. It was early spring—the normal planting time. But a boot? "Poor Rupert must be daft," they whispered. But Rupert cheerfully tended his boot every day. He sang to the boot plant as he weeded, watered, and watched. As it grew, so did everyone's wonder.

By fall, Rupert stood beside a small tree. He loved the little green fruits that hung in pairs. "Boot fruits!" he said proudly. "Bring your children around in a few weeks to try them on. I'll give free fresh boots for any feet they fit!"

Free boots from a tree? Some neighbors still gossiped, but the word spread. Soon, parents brought their children to try on the home-grown boots, which were no longer green. Now they were brown and sturdy on the outside. Even better, they remained soft on the inside—just right for little feet. Rupert handed out free fruit boots, as promised. How do you think next year's crop will turn out?

1. What is another word for *daft*?
   - O A. clever
   - O B. cold
   - O C. crazy

2. Why would Rupert give away free fruit boots?
   - O A. to show his kind heart
   - O B. because they were too small for his feet
   - O C. to earn money before the winter set in

Sentence Mender

Rewrite the sentence to make it correct.

We will bee home by for oclock.

____

BrainTeaser

A *palindrome* is a special kind of word. It reads the same forward and backward.

Write a palindrome for each clue. The first is done for you.

1. Part of the face eye

2. Sound a horn makes ____________

3. A time of day ____________

4. A father ____________

Name ______________________________ Date ____________________

WORD of the Day

Use the word below to write something you long for.

yearn: *feel a deep, sad longing or desire*

____

____

____

WORD Work

C can have two different sounds.
Soft *c* sounds like /s/, as in <u>c</u>ent.
Hard *c* sounds like /k/, as in <u>c</u>art.
Sort the words into each can below.

Word Bank

music	camper	copper
celery	electric	fancy
account	cereal	second
pencil	acid	cider

Hard C	Soft C

Handwriting Helper

Trace the words. Then write them in cursive.

dog

cola

grow

quack

Ready, Set, READ!

Read the passage. Then answer the questions.

Earth is a rocky planet. Rocks make up mountains and other land forms. They can be ordinary stones to kick down a road or to build with. But there is one rock that we eat. Yes, you put rocks in your food! You gladly take it into your body and know its taste. This edible rock is salt.

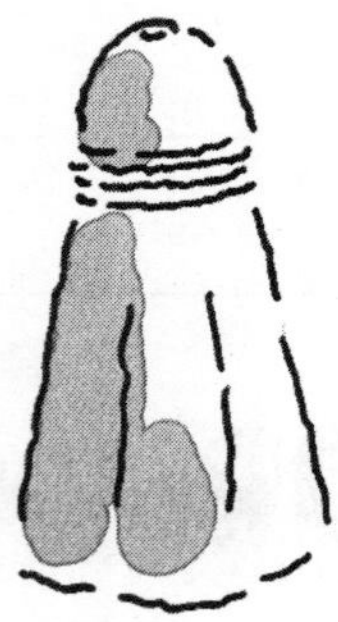

Salt's scientific name is *sodium chloride*. Much of Earth's salt is dissolved in seawater. It is also found underground in mines and in dried-up areas where seas once flowed. It comes in many colors, such as pink, black, and green.

Whatever its color, salt does more than boost flavor. Sodium and chloride help our bodies run properly. They help our muscles and nerves react, and they keep our blood pressure steady.

1. What makes salt different from every other rock?

____

2. How does salt help the body?

____

Sentence Mender

Rewrite the sentence to make it correct.

The tie has red pink and orange flower.

____

BrainTeaser

Hink Pinks are one-syllable word pairs that rhyme to fit clues. Here's a Hink Pink:

What is a skinny hotel?
thin inn

Solve these Hink Pink riddles. Fill in the missing word for each.

1. What is an unhappy father? **sad** ____________

2. What is a library thief? **book** ____________

3. What is a chilly place to learn? **cool** ____________

JUMPSTART 7

Side A

Name ______________________ Date ______________

WORD of the Day

Use the word below to describe a funny scene.

scene: *view or picture; where things happen; certain section of a book, play, or film*

____

____

____

WORD Work

***Th* can have two different sounds.**
***Th* can use only air as in think.**
Or, *th* can use your throat, as in this.
Sort the words by their *th* sound below.

Word Bank

thank	that
theater	them
there	these
those	thunder
third	thumb

Th air only (*think*)		***Th*** with throat (*this*)	

Handwriting Helper

Trace the words. Then write them in cursive.

added

quote

equal

overcook

Ready, Set, READ!

Read the words to the song. Then answer the questions.

The Riddle Song *Traditional Folk Tune*

I gave my love a cherry that had no stone,
I gave my love a chicken that had no bone,
I gave my love a story that had no end,
I gave my love a baby with no cryin'.

How can there be a cherry that has no stone?
How can there be a chicken that has no bone?
How can there be a story that has no end?
How can there be a baby with no cryin'?

A cherry when it's blooming, it has no stone,
A chicken when it's pipping, it has no bone,
The story that I love you, it has no end,
A baby when it's sleeping has no cryin'.

1. How many verses does this song have?

 ____

 ____

2. What other word might you use for a cherry *stone*?

 ____

3. What do you think happens as chickens are *pipping*?

 ____

 ____

 ____

 ____

Sentence Mender

Rewrite the sentence to make it correct.

I love mysterys so does my dad.

____

BrainTeaser

Climb the word ladder to change warm to cold. Change one letter at a time. Write the *new* word on each step.

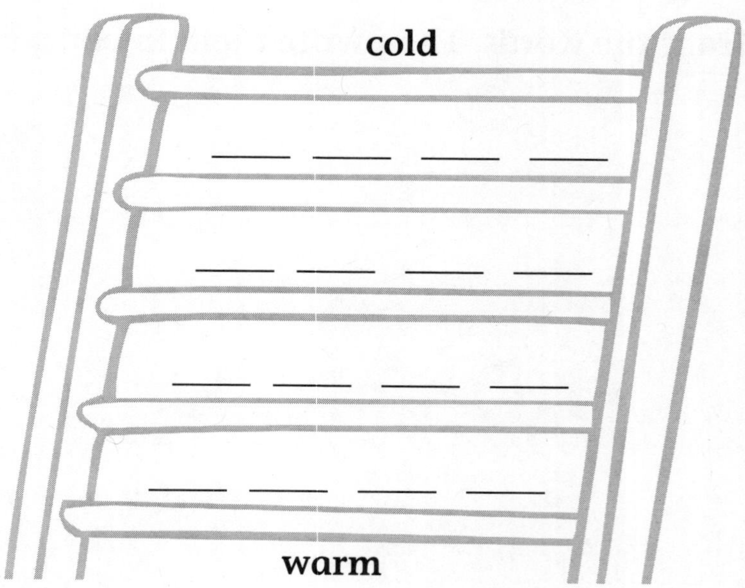

JUMPSTART 8

Side A

Name ______________________________ Date ______________

WORD of the Day

Use the word below to tell about a swift animal.

swift: *fast moving; happening quickly*

____

____

____

WORD Work

Write in the missing consonant digraphs so that each sentence makes sense.

Consonant Digraphs

ch ph sh th wh

1. Blue ______eese is really smelly!

2. ______ich is your favorite baseball team?

3. How many ______ildren need new ______oes?

4. I'd like ______ole ______eat toast, please.

5. I ______ink I'll take a ______oto of my left ______umb.

6. A great white ______ark has many ______arp teeth.

Handwriting Helper

Trace the words. Then write them in cursive.

gold

aqua

dodo

vocal

Ready, Set, READ!

Read the passage. Then answer the questions.

Looking for a fun vacation spot? Try Myrtle Beach, South Carolina. This area has more mini-golf courses than anywhere else in the United States! Mini-golf, or putt-putt, is a sport for everyone. It's a fun game, it's easy to play, and it'll make you laugh.

Most courses are open day and night. You can visit at least 60 different ones. Each course has its own theme and special features. You can putt with pirates or dinosaurs. Follow the holes past jungle animals and volcanos. All you need is a club and a ball. And you get those for free with your ticket.

1. Why do you think mini-golf is such a popular sport?

____

2. What other coast city is north of Myrtle Beach?

____

Sentence Mender

Rewrite the sentence to make it correct.

Ruth asked, "Cood you help me

____

BrainTeaser

Unscramble each word. Write it correctly in the spaces. The letters in the boxes will name an instrument. Write the word on the line below.

The instrument is a

____

OFROL [ ] ___ ___ ___ ___

DABL ___ ___ [ ] ___

REPU ___ [ ] ___ ___

FLET ___ ___ ___ [ ]

LLEEV ___ [ ] ___ ___ ___

JUMPSTART 9

Side A

Name ______________________________ Date ________________

WORD of the Day

Use the word below to describe a character that has to struggle.

struggle: *try very hard; make great effort*

WORD Work

Write in the missing consonant digraphs so that each sentence makes sense.

Consonant Digraphs

ch	sh	th
gh	ph	ng

1. The bar gra_____ shows which team is losi_____.

2. It takes so mu_____ time to bru_____ her long hair.

3. Ral_____ and Jude sat on a ben_____ to wait for the bus.

4. The unlucky mo_____ burned its wi_____ in the lantern.

5. Dad puts reli_____ on every sandwi_____ he makes for lun_____.

6. Drink some warm bro_____ to help calm that nasty cou_____.

Handwriting Helper

Trace the words. Then write them in cursive.

x-ray

valve

zinc

yawn

Ready, Set, READ!

Read the story. Then answer the questions.

Gilda knew it was wiser to stay inside. The ice storm had broken many trees. Power lines crossed the roads like snakes, ready to strike careless walkers. Every surface had a layer of ice on it. News teams told people to stay inside until work crews could clean up. But how could Gilda stay inside with her dad out there on his own?

Gilda's dad was coming home from work. Slippery streets would make it hard for him to roll his wheelchair. Broken branches would block the way. So Gilda decided to meet him at the bus stop. She spread ice melter on the front ramp. She walked to the bus stop with Dad's old cane, just in case. She took each step with care. Then she waited for the bus.

1. Why did Gilda ignore the warning to stay inside?

____

____

____

____

3. Why does the writer compare power lines to snakes?

____

____

____

____

Sentence Mender

Rewrite the sentence to make it correct.

can bill runs up that hill?

____

BrainTeaser

The word bank lists map words. Each word is hidden in the grid. Find and circle each word.

Word Bank

BAY	HIGHWAY	RIVER
CAPITAL	LAKE	ROAD
CITY	MOUNTAIN	SCALE
COAST	PARK	TOWN

R	S	H	M	R	H	C	O	A	S	T
I	C	I	T	Y	S	P	A	R	K	O
V	A	G	W	L	A	K	E	C	H	W
E	L	H	M	O	U	N	T	A	I	N
R	E	W	Y	D	R	O	A	D	R	Y
T	R	A	I	N	T	R	A	C	K	S
B	A	Y	F	C	A	P	I	T	A	L

Name ______________________ Date ______________

WORD of the Day

Use the word below to describe traits of a good friend.

trait: *special feature or quality of mind, body, or character*

____

____

____

WORD Work

Finish each sentence by writing a word from the word bank that begins or ends with *ch*.

Word Bank			
teach	search	stretch	hatch
cherry	chick	cheese	

1. Look at the camera and say "______________."

2. I always ______________ before I go for a run.

3. We saw the baby ______________ ______________ out of its shell.

4. I like to ______________ my dog new tricks.

5. One of my favorite desserts is ______________ pie.

6. A ______________ team looked all over for the lost dog.

Handwriting Helper

Trace the words. Then write them in cursive.

denim

nylon

muslin

velvet

JUMPSTART 10

Side B

Ready, Set, READ!

Read the story. Then answer the questions.

I love chocolate. I think it's one of the best flavors in the world. So how could this yummy treat harm my dog?

Dogs' bodies are not like ours in certain ways. For most foods these differences don't matter. But chocolate is a special case. It contains something called *theobromine* [thee-uh-BROH-meen]. Most humans who eat chocolate handle theobromine with no problem. But this stuff can make a dog very sick, or worse. The smaller the dog, the less chocolate it takes to cause trouble.

Vets know that a tiny bit of chocolate might not hurt a large dog. But the saying "Better safe than sorry" is always the best plan. If any dog eats a bag of chocolates or a plate of brownies, call a vet at once for help. He or she will know what to do.

1. Why is chocolate bad for dogs?

____

2. What should you do if your dog begs for chocolate cake?

____

Sentence Mender

Rewrite the sentence to make it correct.

Maria take a dance class on thursdy.

____

BrainTeaser

How many words can you list that rhyme with able?

1–3 words = Good 4–6 words = Super Over 7 words = Fantastic!

Name ______________________ Date ______________

WORD of the Day

Use the word below to tell ways you can be loyal.

loyal: *faithful; staying true; firmly supporting*

____

____

____

WORD Work

Read the words in each column. Draw lines to match vowel sounds. One is done for you.

bread •	• coat
flat •	• spray
throw •	• view
field •	• light
price •	• grab
huge •	• speak
whale •	• left

Handwriting Helper

Trace the words. Then write them in cursive.

vex

lamb

zero

yogurt

Ready, Set, READ!

Read the story. Then answer the questions.

A great oak tree grew near a river. Its friends were the thin reeds on the river bank. They bent over with the slightest breeze, while the oak stood firm.

"You should rise up straight and tall," scolded the oak. "Don't be pushed around!"

"You are very strong. But we think bending is safer," the reeds answered.

"Oh?" replied the oak. "We'll see."

The next day, a mighty wind blew from the north. The reeds bent their heads as the oak stood tall. But the wind knocked the oak to the ground. The once great tree rolled into the river. The reeds watched their friend float away. "We bent with the wind, and we are still here," they said.

1. Which is the best moral of this story?
   - ○ A. Always stand tall.
   - ○ B. Be willing to bend.
   - ○ C. Don't live by a river.

2. Would you rather be like the oak or the reeds? Explain why.

____

____

____

____

____

____

Sentence Mender

Rewrite the sentence to make it correct.

Thay wont no when to show up.

____

BrainTeaser

Write a synonym from the word bank for each bolded word below.

1. gave **consent** ______________________
2. **delicate** glass ______________________
3. got **enraged** ______________________
4. **frugal** shopper ______________________
5. **plucky** hero ______________________
6. **thorough** cleaning ______________________

Word Bank

brave
thrifty
fragile
furious
complete
permission

JUMPSTART 12

Side A

Name ______________________ Date ______________

WORD of the Day

Use the word below to write about differences between house cats and wild cats.

contrast: *to point out differences in things*

____

____

____

WORD Work

Use silent *e* to change the short-vowel sound in each word to a long-vowel sound. Write the new word next to the old one. The first one is done for you.

Short vowel	Long vowel	Short vowel	Long vowel
1. past	paste	**6.** bath	
2. glob		**7.** shin	
3. them		**8.** rang	
4. slid		**9.** plan	
5. cut		**10.** strip	

Handwriting Helper

Some words end in *i*. Trace the words. Then write them in cursive.

taxi

kiwi

khaki

origami

Ready, Set, READ!

Read the passage. Then answer the questions.

Where the Wild Things Are is a famous picture book. Do you know it? Its author is Maurice Sendak. He wrote the story and drew the pictures. His book is 50 years old, but it's still loved today.

Maurice Sendak was sick a lot as a child. His parents had to keep him at home much of the time. He couldn't play outside with other kids. He could only watch them out the window. Maurice often felt lonely. So he passed the time by drawing pictures. He also made up stories in his mind. He made friends with the characters he met in books, too.

Sendak grew up to be an artist. His first job was helping to make comic books. Then he drew the pictures to go with other people's words.

The first book Sendak wrote and drew was called *Kenny's Window*. It told the story of a lonely boy. Can you imagine where that idea came from?

1. Who was Maurice Sendak?

____

____

____

____

____

2. Why was his childhood lonely?

____

____

____

____

____

Sentence Mender

Rewrite the sentence to make it correct.

Lets supprize them by dressing as elfs.

____

BrainTeaser

Write the words from the word bank in ABC order in the rows of the grid. Then complete the sentence below. (Hint: Read down the column on the far right.)

Word Bank

WOODEN
GAZEBO
TRICKY
USABLE
TUBING
MUSK OX

We need ____________________ to live.

Name ______________________ Date ______________

WORD of the Day

Use the word below to state the subject of a movie.

theme: *the central idea, topic, or subject*

____

____

____

WORD Work

All the words in the word bank have the same vowel sound. Write a word in each blank to complete the story below.

Shirley ____________ as the school ____________. Shirley wears a ____________ uniform. She helps kids who get ____________. She cleans ____________ out of ____________ cuts. On ____________, Earl got a ____________. He ____________ into Shirley's office. She spoke kind ____________ to him. Thanks, Nurse Shirley.

Word Bank
- burn
- burst
- dirty
- germs
- hurt
- nurse
- purple
- Thursday
- words
- works

Handwriting Helper

Some words end in *u*. Trace the words. Then write them in cursive.

tofu

haiku

bayou

kudzu

JUMPSTART 13

Side B

Ready, Set, READ!

Read the poems. Then answer the questions.

Poem 1

Soon the night will fade away,
Darkness soon will change to day.
Time to rub your sleepy eyes
And stretch your legs, begin to rise.

Poem 2

Gold and purple beams
Sparkle in the early dawn.
Robins pipe delight.

1. What is the subject of both poems?

____

2. How are the poems different?

____

3. Which poem do you prefer? Explain why.

____

____

Sentence Mender

Rewrite the sentence to make it correct.

Are that the exact word you writed

____

BrainTeaser

All the words below are made-up.
Write a funny meaning for each one.
The first one will give you the idea.

1. snorzabag a sleeping bag for a noisy sleeper

2. pragging ______________________________

3. unknorbled ______________________________

4. reblatch ______________________________

JUMPSTART 14

Side A

Name ______________________ Date ______________

WORD of the Day

Use the word below to tell one way to be prompt.

prompt: *on time; done quickly; without delay*

____

____

____

WORD Work

Write the word that correctly names each picture.

1.  woll worl waul wall ______________

2.  sard sord sword saud ______________

3. 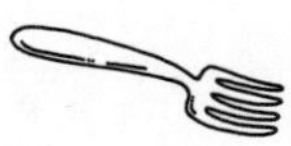 forke fork fark faurk ______________

4.  four fore foor foar ______________

5.  sault sawlt solt salt ______________

Handwriting Helper

Some words end in *z*. Trace the words. Then write them in cursive.

quiz

jazz

frizz

showbiz

Ready, Set, READ!

Read the recipe. Then answer the questions.

How to Make Invisible Ink

You Need

- 1 tablespoon baking soda
- $\frac{1}{4}$ cup water
- mixing cup and spoon
- paintbrush or cotton swabs
- white paper
- purple grape juice

What to Do

1. Mix the baking soda and water. Stir well.
2. Paint a message on white paper with a brush or cotton swab.
3. Let dry. Clean the brush or get a new cotton swab.
4. Now paint the paper with grape juice. Your message will appear!

1. Why does **You Need** come before **What to Do**?

____

2. What might happen if you don't let the secret message dry?

____

Sentence Mender

Rewrite the sentence to make it correct.

Next munth we will flew to chicago!

____

BrainTeaser

✓ the box to show whether the word names *one* thing or *more than one*. If you can't tell, ✓ the last box.

Word	1 thing	2 or more	Can't tell
1. deer			
2. mice			
3. sheep			
4. leaves			
5. social studies			

JUMPSTART 15

Side A

Name ______________________________ Date ____________________

WORD of the Day

Use the word below to tell how to puncture a bubble.

puncture: *make a hole in; pierce; stab*

____

____

____

WORD Work

Circle the correct spelling of long *a*.

1.		tran	trane	trayn	train
2.		flam	flame	flaim	flaym
3.		hae	haye	hai	hay
4.		skayt	skate	scat	skait
5.		sprae	sprai	spray	spra

Ways to Spell Long *a*

a_e

ai

ay

Handwriting Helper

Practice uppercase letters. Trace the words. Then write them in cursive.

Aladdin

Alaska

Boston

China

Ready, Set, READ!

Read the passage. Then answer the questions.

Zero is not just nothing. Zero is a number—a very important one. Zero helps us tell 1 from 10. But zero was not "born" at the same time as the other numbers.

The idea of a number that comes *before* one was hard to picture. When you count things, you start at one. Why have a number less than that? "How can nothing be something?" asked the Greeks of long ago.

Think about the answer to this question. *How many zebras are in your desk?* There are no zebras in your desk. Your desk has zero zebras. Zero is the number you need to answer the question.

A man in India was the first person to use zero for place value. This was a brand new idea. He helped make rules for zero. We use most of those rules to this day. And that is zero baloney!

1. Where in the world was zero first used for place value?

____

____

____

____

2. What does *zero baloney* mean?

____

____

____

____

Sentence Mender

Rewrite the sentence to make it correct.

We be fans of the detroit tigers.

____

BrainTeaser

Each vehicle below lost its vowels! Write *a*, *e*, *i*, *o*, or *u* to finish spelling each one.

1. t _____ x _____

2. w _____ g _____ n

3. r _____ ck _____ t

4. b _____ cycl _____

5. tr _____ _____ n

6. c _____ mp _____ r

7. r _____ wb _____ _____ t

8. st _____ _____ mr _____ ll _____ r

JUMPSTART 16

Side A

Name ______________________ Date ______________

WORD of the Day

Use the word below to write a question about how something is used.

function: *work, job, or purpose of a thing*

____

____

____

WORD Work

Circle the correct spelling of long *e*.

1.		kee	kea	kie	key
2.		seel	seal	syl	siel
3.		queen	quean	quien	quyn
4.		leesh	liesh	leysch	leash
5.		sheeld	sheald	shield	shyld

Ways to Spell Long *e*
ea
ee
ie
y

Handwriting Helper

Practice uppercase letters. Trace the words. Then write them in cursive.

David

Egypt

Flintstones

Frankenstein

JUMPSTART 16

Side B

Ready, Set, READ!

Read this interview between Jerry and his granddad Sid. Then answer the questions.

Jerry: Please tell me about my mom when she was little.

Sid: Your mom always made us laugh a lot. She was very curious.

Jerry: What was she curious about?

Sid: Almost everything. She asked more questions than any other kid in the family. She found humor in things that weren't funny to others. She noticed things and always wondered why.

Jerry: Did Mom tell jokes and ask silly riddles?

Sid: Not so much. But she noticed goofy things.

Jerry: Like what?

Sid: One day she asked why Buffalo wings tasted a lot like chicken.

Jerry: But they ARE chicken!

Sid: Yeah, but she thought they were the little wings of baby buffalo!

1. How is Sid related to Jerry?

____

____

____

____

____

2. How was Jerry's mom different from the other children in the family?

____

____

____

____

____

Sentence Mender

Rewrite the sentence to make it correct.

Their are ate legs on an spider.

____

BrainTeaser

Unscramble the words so that all rhyme.

1. ON ______________

2. OHE ______________

3. WES ______________

4. OWLB ______________

5. ODHUG ______________

6. HUTHOG ______________

Name ______________________________ Date ______________

WORD of the Day

Use the word below to tell why a T. rex is frightening.

fearsome: *frightening; causing great fear*

____

____

____

WORD Work

Circle the correct spelling of long *i*.

1.		bik	byk	bike	biek
2.		fly	fli	fligh	flie
3.		childe	child	chyld	chield
4.		knit	knite	knight	knyt
5.		cris	crys	crighs	cries

Ways to Spell Long *i*
i
i_e
ie
igh
y

Handwriting Helper

Practice uppercase letters. Trace the words. Then write them in cursive.

Garfield

Hawaii

Isaac

Ireland

Ready, Set, READ!

Read the story. Then answer the questions.

The spaceship was cramped. Its small window didn't offer much of a view. But the Isaacs flew through the dark sky, knowing they had little choice. Poor Earth was dying. Food and water were running out. Dense air pollution burned the eyes and lungs. So Dr. Isaac agreed to test a distant home for her family.

The travelers were Dr. Isaac, her two children, and the family cat, Athena. Athena didn't seem to mind the tight fit. But the children were bored, nervous, and eager to arrive at the space station.

"How much longer until we dock?" asked Tina.

"We'll be there by midnight," said Ira. "Unless a comet smashes into us first."

"What comet?" peeped Tina, her eyes wide.

"Ira, don't scare your sister," scolded Dr. Isaac. "You know perfectly well that our course steers clear of comets. But I fear you'll drive us crazy first!"

1. Why was the family leaving Earth?
   - ○ A. The planet was dying.
   - ○ B. They wanted adventure.
   - ○ C. They were being sent away.

2. Why did Dr. Isaac scold Ira?
   - ○ A. He was complaining.
   - ○ B. He was teasing the cat.
   - ○ C. He was scaring his sister.

Sentence Mender

Rewrite the sentence to make it correct.

Pete bys egs milk and tea.

____

BrainTeaser

Fill in the category chart. The letters above each column tell the first letter for each word. Two words have been done for you.

	b	r	i	m
Sports Words		racquet		
Science Words			icicle	
Music Words				

Name ____________________ Date ____________

WORD of the Day

Use the word below to write what a winner might shout.

exclaim: *to speak out with force or feeling*

____

____

____

WORD Work

Circle the correct spelling of long *o*.

1.		crow	croe	croa	cro
2.		glob	gloab	glowb	globe
3.	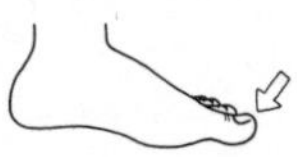	to	toe	toa	tow
4.		sop	sope	soap	soep
5.	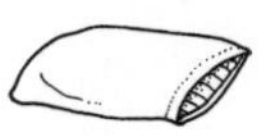	pilloe	pilloa	pillo	pillow

Ways to Spell Long *o*

o
oa
oe
o_e
ow

Handwriting Helper

Practice uppercase letters. Trace the words. Then write them in cursive.

Japanese

Kansas

Korean

Lincoln

JUMPSTART 18

Side B

Ready, Set, READ!

Read the passage. Then answer the questions.

I just saw the cartoon film, *An American Tale*. It is about the Mouskewitz family. They leave Russia because life is hard. They come to America, hoping for a better life. There were no planes then, so they came by ship. A bad storm sweeps young Fievel overboard. But he doesn't drown. He floats to America inside a bottle!

Fievel faces many dangers and adventures in New York City. I won't spoil the ending, but you can expect some happy surprises.

I liked this movie a lot. It's not as funny as other cartoon movies, and the music felt sad. But Fievel Mouskewitz is brave and clever. Even though he is alone, he makes friends and finds his way. That made me admire him. I wonder if I would have been so brave.

I think young children would be scared by this movie. But I liked not knowing what would happen. I saw it with my grandmother. She thought it had many realistic parts. Her parents came to America on a ship, too.

1. What kind of piece is this?
   - ○ A. book report
   - ○ B. film review
   - ○ C. science report

2. Why did the writer like the film?
   - ○ A. It was very funny.
   - ○ B. It told a true story.
   - ○ C. Fievel was smart and fearless.

Sentence Mender

Rewrite the sentence to make it correct.

Witch one of we get to go first?

____

BrainTeaser

A picture pair can make you think of a compound word, like this:

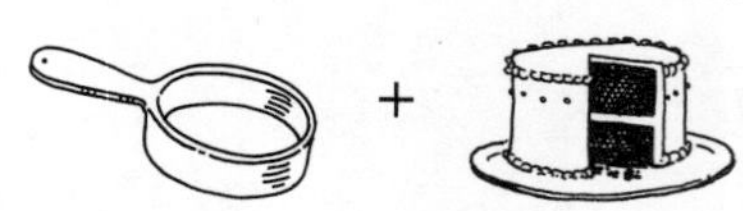

= pancake

Write a compound word that each pair suggests.

1.  +  = ____________

2. I +  = ____________

3.  +  = ____________

4.  +  = ____________

JUMPSTART 19

Side A

Name ______________________________ Date ________________

WORD of the Day

Use the word below to describe a realistic drama.

drama: *play or film with a serious theme; opposite of comedy*

____

____

____

WORD Work

Circle the correct spelling of long *u*.

1. 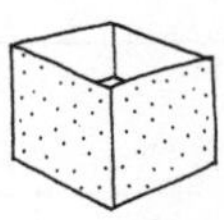 cub cube cewb cueb

2. 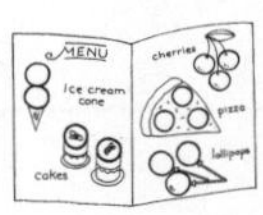

menu menue menew menoo

3. 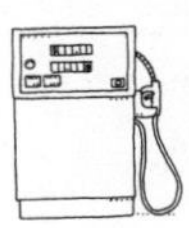 ful fewl fule fuel

4.  scru scrue screw scroo

Ways to Spell Long *u*
ew
u
u_e
ue

Handwriting Helper

Practice uppercase letters. Trace the words. Then write them in cursive.

Mickey Mouse

New Mexico

North Orange

Oxford, Ohio

Ready, Set, READ!

Read the myth. Then answer the questions.

The Myth of Atlas

Wealthy King Atlas was a giant on Earth. He had no rivals to challenge him. He loved his gardens above all else. There, golden apples grew from golden branches. It was a wonder to behold.

One day, a visitor arrived in Atlas's kingdom. He said, "I am Perseus. My father is Zeus, the king of all the gods." Perseus asked Atlas for food and a place to rest.

Atlas had much to offer, but he did not trust Perseus. He worried that Perseus wanted only to steal his golden apples. So Atlas told Perseus to leave.

Perseus flew into a rage, but he would not fight Atlas. Instead, he used his powers to turn Atlas to stone. Every part of Atlas's giant body grew together into a huge mountain. It was atop this mountain that heaven and its stars came to rest.

1. What made the gardens of Atlas special?

____

____

____

____

2. What made Perseus so angry?

____

____

____

____

Sentence Mender

Rewrite the sentence to make it correct.

I like Banana the better of all the froots.

____

BrainTeaser

Each sentence below has two blanks. Both use the *same* letters to form *different* three-letter words. Fill them in. The first one is done for you.

1. Are you sure that your ear feels better?

2. ____________ can you tell ____________ wrote that note?

3. As we left, we ____________ that it ____________ raining.

4. I can bathe in that ____________, ____________ I may splash.

JUMPSTART 20

Side A

Name ____________________ Date ____________

WORD of the Day

Use the word below to tell how to use ample play space.

ample: *more than enough; plenty*

____

____

____

WORD Work

Underline each word with the *oy* sound.
Then fill in the spelling rules in the box.

1. Always avoid tin foil on any voyage.
2. Boil the poison toy for two months.
3. My choice goes to Roy for ball boy.

Ways to Spell the *oy* Sound:

1. __________ 2. __________

Underline each word with the *ow* sound.
Then fill in the spelling rules in the box.

4. Allow a frown only at a grouch.
5. That growling hound scared the scout.
6. I doubt there is a prettier powder blue gown.

Ways to Spell the *ow* Sound:

1. __________ 2. __________

Handwriting Helper

Practice uppercase letters. Trace the words. Then write them in cursive.

Pocahontas

Quinn Quail

River Road

Spring Street

Ready, Set, READ!

Read the speech. Then answer the questions.

Speech at the Opening of the New Library

Good morning, children and teachers. We are here today to launch our new library. We will cut a ribbon to open its doors to one and all. I hope you will think of this day as a great step forward for our school. It will help bring us all into a brighter future.

In olden days, libraries held books, papers, and magazines. Before radio or TV, libraries were the home of fact, fiction, and news. Today's libraries still hold millions of words in print. But we now have new ways to read those words. We use computers and the Internet to make our library more modern.

If you are curious, our library can help open your mind. If you have a question, our library can help you find an answer.

I thank all who made this improvement possible.

1. How does the speaker feel about the new library?

____

____

____

____

2. What is your view of your school's library?

____

____

____

____

Sentence Mender

Rewrite the sentence to make it correct.

You must weight four a peace of cake.

____

BrainTeaser

Use the clues to complete a word that starts with den.

1. Bump or push in D E N ___

2. What jeans are made of D E N ___ ___

3. Very thick, like fog D E N ___ ___

4. Tooth doctor D E N ___ ___ ___ ___

5. False teeth D E N ___ ___ ___ ___ ___

Name ________________________ Date ____________

WORD of the Day

Use the word below to summarize a real-life event you recount again and again.

recount: *to tell about in detail*

____

____

____

WORD Work

The letters *oo* can have two different sounds.
o͞o stands for long *oo*, as in mo͞on.
o͝o stands for short *oo*, as in bo͝ok.
Sort the words in the word bank by their *oo* sound below.

Word Bank

cookie	broom
good	goose
proof	shook
wood	smooth

o͞o as in *moon*	o͝o as in *book*

Handwriting Helper

Practice uppercase letters. Trace the words. Then write them in cursive.

Tyler, Texas

Unique, Utah

Vista Valley

Wedding Walk

Ready, Set, READ!

Read the tall tale. Then answer the questions.

Arizona Weather

I've lived in Arizona my whole life. So I know Arizona weather. I say it's the best weather in the United States. Arizona air is so fine that people drive here just to fill their tires with it. They fill balloons and jugs of it to take home with them. And there's still plenty of air for the rest of us.

Yes, Arizona gets mighty hot. Even the cactus sweat a bit. But with ice from California, our hens don't lay hard-boiled eggs any more. We can still fry eggs on the streets, though.

Rain haters should be Arizona lovers. We haven't seen rain in nine hundred years and seventeen days. It's so dry we give free swimming lessons to our fish. Nobody needs to "save for a rainy day" so there's tons of cash to go around.

1. What is the main idea of this tale?
   - O A. Arizona fish can't swim.
   - O B. It doesn't rain much in Arizona.
   - O C. Arizona has wonderful weather.

2. Has Arizona really had no rain for "nine hundred years and seventeen days"?

   Explain. ______________________

Sentence Mender

Rewrite the sentence to make it correct.

Mikes dad catched her first fish!

____

BrainTeaser

How many different words can you spell with letters from the word earthworm? Every word must have at least three letters. List them here.

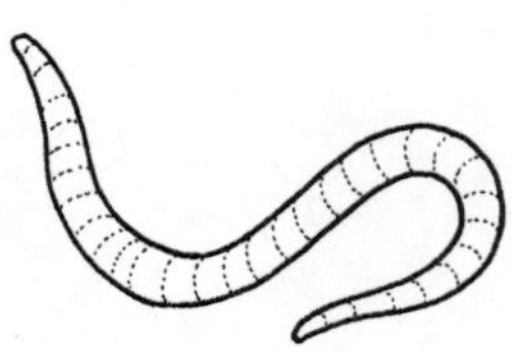

____

Name ______________________ Date ______________

WORD of the Day

Use the word below to write about your favorite TV series.

series: *group of related things following in order*

____

____

____

WORD Work

Read the silly poem at right. Count how many syllables are in each word. Then write the words in the chart where they belong.

Whenever porcupines gather
for their private little picnic,
Nobody need remember
to bring a single toothpick!

1 syllable	2 syllables	3 syllables

Handwriting Helper

Practice uppercase letters. Trace the words. Then write them in cursive.

Xylophone

Yellowstone

Zach Zoller

Ready, Set, READ!

Read the letter. Then answer the questions.

Dear Editor,

I disagree with your article against skateboard parks. You call them risky places that attract rough crowds. You say they waste money and space.

I am a skateboarder. I am not rough. I'm a regular kid looking for fun doing things I like. I'd rather skate in a park with others than alone on the streets. Skateboard parks are built by people who know the sport. They don't take up a lot of space or cost a lot.

I believe strongly that young people need safe places to go after school and on weekends. We learn from each other. We help each other at a sport we enjoy. We also get exercise and fresh air, which everyone knows is smart. Thank you.

Yours truly,
Carlos Gomez, age 13

1. What made Carlos write this letter?

____

____

____

____

2. Do you agree with him? Explain.

____

____

____

____

Sentence Mender

Rewrite the sentence to make it correct.

Mom kepped my first very baby shoo.

____

BrainTeaser

Reorder each word group to make a sentence. Start each sentence with a capital letter and use an ending punctuation mark.

1. window the shut ______________________

2. eat didn't breakfast you ______________________

3. hat seen you my have ______________________

4. to please I Pam speak may ______________________

Name ______________________ Date ______________

WORD of the Day

Use the word below to state a valid reason to miss school.

valid: *based on fact or reason; true; legal*

____

____

____

WORD Work

Solve each riddle by writing a word that starts with a blend from the box.

s Blends							
sc	sk	sl	sm	sn	sp	st	sw

1. A stinky animal? ______________

2. Weighing tool? ______________

3. Not fast? ______________

4. Frightening? ______________

5. A nose noise? ______________

6. Not sour? ______________

7. Spins a web? ______________

8. Horse's home? ______________

Handwriting Helper

Here are four days of the week. Trace the words. Then write them in cursive.

Monday

Tuesday

Wednesday

Thursday

Ready, Set, READ!

Read the story. Then answer the questions.

We rode the trolley to the World's Fair. It was hot in St. Louis that summer of 1904. We got so tired walking around all the displays. Each was better than the one before, but we began to drag. "How about ice cream?" Dad offered. Who could say no to that?

We found the nearest ice-cream stand, but the owner looked wild-eyed. He had plenty of ice cream, he said, but no more cups to serve it in. Cries of "Oh no!" rose from the disappointed crowd. Suddenly, the man at a nearby pastry cart got an idea. He rolled some leftover dough into the shape of a cone. He pointed his finger at the space inside. A problem was solved!

The ice-cream vendor filled cones as fast as the pastry man could make them. It was messy, but it was such fun to slurp the first ice-cream cones in America.

1. When does the story take place?
   - O A. in the past
   - O B. in the present
   - O C. in the future
2. Which best describes the pastry man?
   - O A. frantic
   - O B. creative
   - O C. messy

Sentence Mender

Rewrite the sentence to make it correct.

They wont never solve them riddles.

____

BrainTeaser

Use the clues to complete a word that starts with man.

1. Lion's long hair M A N ___
2. Lots of M A N ___
3. Sweet juicy fruit M A N ___ ___
4. Green "praying" insect M A N ___ ___ ___
5. Large fancy home M A N ___ ___ ___ ___

Name ______________________ Date ______________

WORD of the Day

Use the word below to write about something you hope to convince your parents about.

convince: *make someone believe; win over*

____

____

____

WORD Work

s Blends

scr	squ	str	spr	spl

Solve each riddle by writing a word that starts with a three-letter *s* blend from the box.

1. Kind of owl? ______________

2. four-sided figure? ______________

3. A season? ______________

4. Not crooked? ______________

5. Watery sound? ______________

6. Wash well? ______________

7. Press hard? ______________

8. Drinking tube? ______________

Handwriting Helper

Here are three days of the week. Trace the words. Then write them in cursive.

Friday

Saturday

Sunday

Ready, Set, READ!

Read the passage. Then answer the questions.

I've been begging Mom to share her tablet with me. It's light, bright, and easy to use. You just tap or swipe one finger to move around the pages. You can make pages as big or small as you like.

A tablet is definitely not a toy. It's a computer, so it must be used with care. Mom is very clear on this. I must have clean hands, and I have to be sitting so I don't drop it. Okay, those rules seem fair to me.

Mom reads everything on her tablet. Today she will download things just for me to read! It makes me feel grown-up to read on her tablet. If I come to a word I don't know, I just tap it with my finger. A little box pops up to tell me what it means. If I read the name of a place I don't know, a tap shows it on a map. I don't have to ask questions because it helps me figure out stuff on my own!

1. What rule does Mom insist on when the writer uses her tablet?
   - ○ A. No playing video games
   - ○ B. Always turn it off.
   - ○ C. Wash your hands first.

2. What does it mean to download a book to the tablet?
   - ○ A. Bring it from another computer.
   - ○ B. Use the tablet on a flat surface.
   - ○ C. Plug it in to charge it up.

Sentence Mender

Rewrite the sentence to make it correct.

Mika sayed he feeled to sick to eat.

____

BrainTeaser

Homophones are words that sound the same but have different spellings and different meanings.

Write the correct word in each sentence.

1. The ____________________ of 2 and 2 is 4. **som** *or* **sum**

2. We ____________________ the whole pizza. **ate** *or* **eight**

3. That lizard has a long ____________________. **tale** *or* **tail**

4. Gus ____________________ his bicycle to school. **road** *or* **rode**

5. A postcard costs 20 ____________________. **cents** *or* **sense**

Name ______________________ Date ______________

WORD of the Day

Use the word below to describe a nature photographer at work.

tripod: *a three-legged stand or support*

____

____

____

WORD Work

Pair two words from the word bank to form one new compound word. Use each word just once.

1. ______________________
2. ______________________
3. ______________________
4. ______________________
5. ______________________
6. ______________________
7. ______________________

Word Bank

arm	door
back	finger
bag	night
bean	pack
bird	print
bell	over
cage	rest

Handwriting Helper

Here are four months of the year. Trace the words. Then write them in cursive.

January

February

March

April

Ready, Set, READ!

Read the ballad. Then answer the questions.

The Ballad of the Fox *Traditional Folk Song*
Oh, the fox went out on a very dark night,
He prayed that the moon would give him light,
For he'd many a mile to go that night
Before he'd reach the town-o, town-o, town-o.
He'd many a mile to go that night before he'd reach the town-o.

He ran 'til he came to a great big pen
Where the ducks and the geese were all kept in.
"A couple o' you gonna grease my chin
Before I leave this town-o, town-o, town-o.
A couple o' you gonna grease my chin before I leave this town-o!"

He grabbed a gray goose by the neck!
He threw a duck across his back!
Fox didn't mind the quack, quack, quack
And the legs all dangling down-o, down-o, down-o.
Fox didn't mind the quack, quack, quack and the legs all dangling down-o.

1. What is a ballad?

____

2. This is just part of *The Ballad of the Fox*. What else do you want to know?

____

Sentence Mender

Rewrite the sentence to make it correct.

Peter Paul and mary yous to sing folk songs.

____

BrainTeaser

How many words can you list that rhyme with beam?

1–3 words = Good	4–6 words = Super	Over 7 words = Fantastic!

______________ ______________ ______________

______________ ______________ ______________

______________ ______________ ______________

Name ______________________ Date ______________

WORD of the Day

Use the word below to tell how a fluent reader sounds.

fluent: *can speak smoothly, clearly, naturally*

WORD Work

The passage below has many compound words. Can you find all 11 of them? Circle each one as you find it.

Mom slumped in an armchair. "I can't find my eyeglasses anywhere!" she cried. "They're not in my briefcase or in my coat. But I'm sure I wore them home."

Jaden tried to help. He searched in each bedroom. He dug through mom's handbag. He aimed his flashlight in every wastebasket. No luck.

Then mom got a brainstorm. "I left them on the dashboard of the car!" She raced outside.

"Mystery solved," announced Jaden.

Handwriting Helper

Here are four months of the year. Trace the words. Then write them in cursive.

May

June

July

August

Ready, Set, READ!

Read the passage. Then answer the questions.

Do you know how to thumb wrestle? Can you name the thumb wrestling champ of your class? Have you ever watched *Thumb Wrestling Federation*?

Thumb wrestling may be a small sport, but it is for real. It takes no equipment, no special playing field. You need only two players with thumbs, and maybe a judge. Players sit or stand across from each other to compete. A match can last for a few seconds or more than a minute.

Before wrestling, players agree whether to play lefty or righty. By custom, each player's unused hand goes behind the back. Players link fingers tightly, with their thumbs standing tall. At a start cue, players try to pin each other's thumb with their own.

Try thumb wrestling today. You can find thumb wrestling tips in videos online. Thumbs up for thumb wrestling!

1. What do you think of thumb wrestling?

____

____

____

____

____

____

2. Which word means the same as *compete*?

○ A. agree
○ B. battle
○ C. conquer
○ D. judge

Sentence Mender

Rewrite the sentence to make it correct.

Yes I done all my chore.

____

BrainTeaser

Hink Pinks are one-syllable word pairs that rhyme to fit clues. Here's a Hink Pink: →

What is an empty seat?
bare chair

Solve these Hink Pink riddles. Fill in the missing word for each.

1. What is a boarded-up shack? **shut** ________________

2. What is a lengthy tune? **long** ________________

3. What is a sturdy building material? **thick** ________________

Name ______________________ Date ______________

WORD of the Day

Use the word below to write about an expert you'd like to ask about something.

consult: *to ask the advice or opinion*

____

____

____

WORD Work

Use words from the word bank to form compound words with other words of your choice. Any word you choose can either start or end your compound word.

1. ______________________
2. ______________________
3. ______________________
4. ______________________
5. ______________________
6. ______________________
7. ______________________

Word Bank

book	snow
cup	side
foot	store
pop	work
rain	

Handwriting Helper

Here are four months of the year. Trace the words. Then write them in cursive.

September

October

November

December

Ready, Set, READ!

Read the passage. Then answer the questions.

Have you ever seen balls of ice fall from the sky? It's good that hail doesn't fall often because it brings damage and danger. Hail is a piece of ice. It can be as round as a golf ball, or it can be lumpy. Hail is like rain and snow because all are forms of water that fall from clouds.

Three things must happen at once for a hailstorm to take place.

1. A big cloud must be holding lots of water it has to let go.
2. The sky must be very cold so the water freezes.
3. Strong winds called *updrafts* must push air up.

Hail forms in stages. Water leaves a cloud and freezes hard. An updraft pushes the ice ball back into the clouds. There it picks up more water, freezes again, and falls again. As updrafts continue, the hail keeps getting bigger. Once the hail gets too heavy, the wind can't push it up anymore. It finally hits the ground.

1. What is the opposite of *updraft*?

____

2. What makes hail grow in size?

____

____

____

____

____

____

____

Sentence Mender

Rewrite the sentence to make it correct.

A appel a day keep the doctor away.

____

BrainTeaser

Think of an item for each word part listed below. Look around the room and out the window for ideas. Words can be any length.

Word part	Item
1. -ack	
2. -ash	
3. -eat	
4. -ight	

Word part	Item
5. -ip	
6. -ock	
7. -ound	
8. -ug	

JUMPSTART 28

Side A

Name ______________________________ Date ________________

WORD of the Day

Use the word below to ask a question about a song.

stanza: *group of lines that form part of a song or poem*

____

____

____

WORD Work

Some English words are spelled with silent letters.
Each phrase below has two silent letters. Circle them.

1. signs of autumn

2. talk calmly

3. shepherds and lambs

4. Ghost Island

5. two guards

6. wrap that rhino

7. comb and scissors

8. sword and knife

9. whole school

10. answer column

Handwriting Helper

Trace the names of some famous national parks. Then write them in cursive.

Mesa Verde

Niagara Falls

Grand Canyon

Hot Springs

Ready, Set, READ!

Read the passage. Then answer the questions.

The star-nosed mole is a weird creature. About the size of a hamster, this mammal lives in wetland areas. It eats worms, grubs, and insects. Like other moles, it uses its long claws to dig. So why does it have a fleshy 22-point star around its nose?

Scientists know what great hunters these moles are because they have filmed them in action. Star-nosed moles can search, find, and eat their food faster than our eyes can see! Scientists have to watch the films in slow motion to figure out what the mole is doing.

They know now that the star is a sensitive touch organ. Think of it as a flexible nose with tiny pink fingers! The mole explores with its star, and then gobbles its prey in a flash.

1. Which sentence in the passage does the picture best explain?
   - O A. The star-nosed mole is a weird creature.
   - O B. Think of it as a flexible nose with tiny pink fingers.
   - O C. The mole explores with its star, and then gobbles its prey in a flash.

2. How is this mole like other moles?

____

____

____

____

____

Sentence Mender

Rewrite the sentence to make it correct.

Have you red Mr Popper's Penguins?

____

BrainTeaser

Write an *antonym* (opposite) from the word bank for each bolded word.

1. **sickly** child ____________________
2. **groggy** pilot ____________________
3. **forget** to call ____________________
4. **simple** homework ____________________

Word Bank

alert
healthy
remember
challenging

JUMPSTART 29

Side A

Name ______________________ Date ______________

WORD of the Day

Use the word below to describe a wretched situation.

wretched: *very unhappy or troubled; in terrible condition; miserable*

____

____

____

WORD Work

Write two words as one by removing letters. Write ' where letters come out. Then list those letters. The first one is done for you.

Two Words	Contraction	Letters Taken Out
1. I am	I'm	a
2. what is		
3. let us		
4. you have		
5. they will		
6. who would		

Contract means to get smaller. We often use ***contractions*** when we talk.

Handwriting Helper

Here are silly made-up names. Trace them. Then write them in cursive. Say the names.

Orson Buggy

Eileen Dover

Hugo Furst

Rusty Steele

Ready, Set, READ!

Read the story. Then answer the questions.

Henry was looking after his little sister June while his parents went out to do some shopping. It was such a lovely spring day that Henry decided to go fishing. He gathered up all his gear. And of course, he brought June with him.

Later on, Henry described the afternoon to his parents. "Crazy me! I'll never do that again!" Henry said. "I didn't catch even one tiny fish!"

"Oh, honey," said his mother. "I'm sorry you had no luck. Next time I'm sure June will know to be more quiet and stop scaring away all the fish."

"No, Mom, that's not it at all," Henry replied. "June gobbled up all my bait!"

1. What made Henry go fishing?
   - O A. A friend invited him.
   - O B. He needed food to eat.
   - O C. The weather was so pleasant.

2. Why didn't Henry catch any fish?
   - O A. He just had bad luck.
   - O B. June ate his bait.
   - O C. June scared them all away.

Sentence Mender

Rewrite the sentence to make it correct.

May I sit necks to she

____

BrainTeaser

Fill both sides of each *antonym* (opposite) box with examples. Write three words in each side. Examples are done for you.

Smooth	Rough
glass	brick

Ancient	Modern
pyramid	rocket

JUMPSTART 30

Side A

Name ______________________ Date ______________

WORD of the Day

Use the word below to write about a special object you possess.

possess: *to have or own something*

____

____

____

WORD Work

Underline the contraction in each sentence. Then write the two words it stands for.

1. This doesn't taste good.	
2. They can't finish in time.	
3. I'd never do that!	
4. Here's my favorite color.	
5. She wasn't ready for the test.	
6. You might've called me first.	

Handwriting Helper

English uses words from many languages. Trace the words. Then write them in cursive.

banana

mattress

tangerine

zebra

JUMPSTART 30

Side B

Ready, Set, READ!

Read the passage. Then answer the questions.

The horn is an ancient instrument. The first ones were the horns of animals, such as bulls or rams. People made sounds by blowing into them. Then horns were made of wood or metal.

The first modern horns were made of brass. They started as plain tubes. Soon, the tubes came in assorted shapes and sizes. Those brass horns were so loud that at first, they were played only outside. The players were usually hunters, soldiers, and royal servants.

The French horn is a fancy loop of over 20 feet of brass tubing. A horn player blows air into the *mouthpiece*. He or she can press *valves*, or keys, with the right hand to change notes. The sounds come out the open end of the horn, called the *bell*. Horn players put the left hand in the bell to vary the sound.

1. Why did horn players once play outside only?

____

____

____

____

2. Which parts of the French horn does a player touch with his hands?

____

____

____

____

Sentence Mender

Rewrite the sentence to make it correct.

Clowns loves to make child's laff.

____

BrainTeaser

Use the clues to complete each word that starts with gla.

1. Pleased or happy G L A ___

2. Object to drink from G L A ___ ___

3. Swollen places under the chin G L A ___ ___ ___

4. Kind of donut G L A ___ ___ ___

5. Look at briefly G L A ___ ___ ___

Name ________________________ Date ______________

WORD of the Day

Use the word below to list a sequence you know.

sequence: *the order in which things appear or must be put*

____

____

____

WORD Work

Complete the chart by adding *-s*, *-ed*, and *-ing* to each base word.

Base Word	-s	-ed	-ing
1. swarm			
2. reward			
3. answer			
4. slouch			
5. lengthen			
6. subtract			

Handwriting Helper

English uses words from many languages. Trace the words. Then write them in cursive.

chopsticks

kangaroo

koala

silk

Ready, Set, READ!

Read the story. Then answer the questions.

Rob didn't want to play baseball. He liked being with his friends, but he just didn't care enough about that game to get involved in it. Rob loved a different sort of game. He wanted to play chess.

Rob and his mom had started playing chess when he was five years old. He quickly learned all the pieces and the rules for moving them. He made clay chess pieces, and drew chess sets in his sketch pads. He read books about chess and watched the speed-chess players in the park. He was eager to know more, to become a better player.

But his dad worried that Rob spent too much time on his own. Dad wanted Rob to be more active, to play with teammates in uniform.

Rob played chess with his friend Arun. Arun told Rob about a chess club at the community center. "It meets after school on Tuesdays. Wouldn't your folks let you join a chess team instead of a baseball team?"

1. How did Rob get interested in chess?
   - O A. by joining a chess club
   - O B. by watching speed chess
   - O C. by playing with his mom

2. Which shows Rob's love of chess?
   - O A. He does not play with Arun.
   - O B. He reads books about chess.
   - O C. He doesn't care to play baseball.

Sentence Mender

Rewrite the sentence to make it correct.

We're bin waiting way two long!

____

BrainTeaser

Use the clues to complete each word that has *zz*.

1. Wobbly after spinning ____ ____ z z ____

2. Like a baby chick ____ ____ z z ____

3. Food with sauce and cheese ____ ____ z z ____

4. Jigsaw game ____ ____ z z ____ ____

5. Like curly, bushy hair ____ ____ ____ z z ____

Name ______________________ Date ____________

WORD of the Day

Use the word below to describe what you might see at an elegant party.

elegant: *graceful; rich-looking; tasteful*

____

____

____

WORD Work

Make each word plural. For most words, just add *-s*.

- **For words that end in *s*, *sh*, *ch*, *x*, or *z*, add *-es***
- **For words that end in *y*, change *y* to *i*, then add *-es*.**

Singular	Plural
1. product	
2. berry	
3. crash	
4. index	
5. lengthen	

Singular	Plural
6. trench	
7. jigsaw	
8. trophy	
9. fizz	
10. discuss	

Handwriting Helper

English uses words from many languages. Trace the words. Then write them in cursive.

karate

jungle

shampoo

tsunami

Ready, Set, READ!

Read the passage. Then answer the questions.

Two simple words can make your life better: Plan ahead.

I learned the hard way. I used to leave everything to the last minute. Each school morning was a mad rush. It was no fun, and I often got into trouble—at home and school. So my sister and I started a new habit. I've been practicing it for two weeks now, and it's made a huge difference. Plus, it's really simple.

Each evening before bed, I always do three things:

1. I pick my clothes for the next day. I lay my outfit on my dresser.
2. I pack my lunch, or put lunch money in my bag.
3. I pack my bookbag. I put in homework, permission slips, library books, and whatever else I need. I may forget something, but I'm in better shape than when I tried to do all this each morning.

This idea really works for me. My mornings are much calmer. Now there's even time for a little fun. After breakfast I can play with my rabbit or watch a little TV. So I invite you to join me. Plan ahead!

1. What is *not* in the new routine?
   - O A. Eat breakfast.
   - O B. Pack lunch.
   - O C. Pick clothes.

2. In what way are mornings better now?
   - O A. The speaker can sleep later.
   - O B. There is time to do homework.
   - O C. Things are calmer at home.

Sentence Mender

Rewrite the sentence to make it correct.

We maid plans for Friday Sunday Monday.

____

BrainTeaser

Write *a*, *e*, *i*, *o*, or *u* to finish spelling each color word.

1. r ____ by	**4.** ____ r ____ ng ____	**7.** c ____ pp ____ r
2. r ____ st	**5.** s ____ lv ____ r	**8.** ____ b ____ ny
3. p ____ rpl ____	**6.** l ____ v ____ nd ____ r	**9.** m ____ g ____ nt ____

JUMPSTART 33

Side A

Name ______________________ Date ____________

WORD of the Day

Use the word below to offer a way to modify your room.

modify: *to change or adjust to make better*

____

____

____

WORD Work

irregular = ***not*** regular

Some words have irregular plurals. Draw lines to match each irregular plural with its singular form. The first one is done for you.

dice •	• foot
oxen •	• tooth
men •	• child
teeth •	• die
children •	• trout
trout •	• ox
feet •	• man

Handwriting Helper

These words came from people's names. Trace the words. Then write them in cursive.

Ferris wheel

leotard

saxophone

diesel engine

Ready, Set, READ!

Read the story. Then answer the questions.

Malka didn't like being home alone, especially as the sun was setting. But she had little choice. Her mom had to run to Dr. Hoffman's office with baby Seth, who was running a fever. Malka knew not to answer the phone or the door when she was home alone. But what if someone outside was calling her name?

That's exactly what was happening. "Malka! Malka!" she heard. She couldn't recognize the voice, but it sounded like a lonely child. Malka went to the window and peeked through the curtains. In the fading light, she couldn't see anybody. But that mournful voice kept calling her name, over and over.

Malka paced back and forth, twisting her hair with her fingers. *I'll be fine*, she told herself. *Mom trusts me,* she repeated. *I'm nine years old, after all. Mom and Seth will be home soon, and everything will be just fine.* Or will it?

1. Another word for *recognize* is
   - ○ A. imitate
   - ○ B. identify
   - ○ C. repeat
   - ○ D. stop

2. What time of the day was it?
   - ○ A. morning
   - ○ B. noon
   - ○ C. late afternoon
   - ○ D. night

Sentence Mender

Rewrite the sentence to make it correct.

do you know her fone number

____

BrainTeaser

If athletes get athlete's foot, what do astronauts get?

Solve each clue. Then copy each letter into its numbered box to find the answer to the riddle.

- Signal letters for *Help*! ___ ___ ___ (4, 9, 3)
- Green citrus fruit ___ ___ ___ ___ (6, 5, 1, 10)
- Man's neckwear ___ ___ ___ (8, 2, 7)

1	2	3	4	5	6	7

8	9	10

JUMPSTART 34

Side A

Name ______________________ Date ______________

WORD of the Day

Use the word below to state your viewpoint on voting.

viewpoint: *attitude; a way of thinking*

____

____

____

WORD Work

Use *'s* to indicate belonging. Rewrite each phrase using *'s*.

Kim***'s*** key means:
key that belongs to Kim

1. folder that belongs to Cara ______________

2. bike that belongs to Joey ______________

3. drums owned by Raul ______________

4. office of the principal ______________

5. helmet of the soldier ______________

Handwriting Helper

These words came from the names of places. Trace the words. Then write them in cursive.

frankfurter

hamburger

limousine

manila folder

Ready, Set, READ!

Read the letter. Then answer the questions.

Dear Lindy,

How is everything at your house? We're all fine here in Troy. The weather has been cold and windy, but there's no more snow, so that's great news!

Three weeks from now, on May 7, we're having a block party on our street. If it's anything like it was last year, there should be games, food, music, prizes, and even some surprises. Do you think your family could come visit ours then, and join us at the party? I hope so! Talk to Aunt Viola and Uncle Paul if you're interested.

Remember my watercolor painting of the bird feeder in our backyard? Well, I entered it in the school art fair, and I won third prize. I was proud, and I can show you my ribbon to prove it! How did you do on your oral report? I know you hate to speak in front of the class, but I hope that the time we spent practicing helped.

Please write back soon. Everybody here says hi to everybody there.

Love,

Karyn

1. How do you think Lindy and Karyn know each other? Explain.

____
____
____
____
____
____

2. Which might be the date when Karyn wrote to Lindy?

   ○ A. April 16

   ○ B. May 1

   ○ C. June 23

Sentence Mender

Rewrite the sentence to make it correct.

Dad mist one lunch brake this weak.

____

BrainTeaser

Fill the blank in each sentence with a word that makes sense.

1. Lane dropped his ice cream ____________________.

2. The baby just took her ____________________ step.

3. We ____________________ a long rope bridge.

4. It's better to be ____________________ than to be sorry.

JUMPSTART 35

Side A

Name ______________________ Date ______________

WORD of the Day

Use the word below to tell how birds and jets are alike.

similar: *almost but not exactly the same*

____

____

____

WORD Work

Is it plural or possessive?
Write the correct form.

plural = more than one
possessive = shows belonging

1. Water the ______________ every other day. **flowers** *or* **flower's**

2. Thirty ______________ are in the chorus. **singers** *or* **singer's**

3. Our ______________ new van is silver. **families** *or* **family's**

4. Which ______________ powers are best? **heroes** *or* **hero's**

5. They packed four huge ______________. **crates** *or* **crate's**

6. We froze at the ______________ whistle. **coaches** *or* **coach's**

Handwriting Helper

These words came from myths. Trace the words. Then write them in cursive.

atlas

cereal

echo

volcano

Ready, Set, READ!

Read the words to the song. Then answer the questions.

The Calendar Song

Sixty seconds make a minute,
Something you can learn within it.

Sixty minutes make an hour,
Work with all your might and power.

Twenty-four hours make a day,
Time enough for work and play.

Seven days a week will make,
You will learn if pains you take.

Fifty-two weeks make a year,
Soon a new one shall be here.

Twelve long months a year will make,
Say them now without mistake.

1. What is the main idea of this song?

____

____

____

____

2. How many stanzas are there?

____

3. What would you expect to see in the next stanzas?

____

____

____

____

Sentence Mender

Rewrite the sentence to make it correct.

Avoid that deep whole warned mrs Wu.

____

BrainTeaser

Each sentence below has an extra word. Find it and cross it out.

1. The rusty van drove down the lamp street.

2. How much more time machine will we have?

3. The ruler radio woke me up too soon.

4. Thank you for making songs my favorite pudding.

5. The clown nose did great tricks with a pack of cards.

JUMPSTART 36

Side A

Name ______________________ Date ______________

WORD of the Day

Use the word below in a question to a science teacher.

clarify: *to explain; to make clear*

____

____

____

WORD Work

Write the missing comparing words. The first one is done for you.

1. Mark is **fast**. Derek is **fast<u>er</u>**. Tyrell is the **fast<u>est</u>**.

2. Lil is ______________. Luis is **shorter**. Emilio is the ______________.

3. Jeb was **late**. Bette was ______________. Alan was the ______________.

4. Cars are ______________. Vans are **heavier**. Trains are the ______________.

5. I'm **silly**. Dad is ______________. Aunt Zoe is the ______________.

6. A twig is **sharp**. A pin is ______________. A knife is the ______________.

Handwriting Helper

Each phrase links opposites. Trace the phrases. Then write them in cursive.

freezer burn

never again

science fiction

student teacher

Ready, Set, READ!

Read the memo. Then answer the questions.

TO: All students ages 8 and up
FROM: Principal Bennett
DATE: March 26
SUBJECT: Pet Pals

Girls and boys,

Do you love animals? Then let me share an idea.

Our local pet shelter has a new project. They seek students to help after school and on Saturdays. Many dogs and cats wait there to be adopted. Adult volunteers feed them and clean their cages. But that work doesn't leave time for playing with the pets. Pets need love and attention from a pal—like you!

This project is open to children 8 years old or older. If you wish to help, you need permission from a parent. Ask that person to call 555-5555 by April 5. Ms. James leads the project. She'll be glad to answer any questions. You can also learn more at www.animalshelter.org. Thank you!

1. Who wrote this letter?

____

____

2. What two ways can you get more details about the Pet Pal project?

____

____

____

____

____

____

____

____

Sentence Mender

Rewrite the sentence to make it correct.

Your a grate athlete Victor.

____

BrainTeaser

Each sentence below has two missing words. Both use the *same* letters to form *different* words. Fill them in. The first one has been done for you.

1. I'll cook the meat for the team dinner.

2. The hairy jungle ______________ loves ______________ soup!

3. The scar on his ______________ is about an ______________ long.

4. Please take ______________ of my bike while I run the ______________.

JUMPSTART 37

Side A

Name ______________________ Date ______________

WORD of the Day

Use the word below to give the location of a fire alarm.

location: *position or place where something is*

____

____

____

WORD Work

The prefix *un-* means not. *Un-* turns *happy* ☺ into *unhappy* ☹. Change the meaning of each word by writing *un-* before it. The first one is done for you.

1. not fair	**2.** not sure	**3.** not afraid
unfair		
4. not folded	**5.** not known	**6.** not likely
7. not equal	**8.** not tangled	**9.** not important

Handwriting Helper

These words name kinds of writing. Trace the words. Then write them in cursive.

fantasy

mystery

biography

romance

Ready, Set, READ!

Read the tall tale. Then answer the questions.

Febold Feboldson

Drought was a serious problem for settlers. Crops, critters, and country folk needed water, and lots of it. But over one piece of prairie, clouds just passed by and never left a single drop of rain. It was a dry, dusty time.

Then Febold Feboldson rode by. The famous cloud buster had some tricks up his sleeve that he knew would bring water to the thirsty land. So here's what that big Swede did:

Febold hauled wood and built huge fires around every lake in the area. All that heat turned the lake water into steam. All that steam rose up to make new clouds. Soon, hundreds of clouds clogged up the sky. They crashed into each other and broke open.

Yes, Febold built clouds and then busted them! The drought was over.

1. A *drought* is a

   O A. rainstorm O B. cloudburst O C. fire O D. long time without rain

2. How can you tell that this is a tall tale?

___

Sentence Mender

Rewrite the sentence to make it correct.

My ant Marge teach me to nit.

___

BrainTeaser

The sentence in the box has only five words. But every word starts with the *same* letter.

Abe always adores autumn apples.

Write a sentence in which every word begins with *s*. Make it as long as you can.

___

___

JUMPSTART 38

Side A

Name ______________________ Date ______________

WORD of the Day

Use the word below to write about a defiant person.

defiant: *refusing to obey; strongly against*

____

____

____

WORD Work

The prefixes *dis-* and *non-* mean the opposite of. Read each *dis-* and *non-* word. Write what it is the opposite of. The first word is done for you.

1. disagree	**4.** nonfiction
opposite of agree	
2. disobey	**5.** nonliving
3. discomfort	**6.** nonsticky

Handwriting Helper

These words are synonyms for *big*. Trace the words. Then write them in cursive.

huge

vast

massive

enormous

Ready, Set, READ!

Read the passage. Then answer the questions.

How many famous writers do you know? Did you ever dream that you could be one? Mrs. P might help you. Mrs. P has many ways to excite kids to read and write, maybe even get famous, too.

In real life, Mrs. P is actress Kathy Kinney. She has been in many TV shows and movies. Once she played a librarian. Maybe that role gave her some ideas for Mrs. P.

In 2010, Kinney started a kids' Web site called MrsP.com. You can read books there, or hear classic stories Mrs. P herself reads. That same year she also began the "Be-A-Famous-Writer" Contest. Its rules are simple:

1. You must be between ages 4 and 13, and live in the United States.
2. You must write your fiction or nonfiction piece in English. It must have between 250 and 1,000 words.

The grand prize? Mrs. P will read your story on her Web site!

1. Mrs. P could help you become famous by
   - ○ A. giving you acting lessons.
   - ○ B. reading your story online.
   - ○ C. getting you a movie part.
2. You are 11 years old, you love to write, and you live in Canada. Can you enter the contest? Explain.

____

____

____

____

____

____

Sentence Mender

Rewrite the sentence to make it correct.

Gradys sell phone ringer are cheerful.

____

BrainTeaser

Imagine a huge parade. What passes by? Write a noun for *every* letter of the alphabet, *a* to *z*. The sentence is started for you.

At the parade, I saw **a**nimals, **b**ands, **c**ostumes, **d**______________________________

____

____

____

Name ______________________ Date ____________

WORD of the Day

Use the word below in a sentence about a broken water pipe.

rupture: *to burst open; to break apart*

____

____

____

WORD Work

The prefix *re-* means **again**. The prefix *over-* means **too much**.
Read each *re-* and *over-* word. Write what it means. The first one is done for you.

1. rearrange	**4.** overcooked
arrange again	
2. overeat	**5.** retraced
3. rediscover	**6.** overslept

Handwriting Helper

These words are synonyms for *small*. Trace the words. Then write them in cursive.

wee

elfin

petite

miniature

Ready, Set, READ!

Read the fable. Then answer the questions.

The Turtle and the Eagle *A Fable*

Turtle lay in the sun complaining. "Why won't you birds teach me to fly? I can move about on land, but oh so slowly."

Eagle sat in a nearby tree. He heard the complaining, so he swooped to the ground. "I heard you, Turtle. As you know, I can fly high and far, and am very strong. What reward will you promise me if I agree to take you flying?"

"Why, I promise you all the riches of the sea," Turtle replied.

"Very generous," said Eagle. "Then I shall teach you to fly." Eagle grabbed Turtle in his talons and the two flew high into the sky. Over a rocky mountain, Eagle suddenly opened his talons and let Turtle go. As she fell, Turtle cried, "O foolish me. I should have been content on earth." Turtle crashed on the rocks, where her shell shattered to bits.

MORAL: If we get all we wish for, we may find ruin.

1. Which is another word for *talons*?
   - O A. skills
   - O B. feathers
   - O C. claws
   - O D. legs
2. What does the moral mean to you?

____

____

____

____

____

____

____

Sentence Mender

Rewrite the sentence to make it correct.

Where saw we those huge dear?

____

BrainTeaser

Pick a person to describe. It can be a friend, hero, family member, fictional character, or yourself! Write 26 different *adjectives* (describing words) for that person, from *a* to *z*. Begin like this: [Name] is . . .

____

____

____

____

JUMPSTART 40

Side A

Name ______________________ Date ______________

WORD of the Day

Use the word below to describe a special ability that a superhero might have.

ability: *power; skill or talent*

____

____

____

WORD Work

The prefixes *in-* and *im-* mean not. Add *in-* or *im-* before a word to reverse its meaning. Use *im-* before words that start with *m* or *p*. Use *in-* before words that start with other letters. The first one is done for you.

1. not mature	**2.** not patient	**3.** not possible
immature		
4. not correct	**5.** not direct	**6.** not expensive
7. not perfect	**8.** not polite	**9.** not complete

Handwriting Helper

These sayings use the word *as* to compare. Trace each one. Then write it in cursive.

as cold as ice

as sweet as honey

JUMPSTART 40

Side B

Ready, Set, READ!

Read the passage. Then answer the questions.

Can you buy a book without giving money to a clerk? You can if you buy it from a vending machine. A vending machine is a device made to sell things.

You find vending machines almost everywhere in the world. They look like big cabinets with windows or pictures to show what is for sale. They may be inside or outside.

Vending machines are easy to use. You just put in your own coins or bills. Need some stamps? Drop in the money in first. Then press a button. Out come your stamps, along with any change you need. It's as easy as ABC!

Vending comes from a word that means "to sell." Old machines, like those with gumballs, are plain. Coin in, gumball out! You cannot pick a color or flavor. Newer vending machines give many more choices. They may offer different items, flavors, or sizes. Food vending machines can keep their choices hot or cold.

1. What is the main idea of the first paragraph?
   - O A. Vending machines can keep foods hot or cold.
   - O B. Vending machines are easy to use.
   - O C. Vending machines are for selling things.

2. How are newer vending machines *unlike* older ones?

____

____

____

____

____

Sentence Mender

Rewrite the sentence to make it correct.

"Im so sorry say Gordon.

____

BrainTeaser

Imagine an adventure anywhere in the world. Write 26 different *verbs* (action words) for what you might do, from *a* to *z*. Begin by telling your location.

On my adventure in ____________________, I will ____________________

____

____

____

Name ______________________ Date ______________

WORD of the Day

Use the word below to describe a tranquil place.

tranquil: *calm; quiet; soothing; relaxing*

____

____

____

WORD Work

Write answers that explain the meaning of each underlined word.

1. What is impossible for a rock? ______________________

2. What is used to unlock a door? ______________________

3. Why do you redraw a picture? ______________________

4. What nonliving object is in your desk? ______________________

5. What would you call a dishonest person? ______________________

6. How do you feel if you overeat? ______________________

7. What do you know to be invisible? ______________________

Handwriting Helper

These sayings describe using the word *like*. Trace each one. Then write it in cursive.

eat like a bird

fit like a glove

Ready, Set, READ!

Read the story. Then answer the questions.

Ruby had an extra sense. She could feel, hear, see, taste, and smell like any other person. But Ruby also knew things that nobody else could. She knew when a rainbow would appear, or when Granny would phone. She could awake from a sound sleep and know exactly what time it was without seeing a clock.

Nobody knew of Ruby's ability but her friend Dan. He called it the *preknow*.

Ruby's preknow changed Dan's life one Sunday. Ruby was raking leaves at home. Dan was five blocks away, building a model in his bedroom. All at once, Ruby dropped the rake and raced inside. She phoned Dan and yelled, "Get out of your bedroom NOW!"

Most people would have asked why, but Dan knew to trust the preknow. He ran to the back yard. Within moments, the ceiling of his room caved in.

1. Which other word has the same prefix as *preknow*?
   - O A. preach
   - O B. press
   - O C. pretty
   - O D. preview

2. How did Ruby feel about her special ability?
   - O A. secretive
   - O B. proud
   - O C. bored
   - O D. delighted

Sentence Mender

Rewrite the sentence to make it correct.

Hooray for we yelled Millie.

____

BrainTeaser

Write the words from the word bank in ABC order in the rows of the grid. Then read down the column on the far right to name a music word.

Word Bank

SYSTEM
SCORCH
SQUASH
SAUCER
SPROUT
SLEEPY

The music word is ____________________

Name ______________________ Date ______________

WORD of the Day

Use the word below to tell how to imitate a frog.

imitate: *try to act, look, or be like something or someone else; to copy*

____

____

____

WORD Work

The suffix -*ful* means **full of**. *fearful* = full of fear
The suffix -*ly* means **like**. *ghostly* = like a ghost
-*ly* also means **in a _____ way**. *softly* = in a soft way

Add the suffix each word needs to give the meaning shown.

1. in a **bright** way ______________________

2. in a **clear** way ______________________

3. full of **cheer** ______________________

4. full of **success** ______________________

5. like a **father** ______________________

6. like a **friend** ______________________

Handwriting Helper

Some animal groups have special names. Trace them. Then write them in cursive.

clutch of chicks

____

flock of sheep

____

Ready, Set, READ!

Read the passage. Then answer the questions.

A bracelet is a loop you wear around your wrist. Early bracelets were made of beads, bone, or wood. Some were worn for good luck. Others were worn for fun or fashion, or to show where you belonged in a group.

Bracelet styles may change, but some remain popular. Charm bracelets show off different tiny things the wearer likes. Gel bracelets come in many colors to show support for a cause. Bangles are worn in bunches that move and bump together to sound like wind chimes.

Friendship bracelets have been in style since the 1970s. Most are made of thread or yarn. Friends make and trade them. They tie them onto each other's wrists. There they stay until the person cuts them off.

1. Which kind of bracelet do you wear if you want to make sounds?

____

____

2. How do some bracelets show friendship?

____

____

____

____

____

____

Sentence Mender

Rewrite the sentence to make it correct.

Because he didnt get mutch sleep.

____

BrainTeaser

Climb the word ladder to change hear to boom. Change one letter at a time. Write the *new* word on each step.

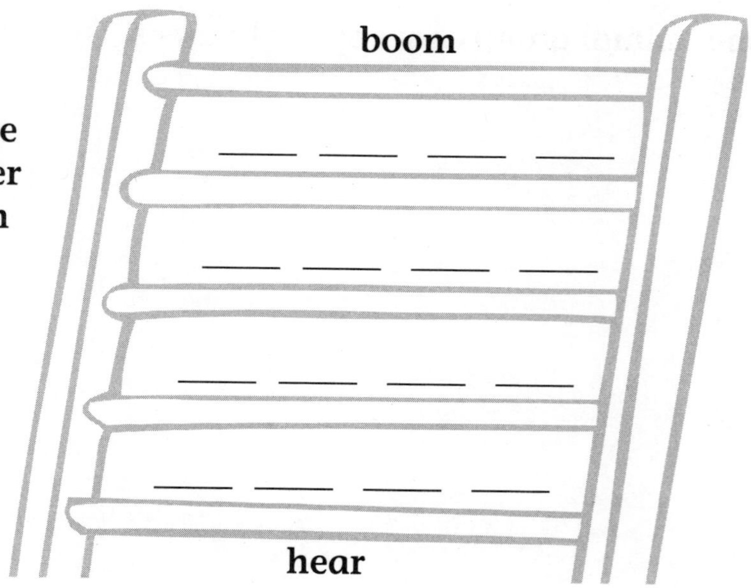

JUMPSTART 43

Side A

Name ______________________ Date ______________

WORD of the Day

Use the word below to ask a question about the past.

origin: *cause or point of beginning; source*

____

____

____

WORD Work

Fill in the chart. Make any needed spelling changes before adding *–er* or *–est*. The first row is done for you.

RULES
- First change final *y* to *i*
- Double the final consonant in CVC words
- Drop silent *e*

Base Word	*–er*	*–est*
1. easy	easier	easiest
2. thin		
3. clean		
4. large		
5. silly		
6. flat		
7. crazy		
8. glad		

Handwriting Helper

These words help describe position. Trace them. Then write them in cursive.

against

toward

between

glad

Ready, Set, READ!

Read the story. Then answer the questions.

On his walk to school, Guy daydreamed about pizza. He imagined piles of pepperoni and soft strings of gooey cheese. But his tasty daydream came to a cold stop when he stepped into a deep puddle. "Arrgh!" he yelled in dismay. Guy got soaked to his toes, and sloshed the rest of the way in a sour mood.

As Guy entered room 3B, everyone turned to look at him. It was bad enough that he was a soggy mess. Even worse, his feet peeped as he walked. Each step made a squishy squeak. He froze in his tracks, rolling his eyes.

"Good morning, Guy!" chirped Mrs. Drenchly. "Did you water ski to school today?" The class burst into waves of laughter.

"No, but I did explore an unknown puddle," Guy said. "Luckily, I found no sharks or sunken ships. But I did get these singing soles!"

1. Why did Guy step into the puddle?
   - O A. It was raining hard.
   - O B. He wasn't paying attention.
   - O C. He wanted to get soaked.
   - O D. He was pretending to water ski.
2. What mood was Mrs. Drenchly in that morning?
   - O A. playful
   - O B. serious
   - O C. angry
   - O D. worried

Sentence Mender

Rewrite the sentence to make it correct.

Us spent sum time runing around.

____

BrainTeaser

What does each saying mean? Read the definitions on the right. Write the number on the line.

1. You're a lone **wolf**.	_______ It's a tall tale.
2. Get off your high **horse**.	_______ You are very stubborn.
3. That's a shaggy **dog** story.	_______ Stop acting like you're special.
4. Take the **bull** by the horns.	_______ Be brave and just do it!
5. You are just so **mule**-headed!	_______ You'd rather be on your own.

Name ______________________________ Date ______________

WORD of the Day

Use the word below in a question about a chair.

authentic: *genuine; the real thing*

____

____

____

WORD Work

Three suffixes identify workers. They signal "someone who acts as."

EXAMPLES
- *-er*, as in bank**er**
- *-or*, as in act**or**
- *-ist*, as in art**ist**

Circle the suffix that ends each word. Write the kind of work.

1. inventor ______________
2. cartoonist ______________
3. teacher ______________
4. violinist ______________
5. director ______________
6. logger ______________
7. machinist ______________
8. investigator ______________

Handwriting Helper

Writers use words to signal *more to come*. Trace the words. Then write them in cursive.

also

next

likewise

secondly

Ready, Set, READ!

Read the passage. Then answer the questions.

Nomads are people who move from place to place. Most nomads follow animals they tend or hunt. Or they travel to find water. So where are their houses? Nomads bring their houses with them! They set them up wherever they stop for the night.

A yurt is one kind of movable shelter. It is a round house that can be set up quickly. A yurt can be cozy in winter and cool in summer. All the parts of a yurt can fold and fit into one wagon.

The walls of a yurt are made of crisscrossed slats of wood. Yurt walls can stretch open and hook together. The yurt's wooden slats connect to each side of a sturdy door. A roof ring in the center has holes to let air in and out. Poles hook into the roof ring to hold it up high. After all the parts are in place, the nomads cover the yurt with cloth or animal skins.

1. What are *nomads*?

____

____

____

____

____

____

2. What makes a yurt easy to move?
   - ○ A. It is made of cloth.
   - ○ B. It is tiny.
   - ○ C. It folds up.

Sentence Mender

Rewrite the sentence to make it correct.

Him never tasted no homemade icecream.

____

BrainTeaser

Decide how the first two words relate. Then copy the word that makes the other pair relate in the same way.

EXAMPLE
Pencil is to **write** as **scissors** is to ___cut___.
sharp print cut

1. **Oven** is to **bake** as **sink** is to ______________.
   hot wash dishes

2. **Piece** is to **puzzle** as **finger** is to ______________.
   toe glove hand

3. **Carrot** is to **vegetable** as **banana** is to ______________.
   fruit peel lunch

JUMPSTART 45

Side A

Name ________________________ Date ______________

WORD of the Day

Use the word below to tell what kids could contribute to help make our world a better place.

contribute: *give help or money for a cause*

____

____

____

WORD Work

A *homophone* is a word that sounds like another word but has a different meaning and a different spelling.

EXAMPLE
ant and *aunt*

Write the best word to complete each sentence. Use the word bank.

Word Bank

pear	sale	wrap
sail	rap	pair

1. I got a new ______________ of sneakers today.

2. Did you hear that ______________ on the door?

3. Jo likes to ______________ her kite on windy days.

4. I love to eat a juicy ______________.

5. The toy store has a big ______________ today.

6. Juan likes to ______________ presents.

Handwriting Helper

Writers use words to change direction. Trace the words. Then write them in cursive.

yet

rather

however

otherwise

Ready, Set, READ!

Read the story. Then answer the questions.

Sally's tenth birthday would soon be here. She didn't want a party, gifts, or even cake and ice cream. Her wish was to walk the brand-new Golden Gate Bridge on its opening day—her birthday. That would be gift enough!

Sally knew the walk would be almost three miles, across and back. She shivered to think of walking 220 feet above the bay. But the bridge had been on her mind for four years. Now it was time to welcome it.

There was no school that day. Dad closed his hat shop. Sally looked forward to crowds, speeches, and a week-long fiesta all over San Francisco. The first day was just for walkers. Sally wanted so much to be in that grand parade.

Over 200,000 people walked the bridge on May 27, 1937, including Sally and her dad. They gladly paid 25¢ each for the walk of a lifetime.

1. Why didn't Sally care to do ordinary things for her tenth birthday?

____

____

____

____

2. Why do you think the San Francisco schools were closed that day?

____

____

____

____

Sentence Mender

Rewrite the sentence to make it correct.

These is the bestest loafs of bread!

____

BrainTeaser

Decide how the first two words relate. Then copy the word that makes the other pair relate in the same way.

EXAMPLE

Cut is to **knife** as **eat** is to ____food____.

lunch food sharp

1. **Album** is to **pictures** as **vase** is to ________________.

   flowers photos water

2. **Artist** is to **painting** as **author** is to ________________.

   book reading statue

3. **Snow** is to **flake** as **water** is to ________________.

   cup drop ice

JUMPSTART 46

Side A

Name ______________________________ Date ____________________

WORD of the Day

Use the word below to describe a good candidate to lead a project.

candidate: *person hoping for a job or an honor, or running for election*

____

____

____

WORD Work

Use prefixes to figure out new words.
How many . . .

1. babies are in a set of **triplets**? ____________

2. shells are in a **bivalve** animal? ____________

3. colors are in a **unicolor** flag? ____________

4. points are on a **bicuspid** tooth? ____________

5. corners are on a **tricornered** hat? ____________

6. cells are in a **unicellular** animal? ____________

Unicycle

Bicycle

Tricycle

Handwriting Helper

Trace the proverbs. Then write them in cursive. Think about what they mean.

Haste makes waste.

No news is good news.

JUMPSTART 46

Side B

Ready, Set, READ!

Read the passage. Then answer the questions.

Earth is so big we need exact ways to label points on it. Our Earth isn't a perfect sphere, but a globe still serves as a helpful model.

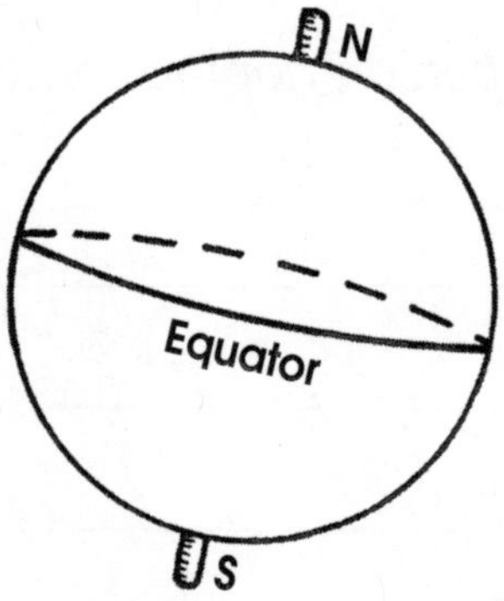

The North Pole is the farthest spot north on Earth. Its opposite is the South Pole—Earth's farthest spot south. Exactly halfway between the poles is an imaginary line that circles the Earth. This "belt" is called the *equator*.

If you could cut through Earth at the equator, you'd get two huge parts. Each part is called a *hemisphere*. *Hemi-* is a prefix for "half," so the word makes sense. Earth has a Northern and a Southern Hemisphere. Which one are you in right now?

1. What clue in *equator* reminds you that it divides Earth in half?

____

____

____

____

2. Why does it help to know where the equator is?

____

____

____

____

Sentence Mender

Rewrite the sentence to make it correct.

Who builded those pyramids in egypt.

____

BrainTeaser

What has a horn but cannot honk?

Solve each clue. Then copy each letter into its numbered box to find the answer to the riddle.

- Kernels on a cob ___ ___ ___ ___ (6 9 8 4)
- Flat garden tool ___ ___ ___ (2 5 7)
- Opposite of *madam* ___ ___ ___ (10 3 1)

1	2	3	4	5	6	7	8	9	10

Name ______________________ Date ______________

WORD of the Day

Use the word below to describe an irregular pattern.

irregular: *not regular or standard; uneven*

WORD Work

Some words we use began as much longer words. Draw lines to match each "clipped" word with its original form. The first one is done for you.

exam •	• hamburger
bike •	• influenza
flu •	• mathematics
gym •	• champion
burger •	• bicycle
math •	• gymnasium
champ •	• examination

Handwriting Helper

Trace the tongue twisters. Then write them in cursive. Try to say them.

A noisy noise annoys an oyster.

The sun shines on shop signs.

Ready, Set, READ!

Read the poems. Then answer the questions.

Two Limericks *in the style of Edward Lear* (1812–1888)

There was a small child dressed in pink,
Who pleaded for something to drink;
Her mom said, "Oh daughter,
I've nothing but water!"
Which saddened that youngster, I think.

There was a complainer from Sark,
Who never made one kind remark;
Neighbors said, "Don't you see
What a beast you can be?
If you were a dog, you would bark!"

1. How are the poems alike?

2. What is the lesson of the second limerick?

3. Which limerick do you prefer? Explain why.

Sentence Mender

Rewrite the sentence to make it correct.

Hey that ones my team jacket!

BrainTeaser

How many different words can you spell with letters from the word brainteaser? Every word must have at least three letters. List them here.

JUMPSTART 48

Side A

Name ______________________ Date ____________

WORD of the Day

Use the word below to explain how music can move you.

inspire: *to cause good thoughts, feelings, or actions; to encourage or affect*

____

____

____

WORD Work

Some English words began as two separate words. Over time, they became one word. Draw lines to match new and old forms. Then circle the key letters from each separate word.

brunch •	• situation + comedy
ditzy •	• dizzy + dotty
flop •	• globe + blob
sitcom •	• breakfast + lunch
glob •	• motor + hotel
motel •	• flap + drop

Handwriting Helper

Trace the riddle and its answer. Then write them in cursive.

Why did the cat get a computer?

____

Answer: for the mouse!

____

JUMPSTART 48

Side B

Ready, Set, READ!

Read the passage.
Then answer the questions.

Orion is the name of one of the best known constellations in the night sky. Orion is also called the Hunter. People in every part of the world notice the stars of Orion. Their stories vary, and they give the star group different names.

The Greeks saw Orion as a tall, handsome, and brave hunter. They told many tales about him. In China he is called Shen the Hunter. In Japan the star group is a drum. Some African cultures see the three stars as steps to heaven. Three facts make Orion special.

1. Orion is easy to spot. It's one of the first constellations kids learn. Most can find Orion's belt—a row of three bright stars.
2. Orion has the star Rigel. It's one of the brightest stars in the sky.
3. Orion helps people find other stars.

1. What is the main idea of this article?
   - O A. Orion was a great hunter.
   - O B. Orion has one of the brightest stars.
   - O C. Orion is familiar to the whole world.

2. In your own words, tell what a constellation is.

____

____

____

____

____

____

____

Sentence Mender

Rewrite the sentence to make it correct.

Its like the sun just sink into the oshin.

____

BrainTeaser

Unscramble the words so that all rhyme.

1. HYS ____________________ **4.** YUG ____________________

2. EPI ____________________ **5.** RTY ____________________

3. YEE ____________________ **6.** GHSI ____________________

JUMPSTART 49

Side A

Name ______________________ Date ______________

WORD of the Day

Use the word below in a question about nature.

environment: *all conditions that surround and affect life and growth*

____

____

____

WORD Work

Circle the vowel pair that spells each word correctly. Write it in place.

1. bel________ve	ee	ei	ea	ie
2. upst________rs	ai	ar	au	ea
3. bl________chers	ee	ea	oa	ie
4. songb________d	ar	ea	ir	ur
5. pion________rs	ee	ei	ea	ie
6. thr________t	oo	oa	ou	oe
7. outd________rs	ee	or	ou	oo
8. ann________nce	oi	oa	ou	ow

Handwriting Helper

Trace expressions with *play*. Then write them in cursive. Think about what they mean.

play hooky

play possum

play second fiddle

Ready, Set, READ!

Read the story. Then answer the questions.

Jett loved two things: waffles and his computer. "Everybody loves waffles," he declared each day. "But I mega-love them. I'd have them at every meal!"

After waffles, there was his computer. Jett used it every chance he had. He did his homework and read e-books on it. He played games and surfed the Internet. He made video calls to his cousins in Maine, and checked the weather forecast.

One day he was doing research on waffles. "Holy ravioli!" he shouted. "Mom, come quick!" His mother rushed to his room. "What's up, Jett? Are you okay?"

"I'm better than okay. I'm mega-okay! I found an amazing machine I never knew about. It's perfect for me. Just look at this rare beauty!"

Mom leaned in to see a shiny waffle maker. "Honey, we already have a waffle maker. Even you haven't worn it out yet," she said as she hugged him.

"But Mom, look at its shape!" Jett exclaimed, his face glowing. "The waffles come out in the shape of a computer keyboard."

1. What got Jett so excited about another waffle maker?

____

____

____

____

____

2. Jett adds *mega* in front of some words. What does he mean?

____

____

____

____

____

Sentence Mender

Rewrite the sentence to make it correct.

Woman offen get there nails done.

____

BrainTeaser

Reorder each word group to make a sentence. Start each sentence with a capital letter and use an ending punctuation mark.

1. name is what her _______________

2. my today team hope wins I _______________

3. is lunch until long it how _______________

JUMPSTART 50

Side A

Name ______________________________ Date ______________

WORD of the Day

Use the word below to describe durable shoes.

durable: *strong and tough enough to last a long time, even with hard use*

____

____

____

WORD Work

Read long words by "chunking" them into parts. Go slowly. Use what you know about base words, prefixes, and suffixes. Then score yourself on each word:

1. Easy!
2. Hard, but I did it.
3. Too long for me.

1. refreshments ________
2. advantage ________
3. continental ________
4. magnificent ________
5. manufacturing ________
6. responsibilities ________

Handwriting Helper

Trace the safety words. Then write them in cursive.

yield

poison

danger

caution

JUMPSTART 50 Side B

Ready, Set, READ!

Read the passage. Then answer the questions.

"Oatmeal makes you smart," our grandparents always said. Are there really *brain foods*—foods that make you brighter? Many people agree that oatmeal is one. Can that lumpy beige stuff be a truly smart choice?

Scientists have been studying this grain to test this claim. Here are some links they have found:

- Oatmeal can boost your memory. It contains folic acid, which helps the brain make and recover memories.
- Oatmeal can help you pay attention. The body digests oatmeal so slowly, you feel full for longer. This helps you to focus.
- Oatmeal can build strength. Athletes who eat oatmeal say they can work out longer and get stronger faster.

Could oatmeal help you? Have some for breakfast to find out!

1. What is in oatmeal that can help a person's memory?
   - O A. focus
   - O B. digestion
   - O C. strength
   - O D. folic acid

2. What kind of food is oatmeal?
   - O A. meat
   - O B. vegetable
   - O C. grain
   - O D. dairy

Sentence Mender

Rewrite the sentence to make it correct.

The Three Stooge is Moe Larry and Curly.

BrainTeaser

Use the clues to solve the puzzle. It has a one-letter word on top and a seven-letter word at the bottom. Going down, each word has the exact same letters as the word above it, plus one more.

Clues:

- right there
- have food
- beef or pork
- water vapor
- creek
- becomes expert at

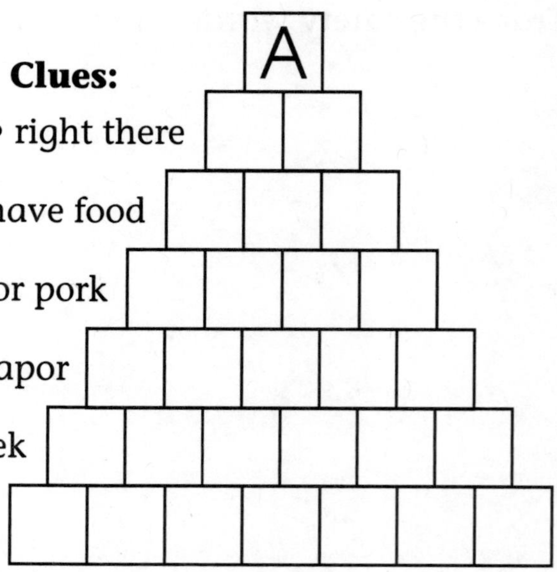

Answers

Jumpstart 1

Word of the Day: Sample response—I like a **plot** where someone gets lost and has to get home.
Word Work: Pairs that rhyme are 1, 3, 5, 6, 8, 10, 12
Handwriting Helper: Check children's work for accuracy and legibility.
Ready, Set, Read! 1. C **2.** C
Sentence Mender: I walked the dog when I woke up.
Brainteaser: 1. cape **2.** ours **3.** plum **4.** flow **5.** study **6.** march

Jumpstart 2

Word of the Day: Sample response—I am **active** when I play chase with my dog.
Word Work: beginning /f/—fantasy, fireproof, fountain; middle /f/—infant, defend, drifter, coughing; ending /f/—sheriff, knife, enough, graph, belief
Handwriting Helper: Check children's work for accuracy and legibility.
Ready, Set, Read! 1. C **2.** B **3.** A
Sentence Mender: Granddad moved back to Canada.
Brainteaser: Sheep shouldn't sleep in a shack. Sheep should sleep in a shed instead.

Jumpstart 3

Word of the Day: Sample response—I'll **vary** my breakfast with cheese toast instead of cereal.
Word Work: 1. rare **2.** pear **3.** pair **4.** bare **5.** tear **6.** air
Handwriting Helper: Check children's work for accuracy and legibility.
Ready, Set, Read! 1. Ethan Clary is turning 10 years old. **2.** Don't give away the secret; don't ruin the surprise.
Sentence Mender: Where do you keep the kitty litter?
Brainteaser: Answers will vary; sample: Cover your sneeze, please!

Jumpstart 4

Word of the Day: Sample response—He walked out on the diving board, but stopped at the **brink** in fear.
Word Work: Possible answers—*bl*: blade, bleach, blare, bled, blown; *cl*: clash, cliff, clone, clown; *fl*: flare, flash, fled, flown, fly
Handwriting Helper: Check children's work for accuracy and legibility.
Ready, Set, Read! 1. B **2.** C **3.** B
Sentence Mender: Do you know Dr. Reed's first name?
Brainteaser: Answers will vary; samples: **1.** jingle **2.** screech, **3.** fizzes **4.** coo **5.** clanks **6.** hisses

Jumpstart 5

Word of the Day: Sample response—On a **dreary** morning, the sky looks empty, sad, and gray.
Word Work: Hard *G*—garden, dragon, wagon, regular, gourd, giggle; Soft *G*—ginger, genius, danger, gem, village, strange
Handwriting Helper: Check children's work for accuracy and legibility.
Ready, Set, Read! 1. C **2.** A
Sentence Mender: We will be home by four o'clock.
Brainteaser: Answers will vary; samples: **2.** toot **3.** noon **4.** dad

Jumpstart 6

Word of the Day: Sample response—She **yearns** for one more chance to ride the horse around the pasture.
Word Work: Hard *C*—copper, second, account, electric, camper, music; Soft *C*—celery, pencil, cereal, fancy, acid, cider
Handwriting Helper: Check children's work for accuracy and legibility.
Ready, Set, Read! 1. It is edible. **2.** It helps nerves and muscles react and it steadies blood pressure.
Sentence Mender: The tie has red, pink, and orange flowers. Note: the series comma before *and* is optional.
Brainteaser: 1. dad **2.** crook **3.** school

Jumpstart 7

Word of the Day: Sample response—The **scene** where the hero gets a pie in his face is totally silly.
Word Work: air only—thank, theater, third, thumb, thunder; with throat—that, them, there, these, those
Handwriting Helper: Check children's work for accuracy and legibility.
Ready, Set, Read! 1. 3 **2.** pit or seed **3.** The chicks are tapping their way out of their shells.
Sentence Mender: I love mysteries. So does my dad.
Brainteaser: Answers will vary; sample answer: harm, hard, card, cord

Jumpstart 8

Word of the Day: Sample response—The **swift** little animal ran by so fast, we couldn't identify it!
Word Work: 1. ch **2.** Wh **3.** ch, sh **4.** wh, wh **5.** th, ph, th **6.** sh, sh
Handwriting Helper: Check children's work for accuracy and legibility.
Ready, Set, Read! 1. Easy to play, no special equipment, fun **2.** Virginia Beach
Sentence Mender: Ruth asked, "Could you help me?"
Brainteaser: (Top to bottom) floor; bald; pure; left; level; flute

Jumpstart 9

Word of the Day: Sample response—The alien ET had to **struggle** to get home to his planet.
Word Work: 1. ph, ng **2.** ch, sh **3.** ph, ch **4.** th, ng **5.** sh, ch, ch **6.** th, gh
Handwriting Helper: Check children's work for accuracy and legibility.
Ready, Set, Read! 1. She wanted to help her dad. **2.** Both can be dangerous to passersby.
Sentence Mender: Can Bill run up that hill?
Brainteaser:

R	S	H	M	R	H	C	O	A	S	T
I	C	I	T	Y	S	P	A	R	K	O
V	A	G	W	L	A	K	E	C	H	W
E	L	H	M	O	U	N	T	A	I	N
R	E	W	Y	D	R	O	A	D	R	Y
T	R	A	I	N	T	R	A	C	K	S
B	A	Y	F	C	A	P	I	T	A	L

Jumpstart 10

Word of the Day: Sample response—The **traits** I like best in a friend are to be honest, fair, curious, and fun.
Word Work: 1. cheese **2.** stretch **3.** chick, hatch **4.** teach **5.** cherry **6.** search
Handwriting Helper: Check children's work for accuracy and legibility.
Ready, Set, Read! 1. The theobromine makes them sick or worse. **2.** Say "NO!"
Sentence Mender: Maria takes a dance class on Thursday.
Brainteaser: Answers will vary; samples: cable, fable, gable, label, table, stable, disable, turntable, unstable, unable

Jumpstart 11

Word of the Day: Sample response—I am **loyal** to my family by helping in good times and bad.
Word Work: (Top to bottom) bread/left, throw/coat, field/speak, price/light, huge/view, whale/spray
Handwriting Helper: Check children's work for accuracy and legibility.
Ready, Set, Read! 1. B **2.** Answers will vary.
Sentence Mender: They won't know when to show up.
Brainteaser: 1. permission **2.** fragile **3.** furious **4.** thrifty **5.** brave **6.** complete

Jumpstart 12

Word of the Day: Sample response—House cats **contrast** with wild cats because wild ones fear or hunt people, but house cats live peacefully with us.
Word Work: 2. globe **3.** theme **4.** slide **5.** cute **6.** bathe **7.** shine **8.** range **9.** plane **10.** stripe
Handwriting Helper: Check children's work for accuracy and legibility.
Ready, Set, Read! 1. He was a famous picture book writer and illustrator. **2.** He was sick a lot and had to stay home.
Sentence Mender: Let's surprise them by dressing as elves.
Brainteaser:

G	A	Z	E	B	O
M	U	S	K	O	X
T	R	I	C	K	Y
T	U	B	I	N	G
U	S	A	B	L	E
W	O	O	D	E	N

Jumpstart 13

Word of the Day: Sample response—The **theme** of *The Wizard of Oz* is "there's no place like home."
Word Work: works, nurse, purple, hurt, germs, dirty, Thursday, burn, burst, words
Handwriting Helper: Check children's work for accuracy and legibility.
Ready, Set, Read! 1. Dawn or sunrise **2.** Poem 1 rhymes and has four lines, not three. **3.** Answers will vary.
Sentence Mender: Is that the exact word you wrote?
Brainteaser: Answers will vary.

Jumpstart 14

Word of the Day: Sample response—Mom leaves 10 minutes earlier than she needs to so she'll be **prompt**.
Word Work: 1. wall **2.** sword **3.** fork **4.** four **5.** salt
Handwriting Helper: Check children's work for accuracy and legibility.
Ready, Set, Read! 1. It lets you get together everything you need before you start. **2.** The grape juice might just mix with the baking soda "ink" and make a mush.
Sentence Mender: Next month we will fly to Chicago!
Brainteaser:

Word	1 thing	2 or more	Can't tell
1. deer			✓
2. mice		✓	
3. sheep			✓
4. leaves		✓	
5. social studies	✓		

Jumpstart 15

Word of the Day: Sample response—Just poke your finger into a bubble to **puncture** it.
Word Work: 1. train **2.** flame **3.** hay **4.** skate **5.** spray
Handwriting Helper: Check children's work for accuracy and legibility.
Ready, Set, Read! 1. India **2.** Zero baloney means no baloney, or no kidding!
Sentence Mender: We are fans of the Detroit Tigers.
Brainteaser: 1. taxi **2.** wagon **3.** rocket **4.** bicycle **5.** train **6.** camper **7.** rowboat **8.** steamroller

Jumpstart 16

Word of the Day: Sample response—What is the **function** of the dial tone?
Word Work: 1. key **2.** seal **3.** queen **4.** leash **5.** shield
Handwriting Helper: Check children's work for accuracy and legibility.
Ready, Set, Read! 1. Sid is Jerry's grandfather. **2.** Possible answers: She asked more questions. She thought things were funny that weren't funny to others. She noticed things and always wondered why.
Sentence Mender: There are eight legs on a spider.
Brainteaser: 1. no **2.** hoe **3.** sew **4.** blow **5.** dough **6.** though

Jumpstart 17

Word of the Day: Sample response—It's that giant mouth and teeth that make T. rex so **fearsome**.
Word Work: 1. bike **2.** fly **3.** child **4.** knight **5.** cries
Handwriting Helper: Check children's work for accuracy and legibility.
Ready, Set, Read! 1. A **2.** C
Sentence Mender: Pete buys eggs, milk, and tea. Note: the series comma before *and* is optional.
Brainteaser: Answers will vary.

	b	r	i	m
Sports Words	basket	racquet	inning	manager
Science Words	battery	rodent	icicle	moon
Music Words	band	repeat	instrument	march

Jumpstart 18

Word of the Day: Sample response—"I jumped higher than I ever did before!" **exclaims** Gabe.
Word Work: 1. crow **2.** globe **3.** toe **4.** soap **5.** pillow
Handwriting Helper: Check children's work for accuracy and legibility.
Ready, Set, Read! 1. B **2.** C
Sentence Mender: Which one of us gets to go first?
Brainteaser: 1. jellyfish **2.** eyeball **3.** paperback **4.** earring

Jumpstart 19

Word of the Day: Sample response—The movie was a **drama** about moving to a new land.
Word Work: 1. cube **2.** menu **3.** fuel **4.** screw
Handwriting Helper: Check children's work for accuracy and legibility.
Ready, Set, Read! 1. They grew golden apples from golden branches. **2.** Atlas refused to give him food and a place to rest, though he was the son of the king of all the gods.
Sentence Mender: I like bananas the best of all the fruits.
Brainteaser: 2. How/who **3.** saw/was **4.** tub/but

Jumpstart 20

Word of the Day: Sample response—If I had **ample** play space, I'd set up a mini-golf course.
Word Work: 1. avoid, foil, voyage **2.** boil, poison, toy **3.** choice, Roy, boy **4.** allow, frown, grouch **5.** growling, hound, scout **6.** doubt, powder, gown; First spelling rules box: **1.** *oy* **2.** *oi* Second spelling rules box: **1.** *ow* **2.** *ou*
Handwriting Helper: Check children's work for accuracy and legibility.
Ready, Set, Read! 1. The speaker is proud, grateful, and enthusiastic. **2.** Possible answer: I wish our library had more computer terminals and e-books.
Sentence Mender: You must wait for a piece of cake.
Brainteaser: 1. dent **2.** denim **3.** dense **4.** dentist **5.** dentures

Jumpstart 21

Word of the Day: Sample response—It's fun to **recount** the story of my first swim lesson.
Word Work: long *oo*—broom, goose, proof, smooth; short *oo*—cookie, good, shook, wood
Handwriting Helper: Check children's work for accuracy and legibility.
Ready, Set, Read! 1. C **2.** No, the writer is exaggerating to add humor.
Sentence Mender: Mike's dad caught his first fish!
Brainteaser: Answers will vary; check students' lists

Jumpstart 22

Word of the Day: Sample response—My favorite **series** is a cartoon show I watch at 7 PM every night.
Word Work: 1 syllable—for, their, need, to, bring, a; 2 syllables—gather, private, little, picnic, single, toothpick; 3 syllables—whenever, porcupines, nobody, remember
Handwriting Helper: Check children's work for accuracy and legibility.
Ready, Set, Read! 1. Carlos disagreed with an article against skateboard parks, and wanted to give his point of view. **2.** Possible answer: I agree that kids need safe places to play, but I think skateboarding is risky.
Sentence Mender: Mom kept my very first baby shoe.
Brainteaser: 1. Shut the window! **2.** Didn't you eat breakfast? **3.** Have you seen my hat? **4.** May I speak to Pam, please?

Jumpstart 23

Word of the Day: Sample response—My broken arm is a **valid** reason to miss school.
Word Work: 1. skunk **2.** scale **3.** slow **4.** scary **5.** sneeze **6.** sweet **7.** spider **8.** stable
Handwriting Helper: Check children's work for accuracy and legibility.
Ready, Set, Read! 1. A **2.** B
Sentence Mender: They won't ever solve those riddles.
Brainteaser: 1. mane **2.** many **3.** mango **4.** mantis **5.** mansion

Jumpstart 24

Word of the Day: Sample response—I hope to **convince** my parents that I'm old enough for a pet.
Word Work: 1. screech **2.** square **3.** spring **4.** straight **5.** splash **6.** scrub **7.** squeeze **8.** straw
Handwriting Helper: Check children's work for accuracy and legibility.
Ready, Set, Read! 1. C **2.** A
Sentence Mender: Mika said he felt too sick to eat.
Brainteaser: 1. sum **2.** ate **3.** tail **4.** rode **5.** cents

Jumpstart 25

Word of the Day: Sample response—The photographer set her **tripod** near a waterfall to take pictures.
Word Work: Sample answers: armrest, backpack, beanbag, birdcage, doorbell, fingerprint, overnight
Handwriting Helper: Check children's work for accuracy and legibility.
Ready, Set, Read! 1. A ballad is a long poem that tells a story. **2.** Possible answers: Will the fox get caught? Will he eat all the animals? How will it end?
Sentence Mender: Peter, Paul, and Mary used to sing folk songs. Note: the series comma before *and* is optional.
Brainteaser: Answers will vary; samples: dream, cream, steam, stream, gleam, seam, team, scream, theme

Jumpstart 26

Word of the Day: Sample response—A **fluent** reader doesn't stumble over words.
Word Work: armchair, eyeglasses, anywhere, briefcase, bedroom, handbag, flashlight, wastebasket, brainstorm, dashboard, outside
Handwriting Helper: Check children's work for accuracy and legibility.
Ready, Set, Read! 1. Answers will vary. **2.** B
Sentence Mender: Yes, I did all my chores.
Brainteaser: 1. shut **2.** song **3.** brick

Jumpstart 27

Word of the Day: Sample response—I'd **consult** a doctor to learn why I cough so much.
Word Work: Sample answers—notebook, buttercup, football, popcorn, raincoat, snowplow, outside, bookstore, workshop
Handwriting Helper: Check children's work for accuracy and legibility.
Ready, Set, Read! 1. downdraft **2.** Updrafts push hail back into the clouds where it picks up more water.
Sentence Mender: An apple a day keeps the doctor away.
Brainteaser: Answers will vary; sample: **1.** backpack **2.** trashcan **3.** seat **4.** lights **5.** paper clip **6.** clock **7.** playground **8.** rug

Jumpstart 28

Word of the Day: Sample response—Do you know all the **stanzas** of "This Land Is Your Land"?
Word Work: 1. signs, autumn **2.** talk, calmly **3.** shepherds, lambs **4.** Ghost Island **5.** two, guards **6.** wrap, rhino **7.** comb, scissors **8.** sword, knife **9.** whole, school **10.** answer, column
Handwriting Helper: Check children's work for accuracy and legibility.
Ready, Set, Read! 1. B **2.** It uses its long claws to dig.
Sentence Mender: Have you read Mr. Popper's Penguins?
Brainteaser: 1. healthy **2.** alert **3.** remember **4.** challenging

Jumpstart 29

Word of the Day: Sample response—They were stuck in the hot elevator for three **wretched** hours.
Word Work: 2. what's, I **3.** let's, u **4.** you've, ha **5.** they'll, wi **6.** who'd, woul
Handwriting Helper: Check children's work for accuracy and legibility.
Ready, Set, Read! 1. C **2.** B
Sentence Mender: May I sit next to her?
Brainteaser: Answers will vary; samples: Smooth—silk, lake, hair, fur; Rough—sandpaper, bark, fish scales; Ancient—mummy, knight, castle; Modern—computer, laser, robot

Jumpstart 30

Word of the Day: Sample response—I **possess** a little wooden boat that my great-grandfather carved.
Word Work: 1. does not **2.** cannot **3.** I would **4.** here is **5.** was not **6.** might have
Handwriting Helper: Check children's work for accuracy and legibility.
Ready, Set, Read! 1. Horns were too loud to be played inside. **2.** The player touches the valves and the bell.
Sentence Mender: Clowns love to make children laugh.
Brainteaser: 1. glad **2.** glass **3.** glands **4.** glazed **5.** glance

Jumpstart 31

Word of the Day: Sample response—I know the **sequence** of planets from nearest to farthest from the sun.
Word Work:

Base Word	-s	-ed	-ing
1. swarm	swarms	swarmed	swarming
2. reward	rewards	rewarded	rewarding
3. answer	answers	answered	answering
4. slouch	slouches	slouched	slouching
5. lengthen	lengthens	lengthened	lengthening
6. subtract	subtracts	subtracted	subtracting

Handwriting Helper: Check children's work for accuracy and legibility.
Ready, Set, Read! 1. C **2.** B
Sentence Mender: We've been waiting way too long!
Brainteaser: 1. dizzy **2.** fuzzy **3.** pizza, **4.** puzzle **5.** frizzy

Jumpstart 32

Word of the Day: Sample response—The **elegant** tables had flowers, lace tablecloths, and fancy candles.
Word Work: 1. products **2.** berries **3.** crashes **4.** indexes **5.** lengthens **6.** trenches **7.** jigsaws **8.** trophies **9.** fizzes **10.** discusses
Handwriting Helper: Check children's work for accuracy and legibility.
Ready, Set, Read! 1. A **2.** C
Sentence Mender: We made plans for Friday, Sunday, and Monday. Note: the series comma before *and* is optional.
Brainteaser: 1. ruby **2.** rust **3.** purple **4.** orange **5.** silver **6.** lavender **7.** copper **8.** ebony **9.** magenta

Jumpstart 33

Word of the Day: Sample response—I'd love to **modify** my room with a four-poster bed and a TV.
Word Work: (Top to bottom) oxen/ox; men/man; teeth/tooth; children/child; trout/trout; feet/foot
Handwriting Helper: Check children's work for accuracy and legibility.
Ready, Set, Read! 1. B **2.** C
Sentence Mender: Do you know her phone number?
Brainteaser: SOS, lime, tie; missile toe

Jumpstart 34

Word of the Day: Sample response—My **viewpoint** is that voting is a fair way to decide things.
Word Work: 1. Cara's folder **2.** Joey's bike **3.** Raul's drums **4.** principal's office **5.** soldier's helmet
Handwriting Helper: Check children's work for accuracy and legibility.
Ready, Set, Read! 1. They are cousins, because Karyn mentions Aunt Viola and Uncle Paul. **2.** A
Sentence Mender: Dad missed one lunch break this week.
Brainteaser: Answers will vary; samples: **1.** cone **2.** first **3.** crossed **4.** safe

Jumpstart 35

Word of the Day: Sample response—Birds and jets are **similar** because both can soar.
Word Work: 1. flowers **2.** singers **3.** family's **4.** hero's **5.** crates **6.** coach's
Handwriting Helper: Check children's work for accuracy and legibility.
Ready, Set, Read! 1. To help you learn basic facts about time. **2.** six **3.** Possible response: I'd expect to see stanzas with names of the months.
Sentence Mender: "Avoid that deep hole," warned Mrs. Wu.
Brainteaser: 1. lamp **2.** machine **3.** ruler **4.** songs **5.** nose

Jumpstart 36

Word of the Day: Sample response—Can you **clarify** the difference between eyelashes and eyebrows?
Word Work: 2. short, shortest **3.** later, latest **4.** heavy, heaviest **5.** sillier, silliest **6.** sharper, sharpest
Handwriting Helper: Check children's work for accuracy and legibility.
Ready, Set, Read! 1. Principal Bennet **2.** You can call 555-5555 and talk to Ms. James, or you can go to www.animalshelter.org.
Sentence Mender: You're a great athlete, Victor.
Brainteaser: 2. ape/pea **3.** chin/inch **4.** care/race

Jumpstart 37

Word of the Day: Sample response—The **location** of the nearest fire alarm is just left of our classroom door.
Word Work: 2. unsure **3.** unafraid **4.** unfolded **5.** unknown **6.** unlikely **7.** unequal. **8.** untangled **9.** unimportant
Handwriting Helper: Check children's work for accuracy and legibility.
Ready, Set, Read! 1. D **2.** Possible answer: It tells a story of something impossible to do.
Sentence Mender: My Aunt Marge taught me to knit.
Brainteaser: Answers will vary; sample: Sue's sister Sara sweetly sang seven silly Spanish soccer songs.

Jumpstart 38

Word of the Day: Sample response—The **defiant** child refused to drink her milk, and knocked over the cup.
Word Work: 2. opposite of obey **3.** opposite of comfort **4.** opposite of fiction **5.** opposite of living **6.** opposite of sticky
Handwriting Helper: Check children's work for accuracy and legibility.
Ready, Set, Read! 1. B **2.** No, you must live in the United States.
Sentence Mender: Grady's cell phone ringer is cheerful.
Brainteaser: Answers will vary.

Jumpstart 39

Word of the Day: Sample response—An old water pipe under our street **ruptured**, causing a flood.
Word Work: 2. eat too much **3.** discovers again **4.** cooked too much **5.** traced again **6.** slept too long
Handwriting Helper: Check children's work for accuracy and legibility.
Ready, Set, Read! 1. C **2.** Possible answer: Be careful what you wish for.
Sentence Mender: Where did we see those huge deer?
Brainteaser: Answers will vary.

Jumpstart 40

Word of the Day: Sample response—I'd love to be a superhero with the **ability** to be invisible.
Word Work: 2. impatient **3.** impossible **4.** incorrect **5.** indirect **6.** inexpensive **7.** imperfect **8.** impolite **9.** incomplete
Handwriting Helper: Check children's work for accuracy and legibility.
Ready, Set, Read! 1. C **2.** Newer vending machines give more choices.
Sentence Mender: "I'm so sorry," says Gordon.
Brainteaser: Answers will vary.

Jumpstart 41

Word of the Day: Sample response—The most **tranquil** place I know is a quiet little cabin on a lake.
Word Work: Sample answers: **1.** A rock cannot speak. **2.** You use a key to open a door. **3.** You might draw another picture if you messed up the first one. **4.** A ruler isn't alive. **5.** A liar doesn't tell the truth. **6.** I feel stuffed if I eat too much. **7.** You can't see wind.
Handwriting Helper: Check children's work for accuracy and legibility.
Ready, Set, Read! 1. D **2.** A
Sentence Mender: "Hooray for us!" yelled Millie.
Brainteaser:

S	A	U	C	E	R
S	C	O	R	C	H
S	L	E	E	P	Y
S	P	R	O	U	T
S	Q	U	A	S	H
S	Y	S	T	E	M

Jumpstart 42

Word of the Day: Sample response—**Imitate** a frog by crouching low and saying "Ribbit!" in a deep voice.
Word Work: 1. brightly **2.** clearly **3.** cheerful **4.** successful **5.** fatherly **6.** friendly
Handwriting Helper: Check children's work for accuracy and legibility.
Ready, Set, Read! 1. bangles **2.** Friends tie them on to each other's wrists.
Sentence Mender: He yawned because he didn't get much sleep.
Brainteaser: Answers will vary; sample: heat, beat, boat, boot,

Jumpstart 43

Word of the Day: Sample response—Scientists think that the **origin** of Earth began with a big bang.
Word Work: 2. thinner, thinnest **3.** cleaner, cleanest **4.** larger, largest **5.** sillier, silliest **6.** flatter, flattest **7.** crazier, craziest **8.** gladder, gladdest
Handwriting Helper: Check children's work for accuracy and legibility.
Ready, Set, Read! 1. B **2.** A
Sentence Mender: We spent some time running around.
Brainteaser: 3, 5, 2, 4, 1

Jumpstart 44

Word of the Day: Sample response—What clues show that this chair is an **authentic** antique?
Word Work: 1. An inventor invents. **2.** A cartoonist makes cartoons. **3.** A teacher teaches. **4.** A violinist plays a violin. **5.** A director directs. **6.** A logger cuts logs. **7.** A machinist runs a machine. **8.** An investigator investigates.
Handwriting Helper: Check children's work for accuracy and legibility.
Ready, Set, Read! 1. Nomads are people who move from place to place. **2.** C
Sentence Mender: He never tasted any homemade ice cream.
Brainteaser: 1. wash **2.** hand **3.** fruit

Jumpstart 45

Word of the Day: Sample response—My scout troop **contributes** to our town pool every year.
Word Work: 1. pair **2.** rap **3.** sail **4.** pear **5.** sale **6.** wrap
Handwriting Helper: Check children's work for accuracy and legibility.
Ready, Set, Read! 1. She preferred to take part in opening day celebrations for the new bridge. **2.** The whole city was celebrating.
Sentence Mender: These are the best loaves of bread!
Brainteaser: 1. flowers **2.** book **3.** drop

Jumpstart 46

Word of the Day: Sample response—The **candidate** should work well with others and follow through.
Word Work: 1. 3 **2.** 2 **3.** 1 **4.** 2 **5.** 3 **6.** 1
Handwriting Helper: Check children's work for accuracy and legibility.
Ready, Set, Read! 1. It's like the word *equal*. **2.** You use it to locate exact places on Earth.
Sentence Mender: Who built those pyramids in Egypt?
Brainteaser: corn, hoe, sir; rhinoceros

Jumpstart 47

Word of the Day: Sample response—My sweater has different color stripes in an **irregular** pattern.
Word Work: (Top to bottom) bike/bicycle; flu/influenza; gym/gymnasium; burger/hamburger; math/mathematics; champ/champion
Handwriting Helper: Check children's work for accuracy and legibility.
Ready, Set, Read! 1. Both use the same rhyme pattern. **2.** People don't like complainers. **3.** Possible answer: I like the second one because I agree with its message.
Sentence Mender: Hey! That one's my team jacket!
Brainteaser: Answers will vary

Jumpstart 48

Word of the Day: Sample response—Bouncy, happy music **inspires** me to get up and dance.
Word Work: (Top to bottom) brunch = breakfast + lunch; ditzy = dizzy + dotty; flop = flap + drop; sitcom = situation + comedy; glob = globe + blob; motel = motor + hotel
Handwriting Helper: Check children's work for accuracy and legibility.
Ready, Set, Read! 1. C **2.** Possible answer: A constellation is a group of stars that form a picture in the sky.
Sentence Mender: It's like the sun just sank into the ocean.
Brainteaser: 1. shy **2.** pie **3.** eye **4.** guy **5.** try **6.** sigh

Jumpstart 49

Word of the Day: Sample response—What will happen to polar bears if their **environment** gets too warm?
Word Work: 1. believe **2.** upstairs **3.** bleachers **4.** songbird **5.** pioneers **6.** throat **7.** outdoors **8.** announce
Handwriting Helper: Check children's work for accuracy and legibility.
Ready, Set, Read! 1. It mixes the two things he loves best. **2.** It was his way to add the idea of *very* to each word.
Sentence Mender: Women often get their nails done.
Brainteaser: 1. What is her name? **2.** I hope my team wins today. **3.** How long is it until lunch?

Jumpstart 50

Word of the Day: Sample response—Work boots are **durable** if they have thick soles, strong laces, and are made of heavy leather.
Word Work: Answers will vary.
Handwriting Helper: Check children's work for accuracy and legibility.
Ready, Set, Read! 1. D **2.** C
Sentence Mender: The Three Stooges are Moe, Larry, and Curly. Note: the series comma before *and* is optional.
Brainteaser: (Top to bottom) at, eat, meat, steam, stream, masters

Printed in Great Britain
by Amazon

16317071R00107

Table of Contents

Foreword

This book is for anyone who wants to learn more about alpine skiing, improve their understanding of the sport and become a better skier.

The goal is to present skiing in simple, easy to understand terms and, ideally, help demolish any roadblocks to the next level that might be standing in your way.

We begin with a look at gear basics and skiing fundamentals, then move on to explore the techniques employed by several high-end demonstrators in a variety of conditions.

Many of the book's illustrations are photo montages designed to help you see exactly what the pros are doing. The descriptive text helps guide your eye to elements explained in the Skiing Basics and Technical Terms Simplified sections.

Keen observers will notice that some of the photos were taken at a time when helmets weren't common and ski gear was different. It's a testament to the fact that good skiing is timeless.

The photo collection was captured internationally on the slopes of Western Canada, Japan and China. The knowledge shared was gleaned from discussions, clinics, lessons, training and study with top trainers around the world and working with students from Canada, Australia, New Zealand, Britain, the United States, France, Switzerland, Germany, Austria, Italy, Japan, Taiwan, Hong Kong and China. Good skiing knows no borders.

As you develop your own skiing, you will see more in these montages each time you look at them. Refer to them often.

... Welcome to Next Level Skier!
Paul Cunnius

Photo | Judy Wang / 熊吉吉
Demonstrator | Paul Cunnius
Location | Wanlong Resort, Chongli, China

Gear Basics

Poles

Poles are used primarily for balance and timing. The pole plant is the trigger to begin a sequence of turns and will help us as we progress to higher levels.

Boots

Boots provide the crucial link between the skis and the body. They need the proper stiffness and comfort. Stiffness is called Flex. Beginners require a soft flex, while experts or racers prefer a stiffer flex. In all cases, the boot needs to allow mobility in the ankle for the skier to remain balanced.

Skis

Choosing the right ski requires a close look at the intended type of skiing. This can include cruising, carving, all mountain, soft snow, hard snow, short turns, medium turns, large turns, etc.

Consideration needs to be given to flex, length, turn radius, shape, width (tip, waist, tail) and main use.

There are endless online reviews of gear and its performance. Many rental shops and resorts offer high end rentals you can try before you buy, which is highly recommended.

Your local ski instructor and the experts at your local shops can help you with gear research and selection.

Photo | Martin Olson **Demonstrator** | Paul Cunnius
Location | Lake Louise, AB

Gear Basics

Poles

The pole plays an important role in timing and consolidating our turns and technique. It all starts with how we grip the pole.

- Put the hand through the strap
- Hold the entire grip with the thumb and all four fingers
- Holding the grip with all four fingers, especially the bottom two, properly affects the arm, shoulder, overall body balance position

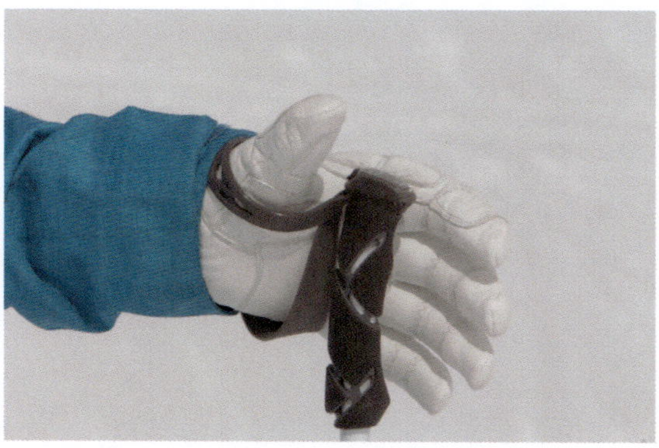

Step 1

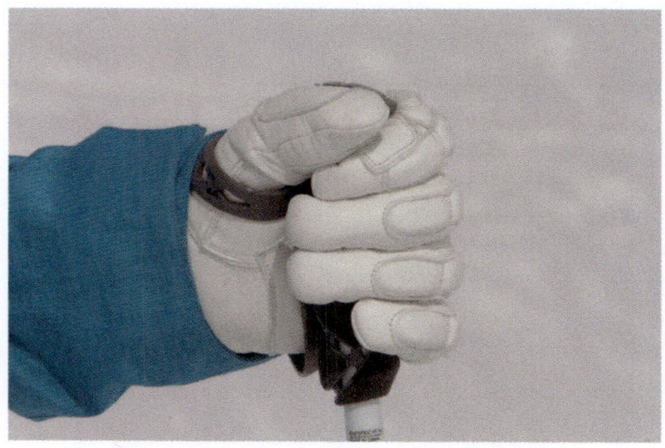

Correct

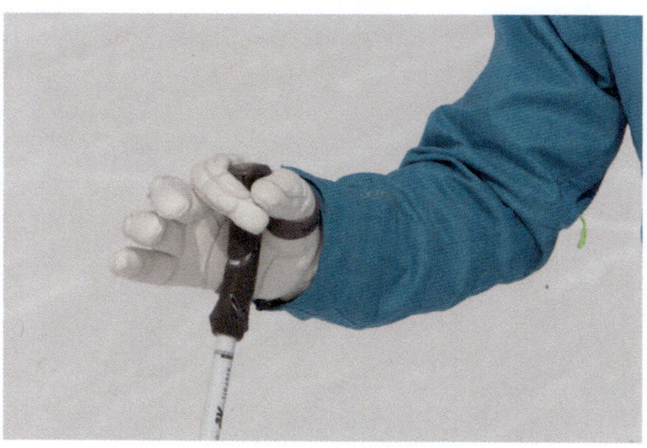

Incorrect

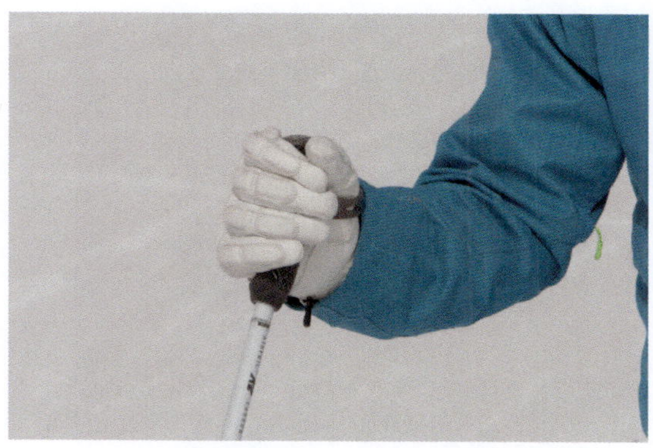

Correct

Photos | Martin Olson **Demonstrator** | Paul Cunnius **Location** | Lake Louise, AB

Gear Basics

Boots

Boot fitting can be a challenge with many theories. Boots should fit comfortably without being too loose or too tight.

Boot companies offer many different sizes and shapes. Try them on before you buy.

- The upper part of the boot (the cuff) should touch the entire leg comfortably
- The back of the boot and the back of the leg (calf) should have comfortable contact (no space)
- The front of the boot (tongue) and the front of the leg (shin) should have comfortable contact (no space)
- There should always be a slight bend in the ankle, providing range of movement without losing the front and back contact points

Incorrect

Incorrect

Correct

Photos | Martin Olson **Demonstrator** | Paul Cunnius **Location** | Lake Louise, AB

Gear Basics

Skis - Turn Radius

Because skis have a narrower waist than tip and tail, they have 'shape'. The more shape a ski has, the more it likes to make shorter turns. Conversely, a ski with less shape prefers larger turns.

Skis come with a number on them indicating the 'Turn Radius'. The same model, with the same tip/waist/tail dimensions, will have a slightly different Turn Radius according to the length of the ski.

Regardless, with the skier's help, skis of varying Turn Radii are not locked in to just one size of turn. They will, however, prefer a range of turn sizes according to their construction and dimensions.

- In the 'Turn Radius' diagram the short ski with a Turn Radius of 10 metres will prefer a shorter range of turns.
- In the 'Turn Radius' diagram the longer ski with a Turn Radius of 25 metres will prefer a longer range of turns.
- In the 'Length' diagram the two overlapping skis have the same shape therefore their turn shapes will be the same.

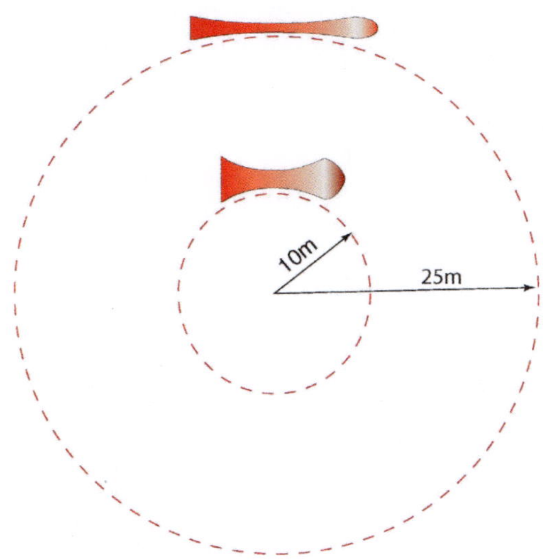

Turn Radius

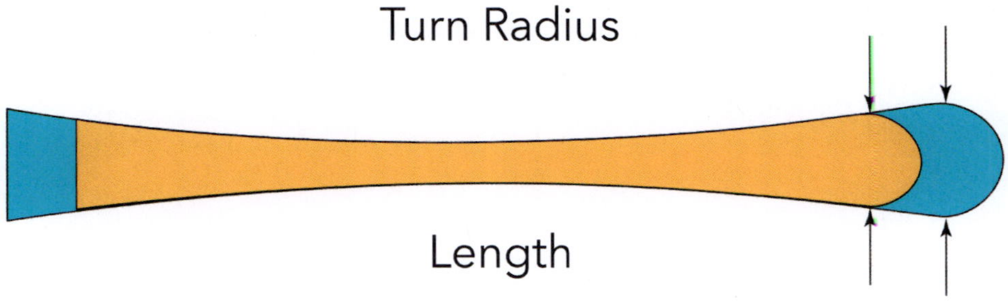

Length

Illustrations | Martin Olson

Gear Basics

Skis - Edging and Ski Bend

Skis turn because they bend, working to get the edge to entirely touch the snow. As the skier moves down the hill, keeping their weight centred, the tip and tail of the ski are pushed by the snow, causing the ski to bend into an arc as seen in the diagram below. When the entire edge touches the snow, it creates a round arc. There are many variables that affect edging, but this is the main principle.

- When the ski is simply tipped up, as in the 'Tipped Ski' diagram, only the tip and tail touch the snow.
- You can actually see the open space under the middle of the ski, shown with the flashlight and shadow in the 'Tipped Ski' diagram.
- When the ski is tipped up and bending, as in the 'Edged/Bending Ski' diagram, the entire edge is touching the snow and this is where turn size, turn shape, grip and actual turning take place.

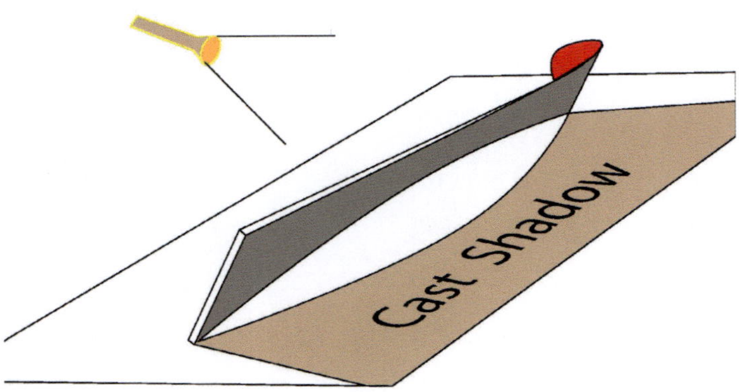

Tipped Ski

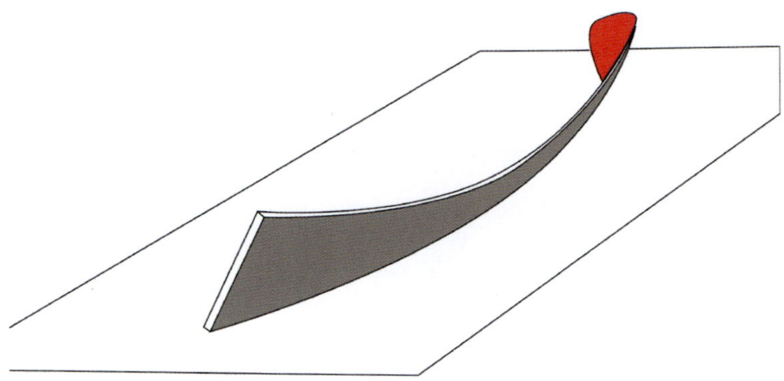

Edged/Bending Ski

Illustrations | Martin Olson

Gear Basics
Skis - Twisting

When a ski is tipped up, force and pressure build and it wants to twist. When there is more twisting, there is less edge grip. When there is less twisting, there is more edge grip.

This is called Torsional Strength or resistance. We want a ski that is torsionally strong enough for the type of conditions we typically ski on. This will give us suitable grip without excessive effort. A torsionally strong ski will provide more grip on hard surfaces.

- We can think of this as sideways bending of the ski, as seen in the 'Twist' diagram.
- The 'Torsion' diagram illustrates torsion as twisting around the longitudinal axis.

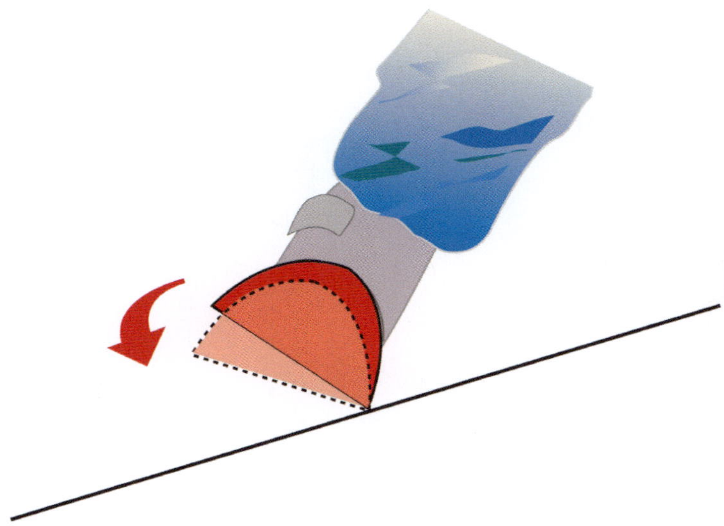

Twist

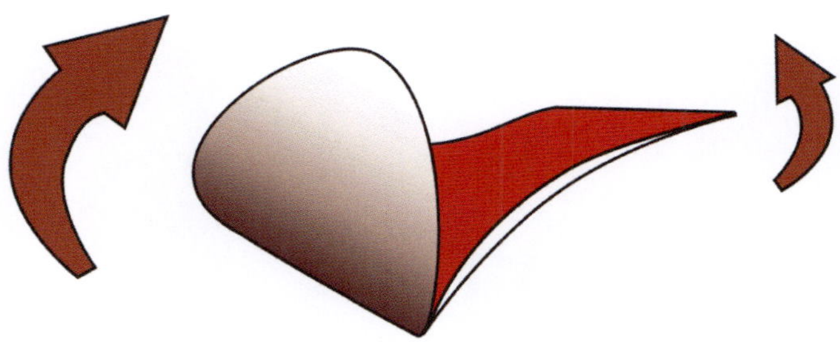

Torsion

Illustration | Martin Olson

Gear Basics
Skis - Ski Width

The width of a ski affects the skier's body in different ways depending on snow conditions.

On firm snow, the ski is mostly on its edge. If the ski is wide, side forces will be transferred to the knee.

By contrast, the same ski in powder will have most, if not all, of its base touching the snow. This manages and dissipates the forces symmetrically through the skier's body.

- Wide skis on hard surfaces (might) make it a challenge to reach maximum turn performance.
- Narrower skis on hard surfaces (might) make it easier to produce and manage performance turns.

Wide skis on groomed snow compared to powder snow

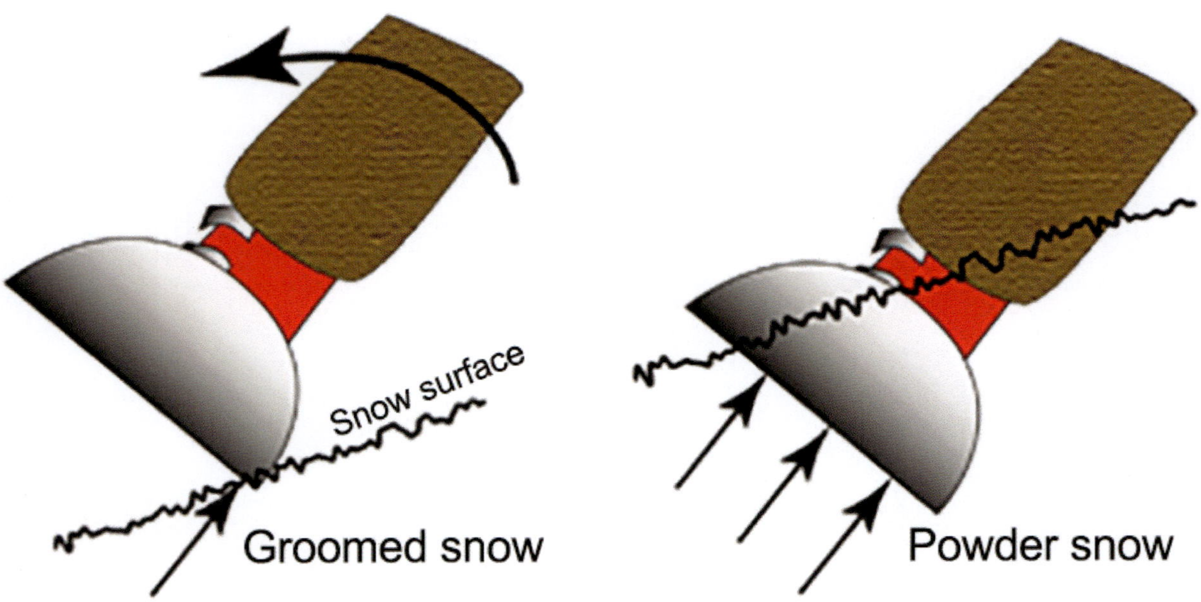

Illustration | Martin Olson

Gear Basics

Skis - Early Rise

Side view, or profile, shows us the camber of the ski from the tip to the tail. The Conventional Profile (Traditional) shows a clear arc from the tip to the tail. When flattened (Conventional Profile flattened), the entire ski base will touch the snow evenly (it's on the way to bending).

Early rise is a gradually raised tip in its neutral, or natural, state. This means there is less edge and ski base touching the snow until the ski begins to tip and bend.

As the edge angle increases, more edge comes in contact with the snow for better grip and control.

The more the ski gets tipped over, the longer it becomes because of the increasing contact the 'Rise' portion makes with the snow.

This is called progressive edge grip and the principle applies to all levels of skiers at all speeds, not just Experts. It can help an Intermediate skier learn how to turn more easily while gaining the grip and control of a ski with more edge as they become confident in tipping the ski over further and further.

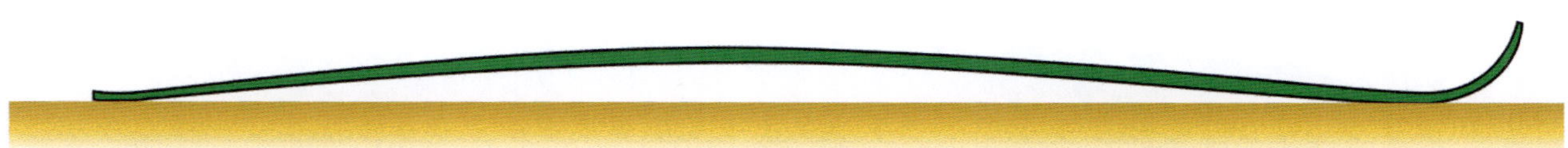

Conventional Profile

Conventional Profile flattened

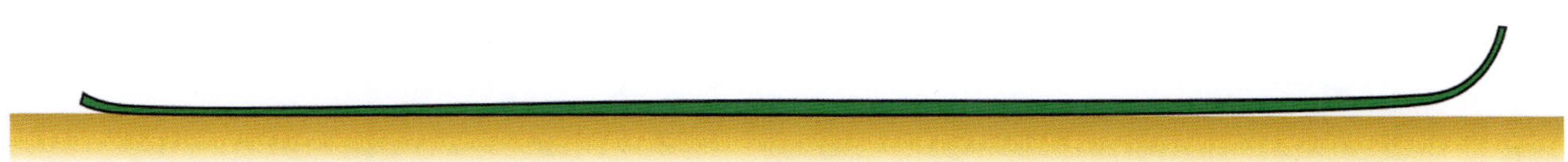

Early Rise Profile flattened

Illustrations | Martin Olson

Skiing Basics

Width of Stance - Lateral Balance

Balance - Forward/Centred/Back

Inside/Outside - Ski the Circle

Balance On/Against the Outside Foot/Ski

Leg Mobility

Centre of Mass (COM) and Base of Support (BOS)

Inclination/COM and BOS Move Together

Transition and Flow

Turn Shape

Weight Transfer

Upper/Lower Body Separation

Early Outside Balance

Turning Effort

Edging

Angulation

Vertical Separation

Steering

Novice

Advanced

Parallel

Flat Ski/Crossover

Photo | Martin Olson
Demonstrator | Paul Cunnius
Location | Silver Star, BC

Skiing Basics

Width of Stance *Lateral Balance*

The feet should be just far enough apart to allow the legs to turn, bend and move inside to get some edge grip. This will also provide the proper Lateral Balance needed on the outside ski.

If the feet are too far apart, leg mobility is difficult. If the feet are too close together, leg mobility is blocked. A proper stance should feel comfortable in all parts of the turn.

Incorrect

Correct

Incorrect

Photos | Martin Olson **Demonstrator** | Paul Cunnius **Location** | Lake Louise, AB

Skiing Basics

Balance *Forward/Centred/Back*

A good stance is centred, slightly bent/flexed at the ankle, knee and hip. Try to avoid being too far forward or too far back.

The body should look supported by, and on top of, the feet (Base of Support).

Incorrect

Correct

Incorrect

Photos | Martin Olson **Demonstrator** | Paul Cunnius **Location** | Silver Star, BC

Skiing Basics

Inside/Outside *Ski the Circle*

Think of a turn as traveling on a circle with the feet straddling the outer circle line.

Refer to body parts and equipment as either inside or outside the circle.

These terms will be used often throughout this book.

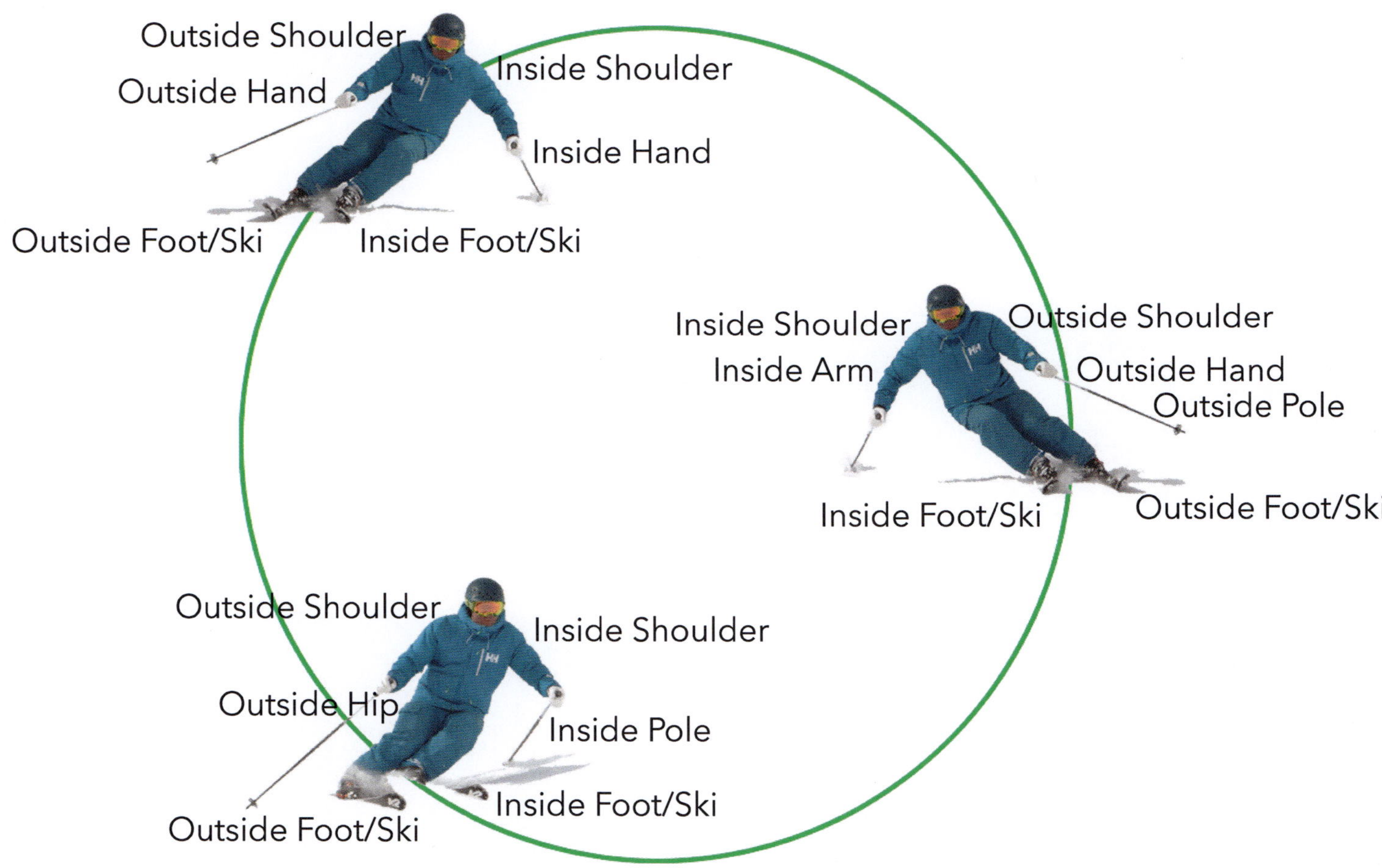

Photos | Martin Olson **Image** | Paul Cunnius **Demonstrator** | Paul Cunnius

Skiing Basics

Balance *On/Against the Outside Foot/Ski*

Balance should be on/against the outside foot/ski. Further, we should be in the middle of the outside foot/ski.

There are many technical reasons for this but, in short, this position best supports the entire body while letting the ski turn on its middle point. And it's true regardless of speed or ability level.

To balance properly, align the skeleton. This is sometimes called 'stacking the bones' - it offers maximum resistance to forces with the least amount of effort. When the skeleton is properly 'stacked and aligned' less muscle power is needed, and skiing is more comfortable and balanced.

It should feel almost as easy to stand against the skis anywhere in a turn as it is to stand on the skis on a flat surface while not moving.

Photo | Martin Olson **Demonstrator** | Misayo Nakamura **Location** | Silver Star, BC

Skiing Basics
Leg Mobility

Legs need to bend and unbend in a turn. We call this Leg Mobility or Flexion and Extension.

The legs should lengthen (straighten at ankle, knee and hip) at the start of the turn, then bend (shorten) moving through the turn. Ideally, the legs should be continually mobile, either flexing or extending.

A high level skier may look flexed most of the time, but their legs are still mobile, allowing them to manage higher speeds and different types of turns and pressure.

Photos | Martin Olson **Image** | Martin Olson
Demonstrator | Misayo Nakamura **Location** | Lake Louise, AB

Skiing Basics

COM and BOS *Move Together/Inclination*

The Base of Support (BOS/feet) needs to support the Centre of Mass (COM/stomach area). The two need to move together as we ski at different levels with changes in terrain and speed.

In every turn, the COM will be inside the BOS, as shown in the illustration. This alignment is called the 'Line of Inclination' and is the basis of dynamic balance. Bending of the ankle, knee and hip (angulation) continue throughout the turn to maintain that balance.

This is the foundation of how we support ourselves. There is inclination in every turn.

Photo | Martin Olson **Image** | Martin Olson **Demonstrator** | Erin Keam **Location** | Sun Peaks, BC

Skiing Basics

COM and BOS *Centre of Mass and Base of Support*

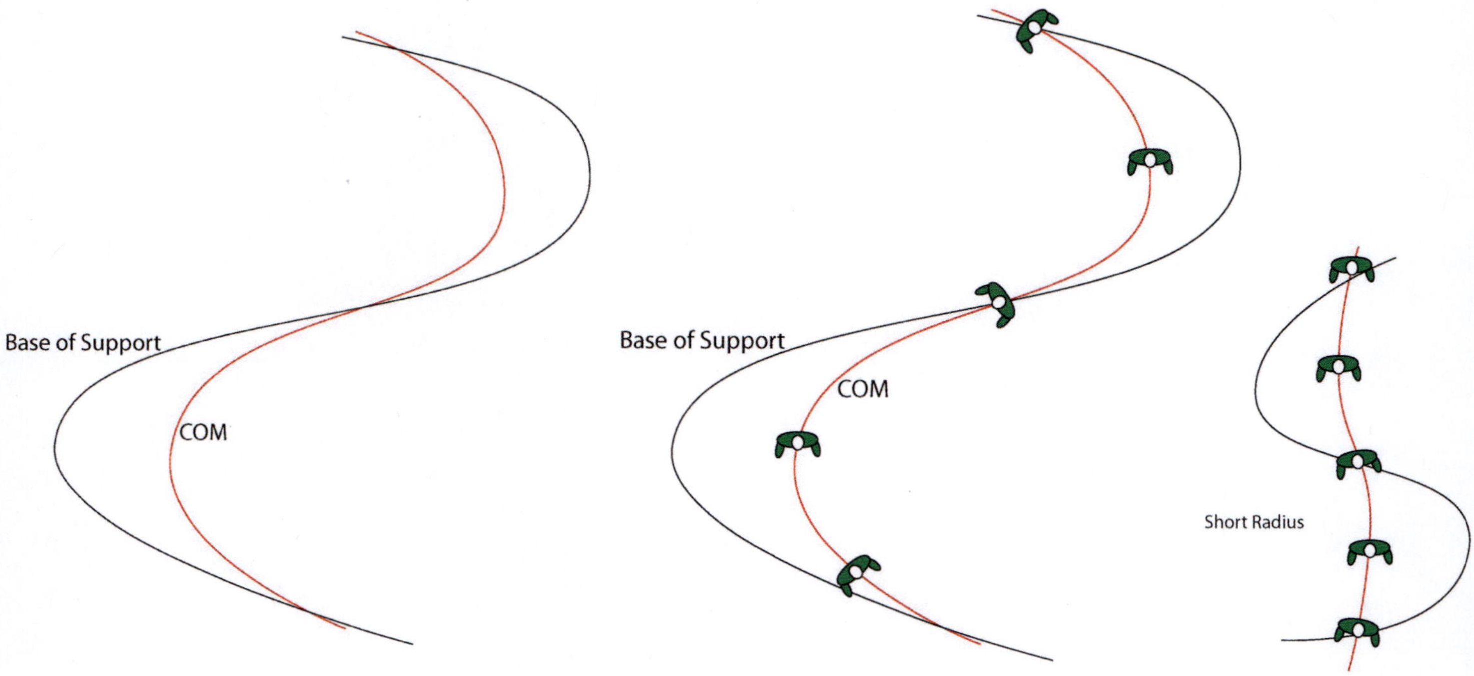

Aerial Views

The diagrams above show aerial views of the different paths the BOS and COM take in a turn.

The COM takes a shorter inside path than the BOS. Between turns, the paths cross in a phase called the transition, crossover or linking phase.

The amount of deflection across the hill is less in a short turn than in a bigger one, so you may feel your body is facing downhill more than it does in bigger turns. In both cases, your body faces the outside of the turn and there is deflection across the hill.

Illustrations | Martin Olson

Skiing Basics

COM and BOS *Centre of Mass and Base of Support*

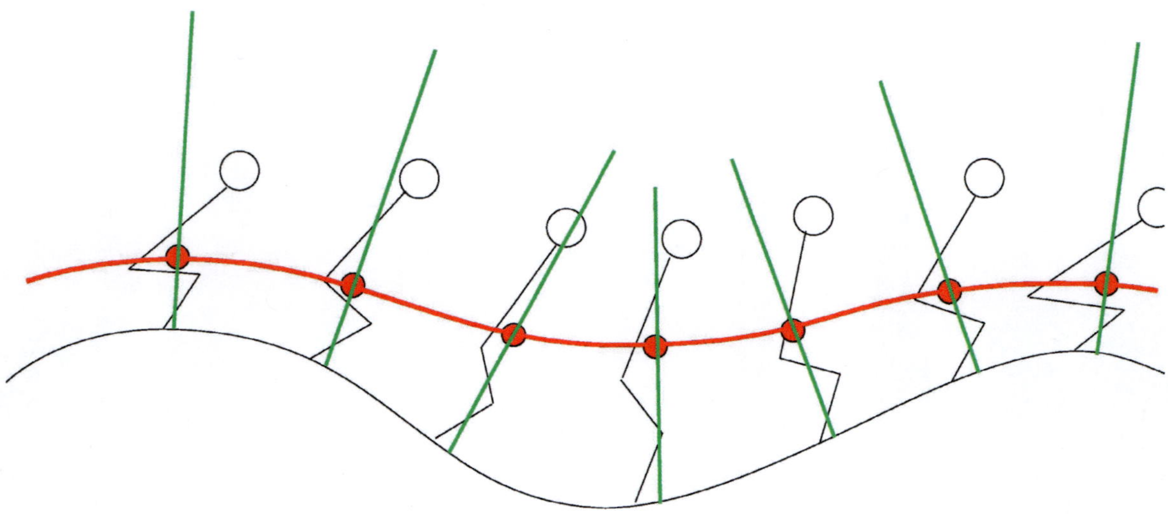

Side View Bumps

The green lines illustrate how the skier moves in changing terrain keeping the BOS and COM in balance.

Illustration | Martin Olson

Skiing Basics
Transition and Flow

Flowing from turn to turn requires well executed blending and timing of the movements: Vertically, Laterally, Rotationally and Fore/Aft.

The demonstration below shows this in detail at moderate speed on moderate terrain.

Photos | Judy Wang / 熊吉吉 **Image** | Paul Cunnius
Demonstrator | Paul Cunnius **Location** | Wanlong Resort, Chongli, China

- Vertically: The legs start in a flexed position, lengthen, then bend and flex again.
- Laterally: As the BOS is steered under the COM, gravity continues to pull the COM down the hill. As the BOS moves to the outside, weight builds on the new outside foot (left), still supporting the COM as they move together.
- Rotationally: The upper body remains calm and quiet. The turning effort (rotational) comes from the legs turning in the new direction.
- Fore/Aft: The BOS moves with the COM supporting the body at every part of the turn, indicating a centred position.

Skiing Basics

Turn Shape

Turn Shape is the track left on the snow in a turn from start to finish. Each turn resembles a semi-circle.

In the diagram below, the Blue Vertical line is the Fall Line. The top of that line is the start of our turn and the bottom, the finish.

Presented here are two typical turn shapes.

- Shallow: The distance from the fall line to the middle (apex) of the turn is shallow and not very far. This would be suitable to a milder or flatter slope.
- Deeper: The distance from the fall line to the middle (apex) of the turn is deeper and further. This would be suitable to a more aggressive or steeper slope.

Constant speed, appropriate to our skill level, should be safely maintained. This requires varying the turn shape according to how the slope changes pitch: Short, Medium or Long.

The Turn Shape is changed by the amount of Edging and Turning Effort applied to the turn.

If the legs turn a lot, with a large edge angle, the result is a deeper, rounder turn.

If the legs turn a little, with less edge angle, the result is a shallower turn.

There are an infinite number of combinations, but the point is to manage the turn shape through technique as needed based on speed, terrain and desired goals.

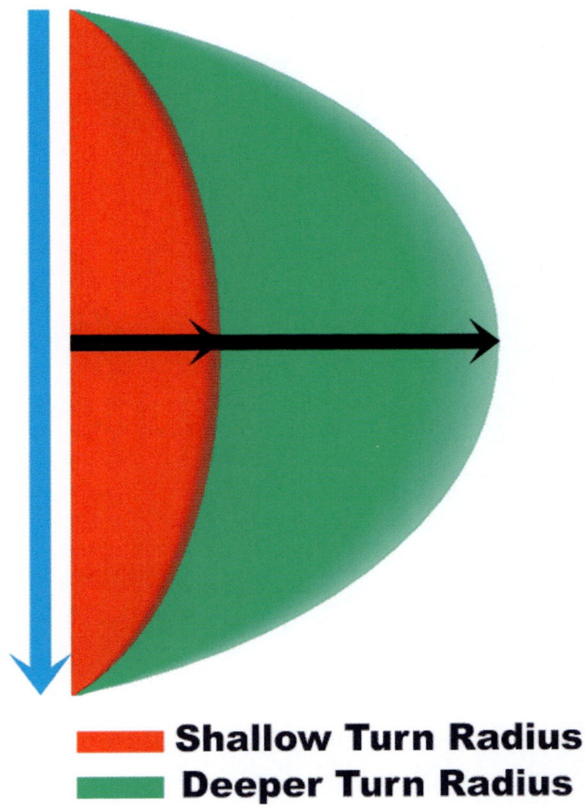

Illustration | Paul Cunnius

Skiing Basics
Weight Transfer

Good skiers show a smooth, easy weight transfer from one outside foot/ski to the new outside foot/ski as they flow from turn to turn. This is vital, as balance, or total body commitment to the outside foot/ski, is key to proper mechanics (edging/balance/control).

Photos | Martin Olson **Image** | Paul Cunnius
Demonstrator | Misayo Nakamura **Location** | Silver Star, BC

Skiing Basics
Upper/Lower Body Separation

There is a horizontal line of separation in the body around the hip area. It divides the upper body from the lower body.

Separation starts by turning the lower body (the legs) first, then letting the upper body follow. This creates upper and lower body separation. Separation is created at the start of a turn and sustained to the end, where it's reduced to cross over into the next turn.

Separation allows us to: Balance against the outside ski on the outside foot, begin the edging process, and maintain the BOS/COM balanced relationship.

Photos | Martin Olson **Image** | Paul Cunnius
Demonstrator | Paul Cunnius **Location** | Lake Louise, AB

In simple terms, the upper body faces the outside of the turn from the beginning right through to the finish, while the lower body carries out the turning effort. The feeling should be comfortable. The upper and lower body travel on a rotational axis, and too much or too little separation usually feels forced or is a strain to maintain. Just the right amount of separation feels comfortable and easy to maintain.

Skiing Basics

Early Outside Balance

Early Outside Balance on the new outside foot/ski helps the skier feel stable and in control. This feeling builds through the turn, allowing the skier to bend the legs and angulate to increase edge performance as they like, while still feeling stable and solid.

Photos | Martin Olson **Image** | Martin Olson
Demonstrator | Lisa Suutari **Location** | Whistler Blackcomb, BC

Skiing Basics
Turning Effort

Turning Effort is a muscular effort of turning both legs from the start of the turn to the finish. Ski sidecut, bending the ski and body angulation determine edging and turn shapes. When we add the turning effort of the legs, the result is a steered turn. Turn shapes can be altered from small to medium to long depending on how much or how little turning effort is applied from the legs.

Too little or no turning effort is simply riding the sidecut of the ski, all edging. The result is one turn shape as dictated by the ski dimensions. Too much turning effort overturns the ski, producing a skidded turn with very little edge grip.

The right combination allows varied turn types and turn shapes to be made: Carved or Skidded; Short, Medium or Long; Fast or Slow - regardless (within reason) of the ski width and Turning Radius as shown on the ski.

Photos | Martin Olson **Image** | Martin Olson
Demonstrator | Paul Cunnius **Location** | Lake Louise, AB

Skiing Basics
Edging

Edges are steel rails located on both sides of each ski. These need to be tuned so they are sharp and suitable for grip.

Ski tuning, like waxing and base structure, should be a regular part of your skiing maintenance routine. While tuning can get very advanced, a good basic 'tune' is the foundation for smooth, grippy turns. It should provide enough grip to enjoy your turns without slipping too much, or too little.

Place the ski flat on the floor. Note that one side of each edge is flat on the floor; this is the 'Base Edge'. The other side is vertical; it's called the 'Side Edge'. Different angles can be placed on each of these two edge sides; this is called bevelling. Typically, the side edge bevel is a bit more pronounced than the base edge bevel.

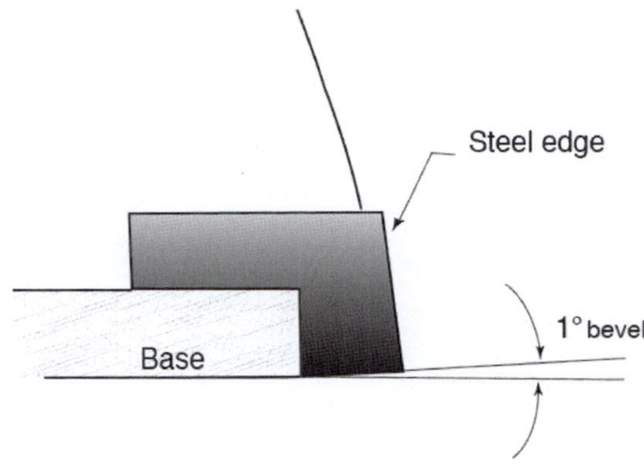

Small Edge Angle

Moderate Edge Angle

Larger Edge Angle

- When the ski is tipped over to engage the edge, it starts gripping the snow. This is called Edge Angle.
- A small amount of edge angle will allow the ski to bend and grip a little.
- A large amount of edge angle will allow the ski to bend more and grip a lot.

Photos | Martin Olson **Demonstrator** | Paul Cunnius **Location** | Lake Louise, AB
Illustration | Martin Olson

Skiing Basics

Angulation

Angulation is the progressive action of bending the ankle, knee and hip down and inside while moving through the turn to create and manage edging. The result is increased edge grip and a settling of the body as it lowers and settles into angles.

This progressive movement keeps the COM supported by the BOS. It also allows the grip needed for different situations. The body lowers as a result of leg bending and, because it is a progressive action, think of it as Angula'ting'.

Angulation = Grip … So, for earlier grip, angulate sooner in the turn. Generally the rate of Angulation should begin and end according to the time spent traveling on the arc (turn).

As Angulation is progressive, timing is important. Angulating too soon or too quickly weakens the second half of the turn. The turn first feels heavy, then light.

Angulating too late weakens the first half of the turn (not enough grip) and lets too much pressure build up too late. The turn feels light, then heavy.

Correct Angulation allows the skier to move through the turn without feeling any sudden heavy or light points.

Photos | Martin Olson **Image** | Martin Olson
Demonstrator | Misayo Nakamura **Location** | Sunshine Village, AB

Skiing Basics

Vertical Separation

Vertical Separation occurs as the inner leg softens (shortens), transferring weight and power to the outside leg and foot.

The feet actually get further apart from each other, but without widening the width between the legs.

It may appear that the stance is wide, but the inside foot is simply moving upward as it gets closer to the outside knee.

Photo | Martin Olson **Demonstrator** | Norman Kreutz **Location** | Silver Star, BC

Skiing Basics

Steering

Steering is the right combination of turning the legs while tipping the skis onto edge. The result is a round steered turn. It is strongly connected to Turning Effort.

Like a car or bicycle, the amount of steering for the desired or required turn size can be controlled.

How much or how little depends on the goal: terrain, turn shape/size, speed.

Too much of one will make the other difficult. If you're turning the skis chiefly by turning the legs, it will be harder to add edge.

Conversely, if you're tipping the skis way up onto the edge first, then it is harder to turn the legs. The action of steering results in the action of turning.

Good steering has the skis turning across the fall line and the skier traveling across the hill, not just down it.

Photos | Martin Olson **Image** | Martin Olson
Demonstrator | Norman Kreutz **Location** | Silver Star, BC

Skiing Basics

Novice

Novice turns begin with a snowplough wedge ending with the skis parallel. It is the middle stage of Beginner to Intermediate Parallel.

The basics covered so far are apparent here. It is important to develop good technical habits early so they can be carried through to higher levels for faster development.

Separation, balance against the outside ski and turning effort are shown here. They result in a complete, balanced, round and coordinated Novice steered turn at a slower speed.

Matching the skis to parallel is the continued effort of maintaining separation, outside ski balance, bending the legs and continuous turning effort.

Photos | Martin Olson **Image** | Martin Olson
Demonstrator | Paul Cunnius **Location** | Lake Louise, AB

Skiing Basics
Advanced

Advanced turns involve more speed and stronger edge performance. The techniques previously mentioned are still employed: separation, balance against the outside ski, turning effort and stronger edging. All are needed for the faster speed and increased performance of a coordinated Advanced steered turn.

Photos | Martin Olson **Image** | Martin Olson
Demonstrator | Paul Cunnius **Location** | Lake Louise, AB

Skiing Basics
Parallel

Parallel turns are the result of turning both legs at the same time through the start, middle, end and linking phases of the turn.

Increased speed and stronger edge grip helps.

Performance varies: Intermediate/Advanced/ Expert

The skis need to flatten in between turns in order to turn them both at the same time, parallel.

As the BOS passes under the COM (crossover or linking phase), they align vertically for a very short time. This is the point when both skis flatten and can be turned most easily at the same time.

Photos | Martin Olson **Image** | Paul Cunnius
Demonstrator | Paul Cunnius **Location** | Silver Star, BC

Skiing Basics
Flat Ski/Crossover

In order to keep the skis parallel, both legs need to turn at the same time. There is a point in between turns called the 'Crossover or Linking Phase'. It is at this point that the COM and the BOS briefly align vertically, and the skis are both flat as a result. This is when we begin turning both legs together.

This carefully timed move is crucial to parallel performance at every level from Intermediate on up to Advanced and Expert.

Photos | Judy Wang / 熊吉吉 **Image** | Paul Cunnius
Demonstrator | Paul Cunnius **Location** | Wanlong Resort, Chongli, China

Carving

Carving is the ultimate ski experience, involving speed and the rush of 'flying' down the hill.

It's where we do our best to get the most out of our edges and where performance can really be defined.

The term 'Ski Performance' involves using your edges, bending the ski and managing to create and complete turns with grip, power, force and confidence.

This is an exciting section of the book, taking a look at many high end demonstrators showing us how to carve at varying levels, in different situations and changing conditions on the hill.

While the demonstrators may show some differences in style, their skills and technique are all built on the same foundation.

Photo | Martin Olson Images
Demonstrator | Martin Olson
Location | Silver Star, BC

Carving

In its simplest form, Carving is tipping the skis over to create angles that bend the ski and allow us to change direction across the slope.

In order to perform a carved turn, we need to be angulating progressively throughout the arc.

Photos | Martin Olson **Image** | Martin Olson
Demonstrator | Norman Kreutz **Location** | Silver Star, BC

Carving

Strong carving includes a great degree of vertical separation. The distance vertically between the feet is a result of increased bending of the inside leg (shorter leg, higher inside foot) and a longer outside leg.

This typically looks as though the inside foot is closer to the hips and the leg separation has widened. In fact, the leg separation remains mostly the same: looks can be deceiving. This is one of the hallmarks of Expert performance.

Photos | Martin Olson **Image** | Martin Olson
Demonstrator | Misayo Nakamura **Location** | Sunshine Village, AB

Carving

Timing of movements is very important to Carving. Angulating and bending the legs, which lowers the body, combine with a lateral movement of the lower legs inside the turn.

Blending these moves together at the right point in the arc (turn) is crucial to getting the best and most performance out of the ski in each turn.

Photos | Martin Olson **Image** | Martin Olson
Demonstrator | Norman Kreutz **Location** | Silver Star, BC

Carving

Carving strength requires a strong and stable upper body. While early steering builds separation, some rotational resistance should be maintained in the upper body. Let it follow the lower body, but with a small delay.

The look should be a strong and stable upper body through the whole turn. Maintaining separation keeps power in the lower body.

Photos | Judy Wang / 熊吉吉 **Image** | Paul Cunnius
Demonstrator | Paul Cunnius **Location** | Wanlong Resort, Chongli, China

Carving

Photos | Martin Olson **Image** | Martin Olson
Demonstrator | Rodger Poole **Location** | Sun Peaks, BC

The degree of movement in the lower body directly affects the angle of the skis on the snow.

This angulation creates a force that the body needs to balance against. The faster the skier goes, and the greater the degree of angulation, the greater the force.

Generating this level of performance requires high levels of athleticism.

Carving

Photos | Judy Wang / 熊吉吉 **Image** | Paul Cunnius

Demonstrator | Paul Cunnius **Location** | Wanlong Resort, Chongli, China

The outside hand is level with the inside shoulder at the start of the turn.

As the edge engages, the outside hand lowers in tandem with the rate of angulation, but doesn't go below the hip. This increases strength on the edge and power to the outside ski.

It is a subtle but powerful move and needs to be timed correctly.

The shoulders should continue to remain relatively level.

Carving

Photos | Martin Olson **Image** | Paul Cunnius
Demonstrator | Misayo Nakamura **Location** | Sunshine Village, AB

Early separation and angulation are the starting points for strong powerful turns.

The progressive movement of angulation can be better thought of as 'angulating' as it is a continual movement.

Softening the inside leg lets the body lower and settle into angles, bending the outside ski in this powerful carved turn.

Carving

Execution of the linking phase into edging in high-speed short turns should remain uninterrupted, even when the skis leave the snow briefly in between turns.

Photos | Martin Olson **Image** | Martin Olson
Demonstrator | Steve Smart **Location** | Silver Star, BC

Carving

Proper alignment of the body is important when skiing fast.

At high speeds, commitment to the outside ski requires entire body alignment to properly balance against the strong forces being generated.

This alignment amplifies the overall 'power image' and is a result of correct COM and BOS placement and separation.

Photo | Martin Olson **Demonstrator** | Casey Bouius **Location** | Lake Louise, AB

Carving

Upper and lower body separation is vital at all levels.

This separation occurs around the hip or waist area, creating an upper and lower body. The upper body should appear to be facing slightly to the outside of the turn, or away from the direction the skis are travelling.

Many skiers look slightly inside the turn in preparation for the next one, but they continue to maintain the proper body separation created earlier.

Photos | Martin Olson **Image** | Martin Olson
Demonstrator | Misayo Nakamura **Location** | Sunshine Village, AB

Carving

Balance on the new outside ski should start early with upper/lower body separation.

As the line of inclination is firmly established, the edge angle increases through angulation and the ski begins to bend. This allows for grip with strong balance as performance increases.

The BOS and COM travel together and a comfortable width between the feet provides stability. Upper/lower Body separation is maintained throughout the entire turn.

Photos | Judy Wang / 熊吉吉 **Image** | Paul Cunnius

Demonstrator | Paul Cunnius **Location** | Wanlong Resort, Chongli, China

Carving

The distance between the feet can change between turns while the commitment to the new outside ski remains the same.

Notice how the tracks (inset) show a varying distance between the feet, but a smooth uninterrupted transition.

Photos | Martin Olson **Image** | Martin Olson
Demonstrator | Norman Kreutz **Location** | Silver Star, BC

Carving

Edge angle produces direction change from left to right and right to left across the hill.

The skier will feel (and look) as though they are travelling with deflection back and forth as well as down the hill.

Photos | Judy Wang / 熊吉吉 **Image** | Paul Cunnius

Demonstrator | Paul Cunnius **Location** | Wanlong Resort, Chongli, China

Carving

Edge angle on the ski can be produced very early in the turn.

The outside ski starts to bend and turn more quickly on a tighter arc. In this case, the resulting force will be felt quickly, but still handled in a relaxing manner.

Photos | Martin Olson **Image** | Martin Olson
Demonstrator | Steve Smart **Location** | Silver Star, BC

Carving

Angulation shows the inside knee moving up towards the chest, creating vertical separation.

The entire body settles down closer to the snow inside the turn.

The result is strong edge grip and bending of the outside ski for a strong, carved, round turn.

Photos | Martin Olson **Image** | Martin Olson
Demonstrator | Norman Kreutz **Location** | Silver Star, BC

Carving

At high speeds, strong angulation and flexibility in the legs lets us manage and ski over rollers.

Sudden rises in the terrain shouldn't upset the stability of the upper body or the roundness of the turn.

Photos | Martin Olson **Image** | Martin Olson
Demonstrator | Paul Cunnius **Location** | Silver Star, BC

Carving

Carving requires a transition where the legs extend and lengthen to start the turn. It's like reaching out to the snow with the feet (BOS).

This lengthening and mobility of the legs, with the COM inside the BOS, allows edge angle to build early. This is the start of a well carved turn.

Photos | Martin Olson Images **Image** | Martin Olson
Demonstrator | Martin Olson **Location** | Silver Star, BC

Carving

Hand position through all phases of the turn should not change very much.

Keeping the hands out front and apart helps provide the rotational stability needed at higher speeds.

Photos | Martin Olson **Image** | Martin Olson
Demonstrator | Misayo Nakamura **Location** | Sunshine Village, AB

Carving

Vertical separation (shorter inside leg) gives the appearance of a wider stance in the middle of the turn. The legs actually keep a mostly similar distance apart through most of the turn.

As the turn progresses and moves closer to the end, subtle bending of the outside leg reduces the vertical separation. The bending angles of the ankle, knee and hip begin to match more closely in both legs preparing for the crossover.

Photos | Judy Wang / 熊吉吉 **Image** | Paul Cunnius

Demonstrator | Paul Cunnius **Location** | Wanlong Resort, Chongli, China

Carving

True carving starts with early commitment to the new outside ski (left ski in this image).

Stable shoulders, arms and separation help keep the power on the bending outside ski for strong steering.

Photos | Martin Olson **Image** | Martin Olson

Demonstrator | Lisa Suutari **Location** | Whistler Blackcomb, BC

Carving

The degree of angulation can be increased to the point of lowering the COM close to the snow.

The skier may look quite far to the inside of the turn, but balance is on the outside ski.

A turn with this high degree of angulation requires a high level of skill and speed.

Photo | Martin Olson **Demonstrator** | Norman Kreutz **Location** | Silver Star, BC

Carving

Expert skiers have the ability to make balance adjustments without interrupting the flow and performance of carved turns.

Bringing the COM over the BOS in the linking phase is often referred to as recentring and is often seen in shorter high performance turns.

Photos | Martin Olson Images **Image** | Martin Olson
Demonstrator | Martin Olson **Location** | Silver Star, BC

Carving

Stability in the upper body requires minimal interruption from the pole plant.

At higher speeds, the pole plant is more of a light 'touch'.

This comes from progressively cocking the wrist, allowing the pole to travel in time with the outside foot. Bring the outside thumbnail back towards the outside shoulder.

When the pole touches, simply ski past the pole basket, keeping the hand up front where it belongs.

Photos | Judy Wang / 熊吉吉 **Image** | Paul Cunnius
Demonstrator | Paul Cunnius **Location** | Wanlong Resort, Chongli, China

Carving

A large degree of angulation is being developed through this turn.

The legs progressively bend and move inside to tip the skis up. This is clear looking at the position of the legs in the first and last frames.

There is an increased bend in the waist and very little change rotationally in the upper body, providing strength and stability.

Photos | Martin Olson **Image** | Martin Olson
Demonstrator | Misayo Nakamura **Location** | Silver Star, BC

Carving

Many skiers 'feel' the snow with the inside pole.

The inside pole basket is kept on the snow in order to feel the terrain angle and measure where the rest of the body is laterally.

Don't confuse this for 'leaning' on the inside pole. It is not being used as a prop.

The 'feel' of the basket on the snow helps adjust the body laterally and rotationally, stabilizing the inside hand, arm and shoulder.

Photos | Martin Olson **Image** | Paul Cunnius
Demonstrator | Paul Cunnius **Location** | Lake Louise, AB

Carving

The linking phase in shorter carved turns often involves a retraction of the feet.

The upper body remains stable and low while allowing the skis to roll off the old edges into the flattening/crossover phase, then quickly onto the new set of carving edges.

Photos | Martin Olson **Image** | Martin Olson
Demonstrator | Norman Kreutz **Location** | Silver Star, BC

Carving

Well executed turns show a change of distance between the feet and the hips.

At the start of the turn the legs lengthen. This creates the longest distance between the feet and the hips. The shortest distance between the feet and the hips is at the end of the turn, as bending and angulation allow the BOS to steer back under the COM.

At higher speeds the skier will feel more 'lateral' than 'vertical' in their overall body position.

Photos | Martin Olson **Image** | Martin Olson
Demonstrator | Paul Cunnius **Location** | Silver Star, BC

Carving

The upper body needs to adjust rotationally to find the strongest feel or position on the outside ski.

When we find the right amount of upper and lower body separation, the outside ski will feel strong.

This rotational adjustment can take place without interrupting angulation or the edge angle of the skis on the snow.

This should not be confused with leading the turn with the upper body.

Photos | Martin Olson **Image** | Paul Cunnius
Demonstrator | Paul Cunnius **Location** | Silver Star, BC

Carving

When the COM and BOS are travelling together properly, the feet can clearly be seen underneath the skier (not in front of or behind).

Good turns illustrate this in every phase of a sequence, especially in the side view.

Photos | Paul Cunnius **Image** | Paul Cunnius
Demonstrator | Martin Olson **Location** | Sunshine Village, AB

Carving

Moving through the flattening phase efficiently is important.

It may appear that the skis change immediately from the old edges to the new, but the flattening phase does take place. It just comes and goes very quickly.

As speed and performance increase, timing the flattening phase is challenging and it is a defining quality of well executed technical skiing.

Photos | Martin Olson **Image** | Martin Olson
Demonstrator | Misayo Nakamura **Location** | Silver Star, BC

Carving

Upper body stability and separation keep strength and power in the lower body.

This strength and power remain on the outside ski to enable bending and high end edge performance shown nicely here.

Photos | Martin Olson Images **Image** | Martin Olson
Demonstrator | Martin Olson **Location** | Silver Star, BC

Carving

When the inside knee moves closer to the chest, it allows the outside leg to angulate further to the inside of the turn. A higher inside knee also creates vertical separation, putting power on the outside ski throughout the turn.

This all happens while the COM and BOS remain in line, with the perfect blend of inclination and angulation.

Photos | Martin Olson **Image** | Paul Cunnius
Demonstrator | Norman Kreutz **Location** | Silver Star, BC

Carving

A low COM in the crossover phase maintains pressure on the skis between turns.

Proper timing results in a quick, strong commitment to the new outside ski well before the fall line for early edge and superior grip.

Photos | Martin Olson **Image** | Martin Olson
Demonstrator | Russ Wood **Location** | Silver Star, BC

Carving

It's common to lift the inside ski early in the turn to develop early edge.

The skier adjusts the body, staying centred while committing to the new outside ski. The result is balance in the middle of the ski for earlier maximum edge performance.

This can only happen with strong balance on the new outside ski early in the flattening phase and usually on steeper terrain.

Photos | Judy Wang / 熊吉吉 **Image** | Paul Cunnius
Demonstrator | Paul Cunnius **Location** | Wanlong Resort, Chongli, China

Carving

Here is an excellent example of early edge grip and vertical separation.

While the feet may appear to be quite far apart, the legs are not.

Taking vertical separation to this degree allows the skier to tip up the outside ski very high, as seen in the last frame.

Photos | Martin Olson **Image** | Martin Olson
Demonstrator | Dave Hay **Location** | Lake Louise, AB

Carving

Retraction of the feet and low COM through the flattening/crossover phase keeps pressure on the skis and allows the edges to change quickly.

Softening the outside leg at transition helps transfer the weight to the new outside ski in preparation for the next turn.

Photos | Martin Olson **Image** | Martin Olson

Demonstrator | Don Kjorven **Location** | Sunshine Village, AB

Carving

Linking carved turns requires good reading of the terrain.

Look ahead to manage shallower turns on flatter surfaces and deeper turns when steeper. Use sidehills to help you grow onto the new edges.

The transition between edges should continue to feel smooth and clean while applying technique to terrain.

Photos | Martin Olson **Image** | Martin Olson
Demonstrator | Paul Cunnius **Location** | Silver Star, BC

Carving

At higher speeds, early angulation will create the force needed to power and bend the outside ski early and throughout the turn.

Maintaining upper and lower body separation is crucial to keeping this power and performance from start to finish.

Photos | Martin Olson **Image** | Martin Olson
Demonstrator | Rodger Poole **Location** | Sun Peaks, BC

Carving

A strong line of inclination is established, followed by a quick rate of angulation.

The progression between these two positions shows how quickly power can be generated in a short carved turn.

Photos | Martin Olson Images **Image** | Martin Olson
Demonstrator | Martin Olson **Location** | Silver Star, BC

Carving

Reorganizing the body and stance from one turn to the next is needed for smooth transition and flow.

Weight is transferred from the old to new outside ski.

Comfortable lateral and inside balance in the rest of the body helps the new outside ski grip and bend. In this case, the upper body looks quiet and comfortable because of the lower body turning and steering effort.

Photos | Martin Olson **Image** | Martin Olson
Demonstrator | Paul Cunnius **Location** | Lake Louise, AB

Carving

Keeping the COM low through the transition phase of short turns ensures that some of the pressure generated is kept and carried through to the new turn.

Precise timing of the lower body turning effort and steering results in nice symmetry from turn to turn.

Photos | Martin Olson **Image** | Martin Olson
Demonstrator | Norman Kreutz **Location** | Silver Star, BC

Carving

Power and carving can be especially fun in softer conditions.

Soft snow provides stronger support because more snow pushes against more of the ski base.

Photos | Martin Olson **Image** | Martin Olson
Demonstrator | Misayo Nakamura **Location** | Sunshine Village, AB

Carving

Gradually increasing angulation creates an image where the outside of the body (from foot to head) resembles the letter 'C'.

The 'C' shape is from bending and increasing the edge angle, moving the ankle, knee and hip inside the turn.

This arc becomes deeper and rounder as the skier continues angulating through the turn.

Photos | Martin Olson Images **Image** | Martin Olson
Demonstrator | Martin Olson **Location** | Silver Star, BC

Carving

Side views allow us to see how the skier aligns and stacks up.

Note there is always a slight bend at the ankle. The outside shoulder lines up over the outside knee and outside foot for an excellent centred position.

Photos | Martin Olson **Image** | Paul Cunnius
Demonstrator | Misayo Nakamura **Location** | Sunshine Village, AB

Carving

Edge transition should look and feel smooth.

Think of rolling the skis from the old to the new set of edges by rolling the ankles and knees down the hill, then further to the inside of the arc.

Be patient and time it correctly. The inset shows edge transition from arc to arc.

Photos | Martin Olson **Image** | Martin Olson

Demonstrator | Paul Cunnius **Location** | Lake Louise, AB

Carving

Subtle retraction of the feet and keeping the COM low in the linking phase allows power to be maintained and carried across the fall line as a line of inclination begins to take shape.

Photos | Martin Olson Images **Image** | Martin Olson
Demonstrator | Martin Olson **Location** | Silver Star, BC

Carving

As angulation movements amplify, so do the forces generated by the increasingly edged skis.

Rotational stability in the upper body is very important. It requires increased physical strength in the core and abdominal area. This provides resistance as speed and performance reach higher levels.

Photo | Martin Olson **Demonstrator** | Rodger Poole **Location** | Sun Peaks, BC

Carving

Symmetry is a goal in all of our turns.

Keep the edge angles equal at the same points on both sides of the turn.
This will help create symmetrical turn shapes.

The turn shape and size should be the same on each side of the fall line.

Photos | Giulia Zhu **Image** | Paul Cunnius
Demonstrator | Paul Cunnius **Location** | Sunac Snow Park, Guangzhou, China

Carving

Alignment of the outside shoulder over the outside knee and toe piece demonstrates the centred position required for control and smooth linking of turns.

A consistent hand position, in front and apart, helps with both a centred position and the resistance to upper body rotation that weakens linking efforts.

Photos | Martin Olson **Image** | Paul Cunnius
Demonstrator | Paul Cunnius **Location** | Sunshine Village, AB

Carving

As the inside leg moves both up and inside, it makes room for the outside leg to move inside and stay strong. The result is a high edge angle and very pronounced arc.

Notice the inner pole basket feeling the snow for lateral balance and reading the terrain.

Photos | Martin Olson **Image** | Martin Olson
Demonstrator | Norman Kreutz **Location** | Silver Star, BC

Carving

This sequence nicely illustrates the mechanics of each phase of the turn.

Upper and lower body separation, followed by well-timed pressure control, builds into a well angulated and very well balanced position on the skis.

The well balanced 'picture' is a result of well timed movements by the skier.

Photos | Martin Olson **Image** | Martin Olson
Demonstrator | Mike DesBrisay **Location** | Lake Louise, AB

Carving

Practicing round arcs to the point of facing uphill is an excellent exercise to improve steering and carving.

Throughout the entire arc, the outside foot (BOS) remains under the core of the body (COM) for the proper support.

This might feel like pushing the feet forward but, in fact, it's not letting them fall behind.

Make sure the slope is clear and safe when doing this.

Photos | Martin Olson **Image** | Paul Cunnius

Demonstrator | Paul Cunnius **Location** | Silver Star, BC

All Terrain

Really good skiers can be put into challenging situations and continue to ski very well. This includes steeps, crud, trees, off-piste, chutes and anything un-groomed off or close to the main trails.

What sets these talented skiers apart is their ability to demonstrate their strength and high level of skill when their surroundings and conditions are most difficult. Their skills don't diminish; if anything, they become stronger, more accurate and powerful.

What also sets them apart is their eagerness to look for and pursue these areas on the mountain. They like them and don't just ski them, they charge!

All Terrain conditions challenge our skiing, resulting in improvement. Make a point of getting off the groomed and onto the un-groomed terrain, safely.

When back on the groomed runs, improvements feel and look very apparent. A balance of skiing all conditions is healthy for all skiers and all levels of skill development.

Photo | Martin Olson **Demonstrator** | Norman Kreutz **Location** | Silver Star, BC

All Terrain

Link the turns in varying snow depths with a little air.

At the end of the turn, a strong short push downward with both feet pushes the body up. With some retraction of the feet, the skis can be redirected while out of the snow into the direction of the new turn.

Photos | Martin Olson **Image** | Martin Olson
Demonstrator | Norman Kreutz **Location** | Silver Star, BC

All Terrain

Clear upper and lower body separation allow the skier to remain stable and strong in changing snow conditions.

Photos | Martin Olson **Image** | Paul Cunnius
Demonstrator | Misayo Nakamura **Location** | Sunshine Village, AB

On steeper slopes, the upper body will face more directly down the hill. Angulating is important to maintain a strong and stable position, even in this soft snow.

Feeling the snow with the inside hand is simply a measure for positioning, not support.

Photos | John Schwirtlich **Image** | Paul Cunnius **Demonstrator** | Paul Cunnius
Location | Mike Wiegele Helicopter Skiing, Blue River, BC

All Terrain

Mobility in the legs keeps the COM well connected to the BOS.

Timing this pressure control properly in the legs makes skiing in rougher terrain look easy.

Photos | Martin Olson **Image** | Paul Cunnius
Demonstrator | Misayo Nakamura **Location** | Sunshine Village, AB

All Terrain

Even in uneven terrain, unweighting is needed to turn the legs properly. This allows the separation needed for proper balance to take place.

Depending on the situation, unweighting can be done by either extending or bending the legs.

Photos | Martin Olson **Image** | Paul Cunnius
Demonstrator | Paul Cunnius **Location** | Sunshine Village, AB

All Terrain

On steeper terrain, the weight transfer and crossover of the COM and BOS require more commitment.

The steeper it gets, the more the COM needs to move down the hill to stay balanced.

A strong pole plant stabilizes the upper body, allowing the crossover to take place so the skier can balance on the new outside ski early.

Photos | Martin Olson **Image** | Paul Cunnius
Demonstrator | Paul Cunnius **Location** | Sunshine Village, AB

All Terrain

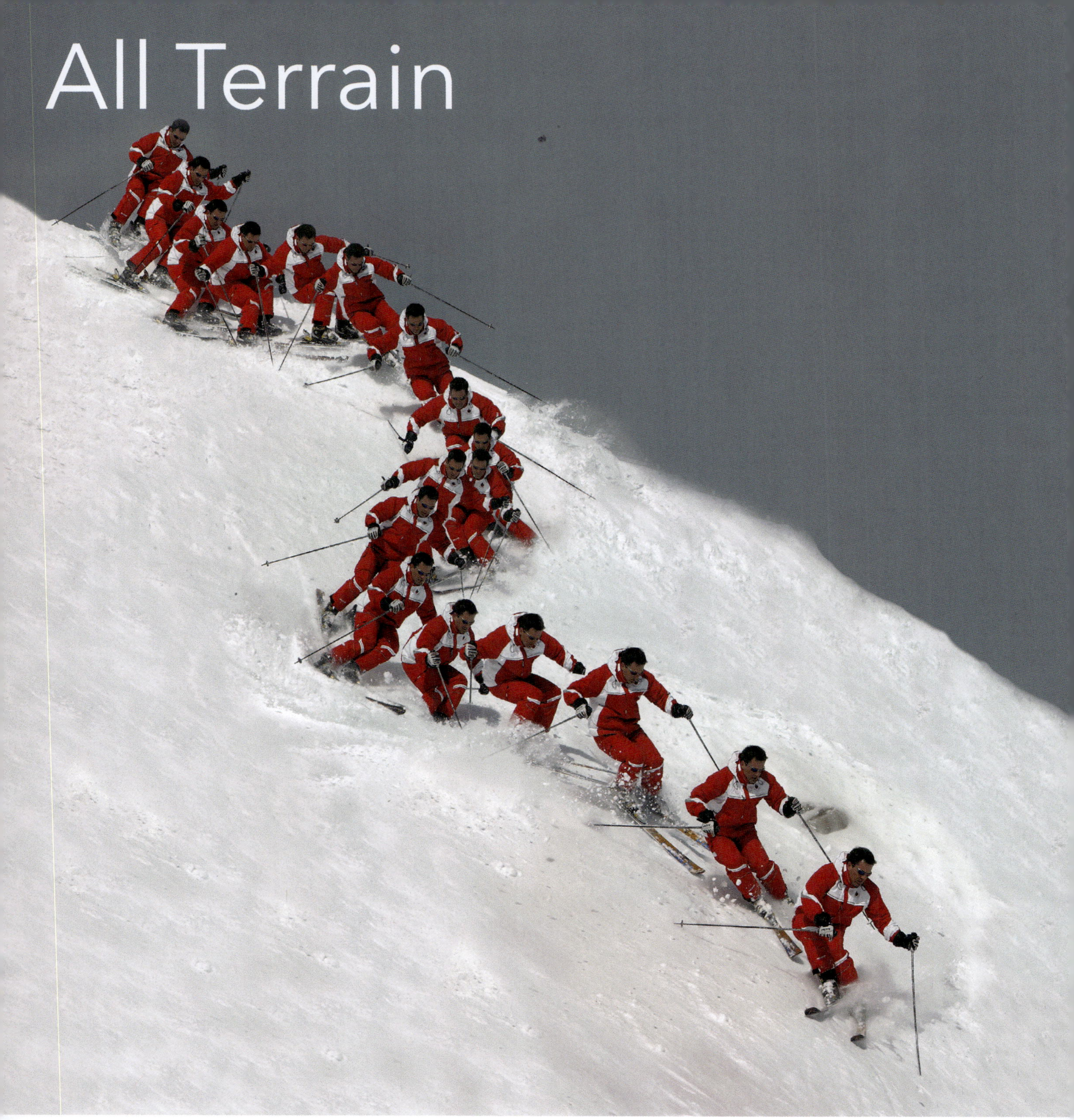

As the COM moves down the steep slope, quick retraction and extension of the legs is required for balance and speed control.

The strong turning effort results in a well angulated and separated position on each turn.

Photos | Martin Olson **Image** | Martin Olson
Demonstrator | Jeff Larouche **Location** | Lake Louise, AB

All Terrain

Linking short powerful turns in snow that wants to throw the skier around requires dynamic leg mobility.

A powerful turning effort in the legs and correct placement of the BOS illustrate how to handle and enjoy rough snow.

Photos | Martin Olson **Image** | Paul Cunnius

Demonstrator | Misayo Nakamura **Location** | Sunshine Village, AB

All Terrain

Be ready for terrain and fallaways that suddenly drop, as gravity will quickly pull you down.

Keep the upper body stable and keep contact with the snow by extending the legs for stability and control.

Photos | Martin Olson **Image** | Martin Olson

Demonstrator | Paul Cunnius **Location** | Sunshine Village, AB

All Terrain

A slight retraction of the feet allows the rotational effort of the legs to begin for a smooth edge transition during the crossover phase.

Even with little or no contact with the snow, the COM and BOS crossover is uninterrupted.

Clear transition from the old to the new outside ski is key, as the outside leg lengthens to make snow contact for early edge and pressure.

Photos | Martin Olson **Image** | Martin Olson
Demonstrator | Paul Cunnius **Location** | Lake Louise, AB

All Terrain

In deeper and denser snow, the rotational turning effort of the legs needs to be especially strong.

Apply the turning effort and be patient. The turning effort will transfer to the skis and help create a turn, but the timing may vary depending on the thickness of the snow.

Photos | Martin Olson **Image** | Martin Olson
Demonstrator | Lisa Suutari **Location** | Fernie, BC

All Terrain

Short turn transitions require a strong stable upper body while the turning effort takes place.

The BOS is placed in front of the COM to stay in balance.

Symmetry can be seen in both the left and right turns, a mirror image of the body position (first and last frames).

Photos | Martin Olson **Image** | Paul Cunnius
Demonstrator | Misayo Nakamura **Location** | Sunshine Village, AB

All Terrain

All terrain skiing should be playful and fun!

Even in the air, keep proportional bends in the legs (ankle, knee and hip). This keeps the upper body centred and ready for touchdown.

Photo | John Schwirtlich **Demonstrator** | Paul Cunnius
Location | Mike Wiegele Helicopter Skiing, Blue River, BC

All Terrain

Let the COM rise between turns for good balance and easier turn initiation.

With good timing, there is minimal interruption to transition and flow in these changing conditions.

Photos | Martin Olson **Image** | Martin Olson
Demonstrator | Lisa Suutari **Location** | Fernie, BC

All Terrain

Skiing through tracked out snow without interruption in turn linking can be a challenge.

The skis will speed up in tracks and slow down in the untouched spots.

Move the BOS ahead when speeding up towards untouched snow. This will prepare you for the coming resistance that will push you forward if not prepared.

Photos | Martin Olson **Image** | Paul Cunnius
Demonstrator | Paul Cunnius **Location** | Lake Louise, AB

All Terrain

Turn sequences and linking in challenging snow require lower body strength both vertically and rotationally.

Early preparation of the pole plant stabilizes the upper body for strong lower body steering to take place.

Photos | Martin Olson **Image** | Martin Olson
Demonstrator | Norman Kreutz **Location** | Silver Star, BC

All Terrain

After the crossover phase place the feet (BOS) to the outside and slightly in front of the COM.

There is no interruption in the flow while the skis leave and regain contact with the snow.

Photos | Martin Olson **Image** | Martin Olson
Demonstrator | Norman Kreutz **Location** | Silver Star, BC

All Terrain

In thick snow, powering the skis through the transition phase may require more body compression and a greater range of leg mobility.

In the transition phase, the body looks low, but the direction change of the skis remains uninterrupted and strong.

Photos | Martin Olson **Image** | Paul Cunnius
Demonstrator | Misayo Nakamura **Location** | Sunshine Village, AB

All Terrain

All terrain often means navigating natural features.

Keep your eyes open and plan your turns to un-encounter any natural obstacles.

In slight wind crust, a little bit of air between turns helps initiate turning the legs to manage the top crusty layer without interrupting the next turn.

Photo | Martin Olson **Demonstrator** | Paul Cunnius **Location** | Lake Louise, AB

All Terrain

For control on steeper terrain, commit early to the new outside ski to maintain snow contact.

This allows for balance, early edging and early pressure necessary to maintain control in steep terrain.

Photos | Martin Olson **Image** | Paul Cunnius

Demonstrator | Misayo Nakamura **Location** | Sunshine Village, AB

All Terrain

The same technique basics apply to skiing both un-groomed and tracked powder. Because there is more snow pushing against the ski bases, you may feel more two footed.

Skiing un-groomed conditions will elevate and improve all of your skills and is an excellent place to practice.

Photos | Martin Olson **Image** | Paul Cunnius
Demonstrator | Paul Cunnius **Location** | Lake Louise, AB

All Terrain

Early separation and a strong turning effort help manage skiing deeper and thicker snow.

Thicker snow makes the upper body want to turn first, but maintain some resistance above the waist and turn with the legs for stable control.

Photos | Martin Olson Images **Image** | Martin Olson
Demonstrator | Martin Olson **Location** | Silver Star, BC

All Terrain

Moving the BOS from side to side and in front of the COM allows for stable linking in dense, thick snow. This placement of the feet in each turn fully supports the COM and the skier's body.

Photos | Martin Olson **Image** | Paul Cunnius
Demonstrator | Misayo Nakamura **Location** | Sunshine Village, AB

All Terrain

Patience is the key to a well-executed turn.

Developing the edge angle early allows the pressure to build up. The ski will bend and begin to arc.

Be patient and react to elements as they build.

Photos | Martin Olson **Image** | Martin Olson
Demonstrator | Paul Cunnius **Location** | Sunshine Village, AB

All Terrain

Look for terrain features to take some air!

Try to feel as comfortable in the air as on the snow. Maintain balance at takeoff, during air time and landing.

Use ankle mobility to keep the skis parallel to the snow.

Photos | Martin Olson **Image** | Paul Cunnius
Demonstrator | Norman Kreutz **Location** | Silver Star, BC

All Terrain

Angulation is especially important in All Terrain conditions.

Even though the snow is deeper and varied, the ski still bends. Angulating allows proper balance and stability against the ski it as it turns.

Photos | Martin Olson **Image** | Martin Olson
Demonstrator | Norman Kreutz **Location** | Silver Star, BC

All Terrain

Use playful terrain features like banks, berms and sidehills to turn a run into a playground.

The lead up requires bending the legs then lengthening them (Pressure Control) in the air to prepare for a smooth landing.

Photos | Martin Olson **Image** | Martin Olson
Demonstrator | Colleen Dunn **Location** | Fernie, BC

Bumps

Bumps, or moguls, are a measure of well-developed skilled skiing.

The bump landscape presents a constant challenge to the skier. Speed, bump size, snow and pitch all determine how great or moderate the challenge will be.

Expert and well managed bump skiing gives the impression of smoothness and control, yet is lively and exciting at the same time. Executing the skills needed to turn and manage the skis while the body constantly adjusts for balance is key to the overall effect.

Great bump skiing demonstrates a lot of snow contact through leg mobility (flexion and extension) and choosing tactical places to turn on and off each bump.

Bump skiing should be fun! Navigating the bump field also includes taking some air. A bump skier can do this without even thinking about it and without interrupting the turning arc they are on.

Bump skiers often get into the back seat as they move the BOS forward preparing to approach the bump. But they possess the skill of pulling the feet back under the body to re-balance and continue.

It is important to look a few bumps ahead to prepare for what is coming. By the time you consult your ski tips, it's too late to make decisions. That moment is already gone.

Great bump skiing means getting out of the zone of 'thinking' and into simply 'doing'. Technical and tactical points need practice, but this is where some of the most impressive and talented skiing takes place.

Photo | Martin Olson **Demonstrator** | Paul Cunnius
Location | Lake Louise, AB

Bumps

When the COM and BOS move together, the upper body looks quiet.

Leg mobility allows the feet to be well placed out in front to maintain stability and balance for the next bump.

Photos | Martin Olson **Image** | Paul Cunnius
Demonstrator | Misayo Nakamura **Location** | Sunshine Village, AB

Bumps

Turn the lower body and steer right from the start of each turn. This provides early grip, helps control speed and keeps the entire body moving while linking from turn to turn.

Steering the skis uphill increases separation in preparation for the next turn.

Photos | Martin Olson **Image** | Paul Cunnius
Demonstrator | Paul Cunnius **Location** | Lake Louise, AB

Bumps

Good bump skiing means going for it! Keep momentum moving forward and into the next turn.

Placing the BOS out in front of the COM prepares you to manage the next bump, even in the air.

Photos | Martin Olson **Image** | Martin Olson
Demonstrator | Matthew Barnes **Location** | Sun Peaks, BC

Bumps

In the spring, bumps can get big and soft.

An aggressive approach still involves patience and timing. Turning the legs through the first half of the turn puts the skier in an ideal position of balance and angulation for the next one.

The large size of the bump can be seen by how high and how low the COM gets in this sequence.

Photos | Martin Olson **Image** | Martin Olson
Demonstrator | Lisa Suutari **Location** | Fernie, BC

Bumps

Vertical Balance lets the entire body absorb the bump, but be ready to extend the legs to maintain snow contact (Pressure Control).

The distance between the COM and the BOS can change dramatically. On the approach, the COM/BOS distance can get quite close (vertically) then expand quickly.

Photos | Martin Olson **Image** | Paul Cunnius
Demonstrator | Paul Cunnius **Location** | Lake Louise, AB

Bumps

Proper balance is needed in both the first and second halves of the turn.

Use leg mobility (Pressure Control) to keep contact with the snow depending on which part of the bump you are skiing.

Photos | Martin Olson Images **Image** | Martin Olson
Demonstrator | Martin Olson **Location** | Silver Star, BC

Bumps

Good bump skiing demonstrates the ability to ski long sequences while maintaining good technique.

A low body (COM) position helps keep pressure on the skis, allowing transition and flow to remain uninterrupted. The legs are active, steering consistently from turn to turn.

Photos | Martin Olson **Image** | Martin Olson
Demonstrator | Norman Kreutz **Location** | Silver Star, BC

Bumps

Contact is the key to control in the bumps. The bump, and the skier, can generate some air time, but putting the tips down quickly re-establishes contact and control for the next set of turns.

As you pass over the bumps, push your toes down to make snow contact with the ski tips.

Photos | Martin Olson **Image** | Paul Cunnius
Demonstrator | Paul Cunnius **Location** | Silver Star, BC

Bumps

Maintain a forward shoulder position and relatively stable hands to help keep the upper body quiet. This helps the legs absorb and extend, maintaining snow contact for control.

Photos | Martin Olson **Image** | Martin Olson
Demonstrator | Joanne Younker **Location** | Sun Peaks, BC

Bumps

Angulate and separate to help prepare for the new bump and turn, even in the air while skiing across the hill.

Make these adjustments while traveling across the fall line, preparing to turn the legs to re-enter the downhill vertical line.

Photos | Martin Olson **Image** | Martin Olson
Demonstrator | Erin Keam **Location** | Sun Peaks, BC

Bumps

The crossover and transition from old edges, to flat skis, to new edges still needs to take place and, with practice, should look easy, even in the bumps.

Photos | Martin Olson **Image** | Paul Cunnius
Demonstrator | Misayo Nakamura **Location** | Silver Star, BC

Bumps

Re-directing the skis, whether in contact with the snow or not, is an active adjustment in bump skiing.

Even when taking some air, the feet turn, preparing for 'touchdown' putting the body into position to bend and angulate on entering the new turn.

Photos | Martin Olson Images **Image** | Martin Olson
Demonstrator | Martin Olson **Location** | Sunshine Village, AB

Bumps

When taking air in the bumps, keep the skis parallel to the snow while 'in flight'.

This requires straightening the ankle and pushing the toes down in preparation for 'touchdown' with the tips.

When done correctly, landing is much smoother, allowing the linking sequence to continue as though uninterrupted.

Photos | Martin Olson **Image** | Martin Olson
Demonstrator | Paul Cunnius **Location** | Lake Louise, AB

Bumps

Sometimes it is easier to simply take some air over a difficult bump section.

When 'airing it out' notice how technique is maintained 'in flight' in preparation for 'touchdown'.

Landing on a long leg allows the skier to absorb as needed when regaining contact with the snow.

Photos | Martin Olson **Image** | Martin Olson
Demonstrator | Norman Kreutz **Location** | Silver Star, BC

Bumps

Keep the hands and shoulders forward, even when only the tail of the ski is in contact with the snow.

Next, push the toes down to get the rest of the ski back onto the snow for contact and control moving to the new turn.

Photos | Martin Olson **Image** | Paul Cunnius
Demonstrator | Paul Cunnius **Location** | Silver Star, BC

Bumps

Approaching bumps often pushes the BOS back. Good skiers expect this and move the feet forward in anticipation. As they pass over the bump, they pull the feet back under the COM for proper alignment.

Photos | Martin Olson **Image** | Martin Olson
Demonstrator | Erin Keam **Location** | Sun Peaks, BC

Bumps

In bumps, the legs get longer and shorter as needed to maintain snow contact. Bending at the waist keeps the COM low and in line with the BOS regardless of the bump challenges that keep coming.

Absorption of the bump, coupled with keeping the COM moving forward, keeps the skier flowing well at impressive high speeds. Fast bump skiing is very athletic.

Photos | Martin Olson **Image** | Martin Olson
Demonstrator | Steve Smart **Location** | Silver Star, BC

Bumps

Use the legs to adjust to the bumps with pressure control and placement of the feet from side to side.

The overall impression is that the skier is in control, moving efficiently from turn to turn.

Notice how the pole plant is always out in front ready to initiate every turn.

Photos | Martin Olson **Image** | Paul Cunnius
Demonstrator | Misayo Nakamura **Location** | Sunshine Village, AB

Bumps

Body compression in the bumps requires bending the legs and waist. Be ready to reverse those movements as you move into the next turn.

The focus should stay on the outside ski through early extension of the outside leg for early balance.

Photos | Martin Olson **Image** | Paul Cunnius
Demonstrator | Paul Cunnius **Location** | Lake Louise, AB

Pole Plant

The primary role of the pole plant is to aid timing and rhythm, but its use goes far beyond that.

The pole plant triggers the start of every turn. The plant, or touch of the pole, begins the sequence of movements needed to make a turn.

The plant should be around 90% wrist action and 10% lowering of the forearm. This ratio avoids gross movements of the arms, hands and upper body.

When the pole is planted, the hand should already be out in front. Keep the wrist supple enough to simply ski past the planted pole, leaving the hand out front.

Cock the outside wrist at the same rate as the turn. At the end of the arc, the pole basket will be in place ready to plant. This subtle skill defines well timed and well executed skiing.

The pole plant also consolidates all of the other movements. When the pole plant stops, or is interrupted, so does the angulation, steering, bending etc.

Every pole plant is typically followed by a turn. So if you want more turns, add more pole plants.

Photo | Martin Olson **Demonstrator** | Norman Kreutz
Location | Silver Star, BC

Pole Plant

Anticipate the pole plant with the 'planting' hand ready out in front. As the turn is made, ski right by the planting hand and the pole basket. This is done by keeping the hand out in front and not letting it fall back or drop down.

Photos | Martin Olson **Image** | Martin Olson

Demonstrator | Roch Newberry **Location** | Silver Star, BC

Pole Plant

The pole plant stabilizes the upper body, allowing lower body turning effort and steering to take place with more power and strength.

The inside shoulder and upper inside arm should feel some tension indicating stability.

Photos | Martin Olson **Image** | Martin Olson
Demonstrator | Lisa Suutari **Location** | Fernie, BC

Pole Plant

Properly timed pole plants are well-prepared in advance.

This keeps the skier balanced and moving into the next turn with minimal interruption.

Photos | Martin Olson **Image** | Martin Olson
Demonstrator | Drew Bragg **Location** | Panorama, BC

Pole Plant

Time the pole plant for the end of the angulating phase, when body position allows maximum grip.

Photos | Martin Olson **Image** | Martin Olson
Demonstrator | Drew Bragg **Location** | Panorama, BC

Pole Plant

With hands apart, gradually bring the outside thumbnail back towards the outside shoulder. You will feel the outside elbow and shoulder lower.

As the outside basket travels and prepares for the next turn, the upper body should remain stable with relatively level shoulders.

Photos | Giulia Zhu **Image** | Paul Cunnius
Demonstrator | Paul Cunnius **Location** | Sunac Snow Park, Guangzhou, China

Pole Plant

In this instance, notice the high degree of flexion (pressure control) and extension (unweighting) in the body from turn to turn, but the right arm position remains virtually unchanged and relaxed from the right shoulder down to the right hand.

What has changed is the position of the planting pole shaft and basket from preparation to completion of the plant. This is due to the quiet supple action in the wrist allowing the pole plant to take place without interrupting the planting arm, the rest of the body and the turn.

Photos | Martin Olson **Image** | Paul Cunnius
Demonstrator | Norman Kreutz **Location** | Silver Star, BC

Pole Plant

Strong pole plants help the body with balance and angulation.
They are key to solid, strong skiing.

Photo | Martin Olson **Demonstrator** | Norman Kreutz **Location** | Silver Star, BC

Pole Plant

If the COM is behind the BOS when linking from turn to turn, push the hands forward to recentre.

Know that the pole plant is coming and use that to time pulling the feet back in the effort to recentre.

Photos | Martin Olson **Image** | Paul Cunnius
Demonstrator | Paul Cunnius **Location** | Silver Star, BC

Powder

Powder, the ultimate skier's prize.

Skiing powder is not something the average skier gets to do every day.

It is a skill unto itself and, like any skill, it takes practice to perfect. However, you don't need to be an Expert to enjoy it.

Deeper snow provides resistance to the sides of the ski (as the ski sinks), requiring a stronger rotational turning and steering effort with the legs.

This resistance varies depending on snow depth, density, conditions (both on and below the surface) and steepness of terrain.

Due to snow resistance, it is tempting to want to twist or turn the upper body first. Resist that so the lower body turning effort can take place.

The pole plant should always be at the ready. All skilled Powder skiers do this, as it is needed for timing and balance.

Often it looks like the outside planting hand is in front of the face. It is in fact on the outside of the turn for balance.

Not every powder day is perfect, but there are rarely complaints when we get the chance to ski the fresh, deep stuff.

Photo | John Schwirtlich **Demonstrator** | Paul Cunnius
Location | Mike Wiegele Helicopter Skiing, Blue River, BC

Powder

Bend and turn the legs lowering the COM in preparation for the next turn.

Strong core body strength helps determine how much we can 'dig in' and enjoy.

Photos | Martin Olson **Image** | Martin Olson

Demonstrator | Norman Kreutz **Location** | Silver Star, BC

Powder

Deep snow can get in your face. Remember to keep looking ahead when this happens!

While navigating trees, terrain and the unknown, stay focused.

In these scenarios, your eyes are your best tools. But if you can't see for a brief moment, your technique will kick in and support you until vision quickly returns.

Photo | Pajaro-Hirosima **Demonstrator** | Paul Cunnius
Location | Hanazono, Hokkaido, Japan

Powder

Technique aside, route planning is essential in powder skiing, especially in the trees.

Look ahead and plan your route without getting too close to the trees. Look for the big untouched 'stash' and hit it!

Photo | Paul Cunnius **Demonstrator** | Misayo Nakamura
Location | Whitewater, BC

Powder

The hands and arms play a key role in keeping the upper body rotationally stable.

Wider skis require more patience and time to turn, so reaction times are different from those of narrower skis on groomed snow.

Hand adjustment is not always perfect, but necessary to counter denser snow applying a twisting force on the upper body and wider skis.

Photos | Pajaro-Hirosima **Image** | Paul Cunnius

Demonstrator | Paul Cunnius **Location** | Hanazono, Hokkaido, Japan

Powder

If you're looking for the freshest snow, the sides of the trails are often your best bet. The majority of skiers ski in the middle of the trails.

Keep the legs mobile to stretch out and regain contact with the snow when needed.

Photos | Martin Olson **Image** | Martin Olson
Demonstrator | Norman Kreutz **Location** | Silver Star, BC

Powder

As deeper snow builds up, speed helps you move through it with more stability.

Use the inside hand as a gauge checking your lateral balance and rotational upper body position.

Photo | Pajaro-Hirosima **Demonstrator** | Paul Cunnius
Location | Hanazono, Hokkaido, Japan

Powder

Preparation of the new pole plant is key for linking turns in deep snow.

Always have it ready to trigger the next turn.

Photos | Misayo Nakamura **Image** | Paul Cunnius

Demonstrator | Paul Cunnius **Location** | Hanazono, Hokkaido, Japan

Powder

Use rebound from the skis and retraction of the feet at the end of the turn to help enter the linking phase.

The skis will come up to the surface where the legs can extend and begin turning.

Photos | Martin Olson **Image** | Martin Olson
Demonstrator | Norman Kreutz **Location** | Silver Star, BC

Powder

At times, comments on technique need to take a back seat so we can simply admire great skiing in spectacular settings …

Photo | Paul Cunnius **Demonstrator** | Misayo Nakamura
Location | Kiroro, Hokkaido, Japan

Powder

'Settling in' is a large part of deep powder skiing.

- Know where you are headed
- Turn the skis without too much initial force
- Be patient
- Take a deep breath
- Enjoy 'settling in'
- Trust yourself, the next turn is coming

Photos | Pajaro-Hirosima **Image** | Paul Cunnius
Demonstrator | Paul Cunnius **Location** | Hanazono, Hokkaido, Japan

Powder

On steeper terrain, be ready to recentre, getting the COM back over the BOS at the start of the turn.

Then place the BOS slightly ahead for the COM to balance against.

Photos | Martin Olson **Image** | Martin Olson
Demonstrator | Norman Kreutz **Location** | Silver Star, BC

Powder

When the skier balances in the middle of the outside ski … it bends, even in deep snow.

This helps the turning effort below the surface as this skier 'Charges' making strong, solid and powerful turns look easy.

Photo | John Schwirtlich **Demonstrator** | Misayo Nakamura
Location | Mike Wiegele Helicopter Skiing, Blue River, BC

Powder

Navigating natural elements can challenge your technique.

Focus on your route and don't be too demanding of your performance.

In deep snow, there may be times when you cannot briefly see. Relax, be patient and keep making your moves.

Gravity will keep you in the fall line.

Photos | Pajaro-Hirosima **Image** | Paul Cunnius

Demonstrator | Paul Cunnius **Location** | Hanazono, Hokkaido, Japan

Powder

Veteran powder skiers know how to keep their focus, regardless of the deep snow. They're thinking about the next turn coming up, not the one that just went by.

Powder skiing also requires rhythm and timing; that's why you see this expert with the new pole anticipating the next turn which shows experience.

Photo | John Schwirtlich **Demonstrator** | Neil MacGillivray
Location | Mike Wiegele Helicopter Skiing, Blue River, BC

Powder

Untouched snow and wide open spaces are very special places to ski.

Enjoy the fresh snow pushing up against your body as you move from turn to turn.

Photo | Misayo Nakamura **Demonstrator** | Paul Cunnius
Location | Kiroro, Hokkaido, Japan

Powder

Using a shallower turn shape in really deep snow helps keep the speed up to overcome snow density and resistance.

When speed and technique match up, it feels like you can 'Power' through anything.

Photo | Pajaro-Hirosima **Demonstrator** | Paul Cunnius
Location | Hanazono, Hokkaido, Japan

Powder

Powder skiing will bring you to some of the most beautiful places in the world.

Seek it ... find it ... and take in every moment.

Photo | John Schwirtlich **Demonstrator** | Paul Cunnius
Location | Mike Wiegele Helicopter Skiing, Blue River, BC

Powder

Powder skiing is better with good friends.

Photo | Martin Olson **Demonstrators** | Dave Hay and Mike DesBrisay

Location | Lake Louise, AB

Powder

Be ready for anything that comes your way. Surprises can lurk beneath the snow.

If you are centred, the 'surprises' are much easier to handle, making them memorable 'powder' moments.

Photo | Misayo Nakamura **Demonstrator** | Paul Cunnius

Location | Kiroro, Hokkaido, Japan

Powder

Always be ready for the 'hot pick up'.

Photo | John Schwirtlich **Senior/Lead Heli Guide** | Crosby Johnston
Location | Mike Wiegele Helicopter Skiing, Blue River, BC

Expert Habits

While equipment changes over time and technique is always scrutinized, the habits of Expert skiers remain embedded. They may be practiced to greater or lesser degree, but they are there and, if developed properly, will help any skier improve.

These habits include exercises, drills, moves made out of necessity and technical targets in any turn shape. It's sort of a skiers' system of 'Checks and Balances'.

The impressive part is how these skiers can move within their movement. Being able to ski on one ski, timing flat skis between changing edges, exaggerating an outside hand position and many more.

Drills take and develop skill and ability. A system of making sure the appropriate skills move at the right time results in a 'good skiing picture'.

Experts keep their skills sharp and improve them by warming up with drills and practicing basic skills regularly.

The Expert picture and overall impression is a result of these habits. It is not an image the skier tries to 'manufacture' and hold, but the consequence of excellent technique, application and, most of all, practice.

Photo | Martin Olson **Demonstrator** | Norman Kreutz
Location | Silver Star, BC

Expert Habits

Uphill turns are excellent practice for steering and keeping the outside foot (BOS) under the body (COM).

Photos | Martin Olson **Image** | Paul Cunnius
Demonstrator | Paul Cunnius **Location** | Silver Star, BC

Expert Habits

Exaggerate an early setup with a high outside hand and early separation for the new turn. With early balance on the outside edge, the entire body can move down and inside for strong angulation and grip.

Photos | Martin Olson **Image** | Martin Olson
Demonstrator | Rodger Poole **Location** | Sun Peaks, BC

Expert Habits

Keep the hands properly positioned in front and apart while moving the feet ahead and under the body from one turn to the next.

Photos | Martin Olson **Image** | Martin Olson
Demonstrator | Paul Cunnius **Location** | Silver Star, BC

Expert Habits

Keep the upper body steady and low when skiing over rollers.

Push the hands further ahead and let the legs really bend to absorb the rising terrain.

Make sure the skis keep contact with the snow before, during and after.

Photos | Martin Olson **Image** | Martin Olson
Demonstrator | Misayo Nakamura **Location** | Silver Star, BC

Expert Habits

Lift the inside ski, then gently put the inside tip down promoting forward anticipation and early steering.

Photos | Martin Olson **Image** | Martin Olson
Demonstrator | Paul Cunnius **Location** | Silver Star, BC

Expert Habits

Lift the inside ski for centred balance on the outside ski.

This is a 'check' of where the skier is standing on the outside ski: forward, centred or back.

Photo | Martin Olson **Demonstrator** | Rodger Poole **Location** | Sun Peaks, BC

Expert Habits

Lifting the inside ski also adjusts the upper/lower body separation and rotational position.

Photo | Martin Olson **Demonstrator** | Paul Cunnius
Location | Sun Peaks, BC

Expert Habits

Lifting the outside ski lets the body adjust laterally and increases awareness of the line of inclination.

As the outside ski is placed back onto the snow, the body is set up and aligned properly.

Photo | Martin Olson **Demonstrator** | Paul Cunnius
Location | Sun Peaks, BC

Expert Habits

Maintain contact with the snow while carrying pressure from one turn to the next.
Feel smooth transitions from the old outside ski to the new outside ski.

Photos | Martin Olson **Image** | Martin Olson
Demonstrator | Misayo Nakamura **Location** | Silver Star, BC

Expert Habits

Pull the feet back at the start to keep the BOS and COM in balance and centred. The feet can then move forward along the arc in tandem with the COM.

Photos | Martin Olson **Image** | Martin Olson
Demonstrator | Paul Cunnius **Location** | Silver Star, BC

Expert Habits

Keep an equal distance between the feet in all parts of the turn.

Practice maintaining an equal width through the completion, crossover and initiation phases.

Photos | Martin Olson **Image** | Martin Olson
Demonstrator | Misayo Nakamura **Location** | Silver Star, BC

Expert Habits

Time the crossover as the BOS steers under the COM and they change sides with each other.

The old edges release at the same rate, leading to both skis being perfectly flat at the same time. Continue to grow onto the new edges smoothly.

Photos | Judy Wang / 熊吉吉 **Image** | Paul Cunnius
Demonstrator | Paul Cunnius **Location** | Wanlong Resort, Chongli, China

Expert Habits

Let the skis come out of the snow and take some air in between turns. Use pressure control and pull the feet up.

Photos | Martin Olson **Image** | Martin Olson

Demonstrator | Norman Kreutz **Location** | Silver Star, BC

Expert Habits

In short turns, even though there is upper and lower body separation, the upper body should appear to be facing down the hill most of the time.

Photos | Martin Olson **Image** | Martin Olson
Demonstrator | Paul Cunnius **Location** | Silver Star, BC

Expert Habits

Increase your speed to the point where the outside ski is bending with edge performance. Maintain the edge angle and body position for symmetry on both sides.

Photos | Martin Olson **Image** | Martin Olson
Demonstrator | Rodger Poole **Location** | Sun Peaks, BC

Expert Habits

With the hands in front, plant the pole then ski right by the hand without letting it fall back.

Take the hand with you in that forward position to stay centred.

Photos | Martin Olson **Image** | Martin Olson
Demonstrator | Paul Cunnius **Location** | Silver Star, BC

Technical Terms Simplified

Advanced	The stage between Intermediate Parallel and Expert Parallel
Angulation	Bending the legs and moving the joints (ankle, knee and hip) inside the turn for balance and edge grip; Angulated, Angulating
Arc	A turn with a round shape
Balance	Comfortable centred stance; BOS and COM aligned
Bevel	The tuning angle on either the side or base edge
BOS	Base of Support; the feet
Camber	The shape of the ski from tip to tail when placed on a flat surface as seen from the side view
Centred	A stance allowing the skier to balance in the middle of the ski while static or turning
COM	Centre of Mass; an area a bit in front of the stomach: in an extreme angulated position the COM could be outside the body
Compression	Bending of the body or specific body parts
Crossover	When the BOS is steered underneath the COM causing them to move laterally in opposite directions resulting in a change of edges and direction
Edge Angle	The degree to which the skis are tipped over; the amount of angle between the ski bases and the snow
Edging	When the skis are tipped up on edge, they grip and change direction
Extension	Lengthening the legs; also referred to as Straightening or Unbending
Flat Ski	When the bases of both skis are flat and/or parallel to the slope surface beneath them
Flexion	Bending the legs; also referred to as Flexing or Bending
Flow	Smooth and well timed movement from one position, or turn, to the next
Grip	How much or how little the ski holds on the snow
Inclination	The amount that the body leans inside the turn; measured by the straight line that goes from the BOS through the COM and continues through the body
Inside	The hand, shoulder, hip, foot, boot, edge or ski that is closest to the centre of the arc of a turn
Linking Phase	The point where one turn is ending and the new turn is starting; crossover or transition
Lower Body	All body parts from the waist area down (legs, knees and ankles)
Lower/Leg Joints	Ankles, Knees and Hips

Technical Terms Simplified

Mobility	Movement of any body part or parts; primarily, movement in the legs
Novice	The stage between Beginner and Intermediate Parallel
Outside	The hand, shoulder, hip, foot, boot, edge or ski that is furthest from the centre of the turn
Parallel Turn	A ski turn performed with skis parallel; Parallel=two lines equidistant from each other
Pressure	The force that builds up as the skis turn across the fall line while gravity pulls the body down the fall line
Pressure Control	Managing the build up and release of pressure through bending and extending leg movements
Range	The distance, limit or scope of a movement
Rate	The period of time it takes performing a body movement, or combined movements
Resistance	Outside factors, like snow, ice, powder or slope angle that challenge a rotational or edging move
Retraction	Pulling the feet up towards the stomach or COM
Separation	The division between upper and lower body; they can move independently of each other
Sidecut / Shape	The difference in width between the tip, waist and tail of a ski
Slip	A ski with less edge angle and less grip slides to the outside of the turn or down the fall line
Stance	How we stand on the skis; where the COM is in relation to the BOS
Steering	A combination of edging and Turning Effort (turning the legs)
Timing	Making specific movements at a specific point in the turn, often in relation to a combination or series of movements made at the same time
Transition	The action of change resulting in a new feeling, position or direction; often relates to crossover and linking turns
Turn Shape	The track left on the snow from the start to finish of each turn
Turning Effort	A muscular effort of turning both legs from the start of the turn to the finish
Unweighting	Reducing the amount of pressure on the skis; can be done through bending or unbending the legs
Upper Body	All body parts from the waist area up (trunk, shoulders, head and arms)

Technical Terms Simplified

Vertical Separation	The inside foot is higher (closer to the hip) than the outside foot; though the legs remain the same width apart, this difference in height makes the stance look wider than it is
Waist	The middle of the ski; its narrowest point of contact
Weight Transfer	Moving the balance from one outside ski to the new outside ski

Bios

Paul Cunnius

Paul has spent his whole life on skis. He put on his first pair at age 2 and has been on the slopes ever since. A Level 4 ski instructor and Senior Course Conductor with the Canadian Ski Instructor's Alliance (CSIA), he has trained and certified instructors at home in Western Canada and around the world in New Zealand, China and Japan. His trainees include candidates, trainers and CSIA staff at all levels.

For 10 years Paul Directed Club Ski, the joint ski school of the world renowned resorts of Banff and Lake Louise, Alberta. He's been a member of Canada's National Demonstration Team, served on the CSIA Western Technical Committee and, for over two decades, tested skis for Canada's longest running ski test. He also held the positions of Technical Editor (Ski Test) and Instructional Editor at Ski Canada Magazine.

Paul holds a BA from Bishop's University in Political Science and Economics and is a member of Mike Wiegele's Silver Buckle Million Foot Club, having heli skied in excess of 1,000,000 vertical feet at Mike Wiegele Helicopter Skiing.

Currently Paul is the Training Director at Mt. Norquay in Banff, Alberta and actively conducts CSIA courses and exams throughout Western Canada and overseas in Asia.

Martin Olson

Martin Olson's career in skiing has spanned a lifetime. Seven years of training and experience in the Mike Wiegele ski school at Lake Louise was followed by twenty-three years working for the Canadian Ski Instructor's Alliance (CSIA), the national body for training and certifying ski instructors in Canada.

For three decades he was fully certified to train and examine all levels of instruction. His roles included 10 years as Western Course Director and more than a decade developing educational material, technical skiing standards and staff training. Martin also attended five Interskis as a demonstrator, delegate or head coach.

Most recently he completed six years as Technical Editor for Ski Canada Magazine and was inducted into the CSIA Hall of Fame. Although officially retired, Martin now spends every winter at a ski resort and is still involved in the ski teaching industry as a consultant. His goal is to ski a hundred days each winter.

Demonstrators

Paul Cunnius
Misayo Nakamura
Norman Kreutz
Martin Olson
Rodger Poole
Lisa Suutari
Erin Keam
Steve Smart
Drew Bragg
Mike DesBrisay
Dave Hay
Matthew Barnes
Casey Bouius
Colleen Dunn
Don Kjorven
Jeff Larouche
Neil MacGillivray
Roch Newberry
Russ Wood
Joanne Younker

Thank You

A very special thank you to Martin Olson for his outstanding contributions to this book.

The photo montages would not have been possible without Martin's talent and endless generosity.

Martin has also provided a great deal of technical guidance for which he needs to be duly acknowledged.

His willingness to share is what makes him a CSIA Hall of Fame Member and a legend within the global ski industry.

A special thank you as well to all the demonstrators. These are talented committed ski professionals and should be recognized as such.

"Good Skiing Feels Good"

Martin Olson

Edited By: Anne Metikosh

Front Cover Photo | John Schwirtlich **Demonstrator** | Misayo Nakamura
Location | Mike Wiegele Helicopter Skiing, Blue River, BC

Aperture increments

Most cameras allow you to change the apertures in 1/2-stop increments. Check the custom function menu in your camera – many models also allow you to set it to 1/3-stop increments if you so wish

MARK BAUER

Shot at f/22

Aperture-priority mode allows photographers to control how much of the scene is sharply in focus.

Shutter speeds & landscapes

Learn how slow shutters speed can add energy and movement to a landscape image

LANDSCAPE PHOTOGRAPHERS understandably give priority to apertures, but in some situations, the shutter speed is just as important to capture the effect of movement within a scene. Due to the relationship between apertures and shutter speeds, you can prioritise a slow shutter speed and still maintain sharpness by maximising depth-of-field with a smaller aperture. Typically the narrower the aperture the longer the shutter speed. By setting your camera to shutter-priority (Tv or S) mode, you can select your desired length of time, while your camera adjusts the aperture accordingly for a correct exposure. So why choose the shutter speed rather than the aperture? Well, setting the slower speed means anything moving when you fire the shutter, such as flowing water or foliage blowing in the wind, is captured as a soft blur, while anything static, like a fence or rock, remains in focus. The effect of setting a long exposure is to give images extra depth and dimension while illustrating a sense of movement. The result is usually closer to how you remember the scene, rather than a lifeless image of grass with every blade in focus.

But remember: even digital cameras can be fooled. Be careful not to overexpose an image when shooting, for example, a field of golden sweeping grass in the evening sun. As you lower the shutter speed, the camera's chosen aperture will eventually flash, indicating that the image will be overexposed. You can, of course, check the image and the histogram on the LCD monitor for blown-out highlights.

For even slower shutter speeds and to elevate your photography to another level, use filters. A polariser cuts out reflections and darkens blue skies to give clouds that 'wow' factor, as well as reduces the amount of light reaching your sensor by two stops. You can enhance movement and blur by using a Neutral Density filter: a neutral grey filter that doesn't affect colour balance but has the effect of reducing the amount of light passing through it, allowing you to select slower shutter speeds.

For optimum results, shoot at dawn and dusk and use a tripod. Shoot on darker, cloudy days, and let nature work for you – less light means slower shutter speeds. On windy days, hang your camera bag from the tripod to keep your outfit stable, and use a remote release/self-timer and mirror lock-up to avoid contact with the camera during the exposure. Wait for the wind, open the shutter and watch you don't get blown away!

Above, polariser and ND grad: Here a polariser and an ND grad filter has been used to hold back the bright sky and ensure a well-balanced, long exposure. The self-timer was used to reduce the risk of camera shake.

Shutter speed comparison: The lens (10-22mm set to 13mm) was focused on the grass in the foreground, then the shutter speed was changed in a sequence from 1/50sec to 1.6 seconds. Note how the grass gets more blurry as the shutter speed becomes slower. Our favourite image from the sequence is the longest exposure, 1.6 seconds, as it captures the most realistic sense of movement.

Final image

Dunstanburgh Castle, Northumberland. The movement in the foreground adds to the impact of the image. Use the histogram and the image on the LCD preview screen to check the exposure and for any clipped highlights.

Exposure: 1.3 seconds at f/29 (ISO 100)

The basic skills for shooting water in landscapes

It's all about technique and the right gear when shooting stunning water scenics: be prepared before you head into the great outdoors

WE'RE NOT SURE if you've ever noticed, but the majority of stunning landscape images usually have some form of water in the scene. Whether it's as subtle as a small river trickling through, or as obvious as a dominating sea in a coastal seascape, water represents a key element in many landscape images.

One of the main reasons for this is because water is such a photographically pliable element. By using filters and/or manipulating the shutter speed, it's possible to record water in all manner of ways, from freezing its movement so droplets are suspended in midair, to using a long exposure to transform it into an ethereal mist. While potentially causing problems with our exposure, the reflective nature of water also plays its part in improving images, too. On days where there is little or no wind, by heading to a lake, reservoir or any other large body of water, it's possible to produce a striking result by capturing a clean reflection of the scene on its surface. The possibilities don't stop there – rivers can be used as strong lead-in lines through the scene or, along with the likes of secluded rockpools and meandering streams littered with rocks, can form highly effective foreground interest.

The list is endless, but here we cover the basics of shutter speeds when shooting water, as well as the gear that should make it easy to take on our water landscape projects on pages 92 - 119. What are you waiting for? Get exploring!

Choosing shutter speeds

The shutter speed you use to capture water will depend on a number of factors: if it's moving; how quickly it's moving; how much of it there is; and whether you want to stop it dead to freeze its movement or let it blur.

For big waterfalls and breaking waves, a shutter speed of 1/1000-1/200sec will guarantee you freeze every droplet. For fast-flowing rivers and smaller waterfalls like this one pictured here, try 1/200–1/500sec, while for slower rivers and streams, 1/125–1/250sec should do the trick.

When it comes to blurring, one second will have a good effect on big waterfalls or try two seconds for smaller waterfalls. Rivers and streams need a slower speed of two to four seconds, though you can go much slower – ten - 20 seconds – if you like.

Overexposure can be a problem when large volumes of water are concentrated in certain areas, so keep an eye on the histogram and use a slower speed if you start to clip the highlights. For coastal scenes, one to two seconds will blur waves, while 20-30 seconds will produce a milky effect.

Essential gear

Wide-angle zoom: An ultra-wide zoom like a 12-24mm or similar is ideal as it allows you to fill the foreground with water and deliver plenty of depth-of-field for scenes that are sharp throughout. The Sigma 10-20mm lens, costing around £300, is hugely popular due to its excellent performance and value-for-money price tag.

Spirit level: If your tripod kit has a spirit level, use it to ensure horizons are even – you don't want to spend ages in Photoshop levelling them if you can avoid it at the picture-taking stage. Otherwise, buy a basic £10 spirit level to slip into a hotshoe or treat yourself to a funky £30 Seculine Action Level (www.intro2020.co.uk).

Filters: If you're serious about landscape photography, it'll pay to invest in a slot-in filter system. Cokin's P-system (www.intro2020.co.uk) represents great value for money, while if quality is paramount, look to Lee Filters' superb 100mm system – the choice of the professionals (www.leefilters.com). A polariser helps boost blue skies and deliver clear reflections off the water's surface. A 0.6 or 0.9ND filter (not ND grad!) is also worth considering, as it will allow you to use long shutter speeds in daylight to blur moving water.

Tripod: When shooting water, you'll be looking to use small apertures to maximise depth-of-field and the slow shutter speeds require you to keep the camera stable to avoid shake. Check out the essential kit section later in this guide for advice on the best tripods to buy for outdoor photography, whatever your budget.

Photo backpack: When you're walking for miles on end, a photo backpack is a far better option for protecting your kit than a gadget bag. Those with an all-weather cover will offer better protection from water and the elements. Take a look at our website for reviews of some of the best: www.digitalslrphoto.com.

Clothing: There's nothing worse than slipping into a river and having to spend the day in wet clothes. Wear decent footwear from reputable brands such as Berghaus and consider waterproof trousers or gaiters from brands such as Paramo, as they allow you to step into rivers and stay dry.

Shoot water like a pro

Dramatic coastlines are the perfect place to put theory into practice when it comes to photographing scenes with water. Follow our advice on the gear to use, the techniques to try and the settings to make and you'll soon be taking landscape images like a pro.

SIGMA 10-20mm F3.5 EX DC HSM

For Sigma. Canon, Nikon, Sony and Pentax
Supplied with fitted padded case and petal type lens hood.
Compatible with APS-C SLRs only.

This super-wide angle zoom lens for digital SLR cameras has a maximum aperture of F3.5 throughout the entire zoom range and its super-wide angle enables breathtaking perspective and one-of-a-kind shots.

ELD (Extraordinary Low Dispersion) glass, SLD (Special Low Dispersion) glass and aspherical lenses provide excellent correction of all types of aberrations. The Super Multi-Layer Coating reduces flare and ghosting and the incorporation of HSM (Hyper-Sonic Motor) ensures a quiet and high-speed auto focus.

Sigma Imaging (UK) Ltd, 13 Little Mundells, Welwyn Garden City, Hertfordshire, AL7 1EW | Telephone: 01707 329 999 | Email: sales@sigma-imaging-uk.com | Website: www.sigma-imaging-uk.com

Learn how to capture sharp images like a pro

Master the fundamentals of focusing, depth-of-field and camera shake to vastly improve your photography

IMAGINE YOU'VE FOCUSED on an object that is five metres away. How sharp will something be at six metres? Or even five-and-a-half metres? The answer is governed by the depth-of-field: the distance either side of the point of focus that is deemed to be acceptably in focus. As long as you control the aperture you are shooting at, you're in control of depth-of-field, and you can use it creatively. There will be occasions when you don't want much of it at all, and you'll get that effect by shooting with a large aperture like f/4. However, for most of the time that you're shooting landscapes you'll want to maximise depth-of-field to get as much of a scene in focus as you possibly can.

Foreground detail is important and has to be in focus, but so does the rest of the scene. This means using small apertures to get good sharpness either side of the focus point. But just consider this last phrase for a moment, and then think about where you might focus when shooting a landscape. Many novice landscape photographers are happy focusing at infinity when shooting a landscape, but don't forget that depth-of-field extends either side of the point of focus. In fact, the area of depth-of-field extends one-third in front of the focused point and two-thirds behind: in other words, you get more depth-of-field behind the subject than in front of it. Obviously there is no benefit to having acceptable sharpness extending beyond infinity, but you can pull the point of focus back towards you, so it's the end of the depth-of-field zone that is at infinity instead. This way you'll get more of the scene sharp. This is called hyperfocal focusing and has been used by pro landscape photographers for decades. The optimum point of focus for any scene relies on the choice of aperture setting and the focal length of the lens you use – and changes for full-frame and crop-sensor DSLRs! There are calculators and pocket reference tables you can stash in your camera bag, or you can use a dependable rule of thumb that suggests you aim a third of the way into the picture with your lens set to a small aperture. We'll be covering both focusing techniques, as well as providing you with advice to ensure you maximise image sharpness. This includes revealing why using the smallest aperture won't necessarily produce the sharpest results, even though it gives the most depth-of-field!

How to maximise your depth-of-field

Including foreground interest can make it difficult to achieve front-to-back sharpness, but Ross Hoddinott shows you how…

Ross Hoddinott: Flick through the pages of any photo or country magazine, and you will quickly notice that foreground interest is an important component in the majority of great landscape images. It provides an entry point into the composition and helps add context, depth and interest to views. As long as it complements the overall scene, practically anything can work as foreground interest – rocks, a stone wall, winding footpath, colourful reflections or reeds. Flowers are another good subject to include in the foreground of your shots. Not only do they help to add scale to wider views, but they also add a welcome splash of colour. There is no better time of year than spring to look for flowers to include in your shots, particularly along the coast where pink thrift grows. Thrift can carpet clifftops, providing colour and interest to views of sandy bays and rugged coastline.

Including foreground interest typically requires a large depth-of-field to render everything from front to back acceptably sharp. Opt for a small f/stop in the region of f/16, but avoid stopping down even further as the effects of diffraction (softening of the image) will grow more apparent. You also need to select your point of focus carefully. Depth-of-field falls roughly two-thirds beyond the point of focus and one-third in front of it. Therefore, if you focus too far into the frame, you waste the depth-of-field available to you. A rough-and-ready method to maximise front-to-back sharpness is to simply focus a third of the way into the frame (see p34 for details). However, a more precise method is to focus on the hyperfocal distance (see panel). It seems like a complicated calculation, but it's much easier than you may think.

To help give your images a three-dimensional appearance, opt for an ultra wide-angle lens – in the region of 17-24mm – and get near to your foreground. This exaggerates the size of foreground subjects and stretches perspective, resulting in eye-catching shots.

Hyperfocal point

The hyperfocal distance is the point where you can maximise depth-of-field for any given aperture – everything from half this distance to infinity will be recorded acceptably sharp. Calculating and focusing on this point is important if you require extensive depth-of-field. Although the hyperfocal distance can seem daunting, it is not actually as complex as it first seems. If you use a prime lens with good distance and depth-of-field scales, simply align the infinity mark against the selected aperture. However, few modern lenses – particularly zooms – are designed with adequate scales, meaning photographers have to calculate it themselves. Thankfully, there are depth-of-field calculators and hyperfocal charts available to download online. Visit www.dofmaster.com – it also offers an app for your smartphone.

Below are two hyperfocal distance charts covering the most popular focal lengths and various apertures for full-frame and APS-C sensors. Photocopy or cut out the chart relevant to your camera type and keep it handy for when you come to compose and focus your shots.

APS-C size sensors

Aperture	12mm	15mm	17mm	20mm	24mm	28mm	35mm	50mm
f/8	3.2ft	5ft	6.4ft	8.9ft	12.6ft	17ft	27ft	55ft
f/11	**2.3ft**	**3.5ft**	**4.5ft**	**6.2ft**	**9ft**	**12ft**	**19ft**	**39ft**
f/16	1.7ft	2.5ft	3.3ft	4.4ft	6.4ft	8.6ft	14.5ft	27ft
f/22	**1.2ft**	**0.9ft**	**2.3ft**	**3.2ft**	**4.5ft**	**6ft**	**9.5ft**	**19.2ft**

Full-frame sensors

Aperture	16mm	20mm	24mm	28mm	35mm	50mm
f/8	3.8ft	5.6ft	8ft	11ft	17ft	35ft
f/11	**2.6ft**	**3.9ft**	**5.8ft**	**7.8ft**	**12ft**	**25ft**
f/16	1.9ft	2.9ft	4ft	5.5ft	8.5ft	17.5ft
f/22	**1.4ft**	**2ft**	**2.9ft**	**3.9ft**	**6ft**	**12.5ft**

1 Find your view Images lacking foreground interest can look flat and boring. Despite finding this impressive vista, by not including anything of aesthetic value in the foreground to complement the view and direct the eye into the photo, this shot is nothing more than a snap.

2 Alter your viewpoint By simply moving a few metres, my next image is much better. By including some flowering thrift in the foreground, the image immediately has more depth and interest. However, the sky is overexposed, so filtration or exposure blending is needed.

3 Set your exposure I take a meter reading from the sky and another from the foreground thrift. The difference in light is around four stops. I don't want to even out the light completely as our eyes naturally perceive the sky to be brighter than the land. Therefore, I attach a two-stop (0.6) graduated Neutral Density filter to help me record detail throughout the scene.

4 Perfect your composition With the correct exposure achieved, it is time to focus on composition. To place more emphasis on foreground, and to create depth, a low, close viewpoint is often best, together with a short focal length. I do this, opting for the wide end of my 17-35mm zoom. The nearest flowers aren't in sharp focus, though, due to inaccurate focusing.

5 Calculate the hyperfocal distance To ensure everything from nearby foreground to the distant view is acceptably sharp, focus on the hyperfocal distance. The chart tells me that, with a focal length of 17mm and aperture of f/16, the hyperfocal distance is just over 2ft. I manually focus the lens to this distance and reshoot. This time, I achieve front-to-back sharpness.

Final image

I switch to a vertical composition as the portrait format usually places more emphasis on foreground subjects. The thrift creates a logical entry point into the composition and directs the eye into the image. Remember, foreground interest shouldn't dominate the composition or be included for the sake of it – it should complement the view, creating depth.

Using small apertures

How to use small apertures for the sharpest landscapes

Lee Frost: We've already explained that small apertures give increased depth-of-field so you can record more of the scene in focus. Ideally, when shooting landscapes you want to record everything in focus, from the immediate foreground to the distant background. Stopping your wide-angle or zoom lens down to its minimum aperture – usually f/22 – and focusing on infinity is a rule of thumb that many use to achieve this. More often than not it works because wide-angle lenses give so much depth-of-field at small apertures. However, it's not best practice to always use the minimum aperture, as it doesn't always give you the sharpest results. The purpose here is to show how you can get the best from your apertures when shooting landscapes, without necessarily always resorting to the lens's minimum aperture.

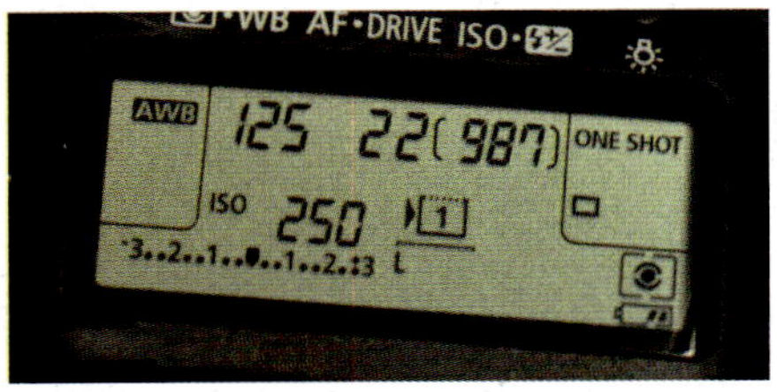

1 Wide aperture This scene was shot using a full-frame DSLR and a 17-40mm zoom at 17mm. The lens was focused manually on the boulders nearest to the camera and the aperture was set to f/4 – the widest aperture. As you can see, the boulders in the foreground are sharply focused, but by the time we reach the middle distance, depth-of-field has run out and the castle in the distance is out of focus.

2 Focus on foreground Stopping the lens down to a smaller aperture will increase depth-of-field so that it extends further and further into the scene. However, with the lens still focused on the foreground, we need to stop right down to the minimum aperture – f/22 – before the castle in the distance is recorded in focus. This is because depth-of-field is reduced when the focusing distance is small, as it is here.

3 Focus on infinity The other option is to focus the lens on infinity, which is a technique that most photographers use when shooting landscapes with a wide-angle lens. If you do this and stop down to f/22 as in the example above, the whole scene is in focus because of the combination of an ultra-wide focal length, minimum aperture and the increased focusing distance.

4 Open up the aperture But do you really need to stop down to f/22 when focused on infinity? We shot this scene with the lens at infinity and opened up the aperture a stop at a time to see how wide open we could go with the aperture before the foreground started to slip out of focus. Actually, we couldn't open any wider than f/22 in this case either, so focusing close to the camera or far away is clearly not ideal.

5 Focus a third in Depth-of-field extends both in front of and beyond the point you actually focus on. That's why focusing on the foreground or at infinity doesn't work so well; you're wasting depth-of-field. So what about using the old trick of focusing a third into the scene? We tried that at f/22 and, as expected, everything is sharply focused because depth-of-field is being utilised more effectively.

Final image

Finally, we opened up the aperture a stop to f/16. In this case, the image is not only sharp from front to back, but also sharper corner to corner because there's less diffraction. So, remember: for sharper images, focus a third in (guess it) and avoid minimum aperture.

LANDSCAPE LIGHTING

Daylight is the most accessible and versatile light source available to photographers. We explore its many forms, look at the factors that change it and tell you how to make the most of it for successful landscapes

LIGHT IS THE SINGLE essential ingredient that allows us to create a photographic image. But light can take on many forms – it can be hard or soft, strong or weak, warm or cold – and each variation has a profound effect, not only on the mood and character of the landscape, but the success of every photograph we take. Time of day and weather conditions are the two main factors that affect the quality of daylight. Throw in seasonal variations and you have seemingly endless permutations that change from one minute to the next. This can be both a blessing and a curse. When things are going to plan, daylight is the most amazing light source there is. But when you crawl out of bed in the middle of the night, drive three hours in darkness to reach a location for sunrise, only to be greeted by thick cloud and drizzle when you finally get there, it can also be the most frustrating.

Be prepared

Planning your shoot puts the odds of success in your favour and is easier than ever these days, thanks to the internet. You can check the weather forecast for the next few days, establish sunrise and sunset times for any day or location in the world, or check tide times if you're heading to the coast. The more information you gather beforehand, the more likely you are to be in the right place at the right time to take advantage of fantastic light. And if things don't go according to plan, you may end up taking photos that are better than you had hoped for – that's because unexpected changes in the weather often produce spectacular conditions that can't be planned for; and by being on location, you can take advantage of them. It's not down to luck that top landscape photographers produce amazing images on a regular basis – it's down to being out in the field, chasing the light.

The ability and willingness to adapt to unforeseen conditions will also help you to make the most of light because different forms of natural light suit different subjects. The flat light of an overcast day may not suit grand wide-angle views, for example, but it's ideal for shooting details in the landscape. Another option is to shoot with the intention of converting images to black & white: in which case, the quality of light isn't so important. You can also employ photographic techniques. No matter how drab the weather is, if you're on the coast you can produce amazing images using a ten-stop ND filter to record motion in the sea and contrast it with static elements, such as rocks, groynes and jetties.

Essential filters

■ **ND grad:** The Neutral Density (ND) grad lets you balance the sky with the foreground so the whole scene is perfectly exposed. Without a grad, you'll end up with a well-exposed sky and underexposed foreground, or well-exposed foreground and blown-out sky. This is especially true at dawn or dusk, when the contrast between sky and land is at its highest. You'll need a 0.9 density (three-stop) ND grad, while a 0.6 (two-stop) is fine for the day.

■ **Polariser:** The second filter is the polariser; in sunny conditions it can make a massive difference to your landscapes, deepening blue sky, cutting through glare, eliminating reflections and boosting both colours and contrast. It's also brilliant for autumnal foliage colour, even on dull days.

The right direction

The direction from which light strikes your subject can make a big difference to the mood and impact of your images. Frontal light, where the sun is to your back, makes the world look lovely but, photographically, it's not very effective because shadows fall away from the camera, making the landscape look rather flat. Just after sunrise, or just before sunset, when the sun is low in the sky and bathes the landscape in golden light, that lack of depth can be forgiven because the light is fantastic, though you may find that you struggle to keep your own shadow out of the composition!

Side-lighting, with the sun at roughly 90° to the camera, works better because you can incorporate shadows, making them an integral part of the composition to reveal texture and detail, and add depth. Again, this is most pronounced when the sun is low, as shadows are very long and weak. Another option is to shoot into the light; a technique

ALL IMAGES: LEE FROST

Light fantastic!
You can get great results on the cloudiest of days if you know how to work those brief glimpses of light to your best advantage.

known as contre-jour. Sunrise and sunset shots are taken in this way because the most colourful area of the sky is generally where the sun's about to rise or the moments after. You can also produce stunning shots when the sun is higher, but you need to choose the right kind of scene. Coastal views or scenes containing water suit contre-jour photography. Winter scenes are also ideal as sunlight reflects off the snow, ice and frost. Mist and fog work well, too, as the light burning through can create images that are incredibly atmospheric.

Ultimately, natural daylight is a law unto itself and no matter how hard you try, you'll never be able to control it. You can master it, though, through planning, patience, practice and perseverance, and once you master light, you master photography.

The time of day

From the moment first light appears to the time when darkness takes over, the quality of light undergoes a myriad of amazing changes and makes a huge difference to your photographs

Predawn First light usually appears 30-40 minutes before sunrise. Ideally, arrive an hour before sun-up to find a viewpoint, set up your gear and start shooting as soon as colour appears. Any light on the landscape is reflected from the sky, so it's soft and shadowless, and tends to have a strong, cool cast. This contrasts well with the warm glow over the eastern horizon.

Water, wet sand and wet rocks pick up the colour in the sky, so predawn is great to shoot coastal or lake views. Ideally, there will be some broken cloud adding colour to the sky, but clear mornings can also be highly productive. Light levels are low, so expect long exposures. The contrast between the sky and land is high due to the lack of direct light, so use a 0.9ND graduate to retain detail and colour in the sky.

Sunrise By the time the sun peeps over the horizon, any colour in the sky may have gone. On clear mornings, the sun will be dazzling once it rises, but you'll be able to shoot into it for a few minutes as the sea and wet sand reflects the light to keep contrast manageable. Features such as piers, castles and lighthouses can also be captured in silhouette. Inland, contrast will be too high once the sun rises into a clear sky. At this point, turn and capture the golden light on the landscape. Ideally, let the sun side-light the scene so you can include long, raking shadows to add depth and reveal texture.

The light is warm at sunrise because the rays pass through the atmosphere at a shallow angle and the light is scattered, with many of the wavelengths at the blue end of the spectrum filtered out.

Early morning Once the sun is up, you have minutes to capture the light at its peak quality before it loses warmth. During the summer, daylight is neutral in colour two hours after sunrise and its colour temperature remains constant for about 12 hours. During spring and autumn, any warmth in the light will have gone by 8am and the colour temperature remains steady until 4pm. In winter, however, the colour temperature hardly ever reaches 5500K, even at midday, because the angle between the sun and earth is shallow all day.

The first two hours after sunrise are the best for landscape photography as the intensity of the light is reasonably low, and long shadows add depth and modelling. A polariser is also effective when the sun is low in the sky and at 90° to the camera.

The middle hours Once the sun has been up for two hours, the quality of the light in clear, sunny weather begins to tail off. The higher the sun climbs, the more harsh and intense the light and the shorter and denser the shadows. By 9am in summer, the sun is at its 'zenith' – its highest point – and stays there until at least 4pm. The landscape looks flat, contrast is high and the light isn't attractive. The urban landscape is better suited to strong light: shoot modern architecture, using a polariser to deepen the sky, and look for abstracts and colourful details. In the countryside, capture trees against the sky from a low angle and look for reflections in water. Infrared photography works in harsh light, especially in spring and summer when there's lush foliage around.

Late afternoon Once the sun begins its slow descent and the light begins to warm up, its intensity is reduced, and shadows become longer and weaker. Shape and character return to the landscape, and the longer you wait, the better it gets. In the morning, the light falls on a cold earth, but in the afternoon, the earth is warm so shadows appear neutral, not cool. The atmosphere is also denser in the afternoon, so light can appear redder than it did at the start of the day. The hour before sunset is often referred to as 'the golden hour' due to the richness of the light. Long shadows reveal texture and modelling to give your pictures depth, and because the sun is sinking and not rising, it's easier to predict how the light is going so you can choose a suitable location.

Everything's rosy
The colours and textures in the sky can be spectacular, especially if you pick the moment as the sun rises above or falls below the horizon.

ALL IMAGES: LEE FROST

GARY McPARLAND

Sunset When a sunset seems likely, get to your location 45 minutes before so you can choose the best viewpoint, get set up and take a variety of pictures as the sun dips. Capture the landscape bathed in golden light. If the scenery is relatively flat, the light will perform its magic literally until the moment the sun sets, whereas in hilly regions, you may lose the sun half an hour before. Shooting into the sun will record anything between the sun and the camera in silhouette: a good technique when shooting water because the sun's glow and colour in the sky will be reflected, creating a backdrop to silhouettes of boats, islands, piers and so on. If flare is a problem, hide the sun behind something in the scene or wait for it to set. If you want to record detail in the foreground, use a 0.9ND grad.

Twilight Once the sun finally disappears below the horizon, light levels quickly fade and the light on the landscape is again reflected from the sky. If you're lucky, there will be a vivid afterglow in the sky created by the sun as it under-lights the clouds above the horizon, but even this will fade quickly. You'll find that colours are muted, the light is soft, shadows fade and light levels fall away. Head to the water's edge where the pastel colours left in the sky look stunning reflected in lakes and rivers. Or use those colours as a background to silhouettes. Long exposures record movement: the swaying of trees in the breeze; the movement of clouds across the sky; the motion of the sea or water flowing in rivers and streams. Keep shooting until those colours fade.

Moonlight The moon can be a lovely natural source of light. Winter scenes work well because snow and frost reflect the moonlight. Coastal views also work if you capture the shimmering silver ribbon of light from the moon on the sea. By increasing exposure, you can create surreal shots that look like they've been taken in daylight. They'll look normal, but the light will have a strange quality. You can even try recording star trails in the sky created by the rotation of the earth while the camera's shutter is open. Obviously, exposures will be long in low light, so use a tripod, and keep the ISO low – 400 or less – for high image quality. Whatever you shoot, unless the moon is obscured by cloud, you should keep it out of frame to avoid it recording as an overexposed white smudge!

Get up early for 'magic hour' lighting

Dawn is the best time of day for taking beautiful, atmospheric shots, says landscape expert Helen Dixon

WAKING A COUPLE of hours before sunrise, which is often in the middle of the night, is not most people's idea of fun. But if you're prepared to make the effort, you will reap the rewards. Planning is essential. Check the weather forecast and the sunrise times on the internet. And check the tide times if you are travelling to the sea – a low tide is usually the best time to visit. If the light fails to materialise, you can always do beach close-ups.

I try to be on location at least half an hour before the sun rises – if not earlier – because it's often before the sun appears that the real magic happens. This also gives me time to set up the camera and to find the best viewpoint. Don't just look for clear days, it's better to have cloud around as this creates wonderful colours in the sky as the cloud reflects the light of the sun. Try to pre-visit and research your location before the day of the shoot. I use Ordnance Survey maps for detailed information on rights of way and parking. Look for appealing places where there will be opportunities for shots that include foreground interest.

Mist mainly develops during a cold night and it only lingers for a short time during the morning or until the heat of the sun burns it away. Something to bear in mind is that, during misty conditions, your camera's metering system will often underexpose the scene, resulting in a dull, lifeless landscape. To compensate, alter the exposure by +1/2 or +1 stop. Check the histogram on the camera's LCD monitor for overexposure.

The use of Neutral Density graduate filters is pretty much standard in landscape photography. They help to control the brightest part of the image, which is usually the sky. Early in the day, there is a noticeable difference between the light in the sky and the light on the land.

Be aware of lens flare if the sun is included in the frame. To help eliminate this, make sure that your filters and lens optics are spotlessly clean. I rarely use a warm-up filter as these filters normally make any green foliage appear a yellow-brown colour. Instead I set my camera's White Balance to Cloudy or Shade to help warm up the scene. Try to avoid using the Auto White Balance (AWB) setting as you are sure to cool down the light, unless, of course, this is the effect you want. There are a number of reasons why I personally prefer dawn light over sunset. I like to capture atmosphere in my shots if I can, and early morning is the best time to do this as you are more likely to have a misty or frosty start to the day. The light is often diffused and softer at this time, but it's also more of a challenge to include the sun in the picture, too, during the morning than in the evening, because at sunset the pollution levels have risen throughout the day, which helps to diffuse the brightness slightly. Another great advantage of early morning is that it's so peaceful; I rarely see another soul. The world belongs to me – it's so satisfying to watch the day unfold and witness the magical light of dawn.

Once the sun has risen and become too strong to photograph, turn to the side or put your back to the sun, being careful not to cast a shadow in the foreground. Now start using the warm light that's illuminating the land. Light is never static but continually changes – it's the main ingredient that allows us to create something beautiful.

Kit watch!

Helen's magic-hour kit

When considering what equipment you will need, a necessity is a sturdy tripod, as at this time of the day you're working with long exposures. I use a Manfrotto MF4 carbon-fibre with 322RC2 head – it's a lightweight but stable support and I can hang my bag from the centre post for extra stability on really windy days.

I always use a remote release but if you don't have one, use the self-timer to stop any vibrations and use mirror lock-up if your DSLR has this facility.

I find my 17-40mm wide-angle zoom and my 70-200mm telezoom particularly useful. These cover most of my requirements. I use the wide-angle zoom when shooting foreground elements. And the telephoto zoom is especially good for compressing perspective and creating layers on misty mornings.

HELEN DIXON

Mirror lock-up

Many digital SLRs have a facility that allows the mirror to be raised prior to the exposure, to minimise shake when the shutter is fired. You'll most likely find this is activated via a Custom Function

Shining through

I waited for the sun to rise above the horizon – I used the small clump of trees to help diffuse the sunlight.

Exposure: 0.5secs at f/22.

Stay out late and shoot stunning sunsets

The other 'magic hour' is at sunset – be prepared and you'll be rewarded, reveals Mark Bauer

ALTHOUGH IT'S possible to take landscape photographs at most times of the day, there are two times when most landscapers agree the light will give the best results – the first and last hours of the day. What makes these times of day special is that the low sun casts long shadows and helps to pick out the features of the landscape. If you're out predawn or post-sunset, you can also see spectacular skies as the clouds are lit from below.

The light is quite similar at these times of day, and your preference often depends on which direction of light suits your subject. For example, the south coast in winter looks best at the end of the day rather than at the start. Having said that, the light in the final hour of the day tends to be warmer and, as the sun sets, the landscape is often bathed in a golden glow. Also, lets not forget, the nice thing about sunset compared to sunrise is that you don't have to force yourself out of bed at a ridiculous hour to make the most of it. Let's be honest, not everyone has the willpower and enthusiasm for sunrises as Helen Dixon (see opposite)!

Almost any type of landscape looks good in the magic hour, but some features really benefit, like stone buildings or rocky cliffs. When the low sun warms everything up and picks out the texture of rock and stone, scenes that might look dull at any other time of day can be lifted out of the ordinary.

Water is also an excellent subject at this time, because if you have an interesting sky, you can double the impact by using reflections. Moving water can sparkle like diamonds or be made to blur during long exposures. Again, the amount and type of light falling on it determines the result.

The direction of the light can have a strong influence on the mood and success of pictures taken at the beginning or end of the day. Front lighting, for instance, can look flat as the direction of the shadows doesn't help to pick out the details of the landscape. With the sun to one side, however, shadows help to create depth in the picture and reveal form and texture. Side-lighting is best if you want to use a polariser to saturate colours, too, as it will have its strongest effect if the camera is 90° to the sun. Backlighting can be very dramatic as well, but exposure is difficult to control and you will have to be careful to avoid lens flare as light falls directly onto your filters or the front element of your lens.

With all this to consider and the weather is notoriously unpredictable, how can you tell if the magic hour will live up to your expectations? Looking at weather forecasts is a good idea – www.metoffice.gov.uk is reliable and you can get a detailed forecast for specific regions. Remember that the longer the range of the forecast, the less reliable it will be. Checking the forecast the night before a dawn shoot gives you the best guide.

If you drive to your location, listen to local radio stations in the car, rather than national ones, and keep an eye on what's happening in the sky. For sunsets you'll need to look to the west, as this is where the sun will be at magic hour. Most of our weather fronts come from the west, too, so by keeping an eye in that direction, it's possible to see if cloud is likely to break up or thicken. Being aware of wind direction, the points of the compass and weather patterns will help enormously and you'll start to recognise the signs of a magic moment.

Kit watch!

Mark's magic-hour kit

Wide-angle lenses are the most popular for landscape work, but longer lenses can also be useful for picking out the kind of patterns and textures that the magic hour reveals.

A polarising filter will help you make the most of side-lighting by improving overall saturation, but is especially effective when used with blue skies.

A sturdy tripod is another essential. If you're shooting in the period after sunset, light levels will be low and handholding will be out of the question. But it's good practice to use a tripod whatever the lighting conditions – it will slow you down, it makes you think and it enables you to make small but often vital changes to composition.

Neutral Density graduate filters are also important, especially if clouds are lit from below and there is no direct light on the land. ND grads help control contrast.

MARK BAUER

White Balance

The White Balance you set has a major effect on the final result. Avoid using the AWB setting. If you shoot in Raw, you can try out all the settings later on your computer and choose your favourite

Get your rocks off

The low sun picks out the details of the rocky ledge and gives the cliffs a warm glow. A 0.6ND grad, angled so as not to cut into the cliff, helps retain details in the sky.

Canon EOS 5D with 17-40mm lens.

Watch the weather

Changes in weather have an even greater influence on the quality of light than the time of day, so if you want to take stunning shots every time, you need to be prepared to take on the elements

"THERE'S NO SUCH THING as bad weather, only inappropriate clothing," so said comedian Billy Connolly, and he was right. If the sun isn't shining and the sky isn't blue, we tend to refer to the weather as 'bad', but photographically, 'bad' can be good because it gives us variations in the quality of light to work with, adds drama and creates atmosphere. So-called 'good' weather is actually not so good for photography because the light is bland and the landscape looks picture-postcard perfect, which gets boring after a while.

Clouds have a dramatic effect on the quality of daylight because they soften and spread it so intensity is reduced, contrast falls and shadows become weaker. Clouds also add interest to the sky, and the sky can make or break a great landscape.

Days when the sky is a blanket of monotonous grey cloud are probably the least exciting for landscape photography as colours appear dull and muted, and a lack of shadows means scenery tends to look flat and uninviting. However, overcast light is ideal for capturing details in the landscape: the patterns and textures in rocks; the smooth shapes and soft colours in sea-worn boulders and pebbles; the rich colours of autumnal foliage or banks of spring flowers. Strong colours look intense in diffuse light because there's no glare to dilute saturation. Dull days are also ideal for slow shutter speed shots of waterfalls – just keep the boring sky out of the shot and you'll get some great results.

White clouds in their many shapes and forms are highly photogenic against blue sky, and you can make them stand out even more by using a polariser to deepen the blue. Keep the sun to your side for the strongest effect. Watch out for cloud patterns on the landscape, too – they can add an extra element that makes a good scene great, and are easiest to spot if you're shooting from an elevated viewpoint.

Stormy weather creates the most dramatic conditions for landscape photography – angry, dark clouds rushing across the sky, strong winds blowing and momentary breaks that allow rays of sunlight to flood through and illuminate the scene below. You can't plan for such conditions, but if you venture outdoors in stormy weather, there's always the chance that you'll be in the right place to capture them. And it will be a blessing if you do.

If the sun does break through during a storm, the landscape ends up brighter than the sky, which is a reversal of the norm. What this means in practice is that you can get away without using an ND grad as the sky won't overexpose. However, it's still worth using a 0.6ND grad to make the sky look even more dramatic than it really is.

Something else to watch out for in stormy weather is a rainbow arching across the sky. Rainbows are created when the sun shines through falling rain, so if that happens while you're out, turn your back to the sun and check the sky ahead. To reveal the colours of the bow at their best, try to catch it against dark clouds and use a telezoom to home in on part of the bow. Alternatively, use a wide-angle zoom and include the whole bow.

Mist and fog reduce the landscape to soft shapes and hazy outlines. Three dimensions become two and aerial perspective means that tones become brighter with distance. The light is diffuse, shadows don't exist and fine detail is lost. Scenes are simplified and your images should reflect that.

Telephoto lenses emphasise the effects of mist and fog by magnifying the scene and compressing perspective, so they're great for shooting the overlapping forms of hills and mountains, or picking out elements like a single tree or church spire fading into the gloom. If you want to relegate mist or fog to the distance, then use a wide-angle lens – visibility close to the camera will be much better than farther away, so you can capture plenty of foreground detail and let the rest of the scene fade away. Dense fog is heavy and damp. It snuffs out colour and turns the world to grey, so you may decide to convert your foggy landscapes to black & white. Mist is more delicate, so instead of destroying colour, it tends to merge all colours together to create very soft hues. Mist is also fine enough to let the light through, so shoot contre-jour at sunrise, when you're more likely to find mist in woodland or over water, and capture golden rays of lights bleeding through. Such conditions aren't common, but the quality of light when you get mist and sunrise coinciding is hard to beat.

Check the web

If you're planning a landscape shoot, whether it's to head out early in the morning for sunrise or to go off into the wilds for a week, use the internet to gather information that will help you make the most of the light. Here are some websites worth bookmarking for future reference:

Weather forecast
www.metoffice.gov.uk
www.bbc.co.uk/weather
www.xcweather.co.uk
www.metcheck.com

Sunrise & sunset times
www.timeanddate.com/astronomy/

Tide times
www.tidetimes.org.uk/
http://easytide.ukho.gov.uk

Planning your shoot
A more sophisticated tool is the Photographer's Ephemeris (www.photoephemeris.com). This is available as a free download for Mac and PC (plus as a paid-for app for the iPhone) and allows you to determine sunrise and sunset times for anywhere in the world, any day of the year, as well as the angle of the sunrise/sunset so you can check if the sun's orb will be blocked by hills, say. Moonrise and set times are also provided.

Below left: Far from ruining the image, clouds can add all-important interest to coastal views.

Below right: Simple scenes suit a misty outlook and are given an ethereal twist.

Right: Rays of light shining through storm clouds can have a really dramatic effect.

LEE FROST

ROSS HODDINOTT

Colour temperature and White Balance

The colour of light is referred to as colour temperature, which is measured in Kelvin (K). The warmer the light is, the lower its colour temperature, and the cooler the light is, the higher its temperature.

Our eyes adapt to changes in the colour temperature automatically, so natural light always looks more or less white – this is known as chromatic adaptation. The photographic equivalent is your camera's Auto White Balance (AWB) setting. If you use AWB, you will find that it produces pleasing results in most daylight situations, but the White Balance does fluctuate so you may not record the colour of the light as it really is. If you want to do that, you should set White Balance to the Daylight preset, which is 5500K. This is the colour temperature of 'mean noon daylight', so in normal daylight situations, your images will come out looking neutral. However, at sunrise and sunset the light is much warmer (lower colour temperature), so by using the Daylight White Balance preset, your camera will record that warmth. Similarly, if the light is cool, as is often the case during predawn or in bad weather, using the Daylight preset will record that coolness.

Remember, also, that if you shoot in Raw, you can adjust the colour temperature of the image later. So if you don't like the cool cast, you simply get rid of it, or if a warm image isn't warm enough, you can adjust the colour temperature to make it warmer.

Conditions	Colour temp (K)	Colour cast (Daylight WB)
Open shade under blue sky	10000K	Very blue
Shade under part cloudy sky	**7500K**	**Blue**
Overcast weather	6000K	Slightly cool
Average noon daylight	**5500K**	**None**
Morning/evening sunlight	3500K	Warm
Sunrise/sunset	**2000K**	**Very warm**

Seasonal landscape light

Although seasonal changes have more of a physical effect on the landscape, the quality of daylight also varies throughout the year. Here's our guide on how to handle landscapes in different seasons…

LEE FROST

1) Winter

The landscape lies dormant and bare during winter. Trees stand skeletal against the sky, while fields are brown and barren. Days are also painfully short, with the sun rising well after 8am and setting before 4pm in January.

Photographically, however, winter is a fantastic season. There are few sights more magnificent than a landscape covered in freshly fallen snow and bathed in crisp morning sunlight. But even if you're not lucky enough to get that, ice and frost are a certainty at some point as temperatures drop well below freezing.

The short days are a benefit, too, because you can shoot sunrise and sunset at civilised times. Plus the sun never climbs more than about 20° above the horizon, so the quality of light remains high from dawn to dusk, with long, weak shadows adding depth – on a clear winter's day you can get eight hours of good light.

Keep a close watch on the weather forecast and if a clear night is predicted, prepare for an early start the next day because that usually means ice and frost come the morning – and, if you're lucky, freezing mist for the sun to slowly burn away. Incredible pictures are guaranteed. Woodland and water locations are your best bet. As well as shooting wide-angle views, look for winter details: cobwebs covered in icy beads; the patterns in ice over ponds and puddles; frosty leaves on the ground; and so on. Dawn on a freezing morning can be magical, with the sky full of pastel colours and the sun rising like a giant orange ball. Its intensity is often reduced by mist or haze, so you can include it in your shots without any risk of flare. Use a long lens to make it nice and big in your shots.

HELEN DIXON

Snow is best photographed when it has just fallen so it's pristine and fresh, and ideally in sunny weather – a glistening snowy landscape under a blue sky is hard to beat. And you needn't head to magnificent countryside to take great snow shots – a visit to your local park can be just as productive if you concentrate on simple scenes, like a single tree standing in the middle of a snow-filled field.

Winter Q&A

Q What should I consider when shooting snow scenes?

A Exposure! All that whiteness in the scene is likely to fool your camera's metering system into underexposure, so take a shot then check the preview image and the histogram. You will almost certainly need to dial in extra exposure using the exposure compensation facility – do that in 1/3-stop increments until the highlight warnings on your preview image start to flash to indicate the images is overexposed. Delete that shot – the one before it should be perfect.

Q Is it okay to use a polarising filter during winter?

A Definitely, but carefully. Blue sky is bluer in winter and because more of it is polarised, the effect of a polarising filter is more obvious than at any other time of the year. In extreme cases, the sky can go almost black if you fully polarise, so you may need to wind back the effect a little.

Q Will my camera work okay in freezing winter weather?

A Yes, but batteries drain faster so make sure yours is fully charged and ideally carry a spare. Also, avoid breathing on your lens or any filters you're using as they will mist up and take ages to clear.

HELEN DIXON

2) Spring

This season marks the dawn of new life as the landscape awakens from the dormant months of winter. Barren trees burst with buds and blossom, woodland floors, hedgerows and riverbanks are carpeted with colourful wild flowers, while desolate fields turn into beautiful patchwork quilts of green.

Scenes that looked grey and drab during winter are transformed within a few short weeks – especially if the weather turns and is mild towards the end of winter. Spring is also time for tulips, daffodils, buttercups and bluebells, turning gardens and meadows into dazzling displays of colour.

The weather during spring is changeable and unpredictable – but this has its advantages for the photographer. Brief showers cleanse the atmosphere and create rainbows arching across the countryside, shafts of sunlight burst through stormy skies to illuminate the landscape below, and light mists hang over rivers and lakes or in valley bottoms at dawn.

As the weeks pass, the days also grow longer. The sun rises at around 6am during the early days of spring and sets at 8pm, but by mid-June, sunrise can be as early as 4.15am and sunset after 10.30pm in the north of Scotland. To make the most of spring conditions, rise early and stay out late. Dawn on a perfect spring morning is hard to beat, with a chorus of birdsong permeating the cool air and the first rays of sunlight slowly burning away the mist. The opportunity for amazing images is one that shouldn't be missed, and nothing quite beats that feeling of getting in touch with nature.

The intensity of colour in the spring landscape can be improved by using a polarising filter to cut through atmospheric haze and glare on the foliage. If you want to capture carpets of spring flowers, ideally wait for a bright but overcast day when contrast is low and shadows weak. This makes it easier to record the delicate colours and fine details of the blooms, especially when taking pictures in woodland where the light is patchy during sunny spells.

HELEN DIXON

Spring Q&A

Q How do I shoot spring mist?
A Mist often occurs when a mild day with rain is followed by a clear night and cold temperatures. If that's predicted in the weather forecast, set your alarm early and head out before sunrise. Mist is common near water and wetlands, and in woodland. Get to a decent location ready for sunrise: if you're lucky, the light from the rising sun will burst through the mist, creating warm rays of light that radiate from behind trees and buildings. A straight exposure should capture this effect perfectly, but, if necessary, increase the exposure in increments up to one stop.

Q What's the best shutter speed to use when shooting waterfalls?
A A shutter speed around one second is usually slow enough to blur the water, but also record some texture – though you can experiment with slower speeds. What you don't want to do is overexpose the water so it comes out white.

Q How do I get backlit shots of flowers?
A You need to shoot when the sun is low in the sky, so during early morning or late afternoon: morning is often more atmospheric. Get down low, use a telezoom to isolate a group of flowers and try to capture them against a dark background so the colours glow.

HELEN DIXON

3) Summer

Summer is the least favourite season for landscape photographers as the light tends to be harsh and bland. Yes, the countryside does look resplendent in its lush coat of foliage, gardens and meadows are alive with colour and the days last much longer. But when the sun does shine, it can be very intense and unflattering, with a high colour temperature that makes images look cool, while heat haze tends to turn blue sky into an ugly washed-out tone. Consequently, the number of effective hours available for landscape photography are no more than on a clear winter's day.

Between 10am and 4pm in summer, the sun is overhead and the light harsh and characterless, while shadows are short and dense. For conventional landscape photography, this isn't great, but if you find scenes containing lots of colour – oilseed rape, poppy fields, sunflowers – on a sunny, blue-sky day, it's still possible to produce striking images. Use a polariser to boost contrast and clarity, and keep your composition simple.

Summer storms are also quite common, with high temperatures leading to thunder and heavy rain. This can produce amazing landscape light, but you risk a soaking to catch it! Once the rain subsides, crisp, clean light will often bathe the landscape and rainbows can appear.

The light is at its best at the extreme of the day, so get to your location very early or be prepared to stay out late. The days do get shorter as summer progresses, but 3am starts and 11pm finishes are not uncommon. You can always grab a sleep in the afternoon when the light's no good!

Wild landscapes can still look dramatic during the summer, and by early September start to turn quite autumnal, so scout out the locations nearest you that will be full of colour. Rocky, barren coastline also changes little during the summer and can be the source of great shots – especially at dawn and dusk when the light is warm.

ADAM BURTON

Summer Q&A

Q Can I do anything about hazy skies?
A Not really. Hazy skies and overcast grey skies lack texture or drama – they're just a blanket, boring tone. Using an ND grad merely darkens that tone, but rarely makes it more interesting. Exclude the sky from your compositions; maybe use a telezoom to shoot selective landscapes or concentrate on smaller details.

Q Is the summer a good time to use my infrared modified camera?
A Definitely. There's plenty of foliage to show the ghostly infrared effect, and it doesn't matter how harsh the light is because infrared photography suits it. Use your IR camera in parks, gardens and woodland, as well as the countryside. For those without an IR modified camera, try using an infrared filter like the Hoya R72.

Q My summer landscapes often have an unsightly blue cast. What causes it?
A High colour temperature – on a sunny blue-sky day, the colour temperature can hit 10000K. If you use Daylight White Balance, set for 5500K, your camera will record the coolness in the light. Setting White Balance to Shade will get rid of the cast – even Auto White Balance (AWB) may work. Or, if you shoot in Raw, you can correct the cast during image processing.

LEE FROST

4) Autumn

Colour – that's what autumn is all about. As days shorten and temperatures fall, deciduous foliage turns a myriad of wonderful rustic colours. Hillsides covered in heather and bracken turn to gold and the landscape battens down the hatches ready for winter. Whether autumn is a hit or a flop colourwise depends on temperatures and rainfall during spring and summer: the first week in November is traditionally a time when colours peak, but the prime period can occur earlier or later.

Clear, sunny days provide the best conditions to capture autumn's beauty, especially during early morning and late afternoon when the sunlight is naturally warm and the sky a deep, velvety blue. Wild landscape looks amazing in autumn – head to regions like Rannoch Moor in Scotland or the Lake District and you can't go wrong.

If you intend to shoot deep inside woodland, ideally choose an overcast day when the light is soft and shadows weak, otherwise high contrast will be a problem. Such conditions reveal the woodland colours at their most intense, especially when enhanced by a polarising filter, which cuts through haze on the damp foliage.

Head for rivers and lakes where you can capture the autumnal colours reflecting in calm water, and as well as shooting wide-angle views, also look for details like the vibrant patterns of fallen autumnal leaves.

HELEN DIXON

Autumn is also good to capture the landscape being brought to life by dramatic, stormy light, with patches of sunlight breaking through the dark, brooding sky. Or why not rise early and make the most of early-morning mist around water or in woodland and valleys? If you're lucky, you may capture the first golden rays of sunlight burning though to create stunning images.

At the start of autumn, the sun rises around 7am and sets at 7pm, so the days are fairly long, but the quality of light remains high throughout. By day one of winter, the sun doesn't rise until gone 8am and it won't set much before 4pm.

Autumn Q&A

Q What causes foliage to change colour in autumn?

A Deciduous trees drop their leaves in readiness for winter when there's too little light for photosynthesis to occur, and they live off sugar reserves stored through the summer. Chlorophyll, which gives leaves their green colour, is necessary for photosynthesis to take place, but as the days grow shorter and the hours of darkness increase, the production of chlorophyll slows down and that's when the colour changes start to occur.

Autumnal colours reach their peak when all the chlorophyll has been destroyed and other chemicals in the leaves are revealed, such as carotenoids and anthocyanins.

Q Can you recommend some top autumn locations in the UK?

A If the colours are good, you can take great autumn shots literally anywhere you find deciduous foliage, but check out Westonbirt Arboretum in Gloucestershire, Glen Affric in Scotland, Stourhead Gardens in Wiltshire, The New Forest in Hampshire, Grasmere and Rydal Water in the Lake District, Gwydyr Forest in North Wales and Kielder Forest, Northumberland.

Giotto's tripods: never leave home without one

Professional landscape and travel photographer Lee Pengelly explains why a good tripod is the most valuable piece of kit a landscape photographer should own

"My landscape photography is, for the most part, about capturing it right in-camera. There are some digital techniques that I sometimes use, such as HDR or panoramic stitching, but it's the tools that I use out in the field that make the image. I run photography workshops, and numerous times I've seen people spend thousands on cameras and lenses, only to skimp on one of the most essential parts of a photographer's kit – the tripod. From experience, I've found that Giotto's range of tripods offer the ideal solution.

"A good tripod and head combination is essential. Not only do they allow you to get creative with shutter speeds for capturing motion or shooting in low light, but they also detach you from the camera, so you can take your time in composing the image. What's more, when the camera is perfectly still you can shoot at a lower ISO for optimum image quality.

"I started using Giotto's tripods two years ago – a few people on the workshops used them and the build quality and strength impressed me. The key features that I look for when choosing the right tripod are weight, portability and stability. I travel a lot so my tripod needs to be able to fold down compact and not take up my luggage allowance. Even when I'm shooting in the UK I don't want to be lugging a heavy set of legs along a coastal path in a gale!

"I'm currently using Giotto's new innovative 10kg carbon-fibre tripod, the YTL8213, with the Giotto's MH5001 three-way head. The Giotto's Silk Road YTL series features a patented Y-tube centre-column that not only reduces the overall weight of the tripod, but also means that it takes up 30% less space when folded down, without sacrificing stability. It's a simple idea but makes such a big difference! The other important factor for me is height; I'm 6ft 2in and finding a tripod that reaches eye level can be a challenge. The Giotto's YTL8213 supports from 15cm up to a maximum height of 194cm, so is perfect for me. What's more, its 10kg load rating makes it ideal for heavier lenses and bodies, and the anodised fittings mean it'll stand up to the harsh elements often encountered in landscape photography.

"If I had one piece of advice to give someone to help improve their photography it would be to know your kit. People often think that shooting landscapes is a leisurely affair; sometimes it is, but quite often that couldn't be further from the truth. This image was taken during a workshop at Land's End, Cornwall. We were perched up on the cliff-top with the wind blowing a head-on gale. I was able to set up quickly thanks to the Giotto's Quick Easy Leg (QEL) Lock system in time to catch the sun basking the cliffs in glorious golden light. I fitted a 0.6ND grad filter to hold back the sky and hung my kit bag from the centre-column hook – the tripod stayed still as rock, allowing me to capture the image. A matter of minutes later and the light was gone."

For further information on Giotto's tripods, visit: www.giottos-tripods.co.uk

GIOTTOS YTL8213
Price: £350
Material: Carbon-fibre
Column: Vertical
Folded height: 69cm
Min height: 15cm
Max height without centre column: 163cm
Max height with centre column: 194cm
Weight: 1.63kg
Weight capacity: 10kg
Leg sections: 3

Lee uses:
Giotto's YTL8213

The YTL8213 is a lightweight and compact professional carbon-fibre tripod offering high stability, 10kg capacity and tall maximum height. The Y-tube centre column saves weight and means that, when folded down, the tripod takes up 30% less space than with a traditional column.

GIOTTOS YTL9383
Price: £125
Material: Aluminium
Column: 3D
Folded height: 68cm
Min height: 20cm
Max height without centre column: 151cm
Max height with centre column: 183cm
Weight: 1.88kg
Weight capacity: 8kg
Leg sections: 3

Lee recommends:
Giotto's YTL9383

A sturdy aluminium tripod that also utilises the innovative Y-tube centre column but adds three-way versatility. The 3D column allows you to position the centre column vertically, horizontally or at an angle in between; perfect for getting the shot, no matter how awkward the position.

Get the shot!

Without my Giotto's tripod I wouldn't have been able to capture both the fantastic golden light and motion of the crashing waves in one image.

RAW & LANDSCAPES

ALTHOUGH YOU PROBABLY don't realise it yet, producing top-notch images is easier now than at any stage in the entire history of photography, thanks to digital technology. Chances are many of you will have come into photography during the digital era, in which case you'll have little or no experience of what life was like pre-pixels. Well take it from us – shooting pictures using digital is a walk in the park compared to taking them with film.

Being able to see your shots seconds after capture is the fast track to success because you can learn as you go, correcting mistakes and making changes so that you need never miss a great shot. This immediacy, and the fact that every press of the camera's shutter button doesn't cost money, also encourages you to take creative risks, which is by far the best way to master new techniques and fine-tune your skills as a landscape photographer.

Of course, tripping the shutter is just the first stage in the creative process as, once home, your images are then downloaded to a computer where you can turn those millions of coloured dots into amazing works of art with the aid of the latest editing software. Successful digital imaging therefore requires a combination of solid camera work and sympathetic processing.

For many creative photographers, there's only one way to achieve both: shooting in Raw. If you've favoured JPEG until now, and can't see how switching to Raw would benefit you, read on as we explain the many benefits you'll gain going Raw.

An introduction to Raw

If maximum detail and control is what you need, then shooting in Raw is the answer. We cover the basics you need to get started

THE MAIN DIFFERENCE between a Raw file and a JPEG is that when you shoot in Raw format, the images recorded on your camera's memory card consist of the raw data from the sensor. Nothing is added, taken away or changed. If you shoot in JPEG, the camera records all the raw data then develops the file in-camera; applying preset parameters to White Balance, sharpening and custom camera styles etc, deleting any unnecessary information and then erasing remaining raw data as well.

In film terms, a Raw file is a bit like a negative, whereas a JPEG is similar to a colour slide. Slides are convenient because they come back from the processing lab finished and ready to view. The same can be said for JPEGs, which are supposedly ready to print straight from the camera. However, this convenience means that you need to get everything right in-camera, so there's less room for error. Negatives are more time-consuming than slides as you need to develop them how you see fit in the darkroom, but are much more versatile with more latitude for error. Raw files are the same. They always require processing using suitable software before they're considered finished, but this allows you to make changes to enhance the images and correct in-camera mistakes.

The key parameters you can control in Raw are:

- Colour temperature can be adjusted to get rid of unwanted casts or to change the mood of an image. This can be done with JPEGs in Photoshop, but not with the same precision.
- Exposure can be corrected – or adjusted for creative reasons – without compromising image quality. Whereas if you make a JPEG lighter or darker, image quality will be affected. You can also optimise image quality by overexposing Raw files in-camera to just before the highlights become blown, as shadow detail is increased and the effects of noise reduced. The exposure can then be 'pulled back' while processing the Raw file. This is only possible because the Raw file contains more data than you need, whereas a JPEG is already compressed, so residual data has been deleted.
- If you do accidentally overexpose a Raw file so the highlights 'blow out', you can recover detail during processing. This isn't possible with JPEGs, so blown highlights appear white and if you try to darken them they simply go grey.
- Sharpening can be applied using the sharpening tools in Raw file processing software or via third-party applications. JPEGs, however, are already sharpened so extra work must be done carefully to avoid spoiling the images.

Any changes you make to a Raw file are non-destructive, because when it's converted to, ideally, a TIFF file, the original Raw image remains unchanged. This means you can return to the same Raw file in the future to process it again. Raw files also contain so much data they can be processed several times then combined either to address exposure and contrast problems, or used as the basis for creative techniques such as HDR (High Dynamic Range), which we'll show you how to do later.

Ultimately, if optimum image quality is what you want, your best chance is to shoot Raw. Raw files support 16-bits of data per colour channel, whereas JPEGs support 8-bits. The difference in image quality won't be obvious initially, but heavy editing reduces quality and 8-bit files will show this more readily than 16-bit.

Many photographers are put off shooting Raw as they assume it's complicated. But using Raw processing software is very intuitive (see panel) and any changes you make can easily be reversed or cancelled. A JPEG, on the other hand, while seen as the more convenient format for beginners, actually leaves more room for mistakes, which beginners will surely make.

What are the downsides to shooting in Raw? Well, aside from spending more time at your computer processing files, there aren't many. And if you get as much right in-camera as you can, a Raw file can be processed in a matter of seconds. Raw files are around four times bigger in terms of megabytes than JPEGs, so take up more storage space. However, memory cards and external hard drives are cheap these days, so if you've spent a fortune on your camera, it's false economy to choose an image format simply to save on storage space. Bigger image files also mean your camera's buffer will fill up faster if you shoot in Raw. While this might prove frustrating when shooting subjects such as sports and wildlife, where lots of shots are taken in quick succession, it isn't a real concern for the landscape photographer.

Troubleshooting

Q I can't open the Raw files from my new DSLR?

A You're having a problem opening Raw files on your new DSLR because camera manufacturers keep changing Raw file formats as they launch new cameras. Adobe releases regular upgrades for Adobe Camera Raw (ACR) for new cameras. Go to www.adobe.com and see if the latest upgrade includes your camera.

Q I processed some Raw files and saved them as TIFFs, but the files are really small. What happened to them and what can I do?

A If you're using ACR, open a Raw file and below the file number for the preview image you'll see a line of text. Click on it and a Workflow Options window opens. To avoid the files being too small, choose Adobe RGB (1998) for Space, 16 Bits/Channel for Depth, 300 pixels/inch for Resolution and, for Size, choose the closest size that matches your camera's maximum pixel resolution.

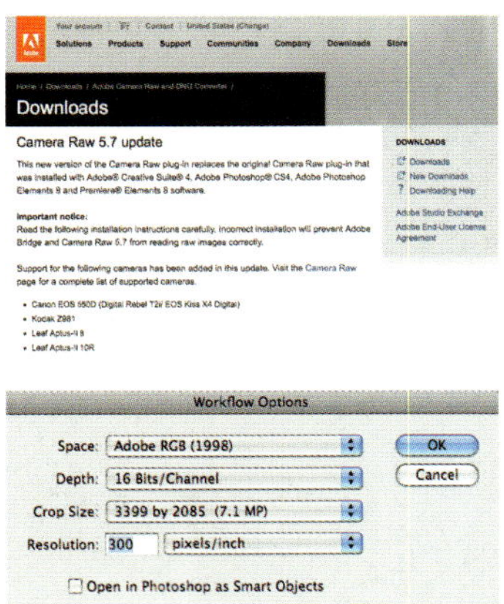

Shoot Raw and JPEG

If you're initially uneasy about shooting Raw, why not set your camera to record every image in both Raw and JPEG? That way, while you get used to processing Raw files, you know you've also got JPEGs of the same images, for reassurance

Shoot & process Raw

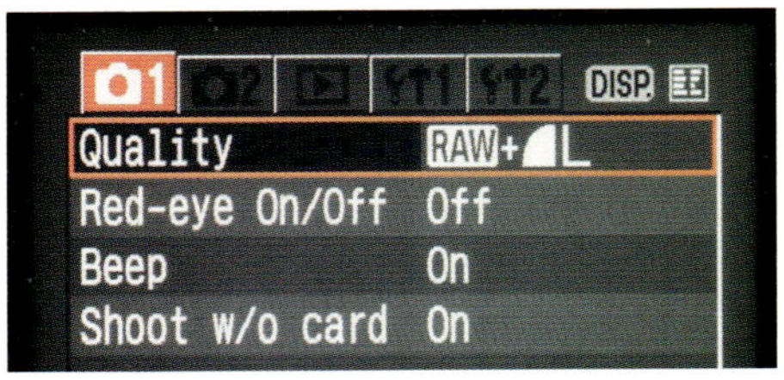

Setting your camera to shoot in Raw is easy: simply select the Image Quality setting via the LCD menu screen and choose Raw (or Raw+JPEG). In terms of how you use your camera and its controls, that remains pretty much the same. The only difference is that when shooting Raw, you give the image as much exposure as you can without clipping or overexposing the highlights. By doing this you'll record as much shadow detail as possible and better image quality as a result. It does mean that the images in their raw state appear overexposed, but this is easily resolved during Raw file processing, which you'll find a step-by-step tutorial for later in this guide. You'll also note that the number of shots you can fit on your card drops dramatically, so carry spares!

Raw processing software

You need special software to process Raw files. When you buy a digital camera, it comes with a CD-ROM containing the camera maker's own Raw processor; Canon has its own system, so does Nikon etc. However, the majority of photographers prefer to use a third-party Raw processor.

By far the most popular is Adobe Camera Raw, found in all versions of Adobe Photoshop from CS2 onwards, Photoshop Elements since version 3.0 and all versions of Adobe Lightroom. Apple Aperture also has its own Raw converter, while Capture One from Phase One is popular with some photographers. SilkyPix is less known but worth trying the free trial download.

- **Adobe Camera Raw** www.adobe.com/products/photoshop/family/
- **Apple Aperture** www.apple.com/uk
- **Capture One** www.phaseone.com/4/
- **SilkyPix** www.isl.co.jp/SILKYPIX/english/

ADAM BURTON

Raw gives you more!
Ever looked at images and wondered how the photographer captured so much detail in the scene? No doubt shooting in Raw played a big part.

The toolbar

At the top-left corner of the interface are various symbols, each with a use to edit your pictures. CS5 has a few new additions to the CS4 arsenal, which we outline below, but the main tools you'll use for everyday Raw editing are the Zoom, Hand, Rotate and White Balance tools. Others, such as Color Sampler, Crop, Straighten and Retouch tools, work well, but unless you're editing solely in Raw, are best left to Photoshop once the Raw file is processed. Red-eye removal is handy if you need it, but you're unlikely to process many portraits shot in Raw that suffer from red-eye!

1) Zoom Tool: Magnify the image to see it in more detail.

2) Hand Tool: Navigate around the magnified image.

3) White Balance Tool: Allows you to correct and set a custom White Balance by clicking on neutral areas in the preview image, such as white.

4) Color Sampler Tool: Allows you to select a colour to adjust by clicking on that area of the image.

5) Crop Tool: Use to crop images.

6) Straighten Tool: Correct a wonky horizon or rotate.

7) Retouch Tool: Gets rid of sensor spots and other unwanted blemishes.

8) Red-Eye Removal Tool: Click on the eye to remove red-eye.

9) Preferences: Click here to access the Camera Raw Preferences dialogue box.

10) Rotate counterclockwise & Rotate clockwise tools: Rotate anti-clockwise or clockwise by 90°.

11) Targeted Adjustment Tool: Instead of using the sliders, drag this tool on the image to make edits (CS5).

12) Adjustment Brush: Use this tool to make localised edits to the image (CS5).

13) Graduated Filter: Draw a line across your image to recreate the effect of a Graduated Filter. You can then adjust the Exposure, Brightness, Contrast, Saturation, Clarity, Sharpness and Color of the filter to suit your picture (CS5).

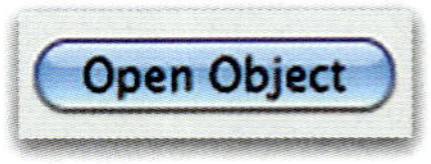

Open object

Once you've done all your necessary Raw editing, press ***Shift*** to turn the ***Open*** button to ***Open Object*** to process your Raw file in Photoshop as a Smart Object. The benefit of a Smart Object is that you can double-click on the layer in Photoshop to reopen the Raw file and continue any Raw edits in ACR. Alternatively, hold down ***Alt*** to turn the ***Open*** button to ***Open Copy*** (so you don't work on the original Raw file in Photoshop) and the ***Cancel*** button to ***Reset*** to revert your image back to its original state.

Understand your Raw converter

To go from an original Raw file to a final image, 'process' it using a Raw converter like Adobe Camera Raw

ANY TECHNICAL process seems complicated and daunting when you try it for the first time. Remember taking your first digital photograph or 'Photoshopping' your first image? Chances are you didn't have a clue what you were doing, but through trial and error and making lots of mistakes, you got there in the end. It's the same with processing your Raw files in software like Adobe Camera Raw.

The main reason why photographers stick to shooting in JPEG is because it's quick, easy and safe: the camera does the complicated stuff and all you're left with are a few tweaks in Photoshop or Lightroom to finish the job off.

Shooting in Raw, on the other hand, involves another steep learning curve because every shot you take needs to be worked on. It's the digital equivalent of going from taking your films to a high-street lab for processing and printing, to setting up a darkroom and doing the job yourself. Do you think it's really worth all the hassle?

In a word, yes! To realise your full potential as a photographer, you need to take control of your photography and the only way to really do this is to shoot and process Raw files. Over the next few pages, we'll give you a rundown of the main controls and tools available in Photoshop's Raw converter – Adobe Camera Raw – with an explanation of what they do and how to use them, starting with the Basics tab which features everything you need for a simple conversion.

The basic tools for Raw conversion

Most of Adobe's Raw controls are adjusted via sliders, making them fast and easy to use. Here are the key features located under the Basics tab:

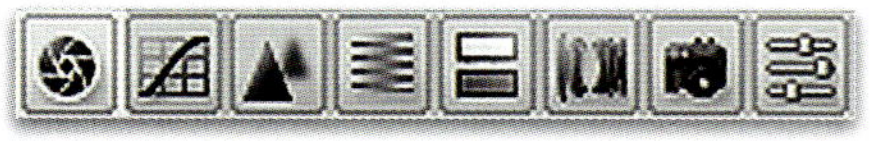

Adjustment panels: The main controls you're going to use when processing Raw files are to be found on the right side of the Raw Interface, between the histogram and the control sliders. There are eight icons covering the following set of options (from left to right): Basic, Tone Curve, Detail, HSL/Grayscale, Split Toning, Lens Corrections, Camera Calibrations and Presets.

Vibrance and Saturation: This tool is an alternative to the Saturation slider, which adjusts all the colours in an image equally. The Vibrance Tool, on the other hand, affects colours that need boosting, having less effect on the colours already high in saturation.

Blacks: This slider shifts the left part of the histogram even more to the left, making the blacks in the image a lot more dominant, and is a useful way of increasing the overall contrast.

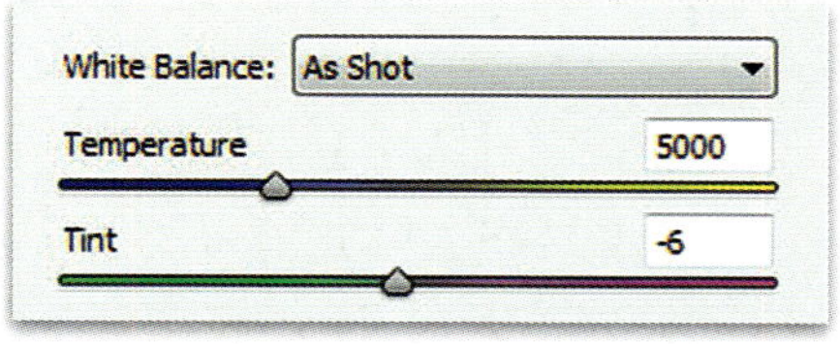

White Balance: Shooting in Raw means that you can control the White Balance in post-production, rather than having to select the right White Balance preset in-camera. Under the Basics tab, you have all the in-camera WB presets available in a drop-down menu to pick from (eg Auto, Daylight, Cloudy etc). You can also use the Temperature and Tint sliders to create your own Custom WB. Alternatively, you could use the White Balance Tool, found in the toolbar.

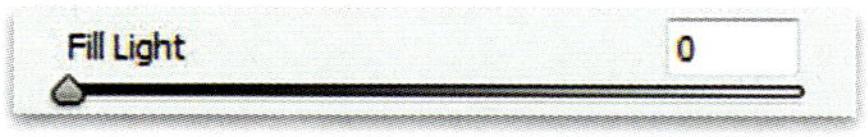

Fill Light: Fill Light attempts to recover details from shadows without brightening any blacks. Similar to using fill-in flash, this tool will cast some light into your foreground. Use it alongside the Blacks slider to add more punch, but be really careful not to overdo it for unnatural results.

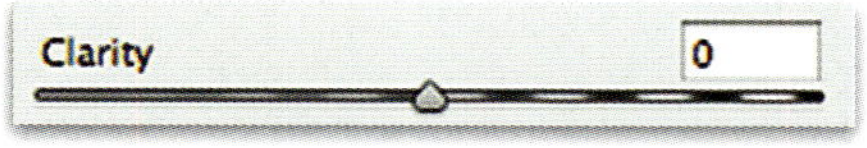

Clarity: Adds depth to an image by increasing local contrast, with the greatest effect on the mid-tones. It works similar to a large radius Unsharp Mask in Photoshop. Zoom into the image 100% to see the effects and stop when you start to see halos appear near the edges in the image.

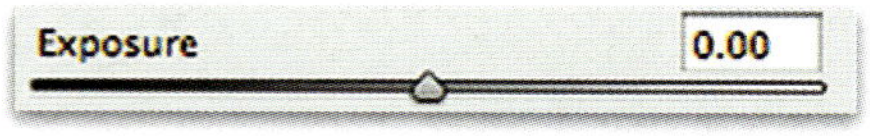

Exposure: Found at the top of the Basics tab, under White Balance, the Exposure slider adjusts the overall brightness of the image, with greater focus on the highlights. The values are in increments equivalent to f/stops. For many photographers, this tool is their saving grace as it allows them to correct their in-camera exposure. Watch out for noise and artefacts creeping in when you push the exposure too far. Use in conjunction with Recovery to reduce the highlight values.

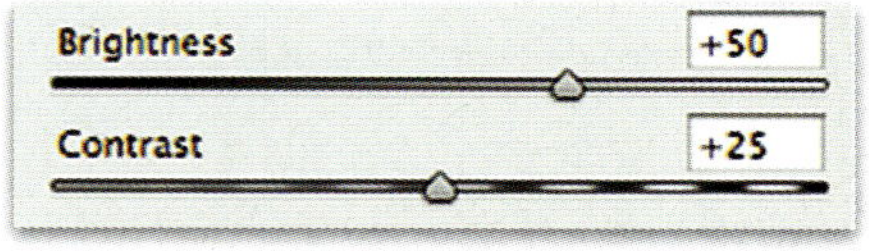

Brightness/Contrast: Brightness works in a similar way to Exposure. However, instead of clipping the highlights and shadows, it compresses and expands the information. Set the overall tonal range first using the Exposure, Recovery and Blacks sliders, then adjust Brightness. The Contrast slider mainly affects mid-tones, causing them to brighten or darken to increase contrast.

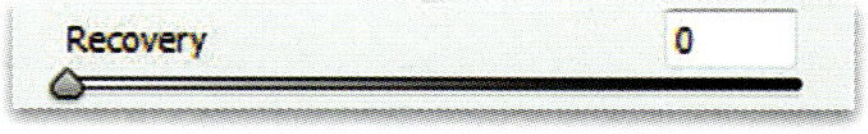

Recovery: This is an image saver for anyone who has slightly overexposed their highlights. This nifty tool should obviously not be relied upon, but is definitely one of the most invaluable features in ACR as it can recover mid-tone detail from clipped highlights. It's not a miracle worker, though: the detail has to be there to begin with.

Raw interface

When you open a Raw file in Adobe Camera Raw, you're presented with this interface. The preview image shows the Raw image in its original state.

14) Zoom: You can vary the size of the preview image and also zoom into it using the tabs in the bottom left-hand corner of the interface.

15) Workflow Option: At the bottom of the screen is the Workflow Option. If you click on this, a dialogue box opens, giving you various options. For ***Space*** (colour space), ***Adobe RGB (1998)*** is most widely used. For ***Depth***, choose ***16 Bits/Channel***. For ***Size***, go for the one that matches the pixel resolution of your camera (no point paying for those megapixels then not using them!). And for ***Resolution***, enter ***300 pixels/inch.***

16) Histogram: In the top right-hand corner is the image's histogram, which shows the distribution of tones in the Red, Green and Blue channels. Where you see Cyan, it indicates a crossover between the green and blue channels, Yellow is the crossover between the red and green channels, and Magenta is a cross between red and blue channels. White shows where all three channels cross over. Use the histogram to judge the exposure as you adjust the sliders.

17) Clipping warning: The two triangular tabs in the top left and right of the histogram tell you if there has been any clipping of the highlights or shadows. If the triangles are black, no clipping has occurred. If the tabs change colour, the colour tells you that a colour channel or a combination of channels have been clipped. If the triangle is white, all three channels are clipped. If you click on the tabs, areas in the preview images will be highlighted to show where clipping has occurred – clipped shadows show as flashing blue and clipped highlights as flashing red.

How to process a Raw file

Get the most from every image by processing in Adobe Camera Raw

Luke Marsh: The best thing about shooting in Raw is that you can process the file to give a far better result than if you had captured the scene as a JPEG. The preview of a Raw file on your camera's LCD monitor may look identical to a JPEG as all the additional information is hidden within the file, and it's impossible to display on your camera's screen. It's only when you open the Raw file on your computer that you'll see the wonders retained in this purest of image file formats. Our guide shows how processing Raw files in Photoshop's Adobe Camera Raw allows you to extract an amazing amount of information, leading to a far superior result than if it had been captured in JPEG.

1 Open the file The first thing we do when we open our Raw file is to see how the histogram looks with the default Camera Raw settings. We can see here that contrast is fairly low with the bulk of the information for this image sitting in the middle. The image looks quite muted and would benefit from extra contrast to add colour and detail.

2 Assess the highlights First check if there's any highlight detail that might be clipped by clicking on the triangle on the top right of the histogram to turn on the highlight clipping display. When active, any clipped areas flash red. The whites of the distant lighthouse here are clipped, which means we might potentially lose some highlight detail.

3 Rescue the highlights You can recover this highlight information using the Recovery slider, but this would be at the expense of highlights elsewhere, which would effectively reduce contrast. The small amount of clipped information isn't that important, so we decide to leave things be. Exposure looks spot on so we don't need to adjust this slider either.

4 Boost the blacks The image probably looks a little flat straight from the camera, like this one does. Adjust the blacks until the histogram spreads towards the far left side by holding down ***Alt/Option*** and moving the ***Blacks*** slider until areas show up black on the white background. You've now created the pure blacks in your image, but be careful not to overdo it.

5 Watch for clipping You'd normally look to avoid clipping any highlights or shadows, but sometimes it's necessary in order to strengthen the dark tones and improve contrast. For instance, here we wouldn't expect to see detail in the rock face cracks. We also set Contrast to +60 to boost contrast further without clipping too much more shadow detail.

6 Boost the colour Now adjust the ***Vibrance*** slider (here we set it to 30), or the ***Saturation*** slider if your software doesn't feature Vibrance, to pump up the colour a little. Press ***I*** to access the ***White Balance Tool*** and check that you have got the correct White Balance by clicking on a neutral white or grey area – the lighthouse is good here.

Final image

It's clear to see the benefits of shooting your images in Raw, as it's possible to extract far more detail than if you had taken the shot as a JPEG.

7 Adjust the White Balance If you're not happy with the image's colour tone (White Balance), adjust the ***Temperature*** slider a little. You can strengthen contrast further if you feel it's necessary by clicking from the ***Basic*** tab to the ***Tone Curve*** tab. Select ***Point*** rather than ***Parametric*** and change the drop-down menu from ***Medium*** to ***Strong Contrast***.

8 Add impact To emphasise areas of colour in the image – in this case the sky and sea – make selective Saturation and Luminance adjustment. Choose the ***HSL/Grayscale*** tab, select ***Saturation*** first and tweak the relevant sliders (we set Blues to +40). Then choose the ***Luminance*** and do the same thing (we set Blues to +40 here, too) until you've reached your level of impact.

9 Sharpen the image Next, negotiate the ***Detail*** tab and use the ***Zoom*** buttons to zoom in ***100%***. Work with the ***Sharpness*** slider to get the image looking crisp on screen. We settle on Amount 100, Radius 1.0 and Detail 30. Sharpening too excessively can cause artefacts and noise to appear, which is why it's important to take pictures at the lowest ISO rating possible.

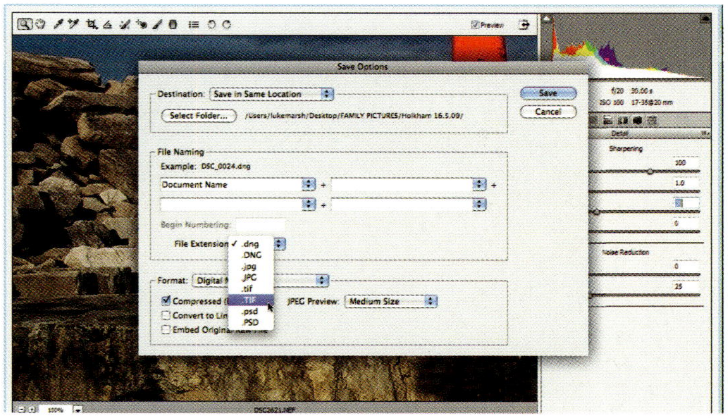

10 Save and open Once you're finished, you can either open the image to continue enhancements in Photoshop or save it for later. By saving the image as a .TIFF or .PSD format you will leave yourself with a 16-bit file as opposed to compressing the image to an 8-bit JPEG, which reduces the amount of information and thus flexibility when editing in the future.

Combining Raw files

Get the perfect image by merging two shots for ultimate quality

Luke Marsh: Setting your camera to shoot in Raw means you're able to recover hidden detail from areas of a scene that are over- or underexposed. The Raw converter in Photoshop Elements, used here, works in much the same way as CS. You need to create two separate images of different exposures from the same Raw file – one for the sky and the other for the foreground – then combine them for the perfect result. Not only will we show how to adjust exposure post-capture, you'll also find out how to use the High Pass filter for sharpening and how to make colour adjustments. This technique is especially efficient as you are only working with image data captured in a single exposure, so you can revisit any of your old Raw files to try it.

1 Open the file When you open a Raw file in Elements the image appears in the Raw control window (above). As the foreground in the original Raw file is well exposed, little work is needed at this stage on the image. Simply click ***Open***, leaving the settings as they are, then go to ***File>Save As*** and create a Photoshop file (.PSD) as we are going to be working with layers.

2 Repeat Reopen the original Raw file, and again the Raw control window appears with the image. This time move the ***Exposure*** slider (circled) left to underexpose the image, pulling back the hidden detail from the original Raw file's overexposed sky. When you're happy with the results, click ***Open*** to take the image into Elements.

3 Copy & paste You now have two files open. One contains the original exposure and the other is the new underexposed image. With the underexposed file active, click ***Select>All*** then ***Edit>Copy***, placing the image into the pasteboard memory. Now you can close this file and use ***Edit>Paste*** to place this image into a new layer on the original file.

4 Remove foreground With the two exposures in place, we now want to combine the correctly exposed foreground with the newly exposed sky. With the sky layer active and using the ***Rectangular Marquee Tool***, select a large area of foreground, just short of the horizon. Next, click ***Edit>Delete*** to remove the area, noting the effect in the Layers palette preview (inset).

5 Clean up Now it's time to tidy up the horizon, so with the ***Eraser Tool*** set to a medium-sized, soft-edged brush and the ***Opacity*** set to around ***55%***, gradually erase areas of the newly exposed layer along the horizon, revealing the original foreground image. The slight feathering between the two layers creates a misty effect that enhances the image's mood.

6 Enhance The initial layer work is complete, so to save your work so far, go to ***Layer>Flatten Image*** then ***File>Save As*** to create a new file. With both layers merged, it's time for some overall enhancement, so click on ***Enhance>Adjust Lighting>Levels*** to lighten up the image and improve the definition. Click ***OK*** to apply the changes.

Final image

Stormy skies overhead! It's clear to see the benefits of shooting your images in Raw, as it's possible to rescue more detail than if you'd captured the scene as a JPEG.

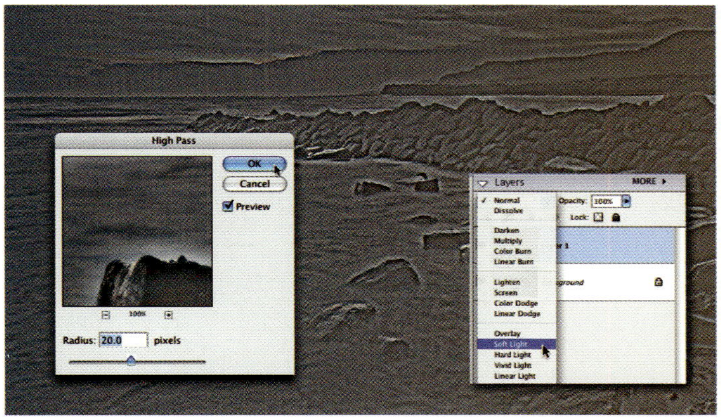

7 High Pass The High Pass filter is a far more forgiving way to enhance detail than sharpening. To use it, first go to ***Layer>Duplicate Layer*** to preserve the original image. Then go to ***Filter>Other>High Pass***, adjusting the ***Radius*** to around ***20*** pixels before clicking ***OK***. Now you need to change the ***Blend Mode*** in the Layers palette to ***Soft Light***.

8 Darken areas Use ***Layer>Flatten Image*** again, saving a copy if required. Now, using the ***Burn Tool*** (inset) with a large soft-edged brush and the ***Opacity*** set to approximately ***25%***, darken the exposure of specific areas, which helps to improve the depth of the image. Focus on the edges of the frame and gradually build the effect up.

9 Select sky The image is predominantly blue in hue and we'd quite like to inject a different tone to the sky area. Using the ***Rectangular Marquee Tool***, select the area above the horizon and go ***Select>Feather***, entering an amount of ***50*** pixels to soften the selection, before clicking ***Edit>Copy*** then ***Edit>Paste***, placing the selection into a new layer.

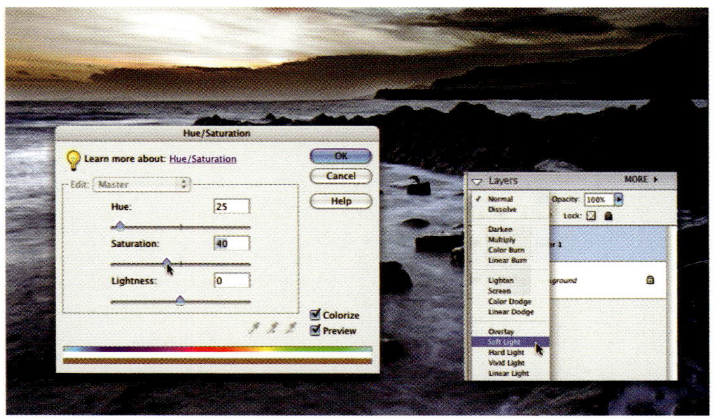

10 Adjust colour Change the ***Blend Mode*** of the new layer to ***Soft Light***, and then go to ***Enhance>Adjust Colour>Adjust Hue/Saturation***. In the window, start by clicking the ***Colorize*** box and immediately see the effect in the preview. Finally, adjust the ***Hue*** and ***Saturation*** sliders until you are happy with the colour, and then click ***OK***.

'Exposing to the right' with Raw

Understand how your camera records tonal information and how to read a Raw histogram

TO MAKE THE MOST of a Raw file, you need to learn to use your camera's histogram. Using the preview image to judge exposure, isn't the best reference. A histogram, on the other hand, provides all the information you need to create the ultimate Raw file. It shows the distribution of tones in a digital image, from the darkest shadows on the far left of the histogram to the brightest highlights on the far right. The general rule when exposing an image is to make sure tones fall within the extremes of the histogram to retain detail. If too much information is to the far left, some shadows lack detail, and if it's to the far right, some highlights may blow out and record as pure white. Making sure neither extremes are clipped gives an acceptable Raw file. To record maximum tonal detail, however, you need to 'expose to the right'. Why? Because sensors record more tones in the highlights than the shadows.

Most sensors record a brightness range of five or six stops. Most histograms are divided into five sections, which represent the five stops in brightness it records. Rather than the tonal values being divided equally across those five stops, 50% of the total number are recorded in the brightest stop, half this number in the next, half as many again in the next stop, and so on, meaning that the brightest 20% of the histogram, on the far right, contains 16 times more tonal values than the darkest 20% on the far left. By 'exposing to the right', you're maximising the information recorded. When you check the preview screen, images exposed to the right look overexposed, so your natural reaction is to reduce the exposure and reshoot, but don't – trust the histogram! You can then adjust the exposure and contrast when processing your shot, retaining the important tonal values and giving a more detailed image with less noise.

1 Watch our for clipping The brightest highlights in the water and sky have been exposed to the point that they've started to lose detail – indicated by the red highlights. The image looks generally washed out.

2 Recover highlights Although you should try to avoid clipping the highlights, you can use the Recovery slider to rescue them – but no more than about 20% should be applied as it tends to flatten the whole image.

3 Reveal the detail Various controls can be used to tone down the image – Contrast, Brightness, Exposure – but the Tone Curve sliders are most effective. Here, the Dark tone was moved to -39 and it looks better already.

4 Adjust tonality The Highlight slider was moved to the right to a value of +26 and the Lights slider to the left to a value of -14. You can see how the Tone Curve has changed from a straight line to a shallow 'S' shape.

5 Improve the colours Clicking back on the Basic tab, the Blacks slider is moved to the right to a value of 14 from its default setting of 5, while Vibrance is set to +22 and Saturation to +8 to boost the colours in the image.

Increasing the exposure

The easiest way to 'expose to the right' is to take a test frame and then assess the histogram. If the graph is centred (ie well exposed), or to the left, increase the exposure by + 1/3 stop via exposure compensation, take another shot and check the histogram. Repeat until the highlight warning starts to flash on the preview image, indicating that the highlights have been 'clipped' and that you've taken the exposure too far. The frame before, where you gave 1/3-stop less exposure, is the file to work on.

A) This is what the histogram for an underexposed image looks like: the tonal graph is pushed over to the left where there are fewer tonal values. If you took a shot like this and tried to recover detail, you'd have problems with noise.

B) There is nothing wrong technically with this image or histogram: the tonal graph is central and neither highlights or shadows have been clipped. If you saw this shot on the preview screen, you'd probably be happy. However...

C) Exposing to the right will record far more tonal values in the Raw files than correctly exposing it. This is what the preview image will look like if you do: overexposed and washed out. But it's the best Raw file of the three examples!

Final image

After saving the processed Raw file as a 16-bit TIFF, a few final tweaks were made in Photoshop and here's the finished image – rather more impressive than the original Raw file it came from.

FILTERS

Lee Frost reveals the importance of filters for landscape photographers

IMAGINE YOU'RE ABOUT to be shipwrecked on a desert island and the captain of the vessel has given strict instructions that you can only take three filters overboard with you. Okay, so it's a rather extreme scenario, but – hey – worse things have happened at sea! The question is, which three would you take?

As a child of the Cokin era, I managed to amass more filters than your average camera shop. I had bits of plastic (okay, okay, C39 resin) that could add fake rainbows to my images, ruin a perfectly nice sky by turning it tobacco, reduce attractive scenes to impressionistic smudges, turn bright points of light into brilliant explosions of colour, and perform all sorts of other weird and wonderful tricks. I never used the things, of course, because most of the effects were horrible. But you weren't a proper photographer unless you carried at least a dozen of them everywhere, and if the worst came to the worst, they were ideal for making a sow's ear from a silk purse. I've got hundred of examples to prove it.

Fortunately, after numerous failed attempts I managed to kick my Cokin addiction, so out went all the filters that weren't essential – which actually left very few. Later still, I jumped on the digital bandwagon, which meant I could jettison even more (mainly the colour correction and conversion filters that have been replaced by White Balance and colour temperature adjustments).

Today I'm left with only three filter types: Neutral Density (ND) grads, a polariser and solid Neutral Density (ND) filters. For landscape and general photography, they're all you need, and all three can be used individually or in combination to help you get the most from a scene.

Some of you may be thinking, 'Why bother with filters at all when the effects can be added in Photoshop?' Well, if you're thinking that, chances are you've never used them, because while the effects some filters have can be replicated in Photoshop, others can't. And anyway, even if they could all be, surely it's better to get your photographs as close to completion in-camera as possible, rather than spending ages at your computer trying to sort them out in post-production?

For information on filter systems, take a look at the panel below, then read on to see the difference my three favourite filters could make to your landscape images.

Which filter system?

Screw-in: These high-quality glass filters screw directly onto the filter thread of your lens, making them fast and easy to use. You'll find numerous polarisers and ND screw-in filters (including B+W's ten-stop ND) but virtually no ND grads. While offering excellent optical quality, screw-in filters have one big disadvantage: if you have numerous lenses, you'll most likely need to buy several sizes of screw-in filters. Brands to consider include B+W, Hoya and Tiffen.

Slot-in: Your best choice when investing in a filter system is the slot-in variety. You buy rings that screw on to your lenses and a single holder that slips on to these rings – this way you only need one filter. Polarisers, NDs and ND grads are all available as slot-in filters. Cokin (P or X-Pro) and Formatt (Hitech) are good first systems, while Lee Filters is the professionals' choice.

Another fine mist

Mystery, drama, atmosphere... using filters in your photography can make your good shots great.

ND graduates

Make bland skies a thing of the past by learning how to use a Neutral Density graduate filter

HOW MANY TIMES have you composed a great shot with a dramatic sky only to discover that when you check the picture you've taken the landscape looks fine, but the sky is overexposed and washed out?

Naive photographers shrug their shoulders and think, 'Oh, I'll rescue that later', which is fine if there's something to rescue. But if the sky's so overexposed that no detail has been recorded, there won't be. More experienced shooters take two photographs of the scene – one exposing for the sky, the other for the landscape – then combine them in Photoshop. This method works well, but does mean more time in front of a computer than a camera. The quickest and easiest solution is to use an ND grad filter.

ND grads are grey on the top half – that's the Neutral Density part – and clear on the bottom half. The idea is that the grey part of the grad tones down the brightness of the sky so that when you expose for the landscape, the sky is also correctly exposed, instead of being completely blown out.

ND grads & exposure

Before multi-zone metering was introduced, exposure readings had to be taken with a light meter and set manually on the camera before attaching an ND grad to the lens in order to avoid getting an overexposed image. Metering systems these days are much more intelligent; now you can compose your shot, align the grad ready for use and meter with it on the lens. The reason for this is that a multi-zone metering pattern takes a number of exposure readings from different parts of the image area, therefore the darkness of the filter doesn't influence the final exposure in a negative way. In fact, it helps your camera obtain an accurate reading, as when an ND grad is fitted, the Neutral Density part of the filter darkens the sky area so that the contrast between the sky and foreground is reduced. Hey presto: a perfectly exposed landscape.

Technique watch!

Choose the right density

To produce a convincing result you need to choose the right density of ND grad. Fortunately, making the right choice isn't difficult as there are only three main densities to choose from: 0.3, 0.6 and 0.9, which reduce the brightness of the sky by one, two and three stops respectively. Some manufacturers also produce a 1.2ND grad, which tones down the sky by four stops. The weakest, 0.3ND, is only of use when you need a very subtle effect, while the stronger 0.9ND is mainly used at dawn and dusk when the sky's really bright but there's no direct light on the landscape. That just leaves the 0.6ND grad, which is the best choice for general use. If in doubt, take a test shot with a 0.6ND grad, check the image on your camera's preview screen, then switch to either a 0.3ND or, more likely, a 0.9ND if the effect isn't right.

Final image

Experienced landscape photographers consider an ND graduate an essential item and not an optional accessory.

ALL IMAGES: LEE FROST

Aligning an ND grad

The key to success with a grad is correct alignment, so it does its job without leaving telltale signs. Many photographers struggle and assume there must be a magic formula, but it's just a case of taking your time.

1 Slide the filter Mount your camera on a tripod and compose the frame. Next, place an ND grad filter in the filter holder on your lens, and while peering through the viewfinder, slowly push the grad down into the holder.

2 Watch carefully As you slide the grad down you should see the top part of the picture appear to get darker. It won't be obvious, even if you're using a strong ND grad, so watch carefully and when you think you've got the ND grad in the right position, stop moving it down.

3 Don't go too far A common mistake is to push the grad too far into the holder. If you do this, the grad will act like a solid ND filter and increase the exposure but it won't balance the difference in light between the sky and foreground. You may also see the line of the grad.

4 Use LiveView If you struggle to align the grad using the viewfinder, try using LiveView. You may find it simpler to do this as you're seeing the exact effect the filter is having on the image, making it easier to accurately align it.

Technique watch!

Hard or soft grads?
There are two types of ND grad: hard and soft. This refers to the way in which the Neutral Density (grey) part of the filter graduates down to clear: with hard grads the change is quite sudden; whereas with soft grads it's gentle. Newcomers to ND grads assume that soft grads are easier to use because if you align them incorrectly it's less likely that you'll see the line of the grad in your picture. However, hard grads are also quite forgiving and give a more defined effect, making them the best choice.

Polariser

A circular polariser will be your best friend, boosting colour impact and reducing reflections

WHEN LIGHT STRIKES a surface, some of the rays scatter in all directions thus becoming polarised, causing reflections and glare that reduce colour saturation – particularly on shiny surfaces such as paintwork and foliage. Polarising filters prevent this from happening by only allowing light rays to enter your lens that are travelling from one direction – effectively blocking out polarised light. Doing this offers three distinct advantages for landscape photography.

The most obvious benefit is that the blue of a sky is deepened because it contains a lot of polarised light. Using a polariser allows you to add visual impact to images by providing a strong, punchy blue backdrop. Another benefit is that glare on non-metallic surfaces is reduced, so the colours in a scene appear richer and more saturated. The third advantage to using polarisers is that reflections are eliminated, so you can see through windows and into rivers.

Using a polariser is easy because you can see the effect it has simply by rotating it slowly in its mount on your lens while looking through the camera's viewfinder. Blue sky goes darker and white clouds stand out, reflections come and go, and glare disappears. When you're happy with what you see, simply stop rotating and fire. To get the best possible results, however, you should also bear in mind certain factors.

Although polarisers generally work best in bright, sunny weather when there's more polarised light around, they can be used in dull, overcast conditions, too, in order to remove glare and reflections. Autumnal woodland scenes usually look much better if you shoot them through a polariser, as glare is reduced, so the rich colours of the foliage really come through.

When using a polariser to deepen blue sky, keep the sun at a right angle to the camera so you're aiming towards the area of sky where maximum polarisation occurs. That way, you'll get the strongest effect. If the sun is behind you, or you're shooting into the sun, a polariser won't make much difference. Polarisation in the sky also tends to be better when the sun is low in the sky – so early morning and evening give better results than in the middle of the day.

Polarisation is uneven across the sky, so take care when using ultra wide-angle lenses or zooms with a focal length wider than 24mm (16mm on APS-C sensors) as the sky in your images may record darker on one side than the other: the effect can look very odd. This can be corrected in Photoshop later, but it's tricky. You should also note that glare will only be removed from non-metallic surfaces such as paintwork, foliage and plastic. To remove reflections from surfaces such as water and glass, the angle between the reflective surface and the lens axis must be around 30°. You can find this by making slight adjustments to your position then rotating the polariser to see what happens.

Finally, polarising filters can give your pictures a slight blue colour cast when used in bright, sunny weather. To remove this, either adjust your camera's White Balance setting or correct the cast when you process the Raw file on your computer.

Technique watch!

Circular or linear?

There are two types of polarising filters available: linear and circular. Avoid linear. You need to use a circular polariser with your digital camera as linear polarisers are used on certain older manual focus film SLRs. Both types do exactly the same job, but a circular polariser is manufactured differently to ensure correct exposure when used with autofocus DSLRs and CSCs.

Polarisers & exposure

When you use a polariser, it reduces the light entering your lens by two stops. This means if you have an exposure of 1/125sec at f/11 without a polarising filter in place, the exposure would drop to 1/30sec at f/11 once you fitted it. Your camera accounts for this light loss automatically, so you don't need to compensate, but you need to be aware of it because the shutter speed can easily become very slow when using a polariser – even in bright sunlight – so the risk of camera shake is increased. That said, this light loss can be a benefit when you want to use a slower shutter speed, as the polariser acts like a two-stop (0.6) ND filter (covered overleaf). When shooting waterfalls, for example, the polariser not only gives you a slower shutter speed to blur the water, but also removes reflections from water and glare from wet rocks and foliage, giving a better result.

ALL IMAGES LEE FROST

Neutral Density (ND) filters

Lengthening exposure times with a Neutral Density filter is one of the simplest ways to be creative with your camera, producing great movement in images

ND FILTERS ARE SPECIALLY made to reduce the amount of light entering your lens without changing the colour balance – hence the name Neutral Density. They do a similar job to ND grad filters, but instead of affecting just part of the image (usually the sky with ND grads), they have a uniform effect on the whole image.

ND filters are mainly used to increase the exposure required for an image, so you can use a slower shutter speed to record motion. The classic subject that they're used for is waterfalls, recording the moving water as a graceful blur. But they can be used to introduce or increase motion in all kinds of subjects – crowds of commuters pouring off a train, traffic moving along busy roads, trees blowing in the wind, waves washing over rocks and so on. They're ideal for use in bright conditions when the lowest ISO rating and smallest aperture aren't enough to give you the slow shutter speed that you desire.

Exposure chart

If you're using weaker ND filters, up to a 1.2 density, your camera's TTL metering will be able to give accurate exposure readings with the filter on the lens. Once density goes beyond 1.2, however, you may find that underexposure occurs because the filter density fools the camera's metering.

To avoid exposure error, take a meter reading without the ND filter on the lens, then calculate the required exposure with it in place and set the exposure on your camera manually. If you have an iPhone, there's a useful app called ND Calc that will do this for you.

Alternatively, refer to the table below. Once the required exposure goes beyond 30 seconds you will have to set your camera to its Bulb (B) mode and time the exposure using the timer on the camera or smartphone, a remote release, your wristwatch or by counting elephants – you decide! We'd recommend that you photocopy and cut out the exposure chart below and keep it along with your ND filter for easy reference.

No filter	With 0.6ND	With 0.9ND	With 1.2ND
1/500sec	1/125sec	1/60sec	1/30sec
1/250sec	1/60sec	1/30sec	1/15sec
1/125sec	1/30sec	1/15sec	1/8sec
1/60sec	1/15sec	1/8sec	1/4sec
1/30sec	1/8sec	1/4sec	1/2sec
1/15sec	1/4sec	1/2sec	One second
1/8sec	1/2sec	One second	Two seconds
1/4sec	One second	Two seconds	Four seconds
1/2sec	Two seconds	Four seconds	Eight seconds
One second	Four seconds	Eight seconds	16 seconds
Two seconds	Eight seconds	16 seconds	32 seconds
Three seconds	16 seconds	32 seconds	One minute
Four seconds	32 seconds	One minute	Two minutes

Technique watch!

Different densities

The amount of exposure increase an ND filter requires depends on its density. The weakest ND worth bothering with is a 0.6ND (4x), which requires a two-stop exposure increase. A polariser also requires an exposure increase of two stops so can be used like a 0.6ND filter. Next up is a 0.9ND (8x), which requires a three-stop exposure increase, followed by a 1.2ND (16x) that requires a four-stop increase. This is where the density of conventional ND filters ends, though you can combine two or more for a cumulative effect – a 0.6ND and a 0.9ND together will require a five-stop exposure increase, for example.

The alternative is to use a more extreme ND filter, with a density of 1.8 (six stops) or more. These filters were originally designed for photographing industrial processes that involved extreme brightness but are now popular with photographers as they allow exposures in daylight of several minutes. Turn over for our favourite: the 3.0ND, which requires an exposure increase of ten stops – that's 1000x more than the unfiltered exposure!

World in motion
Using an ND filter allows you to use longer shutter speeds in daylight: ideal when shooting waterfalls.

Colour casts

While ND filters should be neutral, once you combine them for higher density (and a longer exposure), you'll see that colour casts appear. This is most noticeable with ten-stop ND filters – the B+W 3.0 adds a very warm colour cast while the Lee Big Stopper adds a cool blue cast. These can enhance the look of the image, but if you prefer, you can adjust the colour temperature when you process the Raw file.

Ten-stop ND filters

Use a ten-stop ND filter and you'll find you can create striking colour and black & white fine-art landscapes with ease

THE FIRST THING you'll notice when using a ten-stop ND filter is that it's so dense, you can't see through it. In bright sunlight you might just make out a faint image through the viewfinder, but its brightness is 1000x less than if you didn't have the ten-stop ND in place. To take a photograph you must therefore mount your camera on a tripod, compose the scene, set focus to manual (as AF won't work through it), align your ND grad in its holder if you're using one, then finally position the ten-stop ND. Some of the latest cameras have LiveView that's sensitive enough to see through a ten-stop ND, so if you need to adjust the composition or move the camera and shoot from a different spot, you may be able to do so without taking the ten-stop ND filter off. For most of us, though, removing the filter to see through the viewfinder is unavoidable. That's why a slot-in filter like the Lee Filters Big Stopper or HiTech's Pro Stop is more versatile than the B+W screw-in filter – you can simply remove it from its holder and leave everything else in place, whereas the B+W has to be unscrewed from the lens.

The longest exposure you can achieve using your camera's programmed shutter speed range is 30 seconds. More often than not, you'll be using exposures much longer than that with the ten-stopper, so you'll need to set your camera to Bulb (B) mode in order to keep the shutter open. Trying to keep exposures under 30 seconds for convenience, by opening up the aperture or increasing the ISO rating, is completely defeating the object because you'll get the best effects by using exposures of several minutes.

In terms of subject matter, any scene containing moving elements is ideal. The sky is an obvious candidate: on a windy day, clouds are transformed into ghostly streaks as they drift overhead, and you won't know quite how they're going to record until the exposure ends and you can review the shot. Trees and grass swaying in the breeze also take on a totally different appearance when exposed for several minutes, adding a strong sense of motion to an image.

Coastal scenes are perhaps the most effective subjects for the ten-stop ND. The sea is constantly moving, so over the course of a few minutes, any texture in its surface is lost and it takes on a smooth, milky appearance that contrasts well with static elements such as piers, lighthouses, headlands, jetties and rocks. Clouds work well, too, rendering as streaks in the sky. Or for something completely different, try shooting urban scenes with a ten-stop ND. Anything moving through the scene while the shutter is open – people and traffic mostly – won't record. This means you can capture something that we never see with the naked eye – busy streets completely deserted!

Wide-angle lenses are more effective than telephotos when using a ten-stop ND because you can emphasise the sky and the foreground, which is where most of the motion is recorded. Move in close to a static feature in the foreground and contrast it with moving water, or get down low with a wide lens so you're looking up at the sky.

1/4sec with no filter

Four minutes with a ten-stop ND

Bright sunshine gives the least effective light for ten-stop shots as it's harsh and flat, plus the higher light levels mean you won't be able to achieve really long exposures – even with your lens stopped right down and the ISO rating at its minimum setting. Dawn and dusk, on the other hand, are perfect for creating atmospheric images, along with early morning and evening when the sun's low in the sky and the light is warm. The B+W 3.0 ten-stop ND has a warm colour cast, which is ideal for enhancing shots taken at either end of the day. Stormy weather can produce dramatic results, too, as there's more movement in the sky and sea, while on overcast days the soft light and gentle tones result in simple, graphic images.

Although you'll be shooting in colour, ten-stop shots look amazing in black & white – especially if you're not keen on the filter's inherent colour cast. To maximise the impact and drama, when converting your picture to monochrome, treat the sky and the rest of the scene as separate elements by adjusting their tonality separately, using tools such as Levels and Curves. The end result may look nothing like the original scene, but that doesn't matter because as soon as you put a ten-stop ND filter on your lens, you're taking a step back from reality anyway.

Exposure chart

The chart on the right reveals the increase of exposure times when using a ten-stop ND filter. It's a key reason why you're recommended not to use the Long Exposure Noise Reduction system on your camera, as this function takes the same amount of time as the exposure. For instance, when you shoot a two-minute exposure, you'll need to wait another couple of minutes for the image to write and be viewable on the LCD monitor. We'd suggest you switch Noise Reduction off and control noise in post-production.

Unfiltered	3.0ND (Ten-stop)
1/500sec	Two seconds
1/250sec	**Four seconds**
1/125sec	Eight seconds
1/60sec	**16 seconds**
1/30sec	32 seconds
1/15sec	**One minute**
1/8sec	Two minutes
1/4sec	**Four minutes**
1/2sec	Eight minutes
One second	**16 minutes**
Two seconds	32 minutes
Three seconds	**48 minutes**
Four seconds	One hour

Set the mood

The ten-stop ND is the filter of the moment. Don't leave home without one.

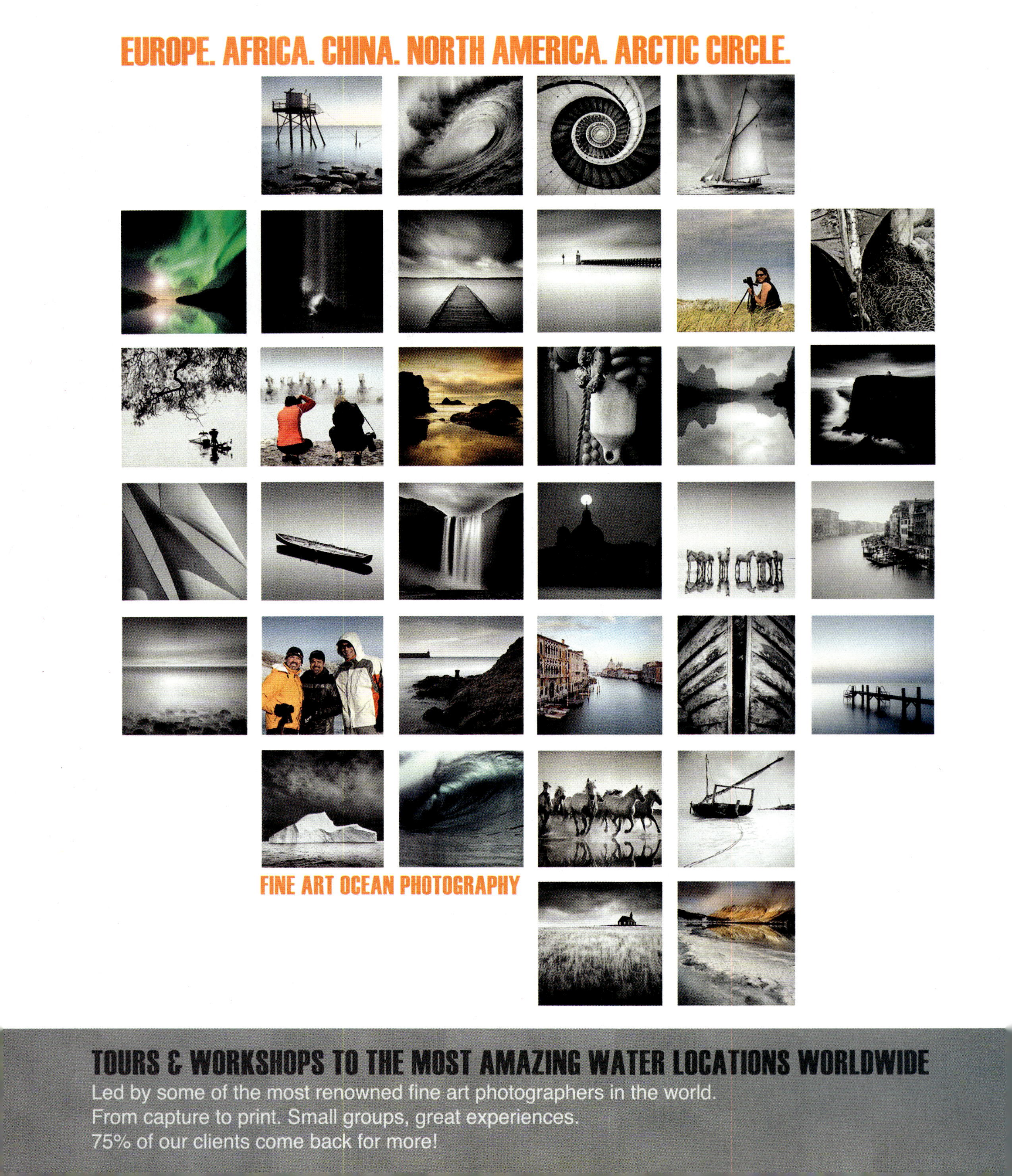
EUROPE. AFRICA. CHINA. NORTH AMERICA. ARCTIC CIRCLE.
FINE ART OCEAN PHOTOGRAPHY
TOURS & WORKSHOPS TO THE MOST AMAZING WATER LOCATIONS WORLDWIDE
Led by some of the most renowned fine art photographers in the world.
From capture to print. Small groups, great experiences.
75% of our clients come back for more!

UNDERSTANDING COLOUR

A LOT OF TIME, energy and thought has been devoted to the study of colour, its practical applications and its psychological effects. Often those applications and effects are linked. It's not an accident that stop signs are red, cool settings on air conditioning are blue or that the environmental movement has adopted the colour green.

Much can be learned about the relationships between colours, too. Colours work together in different ways, with certain combinations creating energy and tension, while others harmonise and create calm. When a colour appears in nature with a greater than normal intensity, the stage is set for great landscape photography. Learning their relationship will reap rewards, helping you to achieve stunning shots that you never before thought possible.

1) Harmony and contrast

There are basically two types of relationship between colours – harmony and contrast. Looking at a colour wheel helps us to understand this. Colours that are next to each other – for example, blue and green – are harmonious, while those that are opposite – for example, blue and yellow – contrast with each other.

Also, colours that are on the 'warm' side of the wheel harmonise with each other, while all those on the 'cool' side also harmonise. Harmonious colours are more calming to look at, and blues and greens in particular are very tranquil. Contrasting colours are more dramatic and create a tension that can challenge the eye – blue and yellow is a strong contrast.

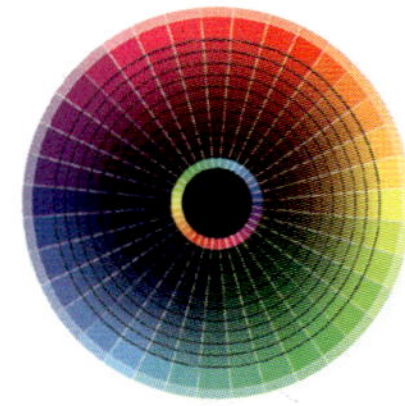

The colour wheel
Contrasting colours, such as yellow and blue or red and green, create tension and drama. Colours adjacent to each other are calming.

ADAM BURTON

ISTOCK PHOTO

CRAIG ROBERTS

MARK BAUER

2) Colour and emotion

As well as having visual impact, colours can suggest different moods, evoke various emotions and can have symbolic significance related to our culture and background. Think about the effect a dominant colour might have on your image. It might be appropriate to subdue a colour, or emphasise it. Consider colour in the composition, the lighting and through careful use of filtration.

R **Red** is an intense colour, especially when contrasted against a dark background. It is a colour universally used for warning or danger and is hard to ignore. Red is the most powerful and attention-grabbing colour in photography, though it can prove distracting if included small within the landscape, for instance, a distant car, boat or letterbox.

B **Blue** is a retiring colour, which can be employed to convey restfulness, sadness or tranquility. In photography, it is commonly used to convey coldness, which works especially well when combined with water and wintry scenes. Blue is a very important colour for landscape photographers as a saturated sky creates a flattering backdrop.

G **Green** is often used to signify health and life. Obviously, green is the predominant colour of vegetation and therefore it is dominant in many scenic images. Green is easily overwhelmed by bright advancing colours like red and, generally speaking, has less impact. However, when isolated, green can still create strong, interesting images.

Y **Yellow** is another bold, advancing colour, often used to represent happiness or brightness. It will add warmth to your image and works particularly well when combined or contrasted with blue. Yellow, along with similarly rich colours, like gold and orange, epitomise autumn. It can prove a good background for still-life images.

ROSS HODDINOTT

3) Using only one colour

Single colours often give an image a particular mood and it's possible to make successful compositions using just one colour – or shades of one colour.

Certain lighting conditions can create this effect and add atmosphere to a scene. An intensely orange or red sunset gives every neutral colour a strong bias, bathing a scene in a fiery warmth.

Also, strong backlighting can desaturate colours, creating an almost monochromatic effect; while at pre-sunrise and post-sunset, there is no single strong light source and the light is diffused and reflected down from the sky.

The two images on the right are really good examples of monochromatic images. Starting over on the far right you can see how backlighting has drained the colours from this scene, resulting in an image that appears almost devoid of colour.

The predawn light bathing the lake and dead wood in the near-right picture is diffused, falling on the scene from virtually the whole sky. It has given the scene a fairly cold cast, but the mood is tranquil. It suits the cold stillness of a winter morning.

Predawn monochrome

Backlit desaturation

ALL IMAGES: MARK BAUER

4) Colour saturation

Okay, if we're going to be strictly technical about this, the term saturation refers to how pure a colour is. But over time, and in practical terms, saturation has come to mean how intense or strong a colour appears in an image. Producing saturated images involves more than simply boosting colours in Photoshop – although much can be done that way, with great results, there are many options at the picture-taking stage. Let's consider those first.

The time of day has an impact on colour saturation. Early-morning and late-evening light, with the sun low in the sky and less glare, produces more intense colours than at other times, as does front lighting rather than side- or backlighting.

A polarising filter, by reducing reflections and cutting down on glare, also improves saturation. A polariser has the maximum effect when the camera is at 90° to the sun. Polarisers are simple to use as the effect is clearly visible through the camera's viewfinder – the most obvious one being the increase in saturation of blue skies.

There are a couple of things to watch out for. It's possible to over-polarise a scene, resulting in near-black skies, and also, when using wide-angle lenses (wider than 28mm on a full-frame DSLR or 17mm on an APS-C sensor), the degree of polarisation can be uneven across the frame.

Of course, you won't always want strong, vibrant, saturated colours. Muted pastel tones are more subtle, but can be just as effective with the right subject matter, creating an atmosphere of calm and tranquility. Early morning mist drains colours and gives a cold, bluish hue to a scene, which you can enhance by tweaking the White Balance in-camera, or later, if you're shooting Raw.

A lot can be done at the processing stage. Experiment with White Balance settings to fine-tune the overall atmosphere and cast. Over the page, we'll show how varying the White Balance of a Raw file can give dramatic results.

Pre-sunrise

Midday

Without polariser

With polariser

Filter choice

Types of polariser

There are two types of polariser: circular and linear. This doesn't refer to the physical shape – they're both actually circular – but the way the light is polarised. Make sure you buy a circular polariser for use with your DSLR as linear types interfere with your camera's metering, which can't handle linearly polarised light.

Using White Balance presets

Learn how to alter the tone of your landscape images by experimenting with different White Balance presets for creative effect

Helen Dixon: Different light sources have different colour temperatures that affect the warmth and coolness of an image's colours: for instance, fluorescent light produces a yellowish cast, while tungsten light is slightly blue. Normally you would set your digital SLR's White Balance to match the lighting conditions in order to eliminate any colour cast, usually most evident in the whites of an image. But while keeping to this rule ensures the whites are actually white, using different White Balance presets on certain types of scenes can give your pictures a deliberate cast that makes them look cooler or warmer for creative effect. It's the digital equivalent of using certain types of film or filters as a way of giving an image more impact.

Auto White Balance (AWB) is the easiest way to maintain a correct White Balance and generally produces acceptable results. However, when you are capturing a particularly warm or cool scene, such as at sunset or twilight, or if your scene is dominated by one colour or hue, AWB can overcompensate, rendering the colours inaccurate and sometimes flat. You're better off taking control over the WB and setting it to match the lighting or setting the WB according to the tone and feel of the shot you want. For instance, setting Cloudy or Shade when the sun's setting or rising can add extra warmth, boosting the oranges and yellows in the sky, while setting Tungsten or Fluorescent WB can make the colours cooler by injecting some blues to the scene.

If you're shooting JPEG, you need to set the White Balance you want to use before you take the shot. For more options, though, we'd strongly recommend shooting Raw + JPEG, setting the correct White Balance and then experimenting with the White Balance afterwards in post-production. The following step-by-step guide will show you how easy it is to do...

Shoot Raw

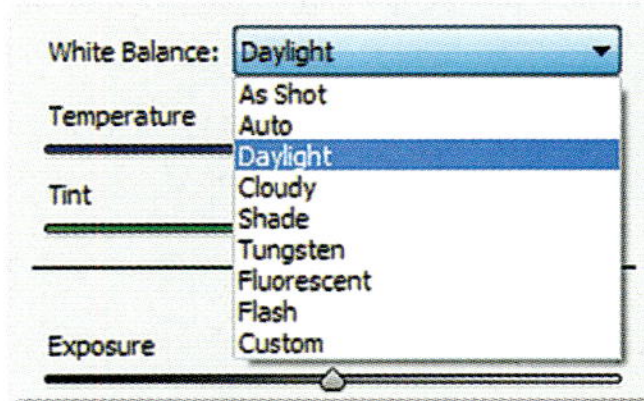

For added flexibility, shoot your images in Raw and adjust the White Balance post-capture in Adobe Camera Raw. Once the image is opened, click on the drop-down menu at the top of the Basic tab and scroll down to select the White Balance preset you'd like to apply to your image. You can change the WB as many times as you want until you find the one you're happy with and even adjust the Temperature slider for more control over a custom WB.

1 Find your location Coastal sunsets or sunrises work well for this type of technique due to their vivid colours. Try to arrive at the location at least half an hour before the golden hour begins. Try out different compositions and look for foreground interest. If you have trouble finding anything, use the wet sand or a rock pool to add a reflection in the scene.

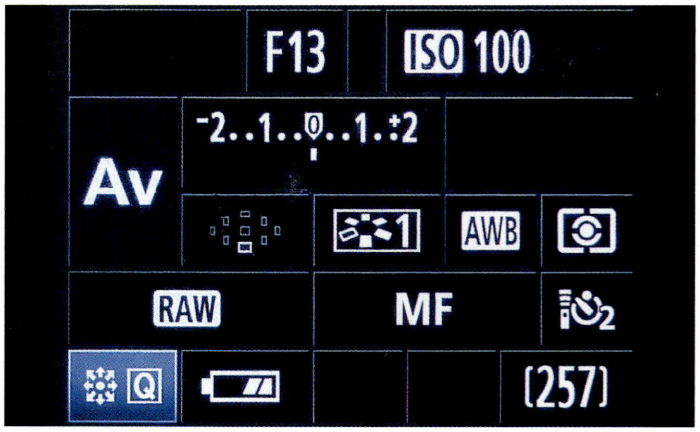

2 Use Auto White Balance Once you've composed your scene, select AWB (see your camera's manual if you're not sure where it is) and set aperture-priority mode to at least f/13 to get adequate depth-of-field. If your autofocus struggles in the low light, switch to manual focus. If you struggle to balance the exposure between the sky and foreground, use an ND grad filter.

3 Try out WB presets As you can see, AWB keeps the colours true to the scene but lacks punch. To warm up colours, I take the same shot using the Daylight, Shade and Cloudy WB presets. The lower the Kelvin (colour temperature), the more saturated the oranges, yellows and reds. Cloudy is the best WB as it boosts the sky's warmth without losing too much coolness.

4 Increase Kelvin As the sun falls just below the horizon, try increasing the Kelvin by setting Tungsten and then Fluorescent WB to enhance the blueness of twilight. To avoid colours looking too unnatural, opt for a WB setting that enhances the blues in the scene but doesn't overpower the whole image. For this scene, Fluorescent is much better than Tungsten (see right).

Fluorescent
Fluorescent WB has rendered the best results, enhancing the deep blue tones and the pinks in the sky.
Exposure: Two seconds at f/13 (ISO 100).

BLACK & WHITE LANDSCAPES

Strip back a scene to its bare essentials by converting to black & white, producing simple, dramatic images that are packed with atmosphere

WHAT'S YOUR OPINION on black & white photography? Do you see it as a fine-art medium that offers endless scope for creative self-expression, or is it irrelevant and old-fashioned? For a long time, the latter view tended to apply, especially once colour film became affordable back in the '70s. Why take photographs in black & white when colour ones are far more realistic? The critics had a point, but fans of the black & white image were quick to point out that it's the very fact they're not realistic that gives them their appeal, and when you study the work of landscape greats such as Michael Kenna, Ansel Adams and Josef Hoflehner, you'll soon see why.

HELEN DIXON

AS WONDERFUL as colour photography is, it can also be too familiar. It shows us what things look like and leaves us feeling reassured and comfortable. But in art, reality isn't always the best solution because it doesn't encourage us to look beyond familiarity and appreciate an image for any reason other than what it depicts. As soon as you remove colour from an image, however, everything changes as it no longer represents reality.

Black & white images are simpler, more dramatic, more evocative and more atmospheric than colour. Our emotional response to a colour landscape image is often rendered superficial by familiarity, but comes from a much deeper place when we take that colour away. Light, shade, texture and shape take centre stage and what's actually in the scene becomes almost irrelevant – it's the impact and effect the image has on you that counts much more.

Digital technology makes black & white landscape photography easier than ever before, mainly because the need for a blacked-out room and smelly chemicals has been removed from the equation without compromising the quality of the final result – now anyone with a digital camera can create amazing black & white images. Putting yourself into the right mind-set to 'see' the landscape in black & white can be tricky, but it's an obstacle that can easily be overcome. By setting your camera to black & white mode and using the LCD screen in LiveView, you can view the scene in front of you in black & white and quickly pick up on which scenes and colours work best in monochrome. Certain colours when rendered black & white look similar grey tones, which can make your shots look flat: learning what colours create contrasting tones will help you recognise what scenes look good in black & white. You can even shoot in both Raw and JPEG – the image

LEE FROST

Above: Misty, blurred water, dramatic looming skies and gritty textures are all great ingredients that add up to an impressive, almost other-worldly, monochrome image.

Right: Don't be afraid to throw the rule book out of the window and include lots of sky in your black & white landscape images. Any interesting cloud formations become the focal point.

The basic rules

Although you don't have to adhere to specific rules when creating black & white landscapes, there are a few worth considering. For example:

- Use foreground interest to add a sense of depth and scale when shooting with a wide-angle lens.
- Look for lines that can carry the eye into the scene – walls, fences, rivers, streams, paths, shadows and other natural or man-made features can be used.
- Use hyperfocal focusing to maximise depth-of-field so you can record the scene with front-to-back focus without having to stop your lens right down to its minimum aperture.
- Use the rule-of-thirds to position the scene's focal point – the top-right third is usually the best place for it. You can also divide the scene into thirds – two-thirds sky and one-third foreground, or vice versa.

Filters for black & white

When you convert an image to black & white, some colours come out as similar grey tones. The solution is to use filters to change the way colours translate to grey and also control contrast. Film photographers did/do this by placing optical filters on their lens (yellow, orange, red or green for landscapes). These filters work by lightening colours close to them and darkening colours opposite them on the colour wheel, so a red filter lightens reds and other warm colours, but darkens blues and greens, for example. As a digital shooter you don't need to use these optical filters on your lens because you can add their effects when you convert an image to black & white during post-production, using Photoshop, Lightroom, Aperture or plug-ins such as Nik Software's Silver Efex Pro 2.

An alternative option is to use the Monochrome Picture Style in your camera – if you have it – to add filter effects to an image as you take it. Or you could set your camera to Monochrome mode then use optical filters on the lens, though you'll produce better images by shooting in Raw (colour) then converting to black & white later.

Here's a quick rundown of the effect that different black & white filters will have on your image:

- **Yellow** Lightens warm colours and darkens cool colours. Also gives a slight increase in contrast, but the effects are subtle.
- **Orange** Lightens warm colours and darkens cool colours, enhances skies and gives a significant boost to contrast.
- **Red** The most dramatic filter of all – blue sky goes almost black, clouds stand out starkly and contrast is significantly increased. Darkens greens in the landscape and lightens warm colours.
- **Green** Lightens greens and blues while darkening warmer colours. Handy for landscapes as it separates out shades of green.
- **Blue** Not a good choice for landscapes generally as greens and blues go very light so it tends to ruin dramatic skies.

There are certain filters that you can use on your lens when shooting images in colour to convert to black & white later, and they include a polariser, neutral density (ND) grads and ND filters.

Polariser Has a similar effect on the sky to a red filter, darkening blue and making clouds stand out, but it also improves clarity and increases contrast, and all of these effects will be seen in the image when you convert it to black & white.

ND grads Reduces the difference in brightness between sky and land so when you expose for the landscape, the sky is also correct. A 0.6ND grad is fine for general use, but a darker 0.9ND grad is better when the sky is bright or for dramatic effect.

ND filters Allow you to increase the exposure so you can record movement in the landscape. Traditional NDs such as a 0.6, 0.9 and 1.2 are handy for blurring the water in waterfalls, rivers and coastal views, but in recent years, extreme NDs such as the Lee Filters Big Stopper have become popular as they allow you to use exposures of a minute or longer in daylight to capture motion in the landscape.

LEE FROST

"Monochrome landscape photography offers endless scope for creative expression"

you see on your camera's preview screen will be black & white, but you'll also have a colour Raw file on the memory card that you can work on later. The other option is simply to shoot as normal, in colour, then decide later which images you want to convert. Some will work, others won't, but there's no reason why you won't end up with some great pictures. The reality is, most of us like to shoot both colour and black & white rather than one or the other exclusively, and we may chop and change between the two while at the same location, or even decide months later to convert a colour shot to black & white. There's nothing wrong with doing this – all that matters is the end result.

The great thing about mono landscape photography is that it offers endless scope for creative expression and experimentation. You've stripped away reality by removing colour, so after that it doesn't really matter what you do. You can go dark and dramatic even if the original scene wasn't, or soft and gentle, and control the mood of the final image. You can also use filter effects to change the tonal relationship in the image and boost contrast (see panel opposite). Basically, you make your own rules.

Black & white suits all types of landscapes, from grand, sweeping views to small details and everything in between, so no matter where you are you'll find mono inspiration. It's also possible to produce stunning black & white images in situations where colour simply wouldn't work, such as on flat, grey days, so it can offer a creative escape route that you may not have thought of. The images used in this feature should give you a good idea of what we're talking about. Black & white can take your landscape photography to a whole new level – all you have to do is throw caution to the wind and give it a go.

Black & white FAQs

Q Does it matter if I shoot in JPEG then convert my images to black & white, or should I ideally shoot in Raw?

It's always better to shoot in Raw as the Raw file is like a black & white negative – it contains all the information you need but you can interpret that information in different ways to control the mood of the final image. With JPEGs, a lot of that information has already been deleted in-camera so it's a less versatile image format. That said, you can still produce great black & white images from JPEGs!

Q What's the best software for converting images to black & white?

The most popular these days is Nik Software's Silver Efex Pro 2 (www.niksoftware.com). It offers lots of presets that give you great effects at the click of a mouse, allows you to tone your images and add the characteristics of specific black & white films, but it also gives you a high degree of control over the image so you can adjust contrast and exposure in localised areas. Photoshop, Lightroom and Aperture are also excellent options.

Q I want to buy a ten-stop ND filter. Which one would you recommend for black & white images?

There are three main options: the Lee Filters Big Stopper (£150); the B+W 110 3.0 (£125 for 77mm thread); or the Hitech Pro Stop 10 (£75). Based on price, the Hitech is the winner, but based on image quality, the Lee Big Stopper is a better option. In terms of versatility, the Lee and Hitech options are better as the B+W is screwed on and therefore tricky to use with other filters such as ND grads (which you will need to stop the sky from overexposing). All things considered, we'd go for the Lee Filters Big Stopper.

Q I have an infrared-modified DSLR. Can you give me a few tips on using it for black & white landscapes?

Follow these steps for the best results:

- Shoot in full sun and include foliage or grass, which really show off the infrared effect well.
- Include plenty of sky and cloud formations; they look amazing in infrared.
- Watch the exposures – you may need to dial in exposure compensation to get well-exposed images.
- When editing images, create a duplicate layer and add a little diffuse glow to it (***Filters>Distort>Diffuse Glow***) to enhance the infrared effect. Adjust the Opacity slider until you're happy with the effect.

Hueless app

Whether you use it purely to shoot b&w or alongside your DSLR for quick analysis of what a scene looks like in b&w, the Hueless iPhone app is highly recommended. It offers live exposure controls, filters and modes. Buy it at the App Store for £1.49.

HELEN DIXON

WEATHER AND LIGHTING

An immediate benefit of shooting landscapes to convert to black & white is that the quality of light becomes far less important than it does when shooting in colour. You still need good light to create great black & white images, but that light may be found in weather conditions that wouldn't suit colour photography. For example, on a dull, overcast day the landscape appears rather flat and lifeless, colours are muted, and other than shooting small details, your colour options are limited. But the quality of light you get on an overcast day is actually very high. The light is soft and contrast is low, so you don't have to battle with deep shadows or shimmering highlights, and it reveals a huge amount of detail that might be lost with stronger light. This makes it perfect for black & white landscapes. The sky may be rather washed out on overcast days, but you can beef it up later if you like. In fact, the same applies to the whole image. Just think of the original Raw file like a digital negative – it contains all the information and detail you need, but how you interpret it is up to you.

Black & white comes into its own in dark, stormy weather. You really need the sun to break through when shooting in colour, to light up the landscape so it contrasts with the sky.

Above: **With such drama in the cloud formations, this shot calls for a black & white treatment. Note the tonal differences in the light across the landscape.**

Right: **A gritty feel is achieved with the use of an ND grad, making the dark and brooding sky even more moody. So many different tones mean the overall effect works brilliantly in monochrome.**

With black & white, though, you can manage well without the sun and just concentrate on bringing out the brooding nature of the scene, perhaps using a strong ND grad filter to intentionally darken the sky more than it was in reality, or increasing contrast during post-production. Black & white landscape photography is about creating a mood, not recording reality.

Sometimes the light is so monochromatic that if you shoot in colour the images still appear to be black & white. When that happens it's a no-brainer as to what you should do with the image. In dense fog or heavy mist, for example, just about every drop of colour is drained from the landscape. Shooting into the sun can have the same effect, especially if there's water in the scene, because you end up with silver patches of light dancing on the water and any solid elements in the scene are reduced to black silhouettes.

LEE FROST

Of course, don't be misled into thinking that you need grotty weather to produce good black & white landscapes – strong, directional light can work wonders when it comes to bringing out the texture in a scene. For example, if you shoot a beach on a dull day it will appear flat, but when light from a low sun rakes across the sand, you'll see every ripple. This is equally important for black & white photography as colour. In fact, in some ways texture is even more important in black & white images because you don't have colour to fall back on. Therefore, it's still worth venturing out early in the morning and staying out late

Pro tip: Lee Frost

"I love shooting in bad weather, capturing the raw power of the elements. This shot was taken on Alnmouth Beach, close to my home on the Northumberland coast. Dry sand was being whipped up by a strong wind and blown towards the sea. As the sun came out it was as though the surface of the beach was alive – I could feel the sand hitting my legs as I walked. I'd never tried photographing this phenomenon before, but decided to give it a go. I experimented with different shutter speeds in an attempt to capture the ghostly effect of the blowing sand and this one, shot at 1/6sec, proved to be the best. I love the contrast between the light tone of the sand and the dark, angry sky, which I emphasised using an ND grad and also by boosting contrast during post-production."

Canon EOS-1Ds Mk III, EF 24-70mm f/2.8L lens at 24mm, tripod, 0.6ND hard grad filter, 1/6sec at f/22, ISO 50.

HELEN DIXON

Above: Snowy landscapes suit monochrome photography really well, with stark, bare trees almost silhouetted against bright white snow and grey skies.

Lighting app

To find out when the best natural light is going to hit your location, download a neat little augmented-reality smartphone app called Sun Seeker. It uses your phone's camera and GPS to show the projected position of the sun at a given date and time, allowing you to return to the location under optimum lighting conditions. Sun Seeker is available from the Apple App Store for £5.99 or the Google Play store for £3.79.

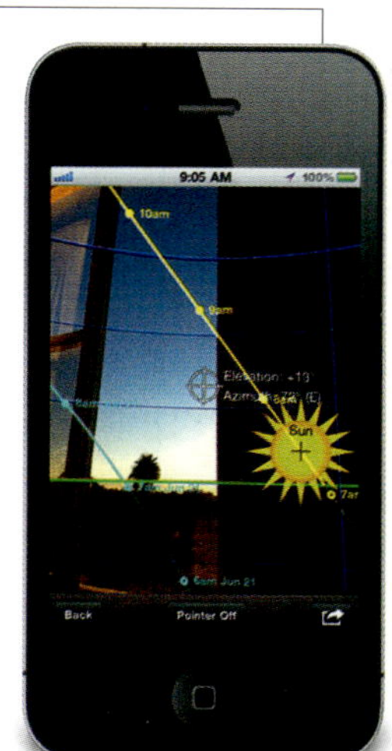

"B&W landscape photography is about creating a mood, not recording reality"

for sundown, so you can take advantage of the low sun raking light and long, weak shadows. Utilising the light from different directions can also pay dividends – shoot with the sun to one side of the camera so shadows are cast across the scene or keep the sun to your back so shadows act as lead-in lines that carry the eye into the scene (taking care not to include your own shadow). Contre-jour photography – shooting into the light – also suits black & white images. Leave the exposure to your camera and any solid shapes will be recorded as stark silhouettes. Alternatively, dial in a couple of stops of exposure compensation to blow out the background and create an atmospheric high-key effect.

When the light is colourful, your gut instinct will be to shoot in colour. At sunrise and sunset, for example, the warmth in the light and the vivid colours in the sky are usually what inspire you to pick up a camera. But don't assume that the same image won't work in black & white. Remove the colour and see what you think. Golden light is fantastic, but it can mask the real beauty of the scene and it's easy to get carried away by colour and ignore the shapes and tones that lie behind it. If you convert a colourful image to black & white, no one will ever know it was colourful anyway, but they will see it in a totally different light.

In a sense, there's a pattern emerging here – namely, when the light's not good for colour it's perfect for black & white, and vice versa. For this reason, you don't have to pigeonhole yourself as one or the other, but simply be a creative photographer who embraces both mediums and switches between the two to make the most of whatever conditions you encounter. Purists may argue that by doing so you're compromised on both counts, but it is possible to embrace both mediums and produce fantastic work.

HELEN DIXON

LEE FROST

Coastlines

For drama, beauty and mood, you can't go wrong with shooting the coast in black & white. It's a scene that constantly changes and evolves thanks to the ebb and flow of the tide and the physical effects of the weather – and it's for that reason that it's earned itself the top location for many a photographer. On first encounter, you might not think to shoot the coast in anything other than colour, but shooting in black & white achieves an atmosphere that colour can't rival. And if you struggle to 'see' in black & white (ie notice the different tones in a scene that lend themselves well to black & white conversion), the coast is the ideal place to begin your monochrome adventures. This is mainly because seascapes are full of tones, contrast, texture and strong shapes; the ideal ingredients for striking mono images. Luckily, many of the thought processes you go through for shooting in colour also apply to shooting in black & white. We'll start with finding your viewpoint.

When capturing the drama of a rocky coastline, find a high view looking down on a bay or inlet and use rocks or boulders in the foreground to add depth and scale to your compositions. The same rules can be applied at sea level, too, where rock slabs extend down to the water's edge and you can use them to lead the eye into the scene, or fill the foreground with sea without getting your feet wet! By shooting in mono and removing the distraction of colour, all emphasis is placed on shape and form – meaning how you compose your image is all-important. You'll find simplicity is often your best bet.

How the sea records depends on how rough it is and the shutter speed you use. If you want to freeze a crashing sea, you'll need to shoot at 1/1000sec or even 1/2000sec. This approach works well if you're using a telezoom lens to fill the frame with pounding waves, or to capture them exploding against the shore and sending spray high into the air. To record motion in the sea, you'll need a slow shutter speed – the slower it is, the softer the sea becomes. Use 1/4sec to one second to record motion in the waves but still retain texture, then gradually slow it down. Once you get to 20 to 30 seconds, waves turn to mist and little texture on the surface of the sea is recorded. To take this idea to the extreme, use a ten-stop ND filter so exposures run into minutes rather than seconds, turning the sea to milk – or wait until light levels are so low that you can achieve exposures of several minutes naturally. Include static elements in the scene to contrast with the soft sea – jetties, rocks, groynes and posts all work well. Converted to black & white, these long-exposure images look sublime.

You can use ripples in the sand to lead the eye, or rock pools reflecting the sky to fill the foreground. Seaweed, driftwood, barnacle-encrusted groynes, old lobster pots, fishing nets, rocks and pebbles found on the beach can also be used as foreground interest.

Above left: Long exposures and ten-stop filters create shots like this. The sea is reduced to a misty blur that gives an air of intrigue.

Above: Rocky outcrops are fantastic for adding a bit of interest. Set a fast shutter to freeze motion in the sea; try 1/1000sec to begin with.

Right: Patterns and ripples in the sea are a blessing for b&w images. Set a long exposure, letting everything appear silhouetted.

Image ideas to try...

HELEN DIXON

■ Receding waves
If you watch waves wash back down to the sea, they often leave streaks of bubbling foam that look amazing in black & white. To capture this effect, use a wide-angle lens and a slow shutter speed – around 1/2sec should be fine. Time your shot to catch the waves receding. A high-contrast b&w conversion will emphasise the effect.

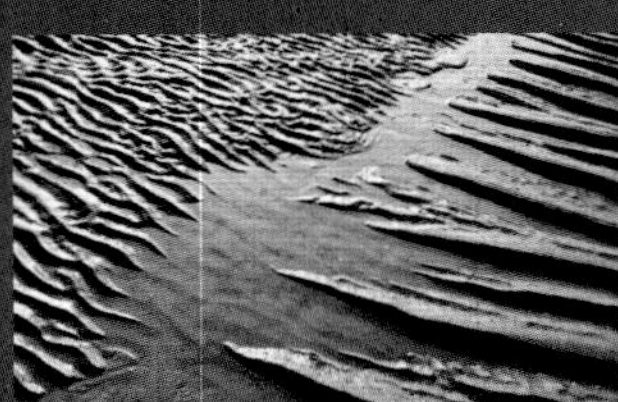
LEE FROST

■ Shooting sand
Ripples in sand are best captured early or late in the day with your camera when the sun is low, or when strong sunlight renders them as silhouettes – use them as lead-in lines in wide-angle shots or fill the frame from close range. Take a closer look in shallow outflow streams, too, where grains of sand are separated to create eye-catching patterns.

LEE FROST

■ Rock art
Rocks are never far away at the coast and offer lots of potential. Pebbles and boulders worn smooth by the sea are ideal for pattern shots, while rocks below the high tide mark are often full of graceful curves and contours. On rock slabs, look for pebbles jammed into cracks and crevices, or move in close to reveal patterns and textures.

HELEN DIXON

■ Piers of the realm
Piers make great seaside subjects. Use them as the focal point in wide-angle views, or as the main element in long-exposure shots that record motion in the sea and sky. Standing under a pier and looking out to sea will reveal the complex pattern of legs, struts and braces. Shoot them in silhouette against the rising or setting sun, or basking under moonlight.

LEE FROST

"Shooting in black & white achieves an atmosphere that colour can't rival"

Set your tripod low to make the most of these elements, use an ND grad to tone down the sky and set your lens to f/11 or f/16 so you have enough depth-of-field to achieve front-to-back sharpness.

Coastal views often need a focal point to round off the composition. This could be anything: a castle or headland in the distance; a person; a boat; a lighthouse or an offshore island. And ideally place the focal point on the top right third to help you achieve a more balanced result for your image.

A final point about light and weather: they have a massive influence on the mood of your black & white coastal images. The great thing about shooting in b&w is that it doesn't matter how bad the weather gets, especially if you're using a ten-stop ND filter. In fact, it's true to say that the worse the weather is, the better your monochrome images because you can never have too much drama when you're shooting the sea! Dawn is a great time for atmospheric light. If the tide has been receding through the night, you'll also have the advantage of beaches being devoid of footprints and delicate sand ripples will still be fresh and wet. Standing water on the sand can reveal beautiful reflections, too.

Pro tip: Ross Hoddinott

"I love b&w photography. However, 'seeing' in b&w comes easier to some than others and I must admit I'm not a guy who naturally 'sees' in mono. But over time, I've taught myself what to look for – and the coast is one of the best places to do so. Simplicity is important. Removing colour places emphasis on shape and form, and composition and light. Often an 'active' sky helps – one with interesting cloud and drama. But failing that, use bold features and foreground interest – large, smooth boulders, piers, lighthouses and weathered groynes. Weather is key. Bad weather suits b&w, as it conveys mood and atmosphere. I also love the effect created by using extreme ND filters. Personally, I use a Lee Filters Big Stopper. With the filter attached, exposures of a minute or longer are possible, reducing the sea to an ethereal blur."

Nikon D800, 17-35mm f/2.8 lens, tripod, Lee Filters Big Stopper, 91 seconds at f/11, ISO 200.

HELEN DIXON

Above: When you're presented with a scene, try to think what it might be like converted to black & white – if there are lots of different tones, as with this shot, it should work particularly well.

Above right: Shadows and highlights are the making of a good mono image, along with a cracking composition. This is a perfect example of how all three combine for a lovely b&w shot.

Landscapes

Landscape photography has always been perceived as an easy option – head into the countryside, find an attractive scene, set up your camera and fire away. Mother Nature's done all the hard work, all you're doing is recording it. Right?

If it were that easy we'd all be master landscape photographers. Clearly there's much more to it. Composition is the Holy Grail of photography. A well-composed landscape shot in average light will always beat a badly composed landscape taken in great light, especially when the final image is monochrome. Why? Because without a strong foundation, creativity crumbles – and composition is the foundation of every photograph we take.

Fortunately, composition isn't rocket science. Common sense, consideration and concentration, that's the crux of it. All you have to do is decide which bits you want to capture and how you're going to arrange it all in your camera's viewfinder.

Although telephoto and telezoom lenses have their place in landscape photography, wide-angle lenses win hands down for 'wow' factor. They give us a view of the world that the naked eye simply can't match. They bend, stretch and distort the truth, and the wider you go, the better it gets. Slight changes of viewpoint also make a huge difference to the impact of elements, while the extensive depth-of-field you get at small apertures such as f/16 and f/22 also guarantees front-to-back sharpness in your shot.

Using a wide-angle lens to exploit foreground interest also helps to make an image look three-dimensional, because as well as providing a logical entry point into the image, it also helps to add a sense of depth and scale. If that rock filling the foreground looks bigger than the cottage in the distance, say, the cottage must be far away, hence distance and depth are implied and a three-dimensional feel is achieved.

To make the most of foreground interest, get close and low. Shooting from eye level is fine, of course, but when the camera is six foot off the ground, interesting elements at your feet lose impact. Kneel down and get in close, however, and that humble mossy rock becomes a giant boulder that dominates the composition and you've bagged a dramatic shot simply by bending your knees.

Lines are another powerful compositional device. Paths, tracks, roads, railway lines, fences, walls and avenues of trees all make great man-made lines. Rivers and streams are ideal natural lines. Diagonal lines work best if they travel from the bottom left of the frame to top right, because that's the natural way the eye looks at a photo. Converging lines are even better. Stand in the middle of a road and look along it through a wide-angle lens. The effect of the parallel sides converging into the distance is dizzying and arresting. Including the vanishing point, where those lines appear to meet on the horizon, brings the composition to a satisfying conclusion. Lines don't have to be straight – the meander of a stream as it travels away from the camera is visually more interesting than a straight line.

Be aware of colours as you're composing and how they might relate when converted to grey tones – what looks great in colour may look flat post-conversion. Conversely, a scene that looks naff to the naked eye could make a fantastic monochrome image.

Confidence has a lot to do with success when it comes to taking cracking black & white landscapes. Digital photographers have a mortal fear of black & white because it's usually an indicator of blocked shadows and

Pro tip: Helen Dixon

"Some of my favourite monochrome images are so simple; often just a lone tree and big sky, like this one that I spotted while driving in the country. I walked around the field to find the best view, looking to incorporate the fence to add interest. The clouds added texture, form and helped the tonal range. Usually I'd opt for my wide-angle lens, but as the field was inaccessible I had to use a telephoto, which kept the shot uncluttered. The Raw image was processed in colour and then I applied a Black & White adjustment layer in Photoshop to adjust the tones. Finally, I used Curves to bring out the contrast and make it punchier."

Canon EOS-1Ds Mk III, EF 70-200mm f/4L lens, 1/20sec at f/13, ISO 200.

Shooting at high ISO

We constantly bang on about keeping your ISO rating low when shooting landscapes to minimise noise, but when it comes to black & white, a bit of noise can be a benefit. Noise on colour images tends to look naff, but once you convert that image to black & white it looks much like film grain, and the stark, gritty feel can look fantastic. Simple images suit the treatment – mist and fog, seascapes, shots taken on overcast days. You need plain areas of tones to really see the noise/grain, so avoid shooting cluttered compositions at high ISO. How high you go depends on how old your DSLR is. The latest DSLRs handle noise so well that even at ISO 3200 you'll get smooth images, and if you want to really go for it you'll need to shoot at ISO 6400 or beyond. With older models, you may see lots of noise at ISO 1600 or 3200. Just experiment. If you find the image looks flat in black & white – high ISO images often do – boost contrast by adjusting Levels or Curves in Photoshop.

LEE FROST

LEE FROST

Right: Meandering lead-in lines are brilliant for providing a fantastic composition, leading the eye on a journey through the image and treating the viewer to a certain amount of intrigue.

Far right: Shooting in black & white requires you to think differently about your picture-taking. Often your image will be above you, so look up – here the clouds form a frame for the church.

LEE FROST

LEE FROST

blown highlights. But you need true blacks and whites in mono images, otherwise all you're left with are various shades of grey and that's just boring!

You have to be bold – don't be afraid to boost contrast, to darken that sky, to make localised adjustments to contrast and exposure (just as they did in darkroom days) by dodging and burning. Remember, you're no longer dealing with reality, so the rule book goes out of the window!

Image ideas to try...

LEE FROST

My home town
We tend to associate the countryside with landscape photography, but the urban landscape is just as interesting – and often far more accessible. Set yourself a project to shoot a series of black & white images of your home town – not just big views, but details that capture its character. You may discover places you didn't know existed.

LEE FROST

Sky high
When we shoot landscapes, the sky usually plays second fiddle to the foreground, but in some situations the sky will be much more interesting than the scene itself. Don't be afraid to tilt your camera up and make a feature of it – dramatic cloud formations look amazing when shot with a wide-angle lens and very often will create incredible pictures.

LEE FROST

Minimalist images
Black & white is a minimal medium so use that to your advantage when selecting scenes. Go for simple, stark compositions such as trees against the sky or reflecting in calm water. The winter landscape lends itself to this treatment, especially when covered in a blanket of snow. Dull days do, too, as they provide a plain, featureless backdrop.

LEE FROST

Moving water
Waterfalls, rivers and streams are a favourite subject among landscape photographers and make great b&w subjects. They're also best shot in dull weather, when the light's soft, so if the weather worsens, find yourself some moving water. To achieve an attractive blurry effect, experiment with shutter speeds from 1/4sec to several seconds.

Convert a Raw file to mono

Stripping a landscape image of colour can give pictures impact and mood. Learn how to create bold mono images from your Raw files

Jordan Butters: The origins of photography are rooted in black & white, but despite the arrival of colour film, and after that the dawn of the digital age, black & white photography still remains a firm favourite of many photographers. Back in the days of film, photographers would have to use dedicated monochrome film combined with colour filters to alter the tonal range of specific colours. Thankfully, when dealing with digital the process is a lot easier and the colour filtration can be done at the post-processing stage. While colour images can use bold, vibrant hues to attract the viewer's attention, black & white photographs rely solely on the core aspects of photography – composition, exposure, lighting and perspective. Monochrome images have an artistic elegance about them, but not every image suits the conversion. It works best with images that have a good tonal range from dark to light – images comprising a lot of mid-tones will end up looking flat and dull when converted to monochrome. You should look to include textures, lead-in lines and interesting shapes in your image. Moody skies and looming clouds work great in black & white, too.

Converting to black & white in Adobe Camera Raw is ideal as Raw files contain more information than compressed JPEGs or TIFFs. However, if you don't have access to ACR or your image is saved as a compressed file, you can get very similar results using a Black & White adjustment layer in Photoshop. While removing colour is as simple as pressing a button, to get the best from your black & white images, the process is more involved. With a bit of time and effort, however, you can produce truly stunning monochrome images.

1 Open up your file First things first, open your original Raw file in Adobe Camera Raw and select the ***HSL/Grayscale*** tab on the right-hand side of your screen. Converting your image to mono is as easy as clicking on the ***Convert to Grayscale*** tick box at the top, but a few more steps will ensure you get the best possible result.

2 Reset your image To get the best out of your black & white image, some adjustment to the tones is required. ACR will automatically adjust some of the settings to tone your image, but we want to tone it ourselves, so click on the word ***Default*** above the sliders which will reset everything to zero.

3 Adjust your colour sliders We'll start by adjusting the Blues slider, as blue was the central tone in our image to begin with. Click and hold on the ***Blues*** slider and drag it to the left to darken the blue tones. Keep an eye on the histogram at the top of the screen to make sure no clipping occurs.

Final image
The strong lighting and interesting textures make this image the perfect candidate for this black & white Raw conversion.

4 Target your adjustments As an alternative to adjusting the sliders, you can target your adjustments. Click and hold on the ***Targeted Adjustment Tool*** button at the top and select ***Grayscale Mix***. Click and hold on any tone in your image and drag up or down to lighten or darken that tone and the surrounding tones, too.

5 Increase Grayscale Mix Some of the warmer tones now look a bit lost, so increasing the Grayscale Mix on the channels for ***Oranges*** and ***Yellows*** brings out the detail in the rocks and creates a strong contrast between them and the sea. This can be done manually or by using the ***Targeted Adjustment Tool*** again.

6 Adjust Curves Finally, select the ***Tone Curve*** button at the top and choose the ***Point*** tab. Under the ***Curve*** tab, select ***Strong Contrast***. If necessary, you can adjust the curve below by moving the individual points as required. This final step just adds extra drama and oomph to our monochrome image.

Turning b&w: a pro's process

Professional photographer Lee Frost explains his process for taking black & white images from Photoshop to print

Lee Frost: The day I captured this picture I was exploring the Northumberland coast, looking for scenes to suit the effect of a ten-stop ND filter. When I saw this old fisherman's hut, I knew a long exposure would work well to record motion in the drifting clouds and swaying grass, while the hut stayed static in the middle of the frame.

The original Raw image looked pretty dull, partly because the light was flat and also because the B+W ten-stop ND filter added a warm cast and some vignetting. However, none of this mattered because I knew the image would be cropped and converted to black & white later.

Bringing out that drama and impact was easy. I'm not one for spending ages working on Raw files and, in this case, I didn't employ any fancy software either – I only used Photoshop CS3. First I boosted contrast by adjusting the Tone Curve: moving the Darks slider a little to the left and the Lights slider a little to the right. I then opened the image in Photoshop and cropped it to square format. To get a basic monochrome image, I applied a Black & White adjustment (***Image>Adjustments>Black & White***). Then I used the Polygonal Lasso Tool, with the Feather set to 100px, to select the sky. To improve the sky's impact, I then added a Levels adjustment (***Image>Adjustments>Levels***), using the Auto button to see if it gave me the look I wanted. Since it did, I stuck with it, but if it hadn't, I'd normally cancel the adjustment and make more controlled alterations using Levels or Curves. I then inverted the selection (***Select>Inverse***), so everything other than the sky was selected, and reapplied the Levels Auto command, which boosted contrast in the shed and grass. The final stage was to bring out detail and texture in the shed, so I selected it with the Polygonal Lasso Tool, the Feather set to 30px, then adjusted Curves (***Image>Adjustments>Curves***) to give the image more 'oomph'!

When it comes to printing my black & white landscapes, I always use the same paper – Hahnemühle Photorag 308. It's a heavy, flat white fine-art paper with a lovely dull finish and brilliant archival qualities. I print with an Epson Stylus Pro 7880 24in printer using Epson K3 Ultrachrome inks. To print black & white, I use the Advance B&W setting on the printer, which uses three black inks to produce pure mono images. I like to print big (usually 20x20in on 24in paper) – then I have the prints mounted in 32x32in window mounts so there's a 6in border on all sides and framed in natural oak frames. The final framed work is 34x34in, so it makes a big statement when hanging on the wall – the best place for black & white landscapes!

Choosing the right products

You can get fabulous results from at-home printing by combining the right products. We recommend trying matt fine-art papers by Hahnemühle, Ilford or Permajet, ideally suitable for black & white images. Also consider using a large-format Epson, Canon or HP printer with only a set of black inks, rather than colour, to optimise details in the shadows and highlights.

Using a Black & White adjustment layer

While some photographers prefer the simplicity of a straightforward black & white conversion, you can get great results using a Black & White adjustment layer (***Layer>New Adjustment Layer>Black & White***...). Not only does it allow you to use the colour channels to adjust the tonality of your black & white image, similarly if you are using colour filters in-camera, any adjustments you make are non-destructive. At any point you can double-click on the Adjustment Layer in the Layers palette and re-edit your conversion, if necessary. It's a very flexible and effective way to edit your b&w images.

Tools for selectively adjusting black & white

Often the monochrome images you get from a basic conversion can be flat and grey. For this reason, make improving the contrast using an Adjustment Layer your first priority: you could use Levels, Curves or Brightness/Contrast for this. If some areas of your image are still in need of help, consider being selective with your adjustments. Either use a selection tool to isolate the target area and apply a Levels adjustment (like Lee Frost has) or duplicate the image layer (***Layer>Duplicate Layer***) and use the Dodge and Burn Tools, set to Midtones and a low Exposure, to reveal detail in shadows and highlights.

Get specific with Silver Efex Pro

Looking for a quick and effective way to convert your landscapes to monochrome? Look no further than Nik Software's Silver Efex Pro 2

Caroline Wilkinson: If you miss the grain quality you got from your Kodak T-Max P3200, the smooth tones of Agfa's APX Pro 100 or the deep blacks and pearly whites from an Ilford XP2 Super 400 roll of film, you'll adore Nik Software's Silver Efex Pro 2. Carefully selecting film had a great deal to do with the art of black & white photography, but that enjoyment doesn't have to end with digital.

While there are a number of ways you can develop a black & white image in Photoshop CS, Elements and Lightroom for grand results, Silver Efex Pro 2 allows you to get more creative and elaborate with your effects. Not only can you replicate the look of your favourite film type with a few clicks, you can also apply colour filters to adjust tonality and pick from dozens of classic, vintage and modern presets for instant results. You can even make your usual selective adjustments to contrast, noise and exposure, and then finish off by picking a vignette, border and toning style. You can make it as classic or as creative as you want with very little effort, so don't worry if you're new to this digital editing malarkey – this software puts the enjoyment back into editing.

As a plug-in, Silver Efex Pro 2 works in conjunction with your main editing suite and is accessible via its Filters menu. This means you can continue to edit your image in Photoshop before and after working on it in Silver Efex Pro: it's one streamlined solution. Personally, while you can yield great results using the techniques we've already shown you in Photoshop, for me, nothing compares to the flexibility and ease of Silver Efex Pro 2. For the time it takes you to get one creative conversion in Photoshop, you could produce a number of different looks using Silver Efex Pro – one of which I'll explain to you here.

Before editing this example image with Nik Software, I cropped the image in Photoshop. It's good to do this first if you plan to add a vignette or border to your finished image to avoid cropping the edge effects out afterwards. Before I made any selective adjustments to the image, I scrolled through the Preset Categories to see which preset best suited the image. Some, like Low Key, made the image look too dark, while others like Pinhole and Antique Plate II looked unusual but were too vintage for what I wanted.

I chose the basic High Contrast preset then increased the Structure to sharpen and boost contrast. To add noise for a grainy high-ISO effect, I set the Grain per pixel slider to 86. You can see the effect of the settings on your image almost instantly in the preview window. To finish off, I added a grunge frame by selecting Type 8 under Image Borders. As soon as I pressed OK, the effect was applied and the image automatically opened in Photoshop's main suite as a separate editable layer within the Layers palette. It really is as simple as that.

You can try before you buy with a Nik Silver Efex Pro 2 15-day free trial, downloadable from the Nik Software website – visit www.niksoftware.com. You can also buy the plug-in on its own for €199.95 (£159), or alternatively as part of Nik Software's Complete Collection for €299.95 (£238.50).

Pro tip: Ross Hoddinott

"As with any creative profession, presentation is everything in photography. Beautifully composed, technically brilliant shots can be totally undermined if poorly printed or presented. Naturally, paper choice is important. There is so much choice when choosing paper, but Ilford's Galerie Gold Fibre Silk is a favourite of mine. The paper has great archival properties and, arguably, is the closest thing you can get to a darkroom print – it looks, feels and even smells like traditional darkroom paper! Cropping is an important part of the compositional process and a square format, in particular, really suits black & white – enhancing its fine-art look. A small border – in the region of 1-2cm – will also help complete the look of your mono masterpiece."

Other ideas to try

Canvas & acrylics If a framed fine-art print is a little too traditional for you, think about getting a stretched canvas print or your image printed on acrylic glass, or even aluminium, for a more contemporary style. Consider brands like White Wall, Jessops, Point101 and Lucy Art.

Professional printers If investing in a quality printer and inks is more money than you're willing to spend for the occasional b&w image, consider hiring a printing company to do it for you. Theprintspace, for instance, offers fine-art Giclèes and silver-based C-type prints that are sure to bring out the best of your image for a reasonable price. Look for companies that offer archival-quality products to avoid the colour fading over time.

Web If you want to add your image to your online portfolio for a wider audience to see, make sure you change the Resolution (***Image>Image Size***) to 72, resize your image and apply a little sharpening before uploading to your site.

LANDSCAPE PROJECTS

How to create a stitched panorama

It's so easy to produce brilliant panoramas with this technique

Lee Frost: Panoramas are so simple to create, you'll use this technique again and again once you know how. All you have to remember is that it's very straightforward providing you stick to a consistent working routine and don't make any silly mistakes along the way. Here, I'll show you how to create a stitched panorama using Adobe Photoshop CS3. First things first, grab your camera…

1 Set up Mount your camera on a tripod in either landscape or portrait format. Make sure the tripod head is level on the legs (a levelling base helps enormously) and also that the camera is level on the head by using a hotshoe spirit level, so that when you rotate the camera between shots it remains level.

2 Test shot Take an exposure test shot from an average part of the scene – not the lightest or darkest. Check the image and histogram; if it looks okay, set this exposure in manual mode. Also switch White Balance from AWB to the preset that suits the conditions. Swing your camera to the left, ready to create the first shot.

3 Start the sequence Focus the lens manually on the scene and make sure the aperture you use provides sufficient depth-of-field to record everything in focus that needs to be sharp – f/8 to f/11 is usually fine. Hold your left hand in front of the lens with your finger pointing right and take a shot; this marks the start of the sequence.

4 Overlap your shots Remove your hand from in front of the lens and take the first shot in the sequence. Immediately swing the camera slightly to the right and take your second exposure. Repeat this until you reach the other end of the scene, making sure you overlap each image by 30-40% to enable easy stitching.

5 End the sequence Hold your right hand in front of the lens with your fingers pointing to the left and take a shot to denote the end of the sequence. When you download the files, you'll know that all the images between the two hand shots are in the same sequence and it will be obvious which ones need to be stitched to create your panorama.

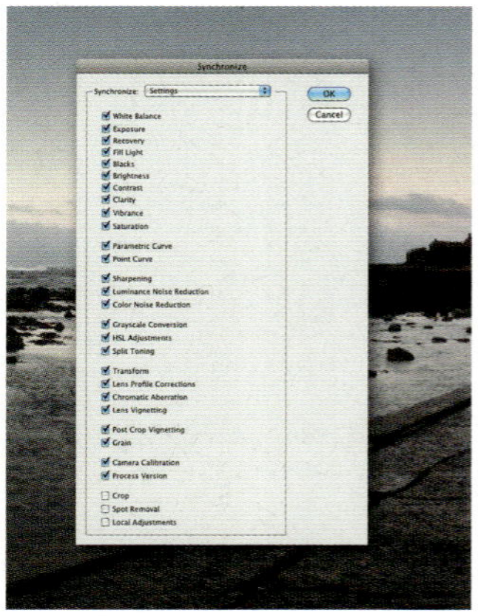

6 Batch-process Download the images to a computer. If you shoot in Raw, open all the files for the stitch together, select ***All*** and click ***Synchronise***, so they all receive the same adjustments to exposure, colour temperature, contrast and so on. It's essential that all the images are consistent otherwise the stitch will look odd.

Final image

This technique is perfect for landscape shots, but it works with all kinds of scenes. Give it a go!

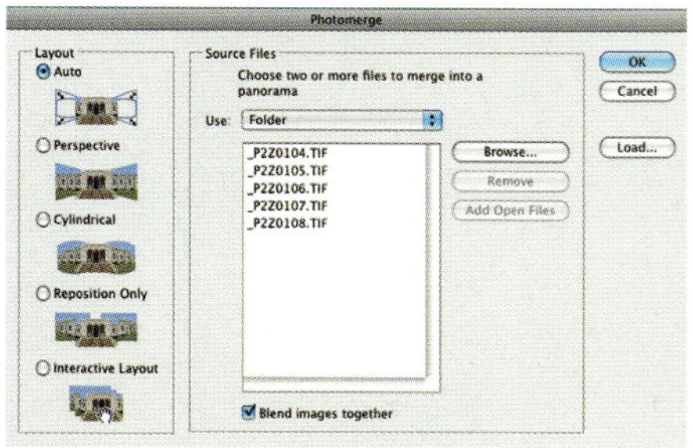

7 Select your layout Put the processed images in a folder so they're in the same place. Next, open Photoshop and go to ***File>Automate>Photomerge***. Select the layout style you want to use – Auto usually works fine, but Cylindrical and Perspective are worth trying. Then click on the ***Use*** tab, select ***Folders*** then click on ***Browse***.

8 Employ Photomerge Click on the folder containing the images you want to stitch and they'll appear in the Photomerge dialogue box. Click ***OK*** and let Photomerge perform its magic. This can take a few minutes, as a series of layers are created and Photomerge decides which bits of each image it will blend together.

9 Flatten image Once the stitch is complete it will look something like this. If the camera wasn't level as you rotated it, you will need to crop the top and bottom edges to straighten them. The file size will be huge, especially if the source images were saved as TIFFs. To reduce it, go to ***Image>Layers>Flatten Image***.

10 Check for seams Enlarge the image on screen to ***100%*** and scroll around it to check that there are no obvious joins where the images meet. If there are, use the ***Clone Stamp Tool*** or ***Healing Brush Tool*** to erase them, though if you overlapped the source images enough, you should find that the stitch is seamless and looks fantastic.

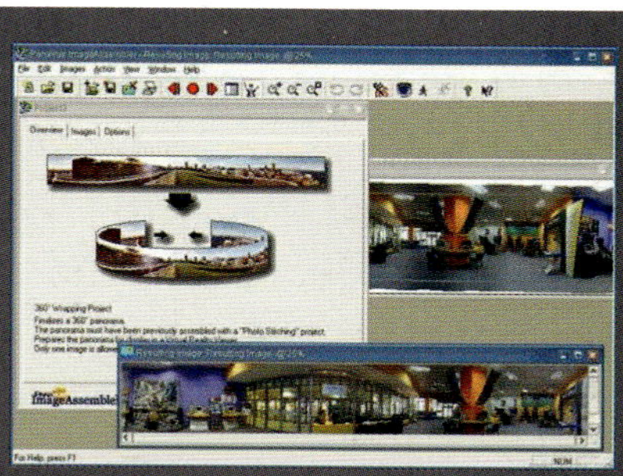

Stitching software

There are various stitching applications available to create panoramas – here's a rundown of the most popular...

■ **Adobe Photoshop**
If you're using Photoshop, Elements or Lightroom, you can stitch images together using the Photomerge function as described on this page. It's quick, easy and effective. Prior to Photoshop CS3 it wasn't so good, but from CS3 on, it does an excellent job. For PC and Mac.
Cost: Free with Photoshop and Lightroom.
Visit: www.adobe.com

■ **PTGui**
(Panoramic Tools Graphical User Interface) Available for both Mac and PC, PTGui is far more capable than Photomerge, allowing you to stitch multiple layers of images, create 360° cylindrical pans, 360x180° spherical pans, HDR pans, gigapixel pans from hundreds of source images and more. The latest version offers an Align to Grid feature that makes it easy to stitch multiple layers, plus you have manual control to fine-tune images when they're stitched. Great if you plan to use this technique often.
Cost: €79 for PTGui, €149 for PTGui Pro
Visit: www.ptgui.com

■ **PanaVue Image Assembler**
Similar to PTGui in that it offers automatic and manual stitching, corrects lens distortion and misalignment, can handle multi-layer stitches and 1x1m pixel stitches, offers automatic cropping, single-step 360° image wrapping, stitches handheld sequences and creates dramatic vertical pans. PC only. Download a free trial from the PanaVue website.
Cost: $64 Std Edition; $129 Pro Edition.
Visit: www.panavue.com

■ **Panoweaver 8**
A good choice if you want to create cylindrical or spherical pans and use them for VR viewing using HTML 5, Flash VR, QTVR and other platforms. You can also use it to create Little Planet images, stitch multiple rows, handle images shot with full-frame fisheye lenses (for spherical pans), create HDR pans to handle exposure/contrast issues and much, much more. For PC and Mac.
Cost: $99.99 Std Edition.
Visit: www.easypano.com

■ **Arcsoft Panorama Maker 6**
Relatively inexpensive and easy to use, it offers five stitching modes: Auto, 360°, Horizontal, Tile and Vertical – just select the one you want then choose your images. You can create panoramas from stills and video, create 360° virtual reality movies, 3D panoramas, export the pans in a range of formats, adjust colour balance, exposure and dynamic lighting. PC only.
Cost: $79.99.
Visit: www.arcsoft.com

Summer landscapes

Wildflower meadows are crying out for your camera – here's all the advice you need to capture them looking their very best...

Helen Dixon: Poppies are the first sign of summer for me. Weeks of rain and heavy cloud cover last year, though, meant all I could do was keep a keen eye out for potential poppy fields and hope for a clear day. So when that day arrived, I wanted to make the most of it in case summer was over before it began (which it usually is in the UK!). Unfortunately, poppy fields aren't as common as they used to be due to farmers spraying pesticides, but they're making a comeback with organic farming. There's no predicting where you might find them either. If you can't find a whole field of poppies, look for bunches growing along the margins. You can often find other wildflowers growing alongside them, too.

Poppies start flowering in June and throughout the summer. I've even seen fields as late as October. I'd been to this area – West Pentire, near Newquay – before, so I knew the sun would set out to sea this time of year and planned my day's shooting to end by the cliffs. If it rains the day before you want to photograph poppies, wait until the afternoon. Rain damages their delicate petals, so give them time to recover: it doesn't take long; usually a morning or a day is enough for new flowers to appear and the broken flowers to be hidden. I set out late morning to start my shoot, as I knew the field I was visiting would look better backlit at sunset than at sunrise.

Camera settings & technique On days when the sky is much brighter than the land, you'll need to use an ND grad to balance their exposures. Start by taking a spot-meter reading for the sky and one for the foreground: make a note of the difference between the two. In manual mode, dial in a mid-aperture to get sufficient depth-of-field for your scene (I usually use f/13) and the shutter speed given by the foreground meter reading. Add a filter to balance the difference between the sky and land; I usually have Lee Filters hard ND grads 0.3 (one stop), 0.75 (2.5 stops) and 0.9 (three stops) to hand. Focus a third of the way into the scene, and use LiveView and the depth-of-field preview button to check that it's sufficiently sharp.

9AM-11AM Walk around the edge of the field to note where the best poppies are growing with the thickest coverage. Look for viewpoints that might work well in the afternoon, too, once the sun changes position. Depending on the weather, you should be able to shoot throughout the day; try to make use of the cloud formations (a sun behind a cloud can give a more even spread of light), and avoid midday when the sun is overhead. It's not always necessary to use ND grads during the day, more so when the sun starts to descend and you have to increase the exposure, but I often find using a 0.3ND grad helps to balance my scene and allows me to record more detail in the sky. For these shots, however, I use a B+W polariser to saturate the colours, intensify the sky and reduce reflections on the foliage. Remember, though, that a polariser will increase your exposure by two stops. Waiting for a bit of cloud coverage, too, makes a huge difference as that little bit of shade draws out detail in the flowers.

Final image

An hour or so before sunset, I head to the cliffs to set up my equipment again; this time I take off the polarising filter and 0.75ND and add a 0.9ND grad, which allows me to record the foreground three stops brighter than the sky to retain detail and stop the highlights from blowing out.

2PM-5PM As the sun has now moved overhead, slightly pointing towards the camera, I change my viewpoint so that it is behind me again by walking down to the bottom of the field. As the cloud has built up, the sky isn't as harsh in the afternoon, so I add a 0.75ND grad to my B+W polariser and lengthen the exposure to balance the sky and foreground. I use a remote release just to be sure that I don't introduce camera shake when pressing the shutter button. Normally it's good to find a focal point in a scene like a tree or distant grouping of trees to add depth, but having changed my viewpoint I don't have any of this. Instead, getting closer and lower to the poppies allows me to emphasise the foreground more and to employ a simple composition. Later in the afternoon is also a good time of day to shoot close-ups as the light is softer and shadows are less harsh. Instead of a macro lens, why not try a telephoto lens like 70-300mm or 70-200mm to compress perspective and isolate poppies with a wide aperture?

Learn how to make the most of summer's luscious lavender

Pro Helen Dixon shares her secrets for shooting lavender landscapes and offers tips for making the most of these heady summer flowers

Helen Dixon: There are quite a few lavender farms in the UK: a taste of Provence right here on our doorsteps. But you better act quickly; they won't be around for long. With such sporadic weather in the last couple of years, lavender has been a bit late arriving but generally is in full bloom between mid-June and the end of August.

Visiting a cultivated lavender farm, just prior to harvest, is a great way to get fantastic pictures as they can offer copious amounts of rich-lilac lavender in beautiful impactful lines. I shot these images all at the Mayfield Lavender Farm in Surrey – see panel on the right to see if there's one close to you, or do a little bit of online research to find out where your local lavender field is located.

Although wild lavender fields are rare and may not grow in rows, they do have the advantage that you can shoot them at any time of day, whereas a farm is restricted by opening hours – check their website first before setting off. Some farms also require you to get permission first for photography, so make sure you do this. Harvest time varies somewhat depending on the type of summer weather we have, so, again, check with the farm you plan to visit beforehand to make sure they haven't already harvested to avoid you making a wasted trip.

There are many ways of shooting lavender and numerous techniques to try – from lead-in lines to selective focusing to the various filters that give different effects – so it's worth taking along a few lenses. An essential lens is a wide-angle zoom (10-20mm if you use an APS-C sensor, 17-35mm for full-frame) and consider a zoom like a 70-300mm lens to compress the flowers, along with a macro lens for extreme close-ups. Taking along a longer lens means you won't come a cropper if you find out that the farm's rules restrict how close you can get to the lavender.

If you want stunning lavender landscapes, you also need to consider the lighting conditions you'll be faced with. As usual, the best time of day to shoot is during the golden hour, either when the sun is coming up or setting. Bear in mind during summer that the evening light lasts a little longer than it does in the morning so you can get a few more shots in before the glow's gone. But if daytime is the only time you can venture out, which is also normally the working hours of farms, avoid visiting between 11am-3pm and hope for some cloud cover to enrich the purple hues of the landscape. Harsh sunlight bleaches lavender, leaving images pale and flat with pink-tinged flowers. Make sure you pack a polarising filter to help enhance the colour impact of your pictures. Happy snapping!

Your nearest lavender farm

- **Snowshill Lavender**, nr Broadway, Cotswolds
- **Long Barn**, nr Winchester, Hampshire
- **Hitchin Lavender**, nr Hitchin, Hertfordshire
- **Isle Of Wight Lavender**, Isle Of Wight
- **Castle Farm**, Shoreham, nr Sevenoaks, Kent
- **Norfolk Lavender**, nr King's Lynn, Norfolk
- **Shropshire Lavender**, nr Newport, Shropshire
- **Mayfield Lavender**, Banstead, nr Sutton, Surrey
- **Lordington Lavender**, nr Chichester, West Sussex
- **Wolds Way Lavender**, Wintringham, North Yorkshire
- **Yorkshire Lavender**, Terrington, nr York
- **Millcroft Lavender**, Argyll, Scotland
- **Wye Lavender**, Rhayader, Powys, Wales
- **Somerset Lavender**, Faulkland, nr Radstock, Somerset

Shooting close-ups Use a wide aperture – f/2.8-f/4 – and focus on a section of lavender using single-point AF to throw the rest of the image out of focus (best done when there's no wind as any movement will be captured). If you use a macro lens, you may be able to use a reflector to bounce light on to it but stop your lens down to increase depth-of-field. For this image, I used a Canon EF 100mm f/2.8 macro lens with the DSLR set to 1/125sec at f/4.5 (ISO 100).

Using filters A polariser will enhance the colour and remove any glare and reflections, although it isn't necessary in this example due to the amount of shade available from the clouds. I did use an ND grad filter here to balance the exposure as the sky was brighter than the land. You will need to use stronger filters if the scene is in shade; I have to fit a 0.9 and 0.75 to retain the detail in the sky area, giving me an exposure of 0.5secs at f/13 (ISO 100).

Composition Lavender is usually planted in rows giving you ready-made lead-in lines, so try to incorporate them in your images and adjust your tripod height for a different view. Experiment with a variety of compositions – portrait format may work, as well as a low vantage point, or alter the position of the vanishing point as central isn't always best. The more you try, the more chance you'll have of getting a winning shot.

Final image

If you can find a focal point in the field then this will add interest. A tree is ideal; a variation in the colour of the flowers will work, too. To achieve sharpness, focus a third of the way into the scene and use a fairly small aperture – f/13 or f/16. Check the zone of sharpness using the depth-of-field preview button if your camera has one.

Exploit the beauty of bluebells

Plan to take a day off in spring and head to a bluebell wood to try out one of several creative techniques to capture striking images

Ross Hoddinott: The UK is the best place in the world to photograph common bluebells – it is estimated that around 70% of their entire population is found here. So, wherever you live in the UK, you will not be far from a bluebell wood. They flower between mid-April and the end of May, but the time when they are at their peak can vary slightly from year to year. Typically, they are most photogenic at the start of May, but it is worthwhile making an early visit just to assess what stage they are at – doing so ensures you time your visit correctly and don't miss them at their best.

Weather and timing are key considerations. There is no bad weather for photographing bluebells, but a bright overcast day can often yield superb results. As the light is low in contrast, it makes it easier to achieve the correct exposure. The quality of light is soft and muted, and the colours of woodland flowers and fresh green foliage look naturally more saturated. Early morning and late evening can produce magical light for woodland photography, too. The light is warmer and the long shadows add depth to your shots. In bright overhead sunshine, the sun-dappled woodland floor can look attractive to the eye, but the level of contrast can often exceed the capabilities of your sensor's dynamic range. With so much contrast, achieving a good exposure can be difficult, if not impossible – so it is often better to avoid shooting in midday sun. It is also a good idea to visit on a still day, when bluebells remain still during exposure.

Identifying 'the shot' in woodland with large swathes of bluebells can prove tricky as your choice of composition is almost limitless. To ensure you take great images, a creative eye is vital. Keep composition simple. Avoid clutter, like fallen branches, and look for interesting woodland detail that you can make a feature of, like a mossy stump or large ferns. Narrow paths winding into the distance can be used to draw the viewer's eye into shot.

Lens choice is important so take a range of focal lengths with you. Wide-angles are great for capturing vast carpets of flowers, but often a mid-telephoto – in the region of 50-100mm – is best suited to photographing bluebells. A short telephoto will shorten perspective, creating the impression that the carpet of flowers is denser than it is. This type of focal length is also good if you wish to focus attention on a particularly photogenic group of trees. A macro lens, or the long end of a telezoom, is ideal to isolate individual flowers.

In overcast light, achieving the right exposure is relatively straightforward. Your camera's multi-zone meter shouldn't have any problems. In early morning or late evening light, it is often preferable to shoot in the direction of the sun, so that it 'bleeds' through foliage. However, when shooting towards the light, metering can be deceived and results underexposed. Keep an eye on the histogram and apply exposure compensation if required.

Shutter speeds are often slow in the shade of woodland, so a tripod is essential. For sweeping, wide-angled images of woodland interiors, opt for a small aperture, like f/13. This creates a large depth-of-field which will render everything in focus. However, a shallow depth-of-field will suit some scenes better. For example, isolate a single plant and select a wide aperture like f/4 or f/5.6 to render background flowers as an attractive blue haze.

UK's best bluebell woodland

Search online for woods in your area. Below are a few, just to get you started.

- **Micheldever Wood, nr Winchester**
  OS Grid Reference: SU530363
  Visit: www.forestry.gov.uk
- **West Woods, nr Marlborough**
  OS Grid Reference: SU163667
  Visit: www.forestry.gov.uk
- **Yoxall Lodge, nr Burton upon Trent**
  OS Grid Reference: SK1521
  Visit: www.bluebellwoodsofyoxall.co.uk

For further information on bluebell woods, visit: www.woodlandtrust.org.uk

Other woodland flowers

Wood anemone: Widespread and locally common woodland perennial, often growing in large clumps. Its white flowers are beautiful and delicate. Best shot individually in close-up or in context with its woodland surroundings using a wide-angle.

Ramsons: Often growing among or near bluebells. They smell strongly of garlic and can grow in vast numbers in damp woodland. Very attractive backlit or in frame-filling close-up. Attach a polarising filter to saturate the colour of the leaves.

Herb Robert: Common and widespread, its photogenic pink flowers appear from April onwards. Using a macro lens or close-up filter will reveal its delicate beauty. A small silver/white reflector bounces natural light and relieves harsh shadows.

Step-by-step to bluebell magic

Bluebells are unquestionably beautiful, but that is not to say they are easy to photograph. Being such a popular, well-photographed subject makes it even harder to produce original, creative images. Ross Hoddinott provides inspiration by visiting his local woodland in order to see what variety of bluebell picture he could shoot. His expert advice will help you know what to look for, techniques to try, and what to avoid when shooting bluebells.

1 Avoid clutter and distraction When I took this image, I was seduced by the vibrancy and colour of the bluebells and overlooked the fallen branches and cluttered woodland floor. Keep compositions clean and simple.

2 Look for compositional aids A winding path or mossy stump can make for a strong lead-in line. This will give your images a three-dimensional feel. Without this, images may sometimes lack depth and interest.

3 Experiment with depth-of-field Shallow focus can work well when photographing woodland subjects. Select a wide aperture to diffuse background detail. This will place emphasis on your point of focus.

Photographer conduct
Always place the welfare of your subject first. Keep to paths and never tread or trample on flowers for the sake of a better composition. Don't pick flowers either. Photographers are getting a bad press for their disregard to wild flowers – don't add weight to the argument

4 Be creative Set a shutter speed of one second and move the camera up and down during the exposure to artistically blur the trees. It is a hit-and-miss technique and may take many attempts to get a result that you like.

5 Try a zoom burst This is another easy, creative technique. Compose your shot using either the zoom's shortest or longest end. Then, during exposure, smoothly adjust the zoom ring to the opposite end of the lens's range.

6 Use a polarising filter A polariser will reduce the glare and reflections from foliage and flowers. The filter helps restore natural colour saturation and gives woodland images added impact. Note it will lengthen your exposure.

Creatively blur trees

The clever use of slow shutter speeds can introduce a sense of motion and bring your landscape and nature images to life

Helen Dixon: Incorporating an element of motion into your landscape shots can add all-important energy and life to an otherwise bland scene. Landscape photographers often use long exposures to blur movement in water, but there's no reason why this technique should be confined to use at the coast; grasses, trees, foliage and flowers all make great subjects, too. When composing your scene, you should look to include one or more static objects that aren't affected by the breeze. This creates a contrast between movement and stillness within your image. Furthermore, it can make the difference between a shot that looks like it includes intentional movement and a shot suffering from bad camera shake. Trees make ideal candidates; the breeze causes the branches and leaves to sway while the thick trunks stand defiant.

Because you'll be shooting using a long exposure, your best option is to head out under overcast conditions. Bright sunlight causes too much contrast between areas in full sun and those in shade during the exposure, whereas a cloudy sky will diffuse the sunlight for a more even exposure. You'll need a breeze to cause movement in the trees, but you don't want to be out shooting when it's blowing a gale as this can cause camera movement, even with a tripod. A tripod is essential for this type of photography; if you try to shoot lengthy exposures handheld then you risk introducing camera shake into your image. Choose a composition where the lighting is diffused throughout the scene as any areas of bright light will cause hotspots in your final image. I chose this row of trees as they provided a consistent canopy overhead to prevent any hotspots and the thick tree trunks made for an interesting lead-in line into the image, with the branches at the top of the image framing the shot nicely.

Setting up and camera settings

In order to use a slow shutter speed without overexposing the result, I set ISO 100 and opt for an aperture of f/13 for optimum front-to-back sharpness. I fit a polariser to eliminate glare from the foliage, which has the added bonus of lengthening my exposure by two stops, although it still isn't enough to capture any real movement. Adding a Lee Filters 0.9ND filter takes me close to the exposure time required to capture the motion of the branches and grass. Stopping down further to f/16 gives a slower shutter speed and the right amount of motion.

Common errors to watch out for

Composition If the composition allows for too much variety in light then it can be difficult to get a balanced exposure throughout the scene. In this image, the light hitting the ground outside of the canopy cover is too bright and distracts from the rest of the shot.

Final image
A perfect mix of movement in the foliage and sharp tree trunks makes for a beautiful artistic shot.

Too much grass The tree trunks are our fixed point of interest in this image and, as such, you should look to compose your shot with this in mind. Here, however, the trees are too close to the edge of the frame and fail to act as an effective lead-in line.

Blown highlights Despite the even canopy cover, the sun breaking through the clouds causes the areas of the ground not in shade to be completely blown out. Just a few minutes later the clouds move back in to place and I can continue shooting.

Not windy enough The exposure is correct throughout and there is movement captured in the foliage, but there are still too many static branches. A smaller aperture and slower shutter speed is required to capture more effective movement in the final result.

Shoot a misty morning scene

Ross Hoddinott reveals how early morning mist provides a wonderful opportunity for you to shoot ethereal, magical scenes

Ross Hoddinott: Misty mornings are one of the key traits of spring. Mist can look magical, filling valleys and hanging atmospherically above fields. By reducing colour and contrast, mist simplifies the look of objects, placing more emphasis on shape instead. There are different types of mist and fog, but the most photogenic is 'radiation fog', which forms during clear, still nights when the ground loses heat by radiation and cools.

The ground chills nearby air to saturation point and mist forms. It often stays confined to low ground, forming a thin white layer at the bottom of valleys. When looking at the local weather forecast, watch for clear skies and cool, still nights – perfect conditions for mist. Also, look at the forecast for clarity. If clarity is predicted to drop to average or poor during the night, then there is a good chance you will be greeted with mist in the morning. Set your alarm early. Allow enough time to get to your intended viewpoint before sunrise, so that you can get set up and ready in advance of the best conditions. If you are driving, remember your journey will be slower due to the conditions.

A high viewpoint, from the top of a hill or valley, is often best; allowing you to get above the mist to shoot atmospheric vistas.

Often, objects are reduced to nothing more than a simple silhouette in misty weather. Therefore, look for strong, bold objects to photograph within the landscape – a church steeple, castle ruin or tree, for example. Longer focal lengths suit misty scenes the most, foreshortening perspective and allowing photographers to isolate points of interest. Light scatters and is more diffused in mist, adding to its mystical effect – often the most dramatic results come from shooting into the light. A medium telephoto lens, in the region of 100mm, is often ideal. Mist – like snow – has a habit of fooling a camera's metering system. This is because it is designed to assume that the subject is mid-tone (18% grey). Subjects that are significantly lighter or darker than mid-tone, like a misty landscape, can be exposed incorrectly. TTL metering has a tendency to underexpose mist, rendering it too dark. Consult the camera's histogram screen regularly when shooting mist. If the graph is biased to the left, this is an indication of underexposure. Apply positive (+) exposure compensation to make the image brighter, and then reshoot. You may only need to apply a +1/3 or +1/2 of compensation, but in extreme instances, you might have to dial in a stop or more of compensation. Again, use the histogram as your guide.

Having dragged yourself out of bed early to shoot the morning mist, don't overlook the picture potential of smaller, less obvious subjects – for example, dew-laden cobwebs glistening in the morning light.

Weather websites & apps

Outdoor photographers rely heavily on local weather forecasts, especially when waiting for ideal conditions leading to mist. While long-term forecasts aren't always reliable, 24- and 48-hour forecasts are often accurate. Therefore, keep a regular eye on them. Mobile phone apps are an ideal source of information but you should also use websites such as www.metoffice.gov.uk

Time	Weather	Temp	Wind			Visibility
			Dir	Speed	Gust	
2100		4 °C	ENE	8 mph		Very Good
0000		3 °C	ENE	7 mph		Good
0300	FOG	2 °C	ENE	6 mph		Very Poor
0600	FOG	2 °C	ENE	6 mph		Very Poor
0900		4 °C	ENE	4 mph		Good
1200		7 °C	NE	7 mph		Very Good
1500		7 °C	NE	8 mph		Good

1 Planning I check the local weather forecast daily and notice that a clear, still night is predicted. Clarity also dropped during the night, so I am optimistic that it will be misty in the morning. I prepare my camera outfit, then set my alarm for just before sunrise.

2 Viewpoint Sure enough, the landscape is shrouded in morning mist. I drive to a high viewpoint, which offers good views over the misty landscape and set up my kit. A telephoto is a good lens choice for mist as it compresses perspective, exaggerating the effect.

3 Metering Mist helps to simplify the look of the landscape, giving it a 'layered' effect. I compose my shot, and release the shutter, but the result is too dark. By looking at the histogram, I can tell the exposure is biased to the left, confirming the image is underexposed.

4 Exposure override The brightness of mist can fool metering systems designed to assume scenes are mid-tone. Using the camera's exposure compensation button, I dial in one stop of positive (+) compensation to lengthen the exposure time. The result is far better, but the scene lacks a focal point.

5 Composition I scan the landscape for a key point of interest to give my shot more purpose and notice a church tower sticking out above the mist. I recompose the picture to make this my main point of interest and also try a vertical composition. The result is a great springtime misty image.

Beware of condensation

If tiny water droplets are condensing out of the air, then they are also likely to condense on the surface of your lens and filters. Keep an eye out for moisture on optics and wipe away with a clean microfibre lens cloth

Final image

I try various compositions but this is my favourite. The short telephoto setting creates an atmospheric, layered landscape image.

Rockpool reflections

Professional photographer Mark Bauer goes paddling among rockpools to show us how to master reflections in water

Framing the shot

Mark Bauer: Reflections make great subjects for landscape images. There's something unique about the symmetry of a perfect reflection in a still lake, but reflections can work equally well in smaller ponds, puddles or rockpools.

They may not always work as the main subject in a coastal shot, but rockpools make excellent foreground interest in wide-angle landscapes, with reflections creating extra depth in a shot and adding brightness and colour, which can break up dark foregrounds.

You'll find rockpools on any rocky coastline when the tide is low – the trick is to find one that will photograph well. If they're too small, they won't have enough impact, and if they're too shallow or if the bottom is sandy and light, the reflections won't be strong enough. The ideal time to arrive is as the tide is going out, so that you can set up as rockpools are being revealed, and shoot while the surrounding rocks are still wet and shiny. This is also easier than having to rush your pictures before an incoming tide covers up the perfect rockpool.

Weather conditions are also important. It needs to be still enough that there are no ripples on the water to break up the reflection, and there also needs to be interest in the sky – dramatic clouds or colours – as unless your rockpool is very close to a point of interest such as a lighthouse, it's the sky that will make the reflection. In terms of technique, accurate focusing and depth-of-field are crucial, as this type of image looks best when both the immediate foreground and the reflection are sharp. This isn't as easy as it may seem, as the focal plane of the reflection is much further away than the reflective medium. One last thing to be aware of is correct filtration, which can be used to balance the light in the scene overall and enhance the reflection itself.

Equipment for reflections

- **An ultra wide-angle zoom** to help you get in close and fill the foreground with your rockpool of choice.
- **A tripod** that allows low-level shooting. A low viewpoint will reveal more of the sky in the reflection and make for a beautifully balanced shot.
- **A polarising filter** to enhance the reflection. Contrary to popular belief, polarisers don't simply remove reflections, but reduce glare too, which can actually enhance reflections. You have to be careful to set the correct polarisation, though, because you can kill the reflection if you get it wrong. Look through the viewfinder and rotate the polariser slowly. Stop when you see the effect you want.
- **ND grads** to help balance contrast in the scene. Take care not to 'overgrad' the scene, however, because in real life, reflections are usually darker than the sky and your picture won't look natural if it's the other way round.
- **Solid ND filters.** If conditions aren't still and there are ripples on the water, you can add a Neutral Density filter to lengthen the exposure and render the water smooth.

Exposure and focusing

Reflective surfaces are by their very nature bright, and this can fool your camera's meter into underexposure. Add +0.5 to +1 stops of exposure compensation, and check the histogram after shooting to make sure. You need to be careful when focusing, as the focal planes of the water's surface and the reflection are not the same. If you leave your camera on autofocus, it could focus on the surface of the water, which means the more distant reflection could fall out of focus. To make sure the scene is sharp from front to back, switch to manual focusing and focus a third of the way into the scene and use a small aperture, such as f/16.

Composition

By taking a low viewpoint, you will be able to fill the frame with the rockpool and also include the reflected sky. Landscape shots usually work better than portraits in these situations

1 Begin early Arriving at dawn, I look for suitable foreground interest. I like the foreground here, but the rockpool doesn't work – it's too small and shallow to reflect the sky well.

2 Try a different viewpoint This one works a little better, but without any filtration, the highlights in the sky have blown, and the shadows in the foreground are beginning to block up.

3 Add an ND grad An ND grad enables me to retain detail in the sky and rays of light are starting to break through, adding drama to the scene. But I feel the reflection can be enhanced.

Final image

All the components come together for a perfect image. As you can see, there's always a bit of time for reflection.

4 Add a polariser My next step is to add a polariser. However, as you can see, if you set it incorrectly, you can kill the reflection rather than enhance it. It's time to tweak the polarisation.

5 Turn the polariser Just half a turn of the polariser helps to make the reflection stand out. However, I feel the image can be improved by smoothing out the water in the middle distance.

6 Add an ND filter Adding a solid ND filter allows me to increase the shutter speed to ten seconds, which smooths the sea and improves the look of the water in the rockpool.

Capture 'natural-looking' waves

Professional photographer Mark Bauer explains the best technique for capturing the movement of breaking waves as they hit the shore

Mark Bauer: There's a lot of debate about how best to photograph wave movement. Long exposures result in a 'misty' look that is popular with many photographers (see over the page), but is certainly not to everyone's taste as it's not authentic. When we watch waves rolling on to the shore, we see the whole movement – we don't see a moment frozen in time or mist drifting over rocks. One way to truly appreciate wave motion as the eye sees it is to use video rather than a stills camera, but by paying careful attention to shutter speeds, it *is* possible to record 'natural-looking' waves on your DSLR.

The trick is to record the right amount of movement: if the shutter is open too long there will be too much motion blur; not long enough and the wave appears too static. You need to find a middle ground where there's misty blur but the waves still keep their shape.

There is no simple recipe for this; the best shutter speed depends on the size and speed of the waves, how they're falling onto the shore, and also personal taste. Experimentation is the key – be prepared to shoot a lot of frames and spend a lot of time looking at the LCD monitor reviewing your images and tweaking the camera controls.

Controlling shutter speeds

Although there's no ideal shutter speed for capturing a breaking wave, as it depends on the conditions at the time, a shutter speed of between 1/4sec and a couple of seconds usually provides the result you'll want.

Unfortunately, though, it's not just a matter of putting the camera into shutter-priority mode and setting the shutter speed. You will also need to make sure you're using the right aperture in order to achieve the appropriate depth-of-field and an accurate exposure. For landscapes, this is usually between f/8 and f/22 for maximum depth-of-field.

There are other ways you can control the shutter speed, too. Apart from waiting for the light to change, for a faster shutter speed, you should increase the camera's ISO rating. Normally this will raise the level of noise, so you do not want to go much above ISO 800 unless you're using a professional digital SLR that handles noise well.

For shutter speeds of more than 30 seconds, you will need to set your camera to Bulb mode and time the exposure manually. However, this can often result in overexposed shots, so you may need to add a solid Neutral Density filter to reduce the amount of light falling onto the sensor. ND filters come in various strengths; the most common being one, two and three stops, and you can use several together, along with a polarising filter, too, for times when you want to set extremely long exposures.

1 Select your viewpoint I compose the shot so that the waves are falling onto the foreground rocks and then check the exposure for the sky and ground separately using my DSLR's spot meter.

2 Use an ND grad As the sky is much brighter than the ground, I add a three-stop ND soft grad filter to balance the contrast. A soft grad means the transition line won't be too obvious.

3 Take a test shot Set to shutter-priority mode, I try 1/100sec but it freezes the movement. For large waves this might convey drama, but with small waves like this it completely fails.

4 Increase filtration To lengthen the exposure, I wait for the light levels to drop and replace the three-stop ND filter with a four-stop ND filter, giving me a ten-second exposure at f/22.

5 Not quite... This time the exposure is still not long enough to give an ethereal misty look to the water, but it doesn't capture the drama of the scene by freezing the water either.

6 Shorten exposure Opening up the aperture to f/11 and swapping the four-stop ND for a two-stop enables me to shorten the exposure time to 0.3secs. The result is almost there, but the wave is frozen just a little too much.

7 Lengthen exposure slightly One more attempt, with the light levels a bit lower, I get the shot I want at around 0.6secs. There's enough movement to create a sense of drama, but the waves still keep their shape.

Final image

Opening up the aperture to f/11 allows me to set a shutter speed of half a second, while still retaining plenty of depth-of-field. The result creates drama and movement but avoids the waves looking like mist. I particularly like the way the spray is rising over the rocks in the middle distance.

Blurring motion in water

Professional photographer Ross Hoddinott demonstrates how to render moving water as atmospheric, ethereal mist for creative effect

Essential kit
Using long exposures to blur water motion is a technique that relies on a sturdy tripod, otherwise camera shake will ruin the results. Quite simply, a tripod is essential not optional

Ross Hoddinott: Blurry water – you either love it or loathe it. I love it. To render moving water milky, the right exposure time is essential; too fast and the water can look messy. A good rule of thumb is to select a shutter speed of around one second or longer. This should create an attractive level of blur. Lengthier exposures create even more atmospheric results.

To generate the longest exposure time for the available light, select your DSLR's lowest ISO together with the lens's smallest aperture (eg f/22 or f/32). In low light, achieving a lengthy exposure is relatively easy, with exposure times naturally longer. But when the light is good, it is not often possible to select a shutter speed sufficiently slow without overexposing the image. The solution is to use an ND filter. The stronger the density of the ND filter, the more light it absorbs, the longer the exposure and the greater the level of blur. For extreme effects, a Lee Filters Big Stopper (ten stops) can generate exposure times of several minutes, requiring the use of your camera's Bulb setting and a remote release. When shooting water movement using long exposures, every image will be different. Take a sequence of images and decide later which one is best.

1 Compose your shot It is evening and the tide is high. To blur the water as it washes over the rocky outcrops and pebbly shore, I carefully arrange my composition, using a tripod to keep my images shake-free. With the camera set to program mode it automatically sets a shutter speed of 1/80sec at f/8 based on the available light – not slow enough to blur water.

2 Select mode To blur the water movement, take control from the camera by selecting either shutter-priority mode and the slowest shutter speed available, or aperture-priority mode and opt for the smallest aperture. Either method sets the longest exposure obtainable in the given light. Also, select your camera's lowest ISO rating; typically ISO 100 on the majority of DSLRs.

3 Lengthen the exposure Having selected ISO 100 and aperture-priority mode, I set the minimum aperture of f/22 and wait for a large wave to wash around the foreground rocks. The exposure of 1/8sec at f/22 is longer, but as the water still isn't rendering milky, I add a polarising filter to help lengthen the exposure.

4 Use a polariser A polariser has a filter factor of two stops, so can be used as a makeshift ND filter by extending the exposure – ideal if you don't own an ND. It also helps remove glare, in this case from the rocks. The result is better, but in this instance, the exposure of 1/2sec at f/22 is still not long enough for the ethereal result I am after.

5 Add an ND filter For the blur I want, I have to add an ND filter. I leave the polariser in place and attach a three-stop ND filter. The camera's TTL metering automatically adjusts for the filter, but it also darkens the viewfinder so you will need to compose and lock the focus for the shot before attaching the filter to your DSLR.

Final image

Thanks to the solid ND filter, and also the lowering light, the exposure time is now six seconds at f/22. Again, I wait for a suitable wave and release the shutter while the water washes around the foreground rocks. I use a remote release to maximise the sharpness in my image.

Capture the best from a coastal sunset scene

For beauty, nothing beats a sunset over the sea. Ross Hoddinott show you how to make the most of it

Ross Hoddinott: There aren't many photographers who can resist a good sunset. Fairly ordinary scenes can be transformed by the extraordinary colour and glow, and one of the best places to be at that time is by the sea. Water reflects light and the sky's warmth, while the movement of incoming waves adds motion and interest to wide-angle shots.

Shooting coastal sunsets is far from easy. In reality, most sunsets are hugely disappointing, barely materialising at all. Perfect conditions are those that don't have too much or too little cloud in the sky – just enough to radiate the sunset's warmth, but not so much that it obscures the sun. Predicting them is almost impossible, too. Great colour can be brief and unexpected. In practice, the only way to guarantee good sunset images is to head out with your camera at every opportunity – sooner or later, your persistence will be rewarded with an amazing sky to photograph.

Winter is a great time of year to try out this technique. Sunset is early, meaning you don't have to be out late, and beaches are quieter, resulting in fewer footprints in the sand. If you are visiting a location for the first time, arrive two hours before sunset to allow time to explore and identify suitable compositions. Look for viewpoints where you will not only be able to shoot in the sunset's direction, but also include interesting foreground – rocky outcrops, sand patterns, a weathered groyne or reflective pool, for example. Also check the tide time – not only is this important from a safety aspect, but the tide's height greatly dictates where you can shoot from.

In terms of kit, a tripod is essential as are ND grads – unless you prefer exposure blending. When there is great colour, you normally want to go wide and include lots of sky, so a short focal length in the region of 17-35mm is a good lens choice. In terms of set-up, aperture-priority mode is best for scenics, giving you full control over depth-of-field, and selecting an aperture of f/11 to f/16 provides good front-to-back sharpness. So with your camera bag all packed, it's time to head to the coast, with fingers tightly crossed for a cracking sunset…

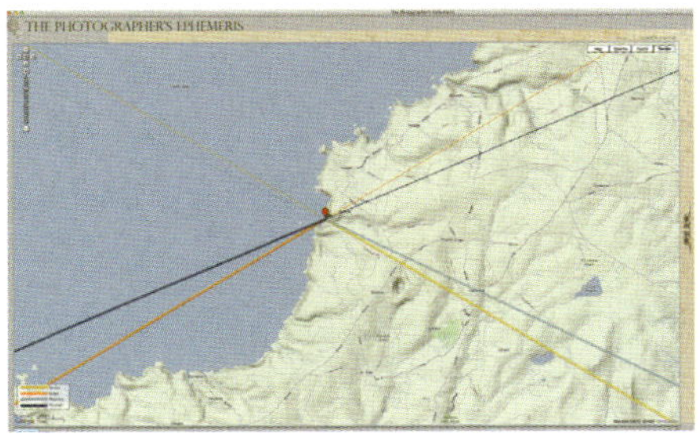

1 Do your research Before you visit, check tide times for the area (www.tidetimes.org.uk) and also plot the sun's position using a sun/moon calculator like The Photographer's Ephemeris. Check the time of sunset and arrive at least an hour beforehand to locate the best viewpoints. If you have a smartphone, I recommend downloading the Sun Scout app to plot where the sun will set once on location, enabling you to select your viewpoint accordingly.

2 Scout the area Look for a good viewpoint where you can shoot towards the setting sun. Rocks, sand patterns and pools are great compositional aids for coastal sunsets. Unless diffused by cloud, the sun's intensity is normally too great to take photos long before the sun disappears below the horizon. Therefore, you need to be patient. If you try to take pictures too soon, your images will suffer from flare and skies will be overexposed and blown out.

3 Use an ND grad filter Even when the sun is low and its intensity reduced, the sky will still be considerably brighter than the foreground. As a result, your camera will either correctly meter for the sky, resulting in foreground that is too dark, or it will meter for the foreground, resulting in an overexposed sky. Unless you fancy Photoshop work afterwards, the only in-camera solution is using graduated ND filters. One with a two- or three-stop density is most useful.

4 Align your filter In this instance, I use a three-stop ND hard grad filter, attaching it to my camera via a Lee Filters filter holder. An ND grad with a hard transition is often best for coastal sunsets, as the horizon is usually fairly even. When using ND grad filters, carefully align the transitional zone with the horizon for seamless results. The image here is much improved, but looks on the cool side, rather than showing off the warmth of the sunset.

5 Adjust the White Balance When shooting sunsets, don't overlook the usefulness of White Balance. Although your camera's Auto White Balance usually does a great job, it can be worth switching to the Cloudy or Shade preset to give sunsets a boost – particularly if capturing JPEGs. Doing so will warm up and enhance your sunsets. If you are shooting in Raw, you can always adjust colour temperature during post-processing.

Final image

Don't pack up and head home too soon, the best colour and conditions often don't appear until after sunset. Beautiful shades of red, orange and pink can form in the sky and you don't want to be walking back to the car if this happens. Exposure times naturally grow longer in the low light, so a tripod is essential. Shutter speeds exceeding ten seconds are not uncommon, rendering water movement as an ethereal blur.

Shoot silhouettes

Backlight your subjects to create stunning silhouetted images – this guide shows you how

Ross Hoddinott: As photographers, we are always striving for the 'correct' exposure, aren't we? However, it could be argued that there is no such thing, as it greatly depends on the subject, the situation and the effect the photographer wants to achieve. For example, a silhouette can create a truly eye-catching image even though, technically speaking, it is the result of a poor exposure.

A silhouette is when the subject is recorded as a black outline, without colour or detail, against a lighter background – in other words, the subject is grossly underexposed. It is the most extreme form of backlighting but, when combined with the right scene or subject, the results can be stunning – particularly when the subject is contrasted against an interesting or colourful sky. Despite the lack of detail and colour, silhouettes can convey much about the subject and they prove that there really is no such thing as a 'correct exposure'.

One of the great things about shooting silhouettes is that they are easily achieved and you need very little in terms of kit to get a good result. I visited Dartmoor's windswept landscape to show you how to shoot perfect silhouettes…

Technique watch

Metering: Your camera's multi-zone meter is designed to render the subject as a mid-tone. While this is perfect for the vast majority of situations, it will rarely produce the results you are looking for when shooting subjects that are considerably lighter or darker in tone. A silhouetted subject can create problems for metering systems. Although highly sophisticated, the camera's exposure system cannot predict the effect you are trying to achieve. Therefore, if the scene is dominated by a black silhouetted subject, the camera will attempt to render it as a mid-tone by selecting a longer exposure – resulting in overexposure. Alternatively, if the scene is dominated by sky and is very light, the camera is likely to underexpose the frame. Thankfully, avoiding this type of exposure problem is simple by switching your camera's spot-metering mode. This metering mode is selected either via a dedicated button or through the camera's menu system. It calculates the overall exposure from just a small portion of the frame – usually a central circle. Point the spot-metering circle at a bright area of the frame and press the shutter release button halfway to take a reading. These are the exposure settings you want to employ to take your silhouette. Pressing the auto-exposure lock (AE-L) button, 'lock' the settings, compose your image and release the shutter. The result should be that your subject becomes underexposed and appears as a pure black silhouette.

Seek strong outlines

In silhouettes, we strive for the main subject to be devoid of detail or colour; so select subjects with a strong, recognisable outline. People, buildings, animals and trees make good choices

1 Get your tripod low When shooting silhouettes, a low viewpoint often works best – helping you to set your subject starkly against a bright sky. Therefore, don't be afraid to get your knees damp and dirty to select a low angle. In this instance, I splay the legs on my tripod wide open, enabling me to shoot from a low perspective.

2 Crop into your subject Trees create a graphic, simple outline – perfect for silhouettes. It is easiest to take silhouettes in mornings and evenings, when the sun is lower in the sky, so having arrived early, I spot these two trees that I think will work well. Using the long end of a standard zoom, I crop in tightly to them, but the camera's multi-zone meter attempts to record them as a mid-tone, resulting in a disappointing, washed-out shot.

3 Use spot metering To ensure that the lovely colours of the sunrise are recorded faithfully, and that the trees are thrown into pure silhouette, I switch the camera's metering mode to spot (this is often illustrated by a dot, as seen in the picture above). If you are unsure how to select spot metering, check your camera's instruction manual. If your camera lacks a spot mode, use partial metering instead.

Final image
By zooming in a little from the last frame, I feel that I've struck the right balance in terms of composition. Placing the trees right-of-centre creates a stronger image than it would have if they had been central. Spot-metering has enabled me to capture the right exposure in-camera – all I had to do post-capture was intensify the sky's colour very slightly by clicking *Image>Adjustments>Hue/Saturation* and adjusting the saturation slider to +10.

4 Lock your settings I remove the camera from the tripod via the quick-release plate, and point the spot-metering circle at a bright area of the sky. I press the shutter release button halfway to take my meter reading, and then lock these settings by using the auto-exposure lock (AE-L) button. I replace the camera on the tripod and check that the composition hasn't changed. Then, using the new locked settings, I take another picture.

5 Review composition Although the exposure is now correct, I am feeling less happy with the composition. It looks a little cramped and I wonder whether I've cropped in too close. The joy of using a zoom lens is being able to quickly change composition without having to move. I zoom out to leave more space around the trees, allowing me to capture more of the sunrise. However, have I now gone too far towards the opposite extreme?

Spectacular star trails

If you're in a remote location, take advantage of clear night skies by capturing stunning star trails

John Patrick: Star trails are rewarding subjects that can add an element of magic to a landscape shot, revealing the scene in a way that isn't visible to the eye. They allow you to extend the day's potential shooting time, and to get out with your camera – especially if you work through the week and can't get outdoors during the daylight hours in winter. If there's any secret to the technique, it's getting the exposure right, but that's simple when shooting digitally...

Get away from the city

The glow from urban areas is known as light pollution and can be seen from miles away on a clear night. This might not be obvious to the naked eye but will show up clearly on a long exposure

Essential kit

Keep it steady
You'll need to keep the shutter open for the long exposure and the best way to do that is to use a remote release with a lock to hold the shutter open. This helps avoid inadvertently knocking or moving the camera. A sturdy tripod is important, too, and a wide-angle lens is handy as it helps you get plenty of sky in the shot. Other than that, star trails don't need any particularly specialist kit. Don't forget plenty of warm clothing, though. Even if you're used to being out in cold weather, standing around for half an hour or more in the dark in sub-zero temperatures can bring a whole new level of chilliness, so pack a few extra layers to keep you comfortable.

1 Find the location If you can, it helps to find your location in advance, in the daylight hours. Midday is a good time to do this for a couple of reasons. One is that it's often dead time in the landscape photographer's day when the light is too harsh for shooting. The other is that, with the sun to the south, shadows will point north towards where the stars will be circling around Polaris later. Visualising that will help you create a good composition. You'll need to ensure that you're a decent distance away from major light pollution, too.

2 Set up Pick your night (a night with a half-moon is a good choice, if possible) and set up the camera on the tripod. If it's too dark to see properly through the viewfinder, you can take a few shots with a high ISO and wide aperture, gradually making adjustments to fine-tune the composition. Autofocus is unlikely to work in very low light, so you'll need to focus manually – either by using the distance scale or by placing a torch somewhere in the scene to focus on.

3 Meter the scene You can meter the scene before taking the final shot by taking test shots at a high ISO and wide aperture. I'm using ISO 1600 and f/4 here. Set the camera to manual and start with an exposure time of around 20 seconds. Take a shot and check the histogram, then simply alter the exposure time and retake test shots until the histogram looks correct. After a bit of experimentation, I find that one stop underexposed works best.

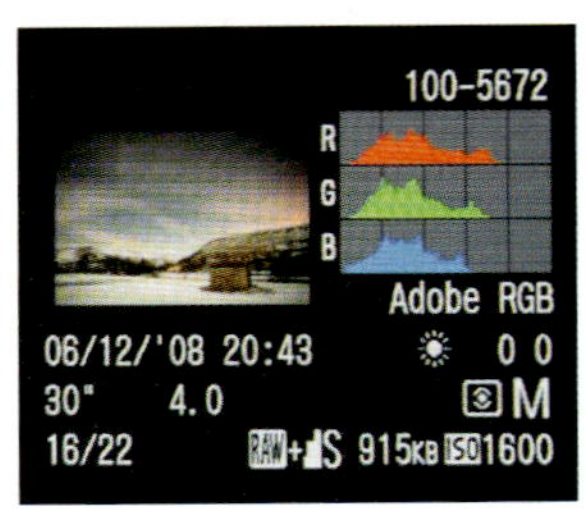

Final image
I've given the final image more contrast using Curves, adjusted the colour balance to make the tones cooler and applied Unsharp Mask in Photoshop.

4 Settings for the final shot When you're happy with the exposure, set the camera to Bulb mode. Select ISO 100 and set a wide aperture. I tend to use f/5.6. Now you can use the exposure time from step three to work out the time needed for the final shot, compensating for the change in ISO and aperture by increasing the time. For instance, if you needed a 30-second exposure in step three: 30 seconds x 2 (for a one-stop change from f/4 to f/5.6) x16 (for the change from ISO 1600 to ISO 100) gives a 16-minute exposure.

5 Take the shot Turn all lights out, note the time and lock the shutter open with the remote release. Get out some coffee and chocolate, have a break for a while and enjoy staring at the stars. Just don't do what I did and discover at this point that the coffee's back down the road, still in the car! If you need to put a light on at any point to read the time, be careful not to illuminate the foreground at all, as it will show up in the final shot (unless you're deliberately attempting light painting, but that's another topic).

Moonlit landscapes

The brightness of the moon can create other-worldly landscape scenes – use it to your best advantage for shots full of mood

JUST BECAUSE THE SUN has gone down doesn't mean you can't capture beautiful landscapes. Using moonlight is in fact simpler than photographing at dusk as the light is less variable. Shooting moonlit landscapes is not that different from shooting in daylight, but a lot easier than shooting at sunset, because moonlight is a lot stronger than the last light of the day. That said, you need to pay similar attention to the angle and position of the moon, as you would the sun. A high moon casts strong downward shadows, while a low moon creates long shadows and much softer lighting. It's the optimum light for landscapes and occurs shortly after sunset, just as the moon begins to rise.

Exposure is a photographer's main challenge when it comes to moonlight, as it's several thousand times weaker than sunlight. A further complication for anyone taking pictures at night is the fact that the moon moves fairly quickly, so exposures that are more than a couple of minutes long can render it a streak in the sky. One solution is to keep the moon out of frame and simply shoot a landscape exposed by its light. Landscapes illuminated exclusively by a full moving moon that softens shadows can make eerie, ethereal pictures. Use too long an exposure, though, and the light becomes flat. If you want the moon in the picture, but the exposure is too long, take the correct exposure for the foreground, immediately followed by a shorter exposure for the sky, and then merge the two in post-production.

The length of an exposure depends on the intensity of the moon: a full moon on a clear night is great for illuminating landscapes where you want extensive depth-of-field. But if the moon isn't as strong or prominent, you'll find you may need to compromise on depth-of-field by using a wide aperture to reduce exposure times. Remember, though, if you use a wide aperture, accurate focusing is critical. The best times to shoot are when there's a full moon or during the two days before and after the full moon, when it wanes into and out of its full phase. Note also that layers of cloud affect the exposure, just like it does during the day.

For extra visual interest in your photographs, try shooting with a river, lake or sea in the foreground, so you can capture the light beams glistening off the surface – you'll find that the reflected light also brightens the whole scene. You could also introduce flash or a torch into your shoot, using it to paint the foreground.

When setting up your camera, apply the same techniques already explained in this guide: use Bulb or manual mode, work out the exposure, focus manually if possible and fire the shutter using a remote release. When working out the exposure for a moonlit scene, multi-zone metering works well. Then follow this technique: take a test shot in aperture-priority mode at your highest ISO rating and widest aperture to give yourself a base shutter speed, then use reciprocity failure to work out the exposure for a decent aperture and low ISO rating. Alternatively, switch to spot metering and meter off the brightest part in the scene, then add two stops of extra exposure because the metering system will otherwise render your highlights as a mid-tone.

Once you've mastered star trails and moonlit landscapes, try shooting auroras, meteor showers or even have a go at deep-space photography – you'll open up a whole world of photo opportunities!

Right: **For every exposure of this scene, the f/stop and ISO had to be adjusted to keep the shutter speed between 15 and 30 seconds in order to freeze the moon's motion.**

Below: **This shot of Swaledale comprises a four-minute exposure for the foreground and a 30-second exposure for the sky.**

JOHN PATRICK

Reciprocity law

With low-light photography, it's important to remind yourself about the interchangeable relationship between shutter speeds and apertures so that you can work out the required exposure.

It takes a bit of brainpower, but you can now download apps to your smartphone that can help you calculate equivalent exposures. Basically, every time you stop down your aperture, you need to increase your shutter speed to double the exposure time, so if you go from f/4 to f/5.6, the shutter speed needs to double from, say, two seconds to four seconds.

Reciprocity law failure is when the camera fails to accurately meter a scene in low light and fails to meter a sufficient exposure time for the length of shutter speed. It's much less common with digital cameras than film, but you may find you need to add an extra stop or two of exposure to ward off underexposure when shooting moonlit shots like the ones on these pages.

GARY McPARLAND

How to shoot the moon

For those of us who don't have the resources for deep-space photography of the Milky Way galaxy, the nearest thing we have to the mysticism of space is the moon. You don't need any special equipment to photograph the moon, only what you'd normally use for most night photography, but a decent telephoto zoom would be an asset – in particular, those extending to at least 300mm. If you don't have a suitable lens, you could invest in a teleconverter to extend the reach. Remember that an APS-C camera has a crop factor of x1.5, so the equivalent focal length of a 200mm lens is 300mm.

It's easy to underestimate the moon's brightness, which is why getting the exposure correct can be quite tricky. Most first attempts at lunar photographs result in an overexposed circle where the moon should be. The first step to avoiding this is to pick a spot where there is no ambient light from traffic or streetlights, on a clear night, with no cloud. There is a little trial and error needed to get the perfect exposure as it changes depending on the shooting conditions, but set your camera to manual mode and use 1/250sec at f/8 (ISO 100) as a starting point. Take a series of bracketed exposures (in one-stop increments) around this setting and review them on the LCD monitor.

We'd recommend you change the shutter speed rather than the aperture. Depending on the phase of the moon, its brightness, your location and the atmospheric conditions, you may find you need to lengthen or shorten the exposure to capture enough tonal detail on the lunar surface.

Position your focus point over the moon, lock on to it using autofocus and then switch to manual focus to stop it hunting. Use a remote release or the self-timer to minimise the risk of shake blurring the result.

You're likely to have to crop the image in Photoshop and do a little work on the tonality by adjusting the Levels to draw out more detail on the moon's surface.

LEE FROST

PHOTOSHOP TECHNIQUES

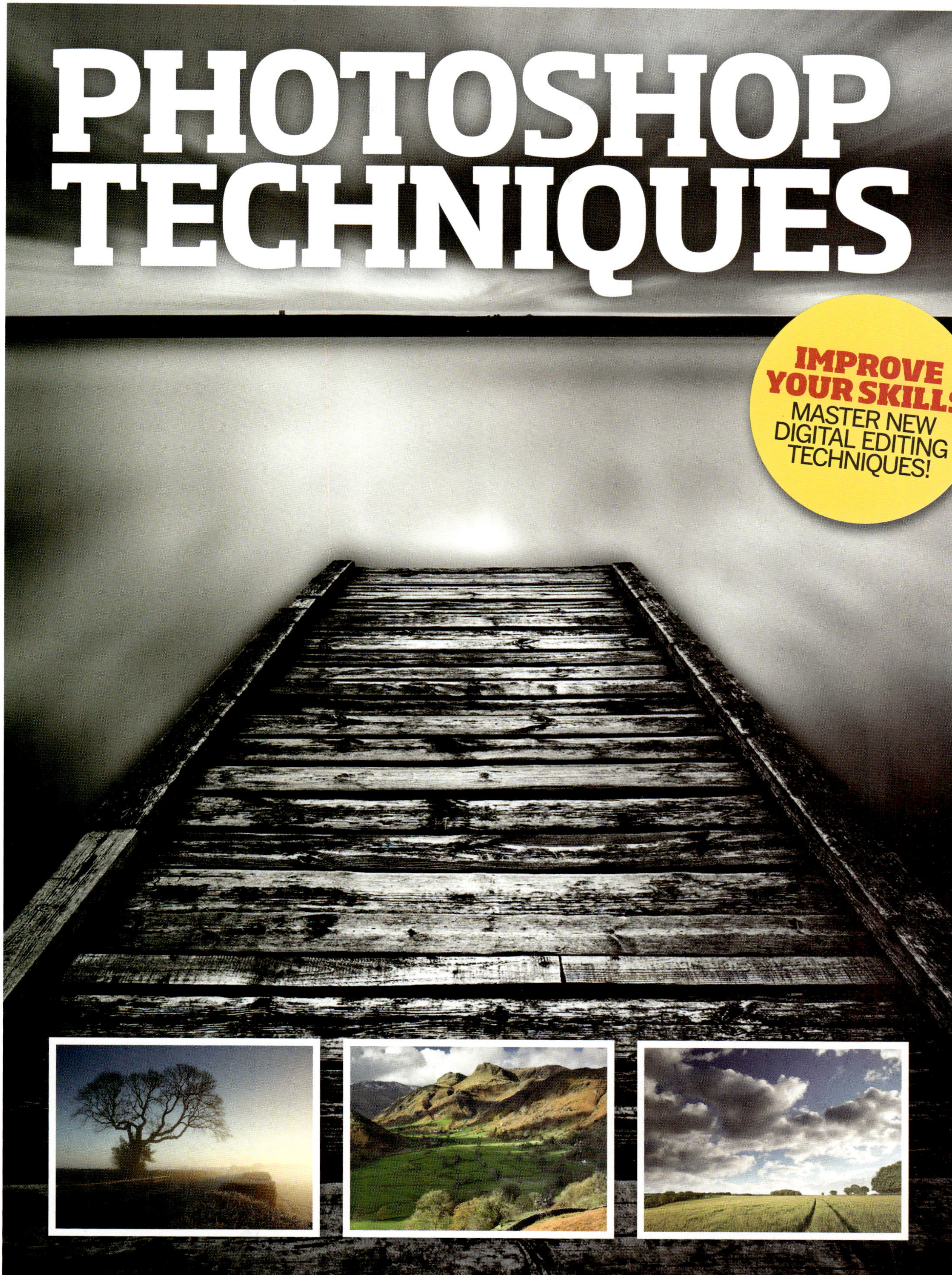

IMPROVE YOUR SKILLS
MASTER NEW DIGITAL EDITING TECHNIQUES!

Increase contrast using Adjustment Layers

Are your images in need of a contrast boost? Find out how to add extra punch to colours using Adjustment Layers and Blend Modes

Jordan Butters: Mist and fog add a wonderful atmosphere to images. Nothing quite conveys the mood of a chilly autumn or winter morning like the early morning sun piercing through a beautiful heavy haze.

More often than not, though, misty landscapes are hindered by a lack of contrast. Not to worry, though, as with the addition of an Adjustment Layer and some experimentation with Blend Modes, you can apply the punch to your misty landscape images. While this tutorial has been done in Elements 10, the same features and methods can be applied to images being worked on in Photoshop CS as well. Similarly, some CS tutorials in this guide can be done in Elements, too.

Working non-destructively

Adjustment layers

We would usually advise duplicating your original image layer before you start editing your photograph, just in case you make any mistakes. However, a major benefit of Adjustment Layers is that they are non-destructive, meaning that any changes you make using them do not affect the original image data. What's more, the parameters and values of an Adjustment Layer can be tweaked in the Adjustment palette at any time throughout the editing process, or if you're not entirely happy with the effect, you can simply delete that Adjustment Layer and start afresh.

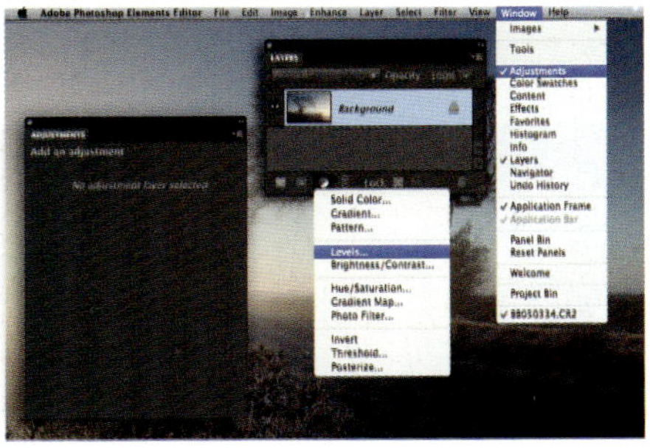

1 Add an Adjustment Layer You'll need the Layers and Adjustment palettes visible, so first go to the ***Window*** menu and make sure that both ***Adjustments*** and ***Layers*** are ticked. Then click on the ***Create new fill or adjustment layer*** button at the bottom of the Layers palette and, in the drop-down menu that appears, select ***Levels***.

2 Try the Auto feature In the Adjustment palette, first try using the ***Auto*** button to allow the software to decide which adjustments are made to your image. This works better on some images more than others. The Auto levels tool adjusts each of the Red, Green and Blue channels independently so you may now notice a colour cast appear in your image.

3 Correct the colour To correct the colour cast, make sure that the ***Levels*** layer in the Layers palette is selected and, using the Blend Mode menu at the top, change the ***Blend Mode*** of the layer to ***Luminosity***. This will remove the image's colour cast by ensuring that the Adjustment Layer only affects the contrast in the image below it and not the colours.

Final image
The contrast increase has cut through the haze and boosted saturation.

4 Try a manual adjustment If you aren't happy with the effect from using Auto levels, delete your Adjustment Layer by clicking on it in the Layers palette and dragging it to the ***Delete layer*** icon at the bottom; this reverts the image back to its original state. Add another Adjustment Layer by clicking on the ***Create new fill or adjustment layer*** button and selecting ***Levels***.

5 Manually set Levels This time, rather than using the Auto adjustment, click and drag on the ***black***, ***grey*** and ***white*** point sliders in the Adjustment palette to tweak the contrast of your image. Be careful how far you push the black and white points so you don't clip the shadows and highlights and lose detail. You can be more liberal with the grey slider for the mid-tones.

6 Experiment with Blend Modes Back in the Layers palette, experiment with the different ***Blend Modes*** to alter the effect. ***Overlay, Soft Light*** and ***Hard Light*** will all offer slightly different effects. You can also use the ***Opacity*** slider at the top of the Layers palette to weaken the effect or you can revisit the Adjustment palette at any time to tweak the parameters.

Learn how to control colour

No one wants dull and washed-out images, but oversaturation can be just as bad. Here's how to take careful control of your colour

Know the difference

Vibrance and Saturation
There's often much confusion surrounding the difference between the Vibrance and Saturation sliders in Adobe Camera Raw. At first glance they can appear to do much the same thing, but there are clear differences in the results you get from each. The main difference is that the Vibrance slider is designed not to affect colours that are already sufficiently saturated. In most cases, this makes it useful for applying a universal adjustment without oversaturating those colours which are already nice and bright. Furthermore, the Vibrance slider will also not affect hues similar to those found in skin tones. This makes it useful for increasing saturation in portrait shots without turning your subject's skin a strange shade of orange. Take a look at the comparison below to see the difference an adjustment of +75 on each slider makes to the original image.

Jordan Butters: Autumn, especially, is a beautiful time of year for capturing colourful landscapes. Deep blue skies, rustic reds, lush green grass and golden oranges. When shooting to capture colour like this, it's only right to assume that we want to do these fantastic colours justice with accurate reproduction. Failure to replicate the hues we see in a scene isn't always down to the photographer – digital cameras are still nowhere near as advanced as the human eye. But there are steps that you can take to ensure good colour reproduction in-camera, such as ensuring that you have the correct White Balance set and shooting under the best lighting conditions.

Most of us want to capture maximum detail in our images, which is why we advise you expose to the right when shooting in Raw format (meaning that you should overexpose your image slightly, but not to the extent that the highlights become clipped). Doing this, though, does sacrifice colour saturation – the brighter the original colour, the worse the image appears bleached. Thankfully, this can be addressed with Photoshop's Adobe Camera Raw, as there are a number of controls that allow you to adjust colours universally and individual hues.

On the surface, many of the controls, such as Luminance and Saturation, seem to have similar effects but there are subtle differences. For the best results, start to learn what each of the sliders do – starting with the areas covered in this tutorial.

1 Open the image This image has been exposed to the right without losing any highlight detail, but the colours are washed out as a result. Open your Raw file in ACR and first make any changes to ***Exposure*** and ***Contrast*** as these parameters will affect the colours in your image.

2 Decrease luminance selectively Select the ***HSL/Grayscale*** tab and choose the ***Luminance*** tab within to target the brightness of the individual colour channels. Reduce the luminance of the ***Blues*** channel to darken the sky. Monitor the image preview to assess the changes.

3 Adjust surrounding channels Quite often you'll find that you need to adjust more than one channel to make the changes look natural. By making subtle adjustments to the neighbouring Aquas channel, the transition in colour between sky and clouds is improved.

Final image
The vibrant, punchy colours that were present on the day have been restored, creating an eye-catching image.

4 Increase saturation manually The Saturation sliders control the intensity of each colour. Click on the ***Saturation*** tab and drag the ***Green*** slider to adjust the channel. Make any changes gradually, as oversaturation can look as bad, if not worse than undersaturation.

5 Adjust the surrounding channels As before, neighbouring channels may benefit from some slight adjustment. In this case, the green grass looked more natural when a small increase is made to the saturation of the Yellows channel as well.

6 Adjust the Hue To change the colour of an area – like these orange hills – select the ***Hue*** tab. Next move the ***Orange*** slider until you are happy with the result. You may find only small changes are needed to alter the hue – but be watchful that it doesn't look unnatural.

Breathe life into flat photos

Want to create an HDR effect but don't have Raw files or a set of bracketed exposures? Don't despair! Use Shadows & Highlights…

Luke Marsh: We all have images that didn't quite render the scene how you remember it. Maybe the sky's not as moody or the ground is too dark, or maybe the overall appearance of the image lacks contrast or is badly exposed. Well, Shadows & Highlights can resurrect these images. This nifty adjustment is a fantastic photographic tool, which is often overlooked by users since dedicated HDR software like Photomatix and Photoshop actions became available from third-party companies. In the simplest terms, the adjustments allow you to recover detail from over- or underexposed areas by adjusting the Highlights or Shadows controls respectively, or you can improve the overall tonal range using the Midtone Contrast slider. It's really very simple.

The key to success with Shadows & Highlights is subtlety. As with any process that plays with tonal range, HDR included, Shadows & Highlights can produce photographic Frankensteins if used too eagerly. So why not give it a go? The controls may seem daunting at first, but after a little experimentation and with a better understanding of what can be achieved, you may find you'll be using this feature regularly.

Hot Key

Alt to reset

When working in Shadows & Highlights, hold down ***Alt*** to change the ***Cancel*** button to a ***Reset*** button in case you want to take the filter back to its default settings. You can also uncheck ***Preview*** to toggle between the blurred and original image.

1 Duplicate original Our chosen image is a bit lifeless, yet clearly has potential texture in the sky and detail in the foreground that could be pulled out using Shadows & Highlights. First, create a duplicate layer from the original by going to ***Layer>Duplicate Layer…***, naming the layer accordingly for reference later.

2 Shadows & Highlights On the duplicate layer go to ***Image>Adjustments>Shadows & Highlights…*** As the image is generally flat, concentrate on the ***Shadows*** and ***Midtone Contrast***, with only minor adjustments to the ***Highlight*** field. At this stage you want to be focusing more on getting the foreground right.

3 Duplicate adjusted layer Now duplicate this edited layer with ***Layer>Duplicate Layer…*** Then add a Layer Mask by going to ***Layer>Layer Mask>Reveal All*** or by clicking on the ***Add Layer Mask*** icon at the bottom of the Layers palette (circled). The purpose of the Layer Mask is so that the next edit only affects the sky area of this layer.

4 Add a gradient Click on the ***Layer Mask*** thumbnail and select the ***Gradient Tool***, ensuring the ***Foreground*** and ***Background color*** are set to the default ***Black*** and ***White***. With the ***Shift*** key held down to ensure a straight line, click near the horizon and drag, letting go at the top of the image. This adds a gradient to the mask.

5 Create a stormy sky With the mask in place, any work done will only affect the sky area. Open ***Shadows & Highlights*** as instructed in step two, but this time work mainly on the ***Highlights*** and ***Midtones Contrast*** to pull all the detail back into the sky. You may want to increase the ***Black Clip*** to improve the overall contrast.

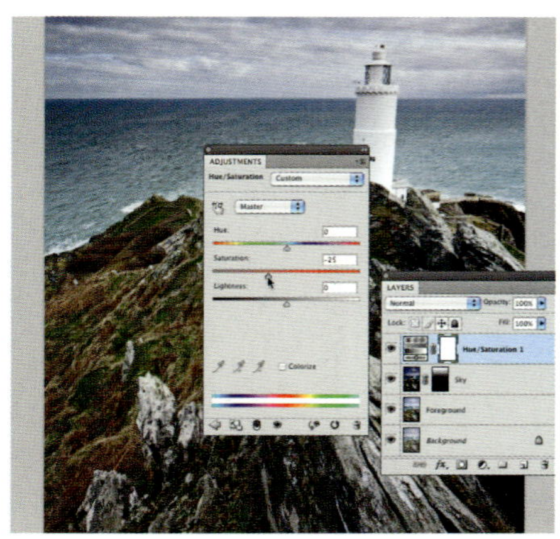

6 Reduce the saturation One final tweak is to remove some of the colour to enhance the storm-like appearance of the image. With the top layer still active, go to ***Layer>New Adjustment Layer>Hue/Saturation…*** and reduce the ***Saturation*** slider by around ***20%***, then click ***OK***. Now save as a ***PSD***, to preserve all the layers.

Final image

From flat to fantastic: Shadows & Highlights has pulled out lots of detail that lay hidden in the JPEG.

Behind the mask

Combining Adjustment Layers and Layer Masks opens up a world of options for selectively tweaking and perfecting your shots

Jordan Butters: Without a doubt, one of the most powerful features of Adobe Photoshop CS is the ability to selectively edit your images in a non-destructive manner using Adjustment Layers and Layer Masks.

Adjustment Layers offer a series of effects and adjustments, each with adjustable parameters to suit your images. Furthermore, they can be applied to the entire image at once, clipped to just a single layer or applied selectively using a Layer Mask.

Layer Masks, as the name suggests, mask the layers that they are applied to, allowing you to edit or affect only selected parts of your image at a time. If you've been using Photoshop but haven't yet delved into the world of Layer Masks and Adjustment Layers, you're missing out on myriad options for improving your images and it's time to harness the full power of CS.

Alternative method

■ Layer Masks
Layer Masks can be applied to image layers as well as Adjustment Layers. For images with two or more layers present, select the layer you wish to mask and check ***Add vector mask*** in the Layers palette. Then use the ***Brush Tool*** to brush over and mask your image. Remember – White reveals the layer, Black masks it.

Top tip

To apply an adjustment to a single layer rather than the whole image, select the ***Clip to layer*** button in the Adjustments palette.

1 Show the Layers palette With your image loaded in Photoshop, make sure the Layers palette is visible by going to ***Window>Layers***. In the Layers palette you will only see a Background layer at present. Duplicate this layer by going to ***Layer>Duplicate Layer***, or by pressing ***Cmd+J*** if you're on a Mac or ***Ctrl+J*** if you're using a Windows-based PC.

2 Add a Quick Mask I want to retain the warm tones in the sky but add a neutral tone to the foreground. Press the ***Q*** key to enable Quick Mask mode, select the ***Brush Tool*** and use the top menu to customise the brush to suit. Brush over the area you wish to remain unaffected by any changes. If you make a mistake, press the ***X*** key and brush back over to remove the mask.

3 Add an adjustment With your area masked off, press the ***Q*** key again to turn this mask into a selection and, in the Layers palette, click on the ***Create new fill or adjustment layer*** button and select ***Photo Filter*** from the drop-down menu. In the Adjustments palette, select one of the three preset ***Cooling Filters*** and adjust the ***Density*** slider to alter its effect.

4 Add another adjustment To bring out detail in the foreground, click on the ***Create new fill or adjustment layer*** button again to create a new adjustment and this time select ***Levels***. In the Adjustments palette, adjust the sliders until you are happy with the effect. These changes will be applied to just the foreground in the next step, so don't worry about the sky for now.

5 Apply a gradient mask Click and hold on the ***Paint Bucket Tool*** to select the ***Gradient Tool*** and press the ***D*** key to make sure that your colour palette is reset. In the top menu, make sure that the ***Mode*** is set to ***Normal***. Click and drag on your image in the direction of foreground to background to apply the mask. The longer the line, the softer the gradient.

6 Tweak the mask Don't worry if you don't get the gradient right first time, you can click and drag as many times as you need to get the right transition. The gradient cuts through the final wooden post in my image and doesn't look natural. Select the ***Brush Tool*** and, with ***White*** set as your ***Foreground color***, paint in the post. If you go too far, press ***X*** to paint back over.

Final image

By selectively adjusting the foreground, the image has far more impact and visible detail.

Create a misty morning

The Gradient Tool is ideal for adding an eerie wintry feel to your images. A few other little tricks are necessary to pull it off, though

Luke Marsh: Mist is one of those elusive elements that rarely appears when you want it to but when it does it can transform the atmosphere of your landscapes. Now this step-by-step is no substitute for the real thing, but it can be used to improve your current landscape images or to occasionally relieve you having to wake early on a winter morning to search for natural mist.

Deep valleys and rolling hills make beautiful scenes for misty landscapes, as do frost-bitten fields. Refer to some example images before you try this technique just to see how mist naturally acts in different situations. Mist tends to look gradually heavier the further it is away from you, which is why you'll notice we handle the image treatment in sections – background, middle-distance and foreground – with each having a different intensity of mist.

Hot keys

Set foreground & background color
When using Layer Masks or the Gradient Tool, use the *X* key to change between the foreground and background colour, which is set to black & white as default.

ADAM BURTON

1 Add a gradient Use *Layer>New Layer...* to create a layer above the original. Select the Gradient Tool and ensure it's set to Linear gradient in the options bar, and that the foreground colour is set to *White* and the background to *Black*. Click and hold, then drag from the top of the image to just under the horizon to create the background layer of mist.

2 Reveal the tree In reality, the mist would be behind the tree. To give it this appearance, add a *Layer Mask* by clicking the icon in the Layers palette (circled). Next, select the *Brush Tool*, set to *Black* and an appropriate *Size*, and begin to work over the tree, removing the mist. If you go too far, you can change the *Foreground color* to *White* and paint over the area to bring back detail.

3 Focus on the middle-distance To add fog to the middle-distance, create another new layer via *Layer>New>Layer...* Use the *Gradient Tool* with the same settings, and draw a line from the top to the bottom of the image and release to create an even gradient across the frame. Reduce the *Opacity* by changing the amount to *50%* in the Layers palette (circled).

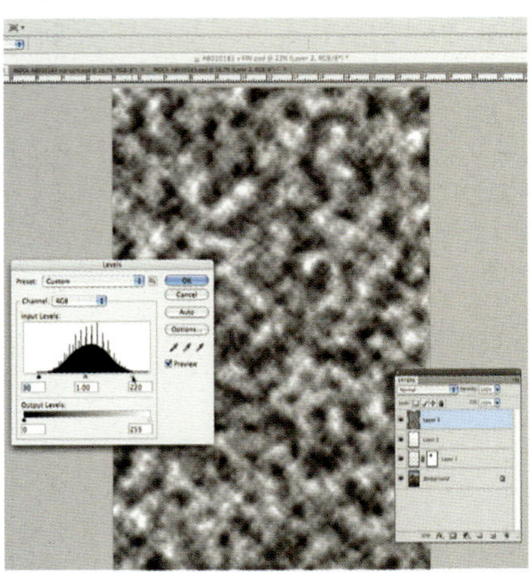

4 Add foreground mist To create eerie foreground mist, again add a new layer (*Layer>New Layer...*), then go to *Filter>Render>Clouds* to fill the layer with a textured cloud effect. Use *Image>Adjustments>Levels...* and the black and white sliders to boost the contrast on the image. Finally, change the layer *Blend Mode* to *Screen* to make the layers interact.

5 Adjust perspective To add perspective, go to *Edit>Free Transform>Scale* and reduce down to the foreground area by dragging the top-centre tab. Before applying, change the transform to *Perspective* and drag one of the bottom corner tabs outside the pasteboard until you're happy. You may need to zoom out to move the tabs out far enough, as shown here.

6 Tweak colour & contrast Create two adjustment layers by selecting the icon at the bottom of the Layers palette (circled). First, create a *Hue/Saturation* adjustment layer, and use the *Saturation* slider to desaturate the colours slightly, and, finally, create a *Brightness/Contrast* adjustment layer to boost the contrast sufficiently to enhance the appearance of diffused misty light.

A mist opportunity!

A few simple steps are all it takes to add a touch of mist to your landscape images.

Add a colour graduated filter

Learn how to control Photoshop's gradients to create a colour graduated filter effect and transform ordinary skies into something glorious

Jordan Butters: In an ideal world, landscape photographers would always have an array of ND grad filters close to hand; one for every conceivable situation and effect that you want to create. In reality, however, this isn't always practical. Thankfully there are a range of effects in Photoshop that simulate the results of using filters, even the coloured graduated variety. This technique is great for emphasising existing colours in the sky or completely changing the mood and feel of your image by emulating a different time of day to when image was taken.

1 Add the gradient Before we begin, press the ***D*** key on your keyboard to reset your colour palette to default. Click on the ***Add new fill or adjustment layer*** button in the Layers palette and select ***Gradient*** from the drop-down menu.

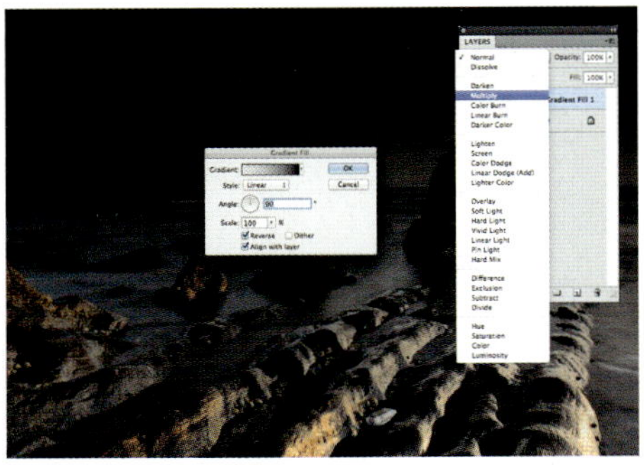

2 Adjust the gradient In the dialogue box, click on the ***Reverse*** tick-box to place the gradient at the top of the image as opposed to the bottom and then click ***OK***. Back in the Layers palette, change the ***Blend Mode*** of the ***Gradient layer*** to ***Multiply***.

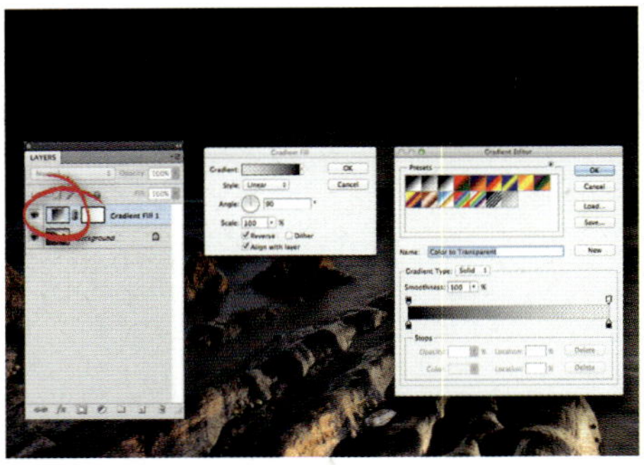

3 Open the Gradient Editor Double-click on the thumbnail on the ***Gradient layer*** in the Layers palette to open the ***Gradient Fill*** menu again and click on the ***Gradient*** thumbnail at the top to open the ***Gradient Editor*** palette.

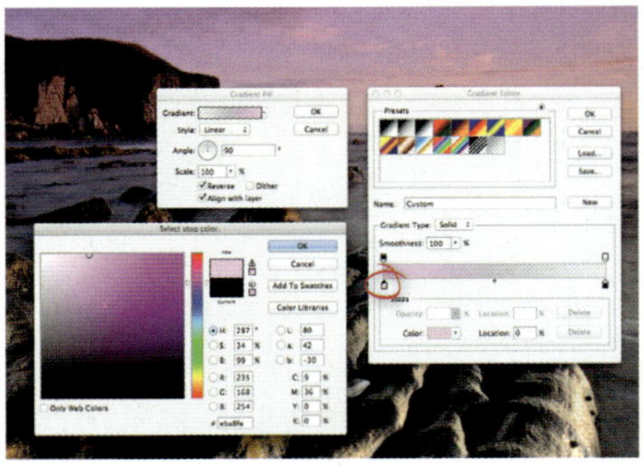

4 Change the colour Click on ***Black Color Stop*** in the bottom-left corner of the gradient. Then click on the ***Color*** thumbnail below to open the ***Color Picker*** window. Select your colour – I chose pink to emulate the sky at dusk. Click ***OK***.

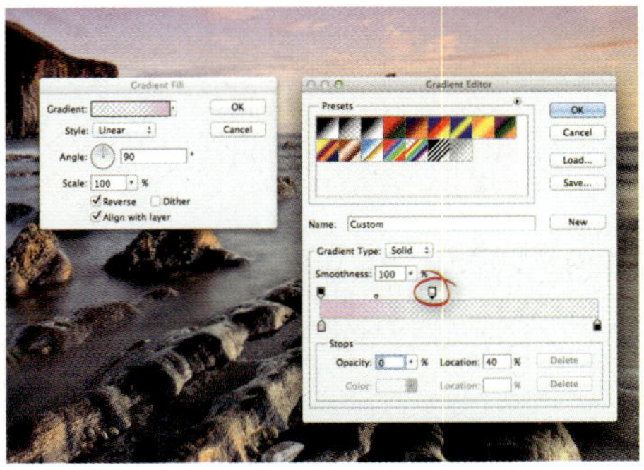

5 Alter the opacity The two ***Color Stops*** above the gradient scale control the opacity of the gradient. Move the ***White Color Stop*** in the top-right corner to control the depth and hardness of the gradient to suit your image. Once done, click ***OK***.

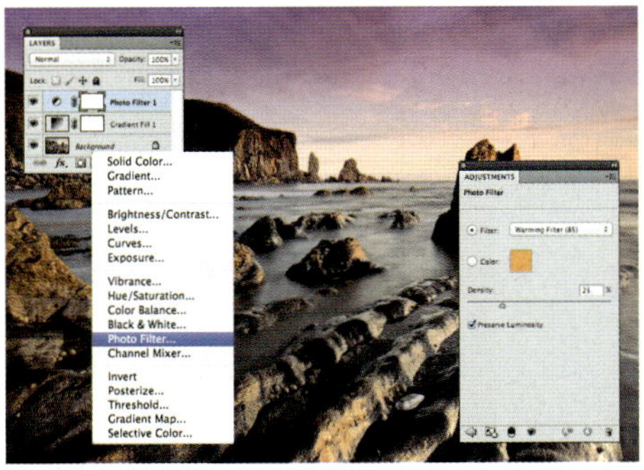

6 Add a Photo Filter Back in the Layers palette, click on the ***Add new fill or adjustment layer*** button again and this time select ***Photo Filter***. Select one of the ***Warming Filters*** and click ***OK*** – this will warm the entire image to suit the dusk colours.

Multiple filters

You could always try adding more than one colour filter to your image. Simply duplicate your Gradient layer by selecting it in the Layers palette and going to ***Layer>Duplicate Layer*** and change the gradient colour as was done in steps three through to five. Try placing the gradients at different angles using the ***Angle*** dial in the ***Gradient Fill*** menu for different effects.

Final image

Caught out without your filters? No fear – when you can create stunning sunsets like this in Photoshop, you've always got a back-up plan!

Duotone your black & white photographs

We reveal how to add colour to your shadows and highlights

Caroline Wilkinson: There is so much you can do with a black & white photograph to alter its look but one traditional technique that's still increasingly popular is colour-toning. All too often it's a technique that's done horrendously badly: images look like they've been dipped in a purple or magenta wash, or like they've been taken using the wrong White Balance.

Subtly altering the temperature of the highlights or shadows with a yellow/orange hue or blue tint can add warmth and a contemporary coolness, respectively. So, as a rule of thumb, err on the side of caution: you want the tint to work with the scene, not overpower it. We're going to split-tone, otherwise known as duotone, a mono image here, which requires you to separately tone the shadows and highlights. The difficulty comes from finding colours that work well together: putting complementary colours in the mix is a good place to start and, after that, experimentation.

Common errors

How not to do it
It can be tempting to take the easy route and colourwash your pictures using a Hue/Saturation adjustment layer or to be too heavy-handed with applying colour. You'll know you've gone too far as you'll start to lose details and will have very little graduation in tone. Often the best results come from picking a colour that isn't so vibrant that it overpowers the scene. You want viewers to see the beautiful photograph first, and then the tint.

1 Convert to monochrome Add a Black & White adjustment layer (***Layer>New Adjustment Layer>Black & White***...) and adjust the colour sliders until you reach the level of contrast that best suits your image. You can also select one of the options under ***Preset*** for one-click effects. Here, I decide to opt for the High Contrast Red Filter.

2 Apply colour Add a Hue/Saturation adjustment layer the alternative way by clicking on the ***Add new fill or adjustment layer*** icon at the bottom of the Layers palette. With the adjustment panel open, click on the ***Colorize*** box and drag the ***Hue*** slider to pick the tint for the shadows, ignoring the effect on the rest of the image for now.

Alternative method

Color balance adjustment layer
Although the results sometimes aren't quite as good, a really quick way to split-tone an image is to use a Color Balance adjustment layer on a black & white image. You're able to control the tinting of tones using the Shadows, Midtone and Highlight settings all in one place.

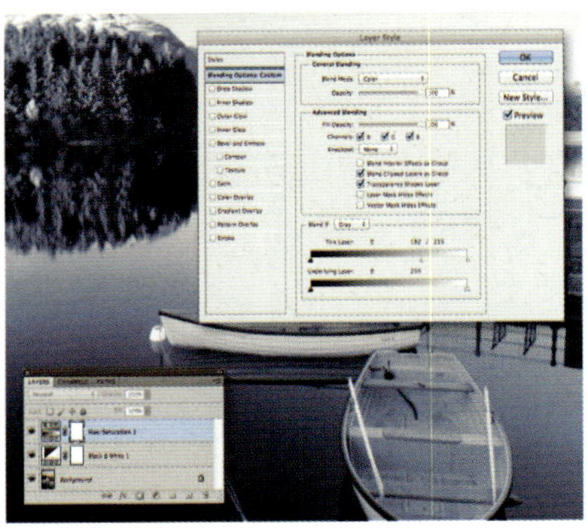

3 Tone the shadows In the Layers palette, change the Hue/Saturation layer's ***Blend Mode*** to ***Color***. Now go to ***Layer>Layer Style>Blending Options***. Hold ***Alt*** and click the white triangle to split it in two and drag them until you find the balance between excluding highlights from the tint and a smooth graduation in tones. Best positions here are around 100 and 200.

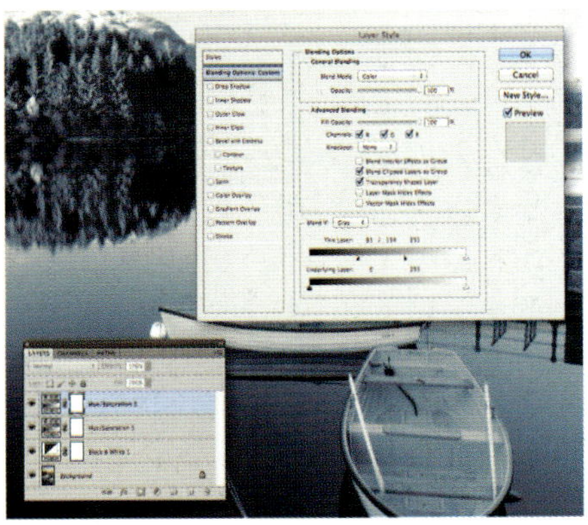

4 Tone the highlight Repeat step three, but focus on the shadows. Add a ***Hue/Saturation*** adjustment layer, change its ***Blend Mode*** to ***Color***, click ***Colorize*** and adjust the ***Hue*** slider to tone the highlights – ignoring the shadows. Access ***Blending Options*** and split the black sliders to remove the tint from the shadows. Good positions here are around 80 and 155.

5 Tweak your contrast One of the reasons for working with Adjustment Layers is so you can revert back to previous adjustments and tweak them once you've finished. The contrast in your black & white conversion greatly affects the duotone treatment, so double-click on the ***Black & White*** adjustment layer to re-edit the sliders and see if you can improve the results.

Final image

A subtle blend of colours in your highlights and shadows can give mono shots warmth or coolness.

Bland to beautiful: learn how to replace a sky

Improve your landscape images ten-fold with this simple technique where you can swap an uninspiring sky for one with more drama

Jordan Butters: The British weather is well known for not doing quite what you want it to and rarely do all of the elements play ball when it comes to landscape photography. You can be perched above a beautiful vista, camera ready on a tripod and remote in hand, but the one thing you can't do much about is a bland sky. All is not lost, though: in a few simple Photoshop steps you can replace the sky and transform your landscapes from drab to dramatic. You'll need to find a replacement sky to swap in, of course, and it's worth keeping a small library of skies in a folder on your computer for such occasions.

Try to shoot a range of different skies from different times of the day: the benefit of this is that it makes it a lot easier when the sky you are replacing is of a similar colour and time of the day to the replacement. You'll often find that trial and error is the key to finding the right sky for your scene.

ISTOCK PHOTO

1 Select the sky Open your image, choose the ***Quick Selection Tool*** and begin painting across the sky. If your image contains objects on the horizon, as ours does, you will need to zoom in and adjust your brush ***Size*** in the options toolbar to make a more accurate selection. If you select an area by mistake, simply hold down the ***Alt*** key and erase the selection. Once happy with your selection, go to ***Select>Inverse***.

2 Refine the selection Go to ***Select>Refine Edge*** to bring up the Options window. Click ***Default*** and the sky will appear white. Using the ***Contract/Expand*** slider, adjust the selection so that it closely follows the lines of the horizon. You can alter the preview that you see by selecting one of the preview options at the bottom. Once done, click ***OK***. Then go to ***Select>Inverse*** again and press the ***Backspace*** key to remove the sky.

3 Bring in the new sky Open your replacement sky image in a new window and, using the ***Rectangular Marquee Tool***, select the sky only. Copy your selection by going to ***Edit>Copy*** and close your sky image without saving. Head back to your original image and paste the sky in by going to ***Edit>Paste***. It's very unlikely that your new sky will fit your image straight away, so don't worry if this is the case.

4 Adjust the proportions Go to ***Edit> Transform>Scale*** and, holding down the ***Shift*** key, drag the corners of the sky image out or in to match the width of your landscape. Once happy, click on the ***Tick*** at the top, or press the ***Enter*** key. Use the ***Move Tool*** to line the sky up so that it completely covers the white area of the image. Don't worry about any overlap onto the horizon at this point.

5 Create a gradient Click on the ***Add Vector Mask*** button in the Layers palette. Select the ***Gradient Tool*** and, at the top of the screen, make sure that the black to white gradient is selected. On the image, click and drag the line from just below the horizon towards the top of the sky, then release the button. This part involves some trial and error, but you can repeat as many times as you need to until you are happy with the effect.

New horizons
The sky typically gets brighter the closer to the horizon it is. Bear this in mind when applying your gradient – if the gradient is too low or too hard, then the effect will lack realism

Final image
We think you'll agree that the new sky adds some much needed drama to the original image.

ISTOCK PHOTO

6 Tidy up the horizon Some of your new sky will still overlap onto the landscape, so to tidy this up, select the ***Brush Tool***, lower the ***Opacity*** to ***25%*** and set the brush's ***Hardness*** to ***25%*** in the brush options toolbar. Select ***Black*** as your ***Foreground color*** and brush over the horizon, building up areas that you wish to reveal. If you go too far or make a mistake, simply select ***White*** as your ***Foreground color*** and brush back over.

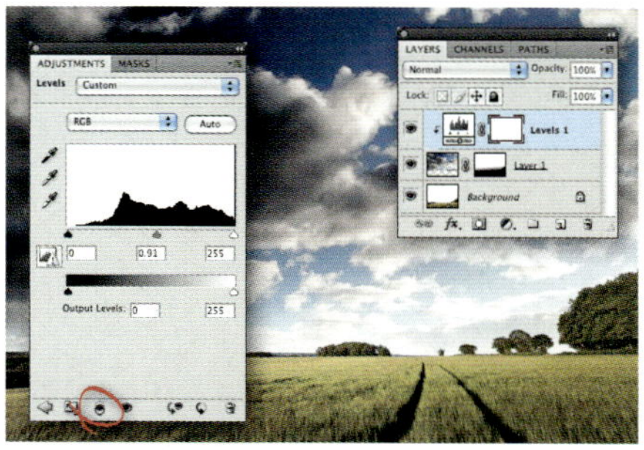

7 Adjust the contrast In the Layers palette, click on the ***Create new adjustment layer*** button and select ***Levels*** from the menu. First make sure that the adjustment is clipped to the layer below only by clicking the button at the bottom of the Adjustments palette. Then adjust the contrast of your sky to match the rest of the image using the middle (mid-tones) level slider. Once done, save your image using ***File>Save As***.

Quick selection

The Quick Selection Tool was released with the launch of Photoshop CS3 and Elements 6, and has featured in all versions since. It works by detecting contrast differences, and makes a selection based on this; ideal for separating skies from horizons. Just be aware of horizons with low cloud or mist cover, as the tool may struggle to separate them accurately.

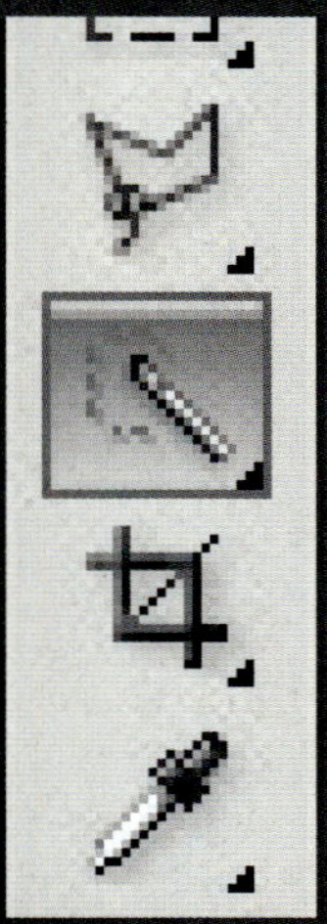

Make the year a blur with a four-seasons special

Give your seasonal landscapes a creative twist with this simple but striking motion-blur technique

Caroline Wilkinson: Every season offers new possibilities to photograph striking colour-filled landscapes, whether it be ruby-red poppies, sun-kissed oilseed rape, blankets of burnt orange leaves or black & white scenes in winter – you're never short of opportunities. While there are a million and one ways to photograph these classic scenes, each as beautiful as the other, it's good to find a technique that gives theses seasonal scenes a fresh, artistic appeal. You may have come across motionscapes before where you pan the camera across a coastal horizon to create streaks of colour. This technique is very similar but applies vertical streaks instead, using Photoshop. You can do a similar technique in-camera using a three-way pan & tilt tripod head to pan the camera up and down in a fluid movement, but it will blur the entire image, whereas here I only want to blur half of it. Plus, while the purists may be cursing, the effect is much easier to control, with better results, using the Motion Blur filter in Photoshop instead.

After some trial and error, it was clear that to get the best results for the seasonal quadtych (series of four images), I'd need images where there was as much interest in the top of the frame as the bottom, otherwise you wouldn't be able to tell what was blurred or in focus. I found that the best scenes seemed to be forests or landscapes where trees fill the height of the frame, so with this in mind the *Digital SLR Photography* team rummaged through their hard drives for suitable images to illustrate spring, summer, autumn and winter.

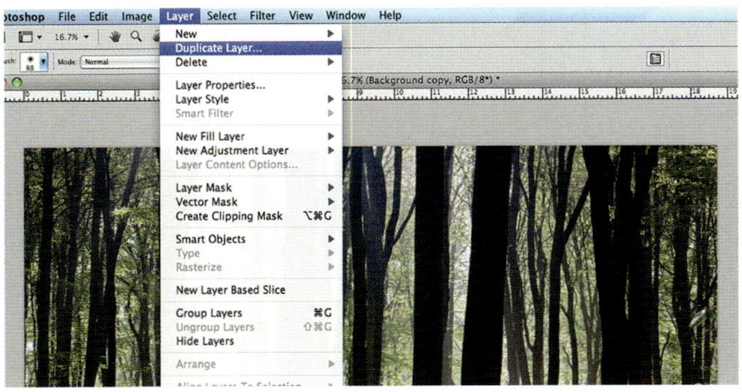

1 Create a duplicate layer Open your first picture and duplicate the image by clicking on the ***Background layer*** in the Layers palette and going to ***Layer>Duplicate Layer***, or by dragging it down to the ***Create a new layer*** icon at the bottom of the Layers palette. From now on you'll only be working on this duplicate layer. Leave the original image untouched.

2 Apply motion blur Click on ***Filter>Blur>Motion Blur*** to open the filter's dialogue box. As you want to apply a vertical blur, set the ***Angle*** to ***90°*** by either typing the amount in or moving the angle finder. You'll notice that by clicking and dragging on the angle finder the direction of the blur will change in the preview screen.

3 Increase the strength Adjust the ***Distance*** slider to increase the strength of the blur effect. The bottom of the image needs to be heavily blurred but not to the point that the subjects become unrecognisable. It will be different for every image (we used 409 pixels). When you're happy, click ***OK***.

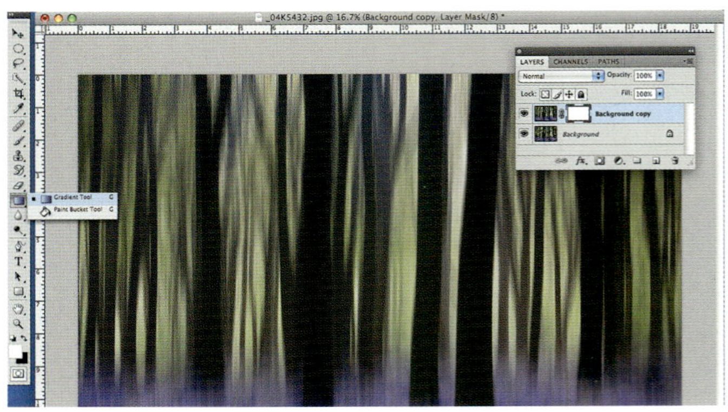

4 Apply a Layer Mask To add a Layer Mask to the blurred image, click on the ***Add Layer Mask*** icon at the bottom of the Layers palette. You'll notice this adds a white box next to your image in the Layers palette. Then select the ***Gradient Tool*** from the toolbar or press ***G***.

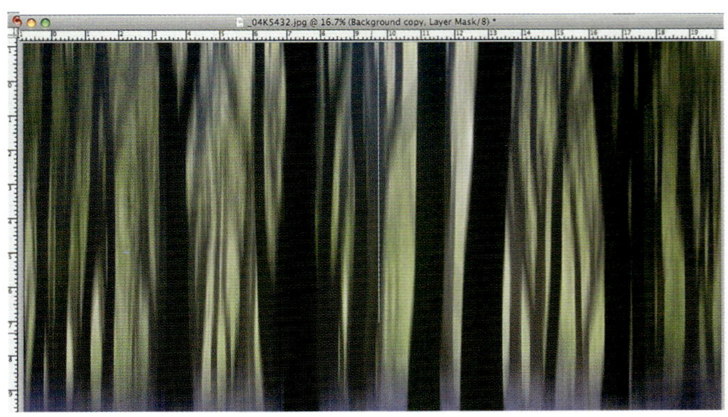

5 Mask off the blur With the Gradient Tool and the Layer Mask selected (black lines appear around the mask's corners when it's activated), click at the top of the image and drag the cursor down to the point where you want the blur to start.

Final image
Print the pictures out and frame them for the wall or why not try having them made into canvas prints or acrylics for a different look?

6 Repeat What you've done is create a gradient in your Layer Mask that allows the blur to graduate through your image. You can change the graduation by repeating step five. You'll find the images look better if the blur is heavier at the bottom of the picture than the top.

7 Apply the technique to all seasons Repeat steps one to six with the other three images of your choice. We've picked a colourful autumn woodland scene, bright sunshine passing through trees for summer and a black & white picture of a snowy forest.

Create a ten-stop ND effect

Neutral Density filters are brilliant, but require a level of dedication to get consistently great results. Here's a technique for those of you who want to trial the effect or don't have the time to attempt the real thing

Luke Marsh: For any of you who aren't already aware, the ten-stop ND filter is amazing! By significantly lengthening a camera's exposure, the filter allows the camera to capture motion so clouds are rendered as streaks and water becomes a fine mist – it's truly magnificent, but it takes skill and patience to perfect. As great as this in-camera technique is, often the key to its success is the location, and with exposure times often more than an hour long, it demands extreme dedication and time – if you're anything like me, those are two things I can't always spare in my hectic schedule.

There is, however, a shortcut to getting a very similar effect using Photoshop's Blur filters, and while it may not be one for the photo-purist, it can produce a very convincing comparison when combined with the right kind of image. Feel free to experiment on any image, but it's usually coastal scenes that produce the most dramatic results. For further inspiration of what images might work, it's worth looking at contributor Lee Frost's Motion Studies (www.leefrost.co.uk), taken with an actual ten-stop ND filter.

How to use

Layer Masks
A Layer Mask allows you to hide detail from the layer it's applied to, revealing the image beneath without erasing it. When the Layer Mask is selected, simply add ***Black*** to the mask to hide image detail and change to ***White*** to restore the detail. Use the ***X*** key to quickly switch between the colours.

1 Create duplicate layers First, create a duplicate layer from the Background layer by going to ***Layer>Duplicate Layer...***, naming the layer accordingly – here, it's called 'Water Blur'. Then click on the ***Add layer mask*** icon at the bottom of the Layers palette to add a Layer Mask. Repeat this process to create an additional duplicate layer – this one was named 'Sky Blur'.

2 Apply Radial Blur On the sky layer, ensure the image thumbnail is selected (circled), then go to ***Filter>Blur>Radial Blur...*** In the Radial Blur window, make sure that the ***Blur Method*** is ***Zoom*** and ***Quality*** is set to ***Best***. Next, enter a large ***Amount*** – no less than ***50*** – and move the ***Blur Center*** to an area where the horizon would roughly be positioned on the image, and click ***OK***.

3 Hide foreground blur The Radial Blur should only affect the sky portion of this layer, so click on the ***Layer Mask*** thumbnail in the Layers palette (circled) and, with the ***Brush Tool*** set to a large soft-edged brush and ***Black*** colour, paint across the foreground area to hide the blur across the water and jetty. Switch to a smaller brush when working near the horizon.

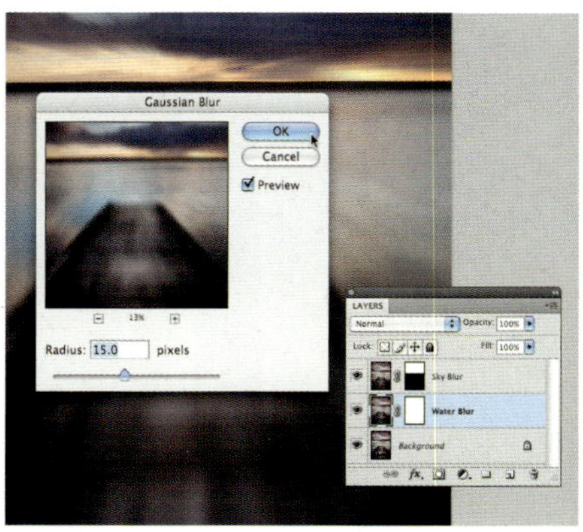

4 Blur the water Switch to the water layer by clicking on it. Add a ***Radial Blur zoom blur***, with all the settings as in step two, but reducing the ***Amount*** down by half, just to make the cloud reflections more realistic. Then go to ***Filter>Blur>Gaussian Blur...***, setting the amount to no more than ***15*** pixels. This adds a hazy sheen to water, common with many long-exposure images.

5 Reveal the jetty Now edit the Layer Mask to reveal the jetty. First, click on the ***Layer Mask*** thumbnail (circled), then select the ***Polygonal Lasso Tool*** and draw a selection around the edge of the jetty. Once complete, go to ***Select>Modify>Feather...*** and add a value of ***1*** pixel to avoid a harsh edge to the selection. Now take the ***Brush Tool***, still set to ***Black***, and paint over the selection.

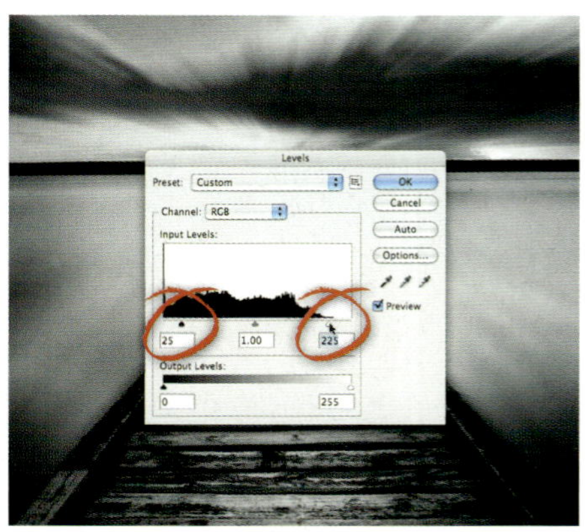

6 Convert to mono To turn the image mono, go to ***Image>Adjustments>Black & White...*** and click ***OK*** to use the default settings. Conversions from colour to mono often leave an image looking a little flat, so use ***Image>Adjustments>Levels...*** to add contrast. Use the black point and white point sliders (circled) to boost the blacks and whites respectively, taking care not to burn out any detail.

Final image

With just a few steps, you could add this beautiful atmospheric effect to your landscape images.

KIT FOR LANDSCAPES

Landscape photographers are a dedicated bunch ready to battle the elements for great images. If you're heading into the great outdoors, our guide ensures you've packed all the key essentials

LANDSCAPE PHOTOGRAPHY is easy, right? You just sling a camera over your shoulder, head into the countryside and great images will be staring you in the face. If only it were that simple! The reality is ridiculously early starts to catch the first light of the day, late finishes to shoot the sunset, routinely being battered by bad weather and tackling long walks shouldering heavy packs with the gnawing knowledge that it may all be for nothing if the light doesn't play ball.

But despite the setbacks, landscapes continue to be one of the most popular subjects to photograph, simply because when things do go to plan, you could be moments away from taking the best photographs of your life. To do that, though, you do need the right gear – and we've got brilliant suggestions right here, whether you're a novice, enthusiast or semi-pro/pro.

Enthusiast p144

Semi-pro p146

Do not forget to pack...

- **Waterproof cover:** Protects your kit if you get caught in a sudden downpour. They're inexpensive and available from most camping shops.

- **Mini groundsheet:** A square of polythene or a bin liner. Make that two – so you can keep your knees and bag dry when they're placed on wet ground.

- **Microfibre cloths:** Pack several cloths to keep lenses and filters clean. Put them in plastic bags to keep them free of debris that could scratch delicate surfaces.

- **Maps and compass:** Handy tools for knowing your location and establishing where the sun will rise and/or set. You can also buy apps for your smartphone.

- **Spirit level:** Helps keep the camera level when it's mounted on a tripod, so you don't get a wonky horizon in your shots. Some cameras offer an electronic level.

- **Snacks & drinks:** Pack high-energy snacks (energy bars, peanuts and chocolate are ideal) and drinks to keep you going. Please don't litter the countryside!

- **Air blower:** Use it to remove sensor dust if necessary. Visible Dust, Giotto's and GreenClean are all specialists with a range of products.

- **Bug spray:** Heading to Scotland between May and September? Take spray to keep midges at bay. You'll find bug spray at Boots and other pharmacies.

- **Camera straps:** Upgrade to a neoprene strap for added comfort. Our favourites are by Op/Tech, but several brands offer a choice of colours and styles.

Contacts

Arctic Butterfly
www.visibledust.com

B+W
www.daymen.co.uk

Canon
www.canon.co.uk

Cokin
www.intro2020.com

Depssi
www.bluepondimages.com

Gitzo
www.gitzo.co.uk

Giottos
www.daymen.co.uk

Green Clean
www.flaghead.co.uk

Hama
www.hama.co.uk

Hähnel
www.hahnel.ie

Hitech
www.formatt.co.uk

Hoodman
www.newprouk.co.uk

Lowepro
www.daymen.co.uk

Lee Filters
www.leefilters.com

Manfrotto
www.manfrotto.co.uk

Nikon
www.nikon.co.uk

Op/Tech
www.newprouk.co.uk

Paramo
www.paramo.co.uk

Really Right Stuff
www.reallyrightstuff.com

SanDisk
www.sandisk.com

Sprayway
www.sprayway.com

Sigma
www.sigma-imaging-uk.com

Slik
www.intro2020.com

Sony
www.sony.co.uk

Tamrac
www.intro2020.com

Tamron
www.intro2020.com

ThinkTank
www.snapperstuff.com

Velbon
www.intro2020.com

1) The landscape novice

So you fancy yourself as the next Joe Cornish or David Noton? You're probably drawn to the landscape by a general love of the great outdoors but have never taken more than snapshots while out on walks or enjoying other pursuits. Now you've added photography to your list of other hobbies it's time to up the ante. Here's a rundown of what you'll need to do just that...

Filter system

In terms of value, the Cokin P System is the best there is. The filters are 84mm wide so the holder is big enough to avoid vignetting on lenses as wide as 14mm on DSLRs with APS-C sized sensors (20-24mm on full-frame) and there are adaptor rings available for lenses with threads up to 82mm. The holder costs around £5 and adaptor rings are £11 each. Whichever brand you buy, make sure you invest in a circular polariser and a set of ND grads. Cokin's P164 Circular Polariser costs £90, while its ND grads cost around £22 each.

Superzoom

Focal lengths from moderate wide to telephoto will cater for all your landscape needs, and if you want to have an easy life and compact kit, this can be covered in a single 18-200mm or 18-250mm zoom (equivalent to 28-300/375mm in full-frame format). Nikon and Canon have superzooms that are worth checking out, but don't write off independents such as the £200 Sigma 18-200mm f/3.5-6.3 DC OS or £180 Tamron 18-200mm f/3.5-6.3 XR Di II.

Backpack

You'll be working with a fairly small kit so there's no need to invest in a giant backpack. You could get away with a 'Zoomster' case for your SLR and lens, like the £43 Think Tank Photo Digital Holster 20, and a belt-mounted pouch or bumbag for your accessories. However, a backpack like the £50 Lowepro Fastpack 350 is ideal as it holds all your kit, plus there's a top section for snacks and spare clothes, a laptop pocket for maps, and mesh outer side pockets for bottles of water.

Entry-level APS-C Digital SLR

There are no poor DSLRs or CSCs – even the least expensive models give you fantastic image quality – so don't worry if your budget won't stretch to a pro-spec model as you really don't need one. What you do need is a relatively compact and lightweight DSLR that you can carry around all day and not notice, that's quick and easy to use and has the features to let you gradually take more control as your knowledge and experience grows. Models to consider include the £500 24.2-megapixel Nikon D3200 and the £400 Canon EOS 1100D.

Memory cards

You'll have to be quite shutter-happy to fill a 4GB card, even on a good day, so one in the camera should be more than enough – though it's worth carrying a spare 4GB card just in case you get carried away.

Remote release

When your camera's mounted on a tripod, firing the shutter with your finger can cause shake. Avoid it with a remote release that plugs into a socket on the side of your camera. Go for a basic model from Hama or Hähnel. The £25 Hähnel 280 Remote Shutter Release is a great choice as your first remote.

Basic outdoor clothing

If you plan to be outdoors all day, you need to make sure you're suitably dressed for the elements. The £25 Sprayway Explore Tee is a comfortable base layer, while the £68 Paramo Challenger is lightweight, reversible and offers excellent protection from wind and rain.

Tripod

You may not like the idea of carrying a tripod around, but trust us, it is worth the effort – especially when you're shooting in low light at dawn or dusk. Better to use a tripod and low ISO for high image quality than handhold at high ISO. Go for a relatively lightweight model like the £100 Slik Pro 700DX or the £110 Giottos MTL 9261B carbon-fibre tripod.

2) The advanced enthusiast

So you've been shooting seriously for two or three years now, you've picked up a lot of knowledge and experience along the way and your images are pretty good. Family and friends are asking you for prints for the wall and you're feeling pretty confident about your photography, so the time has come to upgrade your landscape kit. Here's the gear that you might want to consider...

Remote release

A decent remote release is a must. You could stick with a corded release, like the Hähnel 280 Remote Shutter Release shown on the previous page. However, you might also want to consider a wireless remote too, such as the £50 Hähnel Combi TF. As well as offering a four-second timer, it can be used in the studio to fire your flash system, making it a better choice if you also shoot portraits.

ND grad filters

When shooting landscapes, the sky is almost always brighter than the land so when you expose for the land, the sky blows out and looks horrible. The quickest and easiest way to avoid this is to pop an ND grad filter on your lens. A 0.6ND (two-stop) grad is fine for general use, while the 0.9ND (three-stop) grad is better at dawn and dusk. Cokin's Z-Pro ND grads cost £50 each, while Hitech's ND grads cost from £50 upwards for its 100mm filters.

Filter system

Although you could still get away with using a Cokin P-system holder with lenses as wide as 14mm, the fact that you've bought an ultra wide-angle zoom will probably be encouragement enough to go for a larger 100mm system. Lee Filters will probably be over your budget, but the Cokin Z-Pro system or Hitech 100mm system are a more affordable alternative. Holders cost around £50 each and adaptor rings are under £20 each.

Tripod and head

Serious landscape photography means using a tripod all the time, so go for a well-made and sturdy model that's going to last, but isn't so big and heavy it's a chore to carry. The £260 Manfrotto 190CXPRO3 carbon-fibre is a worthy contender as is the £190 Giotto's MTL 8261B. If you're on a budget, the £110 alloy Giottos MTL 9261B is a fantastic buy. Pair this with a £75 Manfrotto 804RC2 head or Giottos MH1302-652 ball head.

Backpack

It's worth investing in a decent backpack that will take all your gear, offers a good degree of weather resistance and is comfortable to carry when walking long distances over rough ground. The Lowepro Vertex 100 AW is a great buy and can be found under £100, as is the Tamrac £160 Expedition 7x and £130 Lowepro Pro Runner 450 AW.

Top-end APS-C digital SLR

You want the best that you can afford in APS-C format so that you can produce top quality images and print the files to 16x12in or bigger, without worrying about them looking unsharp or grainy. If you're already a Canon user, you're not going to do better than the £1,100 18-megapixel EOS 7D while for Nikon it has to be the £1,100 D300s or the £750 D7000. If you're starting from scratch, you should also consider the 16.2-megapixel £800 Sony Alpha A65.

Standard zoom

If you've been using a kit zoom up to now, it's time to upgrade to a quality standard zoom. Focal lengths around 16mm are ideal for general use as they're wide enough to produce dramatic compositions. Around 35mm you'll get a similar angle of view and perspective to the human eye, while 50mm and beyond takes you into short telephoto territory. Check out the £550 Canon 15-85mm f/3.5-5.6 IS USM or £325 17-85mm f/4-5.6 IS USM, the £450 Nikkor AF-S 16-85mm f/3.5-5.6G ED VR, the £350 Sigma 17-70mm f/2.8-4 DC Macro OS HSM and the £340 Tamron 17-50mm f/2.8 XR Di II VC.

Screen protector

If you want your DSLR's monitor screen to do its job properly, it needs to be kept in good condition, so buy and fit a screen protector. The plastic clip-on variety available for some cameras are okay but are rather on the thick side and with a tendency to take on a 'frosted' look after a while. Self-adhesive protectors, like the £6 protector by Hama, are actually better options and also a lot more wallet-friendly.

Protective clothing

Comfort and protection is a must when your job involves being out in all weather shooting landscapes – if you get wet and cold you won't perform at your best and your work will suffer. Thankfully, technical outdoor clothing is better than ever so there's no excuse for getting caught out. In addition to wearing layers to trap heat and keep you warm, plus a hat to stop heat loss through your head, a breathable waterproof outer layer will protect you from both wind and rain. Regardless of whether you're a beginner, enthusiast or serious landscape photographer, the need to stay dry and warm is the same. Brands to consider include Páramo, Berghaus, The North Face, Mountain Equipment and Mountain Hardwear, among others.

The £190 Velez Adventure Smock pictured here offers one large kangaroo pocket, which can fit an OS map or filters. It's a short, comfortable waterproof top that's also light in weight. As with other Páramo waterproofs, the Velez Adventure pumps away perspiration so that when you stop, you don't get cold as you don't have any liquid close to your skin cooling you down.

While a pair of jeans are ideal for everyday use, they're not a good choice when you're spending a day out shooting as they're not weatherproof and will become clammy and heavy should you get caught in a shower. You are far better off wearing rainpants, which are comfortable, durable and above all waterproof. Shown here are the £40 Sprayway Havana pants, which offer a decent budget option.

In the bag...

1) ULTRA WIDE-ANGLE ZOOM

Though you still tend to reach for your standard zoom first, it's worth adding an ultra wide-angle zoom to your kit as well so you can start to experiment with dramatic compositions, exploiting lines and foreground interest and creating images with a powerful sense of depth and scale. This is likely to become your standard lens as you discover its benefits so make sure you buy a good one. The £459 Sigma 10-20mm f/3.5 EX DC HSM is possibly the best independent option, though the £619 Canon EF-S 10-22mm f/3.5-4.5 USM and the £640 Nikkor DX 10-24mm f/3.5-4.5 G AF-S are both contenders.

2) TELEZOOM

You won't use a telezoom as much but it's worth buying one for effects such as compression of perspective (great in misty weather), reduced depth-of-field and to allow you to fill the frame with details in the landscape. A 70-200mm is effectively a 105-300mm with APS-C sensors, while a 70-300mm equates to 105-450mm – more than powerful enough. Check out the £285 Sigma 70-300mm f/4-5.6 DG OS, £120 Tamron 70-300mm f/4-5.6 DI LD Macro, £413 Nikkor AF-S 70-300mm f/4.5-5.6 VR and £483 Canon 70-200mm f/4L USM.

3) MEMORY CARDS

Though most shoots only last a day, you are venturing further afield and spending weekends on location, so you need extra cards. If you have four good days you could easily shoot 20-30GB of Raw files, so carry at least five 4GB cards.

4) HOOD LOUPE

Viewing images on your digital SLR's preview screen can be tricky in bright light and though you can resort to pulling your jacket over the camera or cupping your hands, the best solution is the £78 Hoodman Loupe as it always gives a bright, distortion-free 1:1 view.

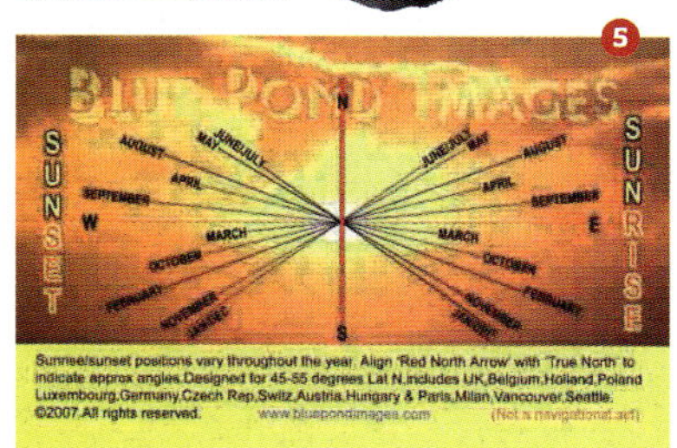

5) DEPSSI CARD

It only costs £2.99, but this handy accessory helps pinpoint the location of sunrise and sunset throughout the year – just align the card with True North and read off the indicator. Turn the card over and you've got a hyperfocal distance chart that tells you where to focus your lens to maximise depth-of-field.

6) ND FILTERS

Use ND filters to increase exposures when shooting moving water to record that lovely blur effect. The Cokin Z-PRO NDs will set you back around £34 each and the ND4 and ND8 will be the most useful. Hitech's ND filters cost around £25 each.

7) POLARISER

A polarising filter will deepen blue sky, reduce glare so colours appear richer, cut through haze and eliminate reflections. The £249 Cokin Z-PRO polariser is the ideal choice for use with the Z-PRO filter system, while Hitech's costs £130. If you can't stretch to a slot-in polariser, consider screw-in circular polarisers. Hoya offers an excellent range of polarisers, prices vary according to size, but expect to pay around £65 for a 72mm or 77mm filter.

3) The semi-pro/pro

Making a good full-time living from landscape photography is very difficult, but some manage it by diversifying – shooting stock images, selling prints, self-publishing cards and calendars, writing books and magazine articles and leading workshops. Semi-pros combine profitable photography with other ways of making money. Either way, if you fall into this category or want to, you're going to need gear that can withstand regular and sustained use in harsh conditions. Think of it as an investment in your future…

Glass polariser

If you've invested in a Lee Filters kit, you might as well complement it with a top-quality polariser. The £220 105mm Lee circular polariser attaches to the Lee filter holder via an optional £33 105mm adaptor ring. However, the polariser has a deep mount so if you use ultra wide-angle zooms or lenses, consider a slimmer polariser, such as the expensive but optically superb £230 Heliopan Kasemann.

Ultra wide-angle zoom

Focal lengths from 16-35mm on a full-frame digital SLR are invaluable for landscape photography. An ultra wide-angle zoom is therefore likely to be your standard lens, so make sure you buy the best there is. From Canon, there's the £1,100 16-35mm f/2.8L Mk II USM and the £585 17-40mm f/4 L USM. The latter offers very high image quality and costs half the price, while its slower maximum aperture isn't an issue for landscape photography. From Nikon, the £1,320 AF-S 14-24mm f/2.8G ED has a good reputation. More practical is the £1,500 AF-S 17-35mm f/2.8D ED-IF, while the £850 AF-S 16-35mm f/4G ED VR is the first ultra wide-angle zoom with Vibration Reduction.

Filter system

There's only one filter system that pro landscape photographers use: Lee Filters. It has no rival in terms of versatility and quality and, though expensive (the basic holder is £55 and adaptor rings £19-£55), it's built to last. More importantly, the 100mm wide holder comes as a kit and can be set up with anything from one to three filter slots, allowing you to adapt it for use with wide-angle lenses. Fit two slots and you'll get vignette-free images with focal lengths as wide as 16mm on a full-frame DSLR. There's also an SW150 system for use with the Nikkor 14-24mm and other ultra wide-angle zooms that have a protruding front element.

Tripod head

Tripod legs are only as good as the head you attach to them, so don't blow your entire budget on fancy pins. A good, solid head is the £125 Giottos MH 5001 head – it's well-made and ideal for both single shots and sequences for stitched panoramas. If you prefer ball heads, professional photographers love Arca Swiss and Really Right Stuff.

Tripod

A solid, sturdy tripod that will keep your heavy full-frame DSLR/zoom combo still in high winds is essential. Carbon-fibre is common now amongst today's tripods, with Gitzo being the most popular brand with pros. Check out the £540 GT2541. If you don't like the Gitzo's twist leg locks, consider the £240 Manfrotto 055CXPRO4, and if you're on a budget you can't beat the classic £114 Manfrotto 055XPROB alloy tripod – heavier than carbon-fibre but as tough as old boots. The £250 Giottos Vitruvian VGR8255 is another great choice.

Full-frame DSLR

In pre-digital days, medium- and large-format film cameras were the weapons of choice among pros, but now medium-format quality can be achieved using a full-frame DSLR, so it has become standard issue. Image quality aside, top-end full-frame DSLRs also boast excellent build quality, including full weather-sealing, so they can cope with daily use in extreme weather conditions and not even flinch. Rain, snow, wind, sand, volcanic ash – you name it. Avoid flagship models, there are more affordable full-frame DSLRs to choose from. You should consider the £1,800 20.2-megapixel Canon EOS 6D and the £1,700 24.3-megapixel Nikon D600. Another model that deserves a look is the £2,600 36.3-megapixel Nikon D800.

Glass screen protector

The rear screen on your DSLR will come in for some punishment so protect it with a £25 Giotto's Aegis Pro Glass screen protector. You won't know there's a screen protector there at all and you can clean it as often as you like, safe in the knowledge that the real screen beneath it is as good as new.

Remote release

Although you can get away with using a basic remote release, being a pro you might want to splash out on something a bit fancier, like the £115 Canon TC-80N3 or £135 Nikon MC-36. Both can be pre-programmed to make long exposures – handy if you use a ten-stop ND filter or shoot sequences of images at set intervals, which is useful for star trail photography. A cheaper option is Hähnel's feature-packed £70 Giga T Pro II.

Ultimate outdoor clothing

It's well worth investing in quality waterproof clothing if you plan to regularly shoot outdoors. Shown here is Paramo's £300 Halcon jacket, which has nine pockets, including large pockets that can fit most filter systems (including Lee), with plenty of room for batteries, memory cards and other accessories. Also shown is the best-selling £115 Paramo Cascada trousers, which offer full weather protection and excellent comfort. You can further preserve body heat by wearing a woollen hat from brands such as Patagonia or Berghaus.

Sensible footwear

When you spend hours on your feet and regularly walk miles over rough terrain – all in a day's work for a landscape pro – you need a decent pair of boots that are comfortable, warm and protective. Check out boots by The North Face, Asolo, Meindl, Berghaus and Solomon. When shooting on boggy terrain, near water or on beaches, a good pair of wellies is far more useful as they will keep your feet bone dry. Aigle and La Chameau are reputable brands to try.

Backpack

Invest in a backpack that's big enough to house all your camera kit as well as have extra space for maps, food, water, spare clothes – and is weather resistant. Lowepro is the brand of choice among landscape pros and the best pack has to be the £120 Pro Runner 450AW. Styled like a traditional rucksack, it has loads of features including mesh side pockets, large front pocket, fully padded interior, laptop compartment and memory card pockets on the inside of its lid.

In the bag...

1) Fast standard zoom

A zoom from moderate wide to short telephoto is a vital part of the pro landscaper's kit. Go for one with a fast f/2.8 maximum aperture so you get a bright viewfinder image. The £1,750 Canon EF 24-70mm f/2.8L II USM or the £1,200 Nikkor AF-S 24-70mm f/2.8G ED are the two favourites, but also consider the £350 Sigma 17-70mm f/2.8-4 DC OS and £345 Tamron SP 17-50mm f/2.8 VC Di II lens.

2) Telezoom

Though it's likely to be your least-used lens, a telezoom is still worth having for compressing perspective and shooting details in a scene. If you're a Canon user you can save a lot of weight, bulk and cash by opting for the £890 70-200mm f/4 IS USM instead of the £1,900 f/2.8 version – you don't need the extra speed for landscapes. For Nikon, consider the £1,550 AF-S 70-200mm f/2.8G ED VR II. We'd also highly recommend Sigma's £900 70-200mm f/2.8 EX DG OS HSM.

3) Back-up full-frame DSLR

If your budget will run to it, a second body is worth having just in case your main one decides to malfunction or you damage it on location. In the ideal world you'd have two of the same model but realistically, a good safe option is an enthusiast-level APS-C DSLR like the £ 1,200 Canon EOS 7D or £800 Nikon D7000.

4) Spare batteries

Goes without saying really – nothing worse than running out of batteries in the middle of nowhere when the light's great. Always set out with two fully charged batteries. As well as branded batteries, Delkin, Hama and Hähnel all offer alternatives.

5) Memory cards

Trips away can last a week or more and with you shooting every day from dawn to dusk when the weather plays ball, you'll soon start filling up your memory cards. Downloading full cards to a laptop is a daily routine, but if you prefer not to reformat cards until you're home, then carry at least 50GB of capacity, in other words six or seven 8GB cards.

6) ND filters

As well as your ten-stop ND filter, it's worth carrying a couple of weaker NDs so you can use slower shutter speeds when shooting waterfalls and rivers to capture motion. A polariser can be used like an ND filter as it loses two stops of light (equivalent to an 0.6ND), but also add 0.9ND (three-stop) and maybe 1.2ND (four-stop) as well so you have more options. Lee Filters ProGlass NDs cost around £110 each.

7) Ten-stop ND Filter

No self-respecting pro would be without one. Go for the £130 Lee Big Stopper or the B+W 3.0ND screw-in filter. Prices vary depending on the filter size – for example, a 52mm filters costs around £41, while a 77mm costs £130.

8) ND grads

The most useful filters of all for landscape photography are Neutral Density (ND) grads as they allow you to produce a well-exposed landscape and a well-exposed sky in one shot, in-camera. Invest in a £200 ND grad set from Lee Filters, which contains 0.3, 0.6 and 0.9 density grads, and we advise going for the hard grads rather than soft grads as they're more effective and easier to use.

9) Piece of card

A sheet of 10x8in stout card is handy to use as a lens shade when shooting in strong sunlight, to shield the front end of the lens and prevent flare. A lens hood would do that, but when using a filter holder, the hood that came with the lens obviously won't fit!

10) Sensor cleaning kit

You may not want to carry it in your backpack, but keep a kit in your car. It's worth having access to a decent sensor cleaning kit in case you should need it, such as the £75 Arctic Butterfly 788 Brite sensor brush.

11) Apple iPhone 4s or 5

Not only invaluable for keeping in touch, and taking decent photos with its eight-megapixel camera, the Apple iPhone 4S is a powerhouse of technology. For example, if you take reference shots using the camera, you can pinpoint their location on Google Maps by tapping the Places option in the Camera Roll. The Apple iPhone's GPS capability lets you know exactly where your landscape shots are taken, so you can find your way back to the same spot – or share the information with others. You can also download the app The Photographer's Ephemeris (http://photoephemeris.com), which allows you to establish the time and direction of sunrise and sunset anywhere in the world.

Types of wide-angles

There are three main types of wide-angle lenses available, each offering its own pros and cons. Here, we explain the virtues of each…

Ultra wide-angle zooms

This group of lenses has become increasingly popular. That's no surprise as the range they cover offers incredible versatility in such a small and inexpensive lens. In fact, the ultra wide-angle zoom is arguably one of the best value lenses you could own. There are a variety of focal lengths available, with those around 11-22mm being the most suitable for cameras with an APS-C sized sensor. In truth, all cover a very similar range, although there are one or two exceptions to note. The Pentax 10-17mm fisheye offers a 180° angle of view at its widest end, so, in a sense, you're getting a fisheye and ultra-wide zoom rolled into one. It's also worth noting that, unlike most ultra-wide zooms, the Sigma 12-24mm can be used on full-frame and APS-C cameras. Finally, while the 16-35mm lens is popular with film and full-frame camera users, the 24-53mm range it covers with APS-C sensors is quite limited, so we'd suggest you avoid it.

Fixed wide-angles

Small, lightweight and compact, with high-quality optics, these are very desirable lenses that are available in various focal lengths and have been designed to offer the ultimate in wide-angles for digital photographers. They start with the ultra wide-angle 14mm, which is particularly suited to architectural photography, when trying to fill the frame with a building from a short distance. Wide-angles from 20mm to 28mm are ideal for landscape photography and are also used by travel photographers. However, their use with cameras sporting an APS-C sensor is limited, especially as a standard kit lens covers this range.

Fisheye lenses

The fisheye offers the most extreme field-of-view. There are two types – the circular and the full-frame fisheye, both producing very different results. Circular fisheye lenses, when used on a full-frame camera, provide round images with a 180° angle of view. They distort perspective, especially when the subject is close and, with close-focusing capabilities, are perfect for comical portraits. The full-frame fisheye (also known as a diagonal fisheye) offers a 180° field of view and can capture incredibly wide vistas. They're very specialist, very expensive and have limited use, so hire one from a pro dealer before you buy.

Anatomy of a wide-angle zoom

1) Petal hood Ultra wide-angles come supplied with a dedicated hood to avoid vignetting and flare.

2) Large, concave front element The front element normally has a prominent curve, leaving it exposed to dust and scratches, so take care to keep it covered in transit.

3) Manual focus ring Normally it's towards the front of the lens and is reasonably wide. You'll rarely need to use it, as wide-angle lenses have excellent autofocus.

4) Zoom ring This is normally found towards the back of the barrel. Most are wide with a grooved surface to allow you to grip it easily.

5) Focus distance Many lenses have the focus-distance scale marked on the barrel, while some of the more upmarket models have a focus-distance window.

6) Hyperfocal scale (see inset) This scale allows you to estimate how much of the scene will appear sharp at your choice of aperture.

7) Internal focusing If you're planning to use filters, lenses with an internal focusing system have the benefit of the front of the lens not rotating when focusing, so you don't have to keep readjusting them.

Why use a wide-angle?

Ever wanted to photograph a subject or a scene and found that you can't fit it all in the frame? Then you need a wide-angle lens. With a field-of-view that extends far wider than the human eye, it's the perfect optic for capturing wide vistas or cramming large objects in the frame. Using such a lens comes at the price of characteristics like exaggerated perspective and distortion, but knowing what to expect and how to use it creatively allows you to take shots that aren't possible with any other type of lens.

Understanding focal lengths: Wide-angles

The focal length stated on a lens usually relates to cameras using 35mm film or full-frame sensors. If your camera has an APS-C sized sensor, then you're effectively cropping the image and so giving the effect of a longer focal length lens. The chart below shows popular wide-angles and how the effective focal length changes when used with digital cameras.

Focal length on lens	Cameras				
	Full-frame	APS-H	APS-C	APS-C (Canon)	Four-Thirds
	1x	1.3x	1.5x	1.6x	2x
8mm	8mm	10mm	12mm	13mm	16mm
14mm	14mm	18mm	21mm	22mm	28mm
15mm	15mm	19mm	22mm	23mm	30mm
20mm	20mm	26mm	30mm	32mm	40mm
24mm	24mm	31mm	36mm	38mm	48mm
28mm	28mm	36mm	42mm	45mm	56mm
10-17mm	10-17mm	13-22mm	15-25mm	16-27mm	20-34mm
10-20mm	10-20mm	13-26mm	15-30mm	16-32mm	20-40mm
10-22mm	10-22mm	13-29mm	15-33mm	16-35mm	20-44mm
11-18mm	11-18mm	14-23mm	16-27mm	18-29mm	22-36mm
12-24mm	12-24mm	16-31mm	18-36mm	19-38mm	24-48mm
16-35mm	16-35mm	21-45mm	24-53mm	26-56mm	32-70mm
17-35mm	17-35mm	22-45mm	25-53mm	27-56mm	34-70mm
17-40mm	17-40mm	22-52mm	25-60mm	27-56mm	34-80mm

Digital-only lenses

When you're choosing a lens, check if it's for use with film/full-frame digital SLRs, or for DSLRs with APS-C/Four-Thirds sensors only. Those made for film and digital are usually pricier; those designed for digital-only are optimised only for sensors. If you're using a DSLR with an APS-C or smaller sensor and never plan to buy a full-frame DSLR, go for a digital-only lens, such as the Canon EF-S range or Nikon's DX.

Nikon AF-S DX 12-24mm f/4 ED-IF

Lens construction: 11 elements in seven groups
Aperture range: f/4 to f/22
Filter thread: 77mm
Dimensions: 82.5 x 90mm
Weight: 485g
Fittings: Nikon only
Website: www.nikon.co.uk

This excellent zoom, for DSLRs with APS-C-sensors only, is compact considering the f/4 maximum aperture. It's partly made of plastic but feels well made. The zoom ring is wide and the focusing ring is adequate; both offer a smooth action. The barrel sports a focusing window and internal focusing. Image quality is very high, delivering very sharp results. Chromatic aberration and flare is barely noticeable but slight barrel distortion is evident.

£800

Canon EF 17-40mm f/4L USM

Lens construction: 12 elements in nine groups
Aperture range: f/4 to f/22
Filter thread: 77mm
Dimensions: 83.5 x 96.8mm
Weight: 475g
Fittings: Canon only
Website: www.canon.co.uk

The Canon L-series lenses offer higher than normal performance, so this zoom, with its constant f/4 aperture, is one of the most popular optics in the Canon stable. Suitable for use with all EOS models, it's larger than most but robustly built, with great handling and fast AF. Optics are excellent, although with full-frame sensors edge detail becomes a little soft. It's a great lens, although the EF-S 10-22mm is a better choice for DSLRs with an APS-C sensor.

£590

Sigma 10-20mm f/4-5.6 EX DC HSM

Lens construction: 14 elements in ten groups
Aperture range: f/1.8 to f/22
Filter thread: 77mm
Dimensions: 83.5 x 81mm
Weight: 470g
Fittings: Canon, Nikon, Pentax, Sigma and Sony
Website: www.sigma-imaging-uk.com

A favourite with landscape lovers thanks to its compact design and sharp optics. Like all Sigma EX lenses, it's well constructed and feels and looks the part. The barrel sports wide zoom and manual focus rings, both of which have a smooth action. Optics deliver high sharpness and only slight evidence of distortion or aberration. It's a better choice than the newer f/3.5 version.

£370

Sigma 8-16mm f/4.5-5.6 DC HSM

Lens construction: 15 elements in 11 groups
Aperture: f/4.5-5.6 to f/22
Filter thread: None
Dimensions: 75x105.7mm
Weight: 545g
Fittings: Canon, Nikon, Pentax, Sigma & Sony
Website: www.sigma-imaging-uk.com

With an effective focal length of 12-24mm (12.8-25.6mm on a Canon), the Sigma provides wide-angle opportunities not previously available for APS-C DSLRs. Build quality is excellent and AF is fast and responsive. Its most impressive aspect is the optics. It boasts four elements in FLD ('F' Low Dispersion) glass and three aspherical elements, and delivers very sharp results.

£550

Voigtlander 20mm f/3.5 Color Skopar SL II

Lens construction: Nine elements in six groups
Aperture range: f/3.5 to f/22
Filter thread: 52mm
Dimensions: 63x28.8mm
Weight: 205g
Fittings: Nikon and Pentax
Website: www.robertwhite.co.uk

One of the most affordable prime lenses on the market, this is one of the smallest and lightest, as well as being manual focus only – which generally isn't an issue for landscape photographers. The manual focus action is smooth and the barrel boasts a clear hyperfocal scale that makes achieving a good depth-of-field a breeze, as well as an aperture ring. A good performer with excellent sharpness once stopped down, this is a great budget prime lens.

£505

Tamron 10-24mm f/3.5-4.5 Di II LD

Lens construction: 12 elements in nine groups
Aperture: f/3.5-4.5 to f/22
Filter thread: 77mm
Dimensions: 83.2 x 86.5mm
Weight: 406g
Fittings: Canon, Nikon, Pentax and Sony
Website: www.intro2020.co.uk

Tamron's 11-18mm zoom has been a popular choice for years but this recent addition, with its extremely wide focal length range, brings even more versatility to wide-angle fans. It's a compact and lightweight option with good handling and an internal focusing system that will please filter users. Optical quality is very good, thanks to the inclusion of aspherical and LD (Low Dispersion) elements and enhanced multi-coatings.

£350

Make the most of wide-angle lenses

Shooting wide ensures your shots are full of detail and impact. Here's why…

Adam Burton: Wide-angles are the lens of choice for the vast majority of landscape photographers for very good reason. These lenses allow you to squeeze as much of a location into your viewfinder as possible and capture a scene absolutely brimming with detail and interest. This is an advantage for landscape photographers as it means you can include foreground interest as well as lots of detail in the far scene, giving your image plenty of depth. By choosing interesting foreground subjects, you can also grab the viewer's attention and pull them in to the picture.

Using wide-angle zooms can be so addictive that you automatically use their widest setting at every opportunity. But this can pose problems. Some lenses can be set so wide that they show the corners of your equipment (lenses, filters and holders) in the frame; this is known as vignetting. Another issue with using extreme wide-angle lenses is barrel distortion, which causes horizons to bend and buildings to lean.

All this can be avoided by training yourself to set your wide-angle lens according to your subject matter. If shooting a straight horizon, like a seascape, then using the focal length a few millimetres up from the widest will reduce the appearance of a bendy horizon. A mountainous terrain, which already has an uneven horizon, can be shot as wide as you want. As well as focal length, pay attention to the height and the angle of your camera when you set it up on a tripod. Trees will lean when composed from low to the ground, so try setting the camera at head height and you may notice a big difference.

The benefits of shooting with wide-angle lenses far outweigh these few considerations. The impact they can give on your photographs is astounding, which is why it comes as no surprise that most pro landscape photographers wouldn't shoot without them.

ABOVE: Choose a format My first image was taken in a horizontal format, which is often the natural orientation for landscapes. However, a vertical format can work just as well with wide-angle shots. It allows more room for foreground details while still including lots of sky.

FAR LEFT: Not too wide Using the widest end of your zoom may cause barrel distortion (when the horizon curves downwards) and vignetting (when dark areas appear in the corners of your frame). The wider your focal length, the greater the chance the camera has of including parts of your kit (eg filter holders). Avoid these problems by not setting your lens to its widest focal length.

LEFT: Go low A viewpoint closer to the ground dramatically increases the impact of the foreground subject matter and provides a more dynamic composition. Now the viewer can focus their attention on the rockpool, which leads their eye into the frame and towards the distant castle.

Maximise sharpness

To ensure the entire scene is sharp, set aperture-priority mode, use a small aperture like f/16 and focus a third of the way into the scene. Make sure to set your digital camera on a tripod for stability

Final image

Wide-angle landscapes are most effective when there's some prominent foreground interest to pull the viewer in to the scene. Don't be afraid to compose so that your foreground is big and bold!

Telephoto zooms

There is no argument that landscape photographers should place a decent wide-angle lens (be it prime or zoom) at the top of their wishlist. However, that's not to say there shouldn't be a little room allocated in the gadget bag for a telezoom.

While you'll predominantly be filling the frame with wide-angle vistas, you'll also find times when a telephoto can prove useful. This will usually be when you want to isolate a specific area or feature within the scene or when you want to create a layering effect through perspective compression (see below). There are a variety of telephoto zooms available but we'd recommend you opt for a focal length of around 55-200mm if you use a DSLR with an APS-C sized sensor, or a 70-300mm or similar zoom if you have a full-frame DSLR. You'll find the Tamron 55-200mm f/4-5.6 Di II to be great value, along with Sigma's 70-300mm f/4-5.6 DG zoom. Both of these will be perfect for filling the frame with any wildlife you may encounter as you roam the countryside.

Perspective compression

Photographers often talk about using a telephoto to compress perspective, but what does it mean?

TECHNICALLY SPEAKING, telephoto lenses don't 'compress perspective', but, practically speaking, you do get a different feeling of perspective from a telephoto shot than from a scene captured with a wide-angle lens. Wide-angle lenses open up perspective and create a sense of depth because nearby objects appear big, and further objects appear to be small, suggesting distance. Wide-angle lenses also create strong diagonals, enhancing the sense of depth. On the other hand, telephotos make distant objects appear larger, apparently compressing the planes of the image and reducing the impression of depth. Lines tend not to stretch into diagonals and parallels remain parallel, increasing the two-dimensional feel. Compared to a wide-angle view, this all adds up to an image that is more static. And, of course, the longer the lens, the greater the effect. So what kind of images benefit from this compression effect of longer lenses? The static character of telephoto images suits tranquil scenes; hilly landscapes are ideal, especially where there are several planes or 'layers' that can be visually pulled together so they appear to be almost stacked on top of each other. The feeling of tranquility can be enhanced by early morning mist, with the tops of the hills rising above the haze. More dramatic images can be created in the right lighting conditions, too – look for alternating bands of light and dark, creating a 'layering of light'. Urban landscapes also work well as you can use compression to contrast elements or suggest a crowded environment.

It's just an illusion!

While telephotos appear to compress perspective, the truth is that they don't. Magnify an area of a shot taken with a wide-angle lens and you'll see that it gives a virtually identical effect!

28-35mm

The apparent distance between the foreground and castle creates a sense of depth, with the hills and village behind the castle stretching away into the distance.

50-85mm

Even at moderate telephoto settings, the perspective seems much flatter, and the castle seems to loom over the distant hills and the village.

105-200mm

As the focal length increases, perspective seems to flatten out, so that the castle and the hills behind seem to be almost on the same plane.

Landscape filters: systems and types

Filters have long been the simplest and most inexpensive way to improve or alter your images in-camera. Even in the digital age, they have their place in every landscape photographer's kit bag. We explain the main types of filter systems, our recommended filter types and the major brands to consider...

THE WORTH OF FILTERS, now that we have Photoshop, is a topic that still divides opinion amongst amateur photographers. But for those that like to get it right in-camera, filters are still invaluable tools, in particular with outdoor photographers.

While some filters can give an image a colour cast, other popular types are neutral in tone and instead enable photographers to balance bright and dark areas of a scene, or have more scope for their choice of apertures and shutter speeds. There are many different uses for filters to suit all types of photography but in this guide, we help you decide which type of filter, as well as what filter system, is the best choice for landscape photography.

Filters come in two main types: screw-in, which attach directly to the filter thread at the front of your lens barrel; and slot-in, which slip into a holder held in place on the front of your lens by adaptor rings screwed on to the filter thread. Both have their pros and cons, which you should consider before deciding which to buy. As you'll no doubt discover as you read on, a combination of both types is often the best solution for most photographers.

Screw-in filters

These are quick and easy to attach and remove from your lens, so are a very convenient choice. As they're made from glass, they are of high optical quality and more difficult to scratch. Screw-in filters come in various sizes, with 52mm to 77mm being the most common. If you own a number of lenses, each with different filter threads, you will either need a filter in each size or take the more affordable option of a stepping ring (see tip below). Another negative point worth considering is that grad filters aren't well suited for use as a screw-in, which will be off-putting for landscape photographers in particular. You also need to take care when using more than one screw-in filter at a time, as you run the risk of vignetting (darkening at the image corners), especially with wide-angle lenses. Another disadvantage is that occasionally you may find a filter won't budge, in which case you'll need a filter clamp to help remove it.

Top tip: Stepping rings

A cheaper option than buying the same type of filter in various sizes is to buy the largest size you need and a step-down ring, which allows you to fit a large filter on a smaller thread. For instance, if you have a 72mm filter and buy a 72-67 ring, you can screw the filter to the ring, which attaches easily to the lens. Don't go for a step-up ring for attaching smaller filters to larger lenses, as these can cause vignetting.

Slot-in filters

With these systems, you only need to buy one filter even if you have several lenses of different sizes. This is because the filter slips into a holder, which attaches to the lens via an adaptor ring. So, instead of needing costly screw-ins in various sizes, you can simply buy affordable adaptor rings in the sizes you need and swap the holder between them. It does mean the initial investment is higher but, over time, it proves to be a far more economical, especially if you have several lenses. You'll find there is an extensive range of filters available, in particular graduates, which are among the most popular types of filter for landscapes. Unlike screw-in filters, slot-in filters are made from optical resin, which is incredibly tough and lighter than glass, although more prone to scratches. Optically, they offer excellent quality, with little discernible difference to screw-ins. For the ultimate quality, look at pro brands like Lee Filters, which use the very best materials.

Top tip: Compatibility

You'll find most brands make more than one size of slot-in system to suit different types of DSLRs. The standard size is 67mm but if you have wide-angle lenses, we'd recommend you consider the 85mm or 100mm formats. Note that as these sizes are standard, similarly sized holders will accept filters from other brands.

Our favourite filter types

There are literally hundreds of different types of filter available, but our shortlist below highlights those that prove most beneficial to your landscape photography

ROSS HODDINOTT

Skylight/UV/ Protection filters

These are essentially clear glass screw-in filters that protect the front element of your lens from dust, marks and damage. The UV filter can also aid in the removal of haze, but all three are more or less the same. We would recommend that you attach one to each of your lenses.

ROSS HODDINOTT

Close-up filters

On bright days when the sun is high in the sky and not particularly suitable for landscape photography, many photographers turn their attention to shooting details in the scenery. Close-up filters are useful if you don't own a macro lens and want to shoot small objects at high magnification.

ROSS HODDINOTT

Neutral Density

These aren't essential filters, but are very useful. A Neutral Density filter is grey in colour and doesn't alter the colour balance of an image but instead reduces the amount of light passing through to the lens. They are mainly used in bright sunlight, when you need to use a wide aperture to minimise depth-of-field or a slower shutter speed to emphasise movement.

Polariser

If you shoot outdoors regularly, buy a polarising filter. It saturates colours, in particular blue sky, as well as minimising glare and reflections from shiny surfaces like foliage or water. The effect of a polariser can't be replicated accurately in Photoshop, which is why most landscape photographers never leave home without one. Avoid linear polarisers – you need a circular polariser; otherwise your camera won't meter correctly. Polarisers have a filter factor of 4x and reduce the exposure by two stops, so watch out for camera shake. While one of the most expensive types of filter, they're definitely worth the investment.

ROSS HODDINOTT

ND graduate filter

Graduates have a dark area that fades to clear and are used to balance bright sky with a darker foreground. They're available in a variety of colours, but we'd say the only grad to buy at first is the ND (Neutral Density) graduate. These have a gradual ND effect that does not change the colour balance of the sky, but allows detail to be recorded in the scene. ND grads are available in various densities, with the 0.6ND grad being a good first choice. You'll find that there are soft- or hard-edged variants, too, relating to how the grad effect falls off – we'd suggest you begin with a soft-edged grad.

ND filter factors: This table explains the relationship between exposures and filter factors. Light loss is stated in stops.

Density	Filter factor	Light loss
0.3	2x	1
0.6	**4x**	**2**
0.9	8x	3
1.2	**16x**	**4**

Using slot-in filters

1) Screw in the appropriate adapter ring
2) Attach the holder to the ring
3) Slide the filter into the holder

Screw-in filters

Guide prices for popular brands

	UV	Polariser	ND
B+W			
52mm	£32	£68	£22
55mm	**£32**	**£77**	**£25**
58mm	£35	£79	£25
62mm	**£38**	**£83**	**£28**
67mm	£45	£99	£35
72mm	**£53**	**£114**	**£40**
77mm	£70	£129	£55
Hoya			
52mm	£30	£45	£28
55mm	**£35**	**£45**	**£32**
58mm	£40	£45	£35
62mm	**£45**	**£55**	**£38**
67mm	£50	£55	£40
72mm	**£55**	**£65**	**£58**
77mm	£65	£65	£68
Kood			
52mm	£8	£18	£12
55mm	**£8**	**£21**	**£13**
58mm	£8	£22	£15
62mm	**£9**	**£30**	**£15**
67mm	£9	£30	£19
72mm	**£10**	**£36**	**£28**
77mm	£12	£38	£29
Tiffen			
52mm	£12	£30	£23
55mm	**£12**	**£30**	**£25**
58mm	£15	£35	£30
62mm	**£15**	**£40**	**£30**
67mm	£18	£45	£35
72mm	**£25**	**£55**	**£50**
77mm	£25	£60	£50

Look after your filters!

Filters can be easily scratched so be sure to return them to their storage case or a filter wallet when not being used. Use a microfibre lens cloth to remove fingerprints and marks.

Filter brands

There aren't too many brands of filter but the choice they offer can be confusing. We've highlighted the tried-and-tested filter brands that offer great value as well as high-quality products

B+W

www.daymen.co.uk

This prestigious German brand is renowned for producing screw-in filters with optimum quality, both in terms of the metal filter ring and the manufacturing process behind its premium optical glass. It's a very popular brand with pros but it does cost around twice as much as other brands. If you need the ultimate in quality from a screw-in filter, then B+W is the option for you, otherwise, Hoya is a great choice. One string in its bow is the ten-stop ND filter, which has proven incredibly popular for daytime long-exposure photography.

Hoya

www.intro2020.co.uk

Hoya produces around 60% of the world's optical glass, so you can be assured it offers excellent quality and value. Hoya offers the most extensive range of any screw-in filter system, with literally every type of filter you can imagine. What's more, for popular types of filter such as polariser or UV, it has a number of options to suit all levels of photographer, from amateur through to pro. Its filters boast several cutting-edge technologies, for instance, the HD series boasts hardened glass and several layers of multi-coating to improve contrast and reduce flare, while the Pro 1 Digital series has been exclusively designed for use with digital cameras. The extensive Super HMC series covers the majority of filter types and provides fantastic quality at a great price. It's worth downloading Hoya's filter brochure to get a better idea of the full range of filters on offer.

Cokin

www.intro2020.co.uk

For many photographers over the decades, the search for high-quality and affordable slot-in filters started and ended with Cokin. This isn't a surprise as this manufacturer was the innovator of creative filters for amateur photographers and has led the way ever since.

Cokin offers four filter sizes: 67mm (A-series); 84mm (P-series); 100mm (Z-Pro); and 130mm (X-Pro). The A-series is aimed more for use with compacts or camcorders, so the P-series is the best introductory option. If you use wide-angle lenses with a focal length wider than 28mm, you should consider the Z-Pro range, while the X-Pro is more for medium-format photographers. All the ranges offer plenty of options but the P-series has everything the DSLR photographer may ever need, with over 140 filters to choose from, including polarisers and a variety of ND grads. Filter rings are available for threads up to 82mm and the P-holder accepts up to three filters at a time. The Z-Pro series is a better choice for landscape photographers – in particular those with ultra-wide zooms. Adaptor rings are available from 49mm to 96mm and filters are 100mm square, except for the grads which are 100x150mm.

All the filters are made from CR39 optical resin and deliver high-quality results, and because it's such a popular range, filters are very well priced. The ND Grad Kit for the P-series is affordable at £50 and consists of a Cokin P filter holder, one P121L ND2 Light Grad, one P121M ND4 Grad and one P121S ND8 Soft Grad filter. The Cokin P164 circular polariser is around £50, while for the Z-Pro, you're looking at around £225 for the Z164! Adaptor rings cost in the region of: A-series: £8; P-series: £11; X-Pro: £50; and Z-Pro: £22.

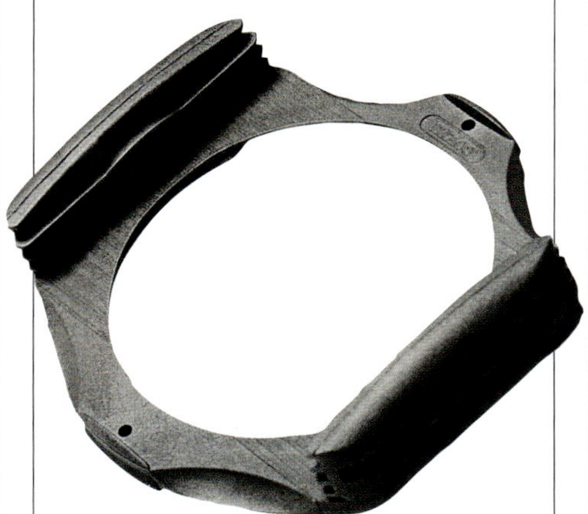

ADAM BURTON

Lee Filters

www.leefilters.com

Lee Filters is the ultimate choice for the discerning photographer. Loved by pros and relished by enthusiasts, Lee Filters are as good as it gets in terms of optical quality, but due to the stringent manufacturing processes involved, expect it to command high prices. Its brilliant 100mm system is the cornerstone of its success, with a high-quality and versatile holder that can be made to your own specification to hold varying numbers of filters. The filters themselves are brilliant quality and are manufactured from a number of materials, including glass, resin and polyester. Various kits are available and we'd recommend the £200 Digital Starter Kit, which comprises an assembled holder, 0.6ND ProGlass ND hard grad, 0.6ND and cleaning cloth, all packed neatly into a pouch. The other kit is the £150 Starter Kit, which includes an assembled filter holder, 0.6ND grad, cleaning cloth, Coral 3 grad and pouch. Its ten-stop 'Big Stopper' ND (around £130) is the best on the market. Adaptor rings from 49mm to 77mm cost £19; 82mm and 86mm are £41; while 93mm, 95mm and 105mm rings are £55. The filter holder (the Foundation Kit) is £55. If you intend making a living from photography and investing in expensive lenses, then these are the filters you should aspire to own.

ROSS HODDINOTT

Filter aid
Do not underestimate how filters can be used to improve your images, especially if you're keen on shooting landscapes.

Formatt (Hitech)

www.formatt.co.uk

Formatt makes a range of filters for movies and stills photography. Its Hitech filters are aimed specifically at digital SLR photographers, made from optical resin and are manufactured in the UK to extremely high standards to provide excellent optical quality. The 67mm, 85mm and 100mm filter systems are compatible with other slot-in brands and include an extensive range of graduates. As well as hard- and soft-edged ND grads (from 0.3-1.2), it offers a huge choice of colour grads, as well as the Blender, which graduates the effect through the entire length of the filter. Hitech also boasts the Pro Stop, a ten-stop ND filter that costs only £50 for the 85mm version, or £75 for the 100mm. An ND grad kit with 0.3, 0.6 and 0.9ND grads cost £38 (85mm); £85 (100mm); and £111 (100x150mm). The circular polariser costs £133 (85mm) or £139 (100mm). A plastic holder costs under £10 and plastic adaptor rings cost around £5 from 49mm to 77mm.

Kood

www.kood-international.com

Kood has its own range, with screw-in filters imported from Japan and slot-in filters manufactured in the UK. The range of screw-in filters isn't large but includes polarisers, protection and close-up filters, as well as various special-effect items such as starburst and colour-correction filters. Kood also has a good range of stepping rings, too. Kood offers four sizes of slot-in filters – 67mm, 84mm, 100mm and 130mm – so its filters are compatible with all the major slot-in brands. Made from CR39 optical resin, they offer decent quality and are a good budget buy. Kood isn't available from all high-street outlets, so visit its website for your nearest stockist. Kood's Circular Polariser and ND grads in sizes 84mm to 130mm cost between £25 and £35, and can be purchased from Kood direct as well as a number of camera dealers.

Unknown brands

Search the web and you'll find filters from little-known brands like Helios. Most stem from China and as there are no official UK importers, it's hard to judge optical quality – the safest bet is to stick with recognised filter brands

Tiffen

www.tiffen.com

Tiffen is an American brand that has been around for decades and is particularly popular in the movie industry. Its range of screw-in filters isn't as comprehensive as Hoya's, but it does cover all the key types including protection filters, polarisers and Neutral Density filters. It also has a number of special-effect filters, in particular lots of diffusion filters including soft-focus, mist and fog, but these aren't filters you'd use on a regular basis. While the range is relatively small, quality is very high and Tiffen filters come with a ten-year guarantee. You'll also find that prices are competitive, too, making them a decent alternative to brands like Hoya, although the latter is more likely to be stocked by your local photo dealer.

Tripods for outdoor use

Don't leave home without a three-legged friend

A TRIPOD SHOULD be viewed as an essential part of your outfit. You'll usually be using a small aperture setting to maximise depth-of-field, along with a low ISO rating to give the highest quality results, which will result in long shutter speeds. Handholding might be feasible with some shots, but with a tripod you never need to worry about the shakes. You'll also find that, by using a tripod, you can spend more time and attention on fine-tuning the framing of the scene to get the best possible composition.

There's a huge variety of tripods on offer, so choosing one isn't straightforward, but there are two key factors to consider. The first is stability – while cheaper models may be tempting, they may not provide a stable platform, so ensure you pick a model that is sturdy enough to keep your kit totally still when shooting. The second factor to think about is how much a tripod weighs, which is important as you'll be carrying it, along with the rest of your gear, for considerable distances. Most tripods are made from aluminium, which is sturdy and fairly lightweight, although decent models weigh around 2kg or more. If you want a tripod that's as sturdy but far lighter, you'll want a carbon-fibre model, although you'll have to be prepared to pay a premium. Our selection of tripods have all received the highest ratings in *Digital SLR Photography* magazine. We've chosen examples that cover various street prices (not the manufacturer's RRP) to ensure you find one that suits your budget. Bear in mind that with the more expensive models, you buy the tripod and the head separately.

Features

1) Head There are various tripod heads available, from ball-and-socket to three-way pan & tilt. Some are also interchangeable. When choosing a tripod, attach your DSLR securely and ensure the head is free from movement.

2) Quick-release plate These allow you to quickly attach and detach your DSLR to/from the tripod. All of the tripods in this review have one.

3) Leg locks Most of the tripods here feature 'clip' locks, which are easy to use and are secure.

4) Leg sections Tripods with three leg sections or fewer tend to be the most sturdy, as the more sections you have, the less stable they can become.

5) Spirit levels Useful for landscape photography, many tripods feature built-in spirit levels to make sure your images are straight. If not, your local photo store should sell one that slots straight on to your hotshoe.

6) Bag hook Some tripods have hooks on the central column, from which a bag can be hung, using its weight to add stability to the tripod in windy conditions.

7) Tripod feet Spikes are good for grip outdoors but will scratch flooring. Rubber feet, on the other hand, offer good grip indoors and outside and are the best choice for general use.

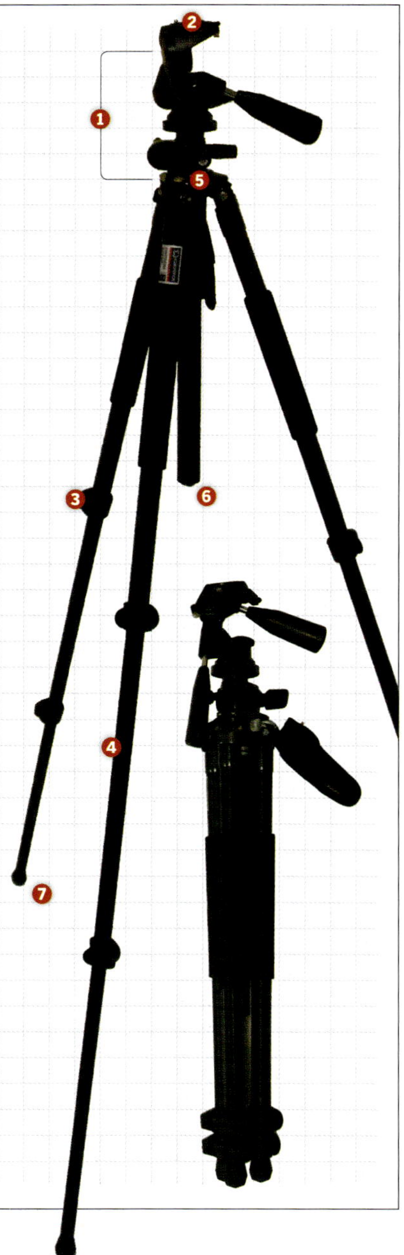

Kit watch!

Interchangeable tripod heads
Most high-end tripods aren't supplied with a head, allowing users to choose their preferred legs and a specialist or general-purpose head. The two most common types of heads are as follows:

Ball-and-socket: These range from simple heads with one control to complex units with panoramic locks and gauges, grip-locks and hydraulic ball-locking systems. Usually stronger and quicker to adjust than pan & tilt heads, they allow free movement in all directions.

Three-way heads: Commonly known as pan-and-tilt heads, these are great for all types of photography. Panning gauges are useful for panoramic shots and fluid heads have the smoothest panning motion.

Giottos MTL 9261B

Length (closed): 66cm
Height (legs extended): 171cm
Number of leg sections: 3 **Weight:** 1.9kg
Maximum load: 8kg **Website:** www.giottos-tripods.com

It all came together for Giottos with its justly popular MTL 9261B. A chunky platform and large 28mm diameter top sections offers good stability, with some flex when the tripod is at full height, but that's to be expected at 148cm, tall enough even for six-footers. Reducing the height a little stiffens up the legs and lessens the flex in the joints, making a solid base. Minimum height is not the lowest at 33cm but at 1.9kg, its weight is very reasonable for a taller tripod. Some nice finishing touches include a ballast hook, spirit level, a handy metal loop on the platform to attach a carrying strap and adjustable lever locks. It's a quality tripod with a lot of functionality and value.

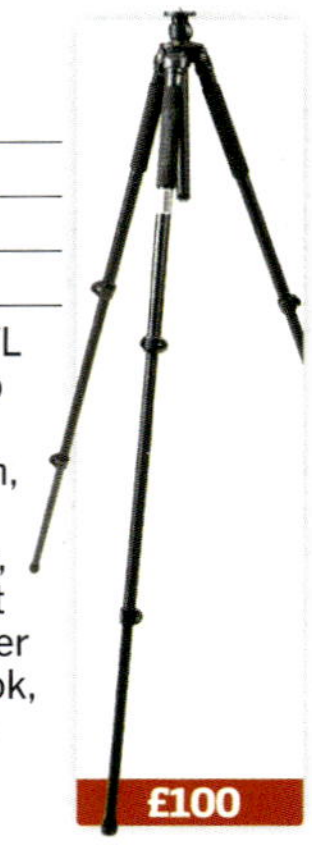

Velbon Sherpa 435 + PHD-41Q head

Length (closed): 53cm
Height (legs extended): 161cm
Number of leg sections: 3 **Weight:** 1.92kg
Maximum load: 3kg **Website:** www.intro2020.co.uk

At the more affordable end of the market is this combined head-and-legs set from Velbon. The tripod's aluminium legs have three sections, locked in place with easy-to-open, clip-style locks. The centre column is adjustable and reversible for low-angle shooting. For an entry-level model, the PHD-41Q head is a good buy, too. It's bigger and sturdier than others in this bracket and takes up to 3kg, no problem. We like the relative simplicity; using it quickly becomes second nature. Two padded handles control movement, and one unscrews and fits inside the other when the tripod is stored. A well-designed quick-release plate completes the package.

Manfrotto 804RC2 head

Weight: 712g
Height: 110cm
Base diameter: 60mm
Maximum load: 4kg
QR system: Manfrotto RC2
Website: www.manfrotto.co.uk

This is a simple three-way head that does the job well and is one of Manfrotto's bestsellers. It's a good size, about average weight, with ample load-bearing capacity. The three axes each have graspable control handles, are logically positioned, and marked with degree scales and a spirit level. The RC2 quick-release plate is one of the best, slotting in easily and locking automatically. A neat feature is that the up/down movement is spring-loaded, increasing resistance as the camera is tilted forwards or backwards. If you're looking for a tripod for video use, though, you'll be better off looking at other options.

Slik Pro 700DX + 700DX pan & tilt head

Length (closed): 76cm
Height (legs extended): 190cm
Number of leg sections: 3 **Weight:** 3.2kg
Maximum load: 6.8kg **Website:** www.intro2020.co.uk

The largest tripod on review, the Pro700DX feels like it could withstand any treatment. It's sturdy and stylish, and certainly looks a tripod for serious use. Although it's heavy, it is still portable. The locks are strong and secure, yet easy to open, while the reversible central column allows users to take low-level and macro shots with ease. It is particularly effective when used with the legs open wide, which is easy if using the three-position locks to hold them firmly in place. The pan & tilt head features a panning lock and a smooth panning motion. The quick-release plate is circular, making it easy to attach and detach the camera. There are two spirit levels but no bag hook.

£150

Giottos Vitruvian VGR8255 kit

Length (closed): 40cm
Height (legs extended): 136cm
Number of leg sections: 5 **Weight:** 1.28kg
Maximum load: 4kg **Website:** www.giottos-tripods.com

The legs of the Vitruvian fold 180° to surround the centre column, reducing the length to 40cm. Open the legs and it extends to an impressive 1.36m (1.57m with centre column raised, too). Made from six-layer carbon-fibre, it's lightweight and stable with aluminium alloy in the main casting increasing robustness. Twist locks are fast and easy to use and the centre column can be removed to turn it into a monopod. The supplied ball-and-socket head moves smoothly and has a friction lock, spirit level and quick-release plate with safety lock. A maximum load of 4kg makes this a suitable choice for most. There's also a cheaper aluminium version (VGR9255).

£250

Giottos MTL 8261B

Length (closed): 66cm
Height (legs extended): 169cm
Number of leg sections: 3 **Weight:** 1.6kg
Maximum load: 8kg **Website:** www.giottos-tripods.com

You can't have it all, and the ideal requirements of high strength, low weight and competitive price tend to be mutually exclusive. Compromise is the name of the game, and some tripods make a better fist of it than others – like this Giottos. It's tall and strong, very light at only 1.6kg, and although it uses pricey carbon-fibre to achieve that, the cost is reasonable at just under £200. This is a classic three-section tripod, which puts it in the middle of the popular size scale as the best all-rounder. It's more than big enough for most, strong enough to take anything short of the heaviest super-teles and light enough to be carried anywhere. It does everything you need.

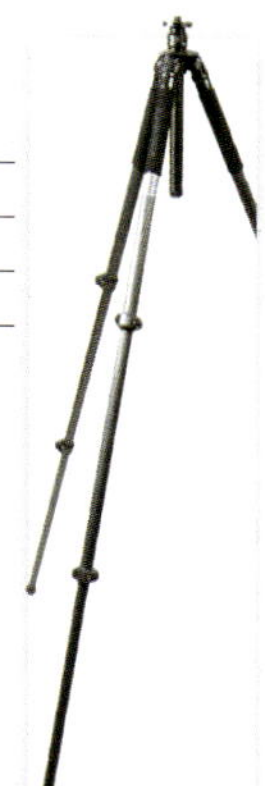

£192

Manfrotto 190CXPRO3 + 494RC2 head

Length (closed): 58cm
Height (legs extended): 146cm
Number of leg sections: 3 **Weight:** 1.62kg
Maximum load: 5kg **Website:** www.manfrotto.co.uk

This Manfrotto is light and its sleek design looks fantastic. Despite its thin legs, it was sturdy and supported our test camera with ease. The twist locks are strong and quick to use. The central column can be raised and moved into horizontal position without removing it from the legs, making the tripod perfect for macro and low-level shots. The multi-position leg locks have a depressible button, making them easier to use than those with clips that must be lifted. The ball-and-socket head is smooth and one switch controls everything, so it's ideal for quick positioning, but not as precise as some of the other heads on test. There is a spirit level and a bag hook.

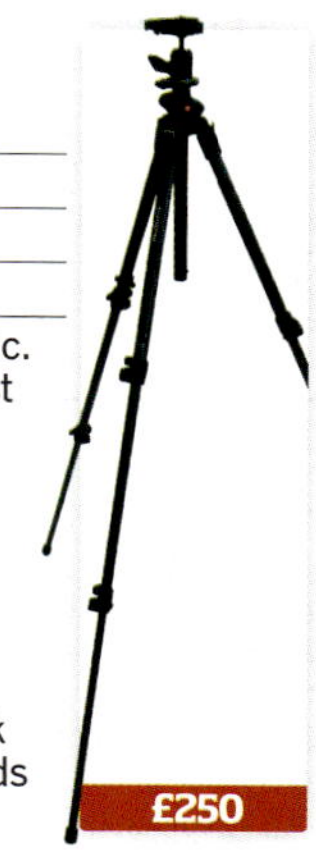

£250

Manfrotto 055CXPRO3

Length (closed): 66cm
Height (legs extended): 175cm
Number of leg sections: 3 **Weight:** 1.7kg
Maximum load: 8kg **Website:** www.manfrotto.co.uk

Manfrotto is actually part of the same company as Gitzo, owned by the UK-based Vitec Group. Between them, they've got everything covered. This Manfrotto, part of the popular 055 series, is a decent size for serious work, similar to the Giottos MTL 8261B, and capable of handling all but the heaviest outfits. It's available with three or four-section legs, with or without the tilting column. This is a simplified version of the tilting column idea, and while it can only be locked upright or horizontal, in practice that doesn't compromise versatility. You can still get to ground level by adjusting the height with the normal leg levers or by selecting one of the four leg angle positions.

£220

Gitzo GT3541 Mountaineer

Length (closed): 54cm
Height (legs extended): 168cm
Number of leg sections: 4 **Weight:** 1.9kg
Maximum load: 18kg **Website:** www.gitzo.co.uk

You can tell this is a really good tripod just by looking at it. Another clue is the price. Gitzo makes nothing but the best tripods, and while some Chinese clones run close by on performance, and beat them on price, there's none better than this classy Italian brand. Weight is low, yet everything feels taught, rigid, locking solid. Making a good tripod is not rocket science; they all have three telescoping legs hinged to a central camera platform. The difference is in the design integrity of the joints, quality of materials and manufacturing precision. Gitzo has all that totally sorted. If £600 is too much, Gitzo's aluminium and basalt versions are significantly cheaper and only a bit heavier.

£600

Giottos MH 5001 head

Weight: 848g
Height: 109cm
Base diameter: 59mm
Maximum load: 6kg
QR system: Giottos
Website: www.giottis-tripods.com

£60

This three-way Giottos head is substantially built, getting on the heavy side, and with large handles that offer plenty of leverage for fine control – although they can be unscrewed for packing away and storage. Where it scores over the Manfrotto 804RC is in the smoothness of operation. It doesn't really make that much difference for stills, but it's not far off the standard of a fluid damped head, offering just the right amount of gentle resistance as you pan, without any jerkiness. So if you're amongst the growing ranks of photographers who like a bit of video, too, the Giottos makes for a more versatile choice.

Slik SBH-280E

Weight: 303g + 39g
Height: 100cm
Base diameter: 51mm **Ball size:** 25mm
Maximum load: 5kg
QR system: Slik 6183
Website: www.intro2020.co.uk

£100

Very well made, with a design that's slightly unusual, the Slik comprises one large knob to control everything, including locking the smallish 25mm ball. It's rated for a modest 5kg load but can take much more. This is a tough head and works well. There's minimal shift on locking down – in fact, we found it to be one of the best tested. It's nice to use, too.

The main knob has a finely machined grippy surface, locking solid in only 1/8th of a turn. The quick-release plate has a non-slip cork surface and drops easily into place as the lever snaps shut. All in all, this is a good offering from Slik at a reasonable price.

Bags and backpacks

Expert advice on storage to protect your camera gear

MOST OUTDOOR PHOTOGRAPHERS prefer backpacks as they distribute weight over your shoulders and back, making it far easier to carry gear over long distances. The daypack holds photo gear in the bottom section and general items in the top compartment, while dedicated photo backpacks are designed with larger kits in mind. Consider the following:

Comfort: As you carry more kit, the weight increases, so shoulder straps are important. The wider and more padded they are, the less they dig into your shoulders. Waist straps are useful, as they relieve tension from the lumbar region and help keep your back straight. Another important factor is the bag's frame. Some are sturdier than others which may seem uncomfortable at first, but it helps keep your back straight on long treks.

Capacity: Think about how much kit you plan to carry. All the bags here have adjustable compartments, so are quite versatile.

Build quality: How well the backpack is put together, including the stitching, zippers and weatherproofing, determines how long it ought to last, how strong it is and how well it protects your equipment.

Features (see panel below): Some photographers just want a bag with lots of space, others are more demanding over specific features. Most have front pockets, designed to help you organise your memory cards and batteries into used and unused.

Price: We have stated the average street price from a number of popular retailers and not the manufacturer's guide price.

Features

1) Straps Check to see if the straps are adjustable, padded and wide to stop them from cutting into your shoulders on long journeys. Also look for waist straps.

2) Padding Some bags have pressure pads on the back, which will take a lot of the strain out of long journeys and spread the weight of the gear over a larger area.

3) Storage/capacity Does the bag hold all the equipment you need for your photography? If there is too much empty space, the bag will be unbalanced, which can be bad for your back. All the bags featured here have adjustable dividers and offer quite a bit of versatility.

4) Weatherproofing/ rain cover Most bags are weather resistant. Some are weatherproof, and others have all-weather covers that can be pulled out from a hidden compartment, usually on the base.

5) Laptop compartment Make sure that the laptop compartment is big enough for your computer, as they vary in size. The padding is also important here.

6) Accessory clips Some bags allow you to attach further bags, tripods and monopods, but be aware that some are only compatible with the bag manufacturer's own clip systems.

7) Zips If you go out a lot in bad weather or near water, make sure that the zips are up to it. Wildlife photographers should also consider the noise made by the zips as animals can be easily frightened off.

Kit watch!

Fitting and wearing a bag properly
If you're carrying a lot of heavy kit, it's important that your bag sits correctly on your back or at your side. This advice can prevent all kinds of back and posture problems. With a backpack, ensure that both straps are over your shoulders and tightened so that the bag sits in the centre of your back. If it has waist and chest straps, make sure you use them to distribute the weight evenly across your back, rather than just your shoulders. For shoulder bags, pull the strap over your head to the opposite shoulder. This should distribute the weight better than if it were on the closest shoulder and stop it from slipping off your shoulder or being easily snatched.

Lowepro CompuDay Photo 250

Dimensions: 40x32x18cm
Weight: 900g
Warranty: Lifetime
Contact: 01902 864646
Website: www.lowepro.com

This laptop bag has plenty of room for everyday items and a padded side compartment big enough for a DSLR with standard zoom. While the camera aspect is not exactly an afterthought, the large and deep main compartment is better suited to a flask and sarnies than anything specifically photographic. There are no dividers, but there's room for a spare lens or flashgun if protected in a soft wrap. The top zip also has a rain flap. It's a great concept for carrying a camera alongside your general workday kit. There are pockets for documents and a separate interior bag for a laptop charger and leads. The harness is simple, just shoulder straps, though the contoured shape makes it easy to carry the bag over one shoulder with quick access to the camera.

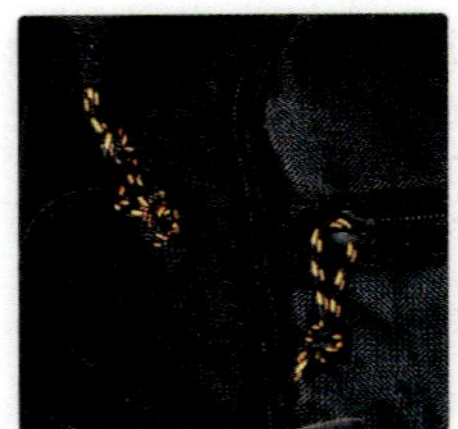

£50

Tamrac Evolution 6

Dimensions: 42x26x19cm
Weight: 1,510g
Warranty: Lifetime
Contact: 01628 674411
Website: www.intro2020.co.uk

This is one of Tamrac's clever Evolution series, which includes two larger versions in the range. There are three ways of carrying it: as a backpack, or as either a left- or right-handed sling. There are three entry points to the main camera compartment: from both sides and the front. It works well as a sling for fast access, with the other shoulder strap and waistband tucked away behind the rear padding. Camera access is through the side, where there's room for a DSLR and medium-sized zoom. There's also enough space for another lens or maybe two, plus flash, and you can get at those either through the front flap, or from the opposite side. The top compartment has useful extra capacity, wide enough for a 70-200mm zoom. The outer is well padded, but any equipment in there would need its own protection.

£75

Vanguard UP-Rise 45

Dimensions: 43x32x22cm
Weight: 1,600g
Warranty: Limited lifetime
Contact: 01202 651281
Website: www.vanguardworld.co.uk

The UP-Rise tag refers to Vanguard's expansion system, supposedly unzipping extra space when needed but, in practice with the 45, it makes barely any difference. Not that it is short on space, or features. The main compartment is large enough for a DSLR with up to 70-200mm zoom attached, plus two or three extra lenses and a flashgun. Grabbing the camera through the side flap is easy, with lesser-used items accessed by unzipping the back. The padded top compartment is large, and the bottom can be detached to swing down and form one very large holdall. There are a number of thoughtful touches, like the camera compartment secured with fast-pull twin zips, plus Velcro and a clip. There are dual grab handles, a rain cover and a good tripod slot with adjustable straps.

£90

Vanguard Heralder 33

Dimensions: 42x27x35cm
Weight: 1,620g
Warranty: Lifetime
Contact: 01202 651281
Website: www.vanguardworld.co.uk

You get a lot for your money with Vanguard: this bag is just crammed with features, too many to mention here. Take for granted that this is a big bag with all the normal stuff, plus a generous helping of extras. For instance, the top zip opens wide for direct access to the main compartment, which can be removed completely so that the bag becomes a general holdall. The padded laptop pouch lifts out, too.

A decent-sized tripod sling appears like magic from the front, and a rain cover from the back. The shoulder strap has an extra support strap that you may need when this heavy bag is full (or go for the optional-extra full shoulder harness) and there's a handy mini-bag included for things like batteries and cables, too.

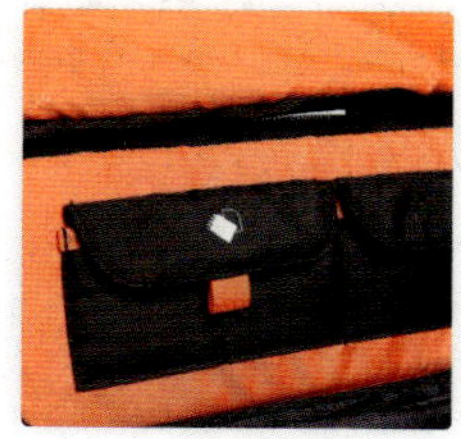

£110

Lowepro Flipside 400 AW

Dimensions: 45x30x24cm
Weight: 1,540g
Warranty: Lifetime
Contact: 01902 864646
Website: www.lowepro.com

This is a serious backpack, designed for carrying lots of camera gear with comfort and security. The whole of the back unzips to open a storage area the full size of the bag, large enough for a couple of cameras, four or five lenses up to almost any length, flash and accessories. When you're carrying it, there's no access to the main compartment – for you or anyone else. Comfort is assured by shoulder straps and a chest strap, the waist band is deep and heavily padded, and includes accessory loops. Lowepro claims you can rotate the bag around to your front and access gear while it's attached to your waist, but that's asking a lot when it's full. The front compartment is quite shallow and thinly padded, but deep and large enough for small personal items and an iPad, but not a laptop.

£100

Lowepro Pro Runner 450 AW

Dimensions: 34x29x50.5cm
Weight: 2,700g
Warranty: Lifetime
Contact: 01902 864646
Website: www.lowepro.com

The Pro Runner 450 AW holds a lot of gear, with room for two large DSLRs with zooms attached, and space for several extra lenses, flashguns, a third body and a 17in laptop, too. The shoulder straps are thickly padded and adjustable, and the waist belt and carry handle will be appreciated when carting about all that weight. The compression straps help reduce the bulk on the 450 AW for easier transportation, there's a built-in all-weather cover and loops are handy for carrying a tripod. The front pocket will hold a few personal items, the three internal pockets feature windowpane panels to help keep things like filters on display, and there are two dedicated memory card pouches, too. This bag is a great option for carrying a large outfit as well as personal gear.

£120

Tamrac Adventure 9

Dimensions: 28x33x51cm
Weight: 900g
Warranty: Lifetime
Contact: 01628 674411
Website: www.intro2020.co.uk

Tamrac's Adventure range includes four backpacks and this is the smallest, with light weight and mobility in mind. It features a clamshell design – the main compartment unzips and hinges open to reveal a modest space just big enough for a smaller DSLR with kit zoom and maybe an extra lens or flash, but no more. Protection is good. The top compartment is roughly the same size, and large enough for lenses up to a 70-200mm zoom, plus another lens or a flashgun, but the outer fabric has no additional padding. The front pocket takes a couple of filters and a phone, and drinks can be tucked into the side pockets. The harness makes no concessions to size, offering good support and comfort. It's a full three-point jobbie with adjustable chest and waist straps, including accessory loops.

£110

Tamrac Ultra Pro 13

Dimensions: 46x31x31cm
Weight: 2,584g
Warranty: Lifetime
Contact: 01628 674411
Website: www.intro2020.co.uk

This Tamrac is fabulous value at around £120. Instead of a separate laptop case, there's a large slot in the front, plus two good ZipDrop front pockets and two more under the lid, all with Tamrac's see-through Windowpane-mesh. When the bag is set down and open, there's good access to everything. The standard layout is to have two pro-size DSLRs with lenses attached across the top, though the dividers can be customised. The top is secured by a zip, four clips and Velcro tabs to take the weight, with a large central handle. The rain cover is in an accessory pouch on the side where there are twin loops at either end. Tamrac's Strap Accessory System is similar to Lowepro's SlipLock and Think Tank Skins – good for expanding capacity.

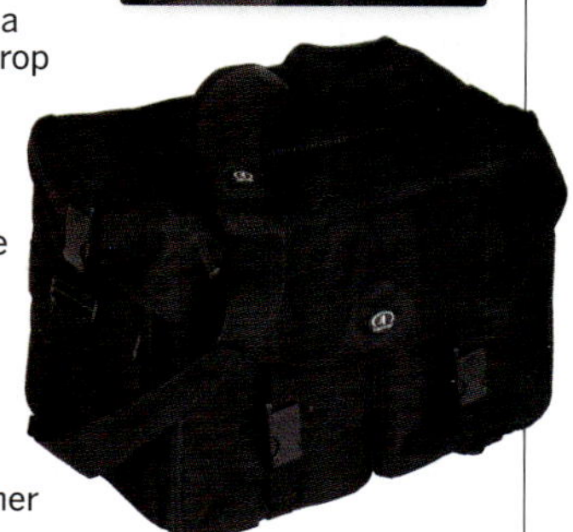

£120

ADAM BURTON

Be sure to bracket!
Whether you use the grey card or not, in tricky lighting conditions, bracket your exposure by +/-1 stops using your camera's exposure compensation or AEB functions to ensure you get the shot

Metered to perfection!
Scenes with bright skies can lead to exposure error. Use a grey card and you should have no problems.

How to use your metering & White Balance cards

The 18% grey card can be used to ensure perfect exposures when shooting in tricky lighting conditions. Both reference cards can also be used to set a custom White Balance. Depending on the camera you use, you need to take a White Balance reading off the grey or the white card (your camera's instructions will show you how)

DIGITAL SLRS USE SOPHISTICATED exposure systems and all work using the same assumption that the average of the scene that is being metered from is a mid-tone, or 18% grey to be exact; ie the average of all dark, light and mid-tones mixed together is 18% grey. It's the basis of all metering patterns and works surprisingly well, but while it's fine for the majority of shooting situations, it can lead to incorrect exposures when the scene or subject is considerably lighter or darker in tone than 18% grey. For example, very dark areas can fool the metering system into overexposure. Similarly, very light subjects, such as a snow scene, can fool the camera into underexposing them – making them appear darker than they are – as the light meter will take a reading designed to render them as a mid-tone. As a camera is trying to render an image 'grey', it's your job to ensure you compensate to keep the tones true to life. You can do this by using one of your DSLR's exposure override facilities, such as exposure compensation or the AE-Lock button, or by metering from an area of the scene that has a mid-tone. And that's where our grey card comes in. Using it is very simple as our step-by-step guide below illustrates. Remember that you need to place the grey card in similar lighting to your scene: for instance, don't place it in a shaded area if your scene is bathed in sunlight. Also make sure that the card fills the metering area – we recommend you use spot or partial metering as the card won't need to fill the entire image area, but any is suitable. You can either lock the exposure using your camera's AE-Lock facility or note the aperture and shutter speed, and then switch to manual mode and set these (although this method isn't suitable to days where lighting is variable). The card has AF reference lines to help your camera's autofocus lock on to it. However, you don't necessarily need it to be in focus to work correctly. The grey card (as well as the white card) can also be used to take a custom White Balance reading from, too.

1 Getting started Place your grey card on the ground angled towards you and ensure it's located in a spot that is bathed in the same light as the majority of the scene you plan to shoot.

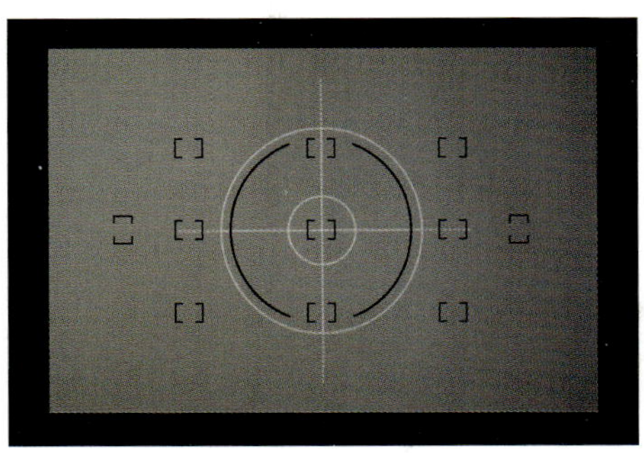

2 Take a meter reading Ensure that the entire metering area is filled by the grey card (in this instance we're using multi-zone metering) and lock the exposure with the AE-Lock button.

3 Compose & shoot With this exposure locked, you can compose your scene and take your shots. When you check it on your LCD monitor, the exposure should be perfect.